# THE SUPPLIANT.

This is the story of a British Army intelligence officer who in the 1970's took part in both hoaxes and covert struggles with left-wing politicians and corrupt civil servants.

In the ambitious selfish and delectable daughter of a Lowland Scottish land-owner, he finds a secret and potent weapon of revenge.

Under his auspices the egotistical perversities of this thwarted and unsuccessful actress are retargeted to do battle with the treacherous hordes who oppose him. She is enticed by sustaining an illusion of success and by the glowing fires of ruinous sin into fury-like savagery and nihilism ... until her bubble bursts.

The plot is overshadowed by the vivid insights into the defiance and hubris of its main character and as the deepest part of the story is revealed, the reader comes to know intimately and even love this tormented girl, despite her pitiful aberrations of self-love and her wicked and succubus-like deeds.

# THE SUPPLIANT.

Peter Morris.

Saxum Books.

Published in Great Britain in 2006
by Saxum Books.



A catalogue record for this book is
available from the British Library.

Printed in Great Britain by
Antony Rowe Limited,
Chippenham, Wiltshire.

ISBN 0-9553041-0-5
ISBN 978-0-9553041-0-1

Saxum Books,
P.O. Box 238,
Beverley,
HU17 6AT,
Great Britain.

e-mail : saxum@hotmail.co.uk
www.saxumbooks.co.uk

# PROLOGUE.

Minuscule blue flowers cascaded down the bleached ancient stones of the wall. By its foot, a fluorescence of apricots and a worn runnel of clear flowing water, lent an air of delight and abundance to the garden.

Hassan al-Uzza lifted a sun-scorched hand and inserted half a dried fig, dipped in rose sherbet, in between his flashing teeth.

'It voz not chance zat zat Hollandisch salveege togg voz stopped off sous-vestern Eerlant, near ze Fastnet Rock. No. Zat Breetisch freeget voz only pretending to be shadoving ze Sofiet crooser in ze Atlantisch Osion. It voz reely votching ze togg,' said the German girl volubly.

Al-Uzza returned his hand to the midge-attended folds of his black woollen jellaba, where reflectively and indiscreetly, he scratched his groin. Under his dirty white kefia and from either side of his hawkish nose, two small eyes peered furtively at his guest.

She shifted petulantly under the parasol and sipped her glass of rough red paraffino. 'I know zay dumped ze veppons overboard before ze vorship clohsed, but viz all ze rardars and sattaleets today, it is too easy to votch sheeps.'

Her harsh tones did not echo in the parched exotic stillness, nor ruffle the timeless Coelo-Syrian balm, but floated away like chaff.

The acrid spicy smell of qahwa tobacco in her host's shrouds, could not entirely quell the fetid odours of his festering sex and sweat glands. Everyone sweated in Damascus in August, but Ingrid at least was moistened only with fresh clean sweat.

'I am unhappy for you. And today morning, I ringing my chief and he too, very unhappy. Vee sink vee should arrange for you a ... how you say ... overland corrier, uzzervize you suffer maybe furzer losses.' She eyed him sternly for an instant.

Under a searing noon sun, the fronds of a gnarled terebinth tree cast dark shadows across the Libyan's charred facial parchment, making it even harder to discern its obscure moods. The flecks of light seemed to hint at a smile, but did it imply the weighing of her advice or the relish of some maturing deceit?

To elude her scrutiny he nodded sagely, for his dealings with Westerners had taught him the advantages of enacting some play of sincerity, even though deep in his barbaric heart he was no less corrupt or quixotic than his rougher nomadic kin. He could tolerate Europeans for a short while, so long as they did not excavate too closely around his ultimate motives.

'So if you vish it, I can take contact for you viz somevun who transfers sings across ze Continent.'

Ingrid's tall figure, whilst not overtly sexy, exuded a calculated indolence which hinted at events in the middle of the night, able to make even the most rabid of men blush.

Al-Uzza indulged in another scratch round his gonads and Ingrid wondered if he too had green-fly, like the flowering pomegranate beside her. He moulded his aquiline features into that *nice* smile which often conceals dislike.

'Do you have a boyfriend, Miss Axt?'

'Uha.' The drawn-out wink was intentionally indecipherable.

Her hard thirty-one-year-old form still appeared young and athletic. Her dark brown hair, swept back into a long plait looked girlish, but her pale face with its exposed ears, thin lips and long neck, was common and cruel.

# 7

'What is he like?'

'He *voz* like you,' she paused, 'Ugly.' Something raw and discourteous in her manner, suggested that she enjoyed stimulating him. She shuffled her bottom sinuously as a goading carrot, helped herself to a second chocolate biscuit from the white fretwork table and drank more orange juice.

Al-Uzza smiled intently. She seemed to be wholly flesh and wonderfully devoid of soul. The Arabs have a saying – 'A girl for fun, a boy for pleasure and a goat for ecstasy'. Hassan all at once wanted fun. He extended a bare horny foot and tickled her long shiny leg. 'You have an itch for me?'

Ingrid actually *did* want to copulate, but decided on balance that the lure of fondling his big black maggot-infested balls was outweighed by the stench of his pungent oily secretions and so after a delay she retracted her leg and smiled with a faint blasé smugness. 'On ze contery.'

Al-Uzza's cavernous nostrils twitched as a prelude to a long rumbling snort, which ended in a short explosion somewhere between a cough and a sneeze, like a camel spitting.

Ingrid saw with sudden fright, how his nasal hairs were vibrating in their dilated orifices and that his scowl of ill-temper was verging on the uncontrollable. As he rose – quite possibly to hit or rape her – she threw herself at him to defuse his rage. Her bid consisted of saying, 'Pleese! I voz only teesing! You can haff me if you vont,' and forestalling kisses on his stubbly left cheek. This just placated him sufficiently.

He clasped her hand and strode to some oversized pillows behind a screen of dark green orange bushes, dragging her with him. He performed his act using a minimum of energy, with a few rough pokes. It was over in a minute. Still though, the deep impiety of these infidel whores evoked his scorn. He found it extraordinary that Allah let such shameless behaviour pass unpunished. She would be rot in a man's bones.

Ingrid did not object to the *act* – in fact his massive black prong had stimulated a twinge of enjoyment in her desensitised body – it was the loss of esteem and bartering power which hurt.

As he rose, his sticky effluent drained itself all down her left thigh. 'Scheiss,' she muttered as she tried to wipe it off with some rough pink sacking. Being able to make fools of and laugh at pimply Western youths had led her into this blunder. What a mess she looked. Fuck these bloody Arab scum-bags!

With minimal savoir-faire, the Atabeg thanked her for the East German offer of help and undertook to review it. Their barbed smiles of parting, acknowledged across the gulf of their dislike that they might none the less be useful to one another. Al-Uzza noted too, that as well as her divergent squint which had seemed mysterious and attractive at first, one of her eyes was yellow and the other pale blue – most unusual.

The heavy vertically-planked door swung to behind her, in the high sand-eroded wall of this outwardly unpretentious house in a quiet sector of the city.

She guided herself towards the Great Square using as a landmark the Mosque of Paradise, once a Byzantine church built by the Empress Helena, but before she reached its babbling caftaned throng and its mesmerising oriental aura, she turned off down the rubbish-strewn Rue de el-Mo'allaqa. On one side, beneath neatly kept linden trees and rose-granite arches with grey acanthus-leaved capitals, plain-robed students of the Quoran sat in coteries with wizened mullahs in gleaming silks, discussing theology. On the other were mud-coloured buildings and a bazaar where she glimpsed stalls crammed with intricate ornaments and domestic utensils, sandals and the shoddiest of Western goods. She smelt the aroma too of cloves and peppermint and succulent bits of roasted lamb until an old French bus tore by, kicking up dust and exhaust fumes. Above the street drooped scores of curtseying telegraph wires, strung up on brackets with antiquated insulators of baked clay. These led to a neo-baroque colonial structure with 'Central Téléphonique' etched into its lintel.

Ingrid entered warily through its fretted door-arch and saw off the nicotined corridor a vault with old-fashioned switchboards operated by earphone-wearing natives, jabbering and clicking. She approached a beefy turbaned Damascene in a green waistcoat, who sat twiddling his thumbs behind a vast ink-stained desk of editorial dimensions. On a slip of paper she wrote the West German number she required and then proffered a fifty Deutschmark note as bakhshish. With unsmiling lassitude he rang the number and handed her a fusty pre-war bakelite hand-set.

Ingrid wished to avoid telephoning from the plush Oxus Hotel, in case her room telephone should be tapped.

She heard the discontinuous buzz of the German exchange and then a familiar voice.

'81102.'

'Leonore Uff?'

'Nein.'

'Entschuldigung. Ich versuche ... '

Outside, the plaintive wail of a boy singing to a one-stringed rebab and the smell of mule dung hung round a squalid fountain, where old men smoked Turkish pipes with thin bony fingers and bearded cross-legged fortune tellers gazed up at a cloudless sky.

She ruminated both on her lack of knack in dealing with the natives and on her meeting with the shifty and unstable al-Uzza. She would send Ute to see him next time.

With nothing to fetch from her hotel, she took a jarring springless Citroën taxi out to the airport. From there she would fly to Rome with a break of journey at Athens.

* * *

Ute Steyer wrote out a blue-green cheque in her slow calligraphic hand, using her Luzern account in the pseudonym of Nicole le Saige. It would pay for a third pile of a thousand gold coins, each nominally worth twenty Swiss francs, which she had ordered and was now due to collect from another bank in Luzern.

Her cogitations digressed to the ocean-going tug, which her accomplice had earlier that day mentioned to the self-styled effendi in Syria.

Ingrid had learned of this sea-borne gun-runner from a Russian naval pilot back in June, whilst playing with his joy-stick one night after a meeting at the H.V.A. headquarters on the Gross-Berliner Damm in East Berlin.

She had guessed that he was planning to flee to Sweden at some point in a forthcoming training session, for he was most willing to give her the information she wanted in exchange for certain peculiar details about the exercise.

Whilst Ingrid had been back in East Germany again a week later, Ute had anonymously telephoned a British Army depot on the Lüneburg Heath, near to the village of Fassberg where she had spent her childhood and most satisfactorily for their plans, the Royal Navy frigate *Charybdis* had hooked this shark.

With her felt-tips on a sheet of paper dotted with practised forgeries, she sketched a bride with a bouquet of red roses. Around her, she formed a border of alternate pink hearts and yellow lozenges and then with her blue roller-ball wrote, 'La mariée? Oui!'

Ute recalled another hapless Dutchman, whose membership of the arms smuggling club they had brought to an abrupt end. Jan van der Rotte had been coaxed to a derelict copper foundry near Osnabrück one warm July evening and she and her kinky lover Ulrich had pretended to be concluding a deal with this prosaic little tea importer, when as a goods train had roared through the night on an adjacent embankment, she had shot him in the back with an ancient Husqvarna pistol. Her boyfriend – a cousin – had bound and weighted the body, dragged it out onto a rusty gantry spanning a disused spur of the Mittelland Kanal and toppled it off. Ute, who had stood on a ladder and peered over an old wall of scorched and crumbling brick, could still see the shiny black hole where the corpse's splash had driven back the duckweed on the stagnant surface below.

On his snazzy motorbike with its false number-plate, they had hurtled away unnoted, wearing their heavy motorcycle suits of gleaming dark blue leather and their black boots and mittens, but shunning those freedom-spoiling helmets which their nursemaid government had recently made obligatory. After an hour, they had stopped off in a forest for their inevitably frequent fusion. Ulrich liked it outdoors with the scents of pine resin and dank earth, matted needles and epigeous herbs. A spotlight of pale moonlight had probed their black domain of toughness and sex and glinted off her large-lensed spectacles which she had laid on a fallen log and off their rippling leather, especially where it ebbed and flowed concertina-like round their elbows and shoulders. Their leather suits had those new stretch sections of ribbed finely-pleated leather in them – a strip down the outside of each leg and an oblong at waist-level in the back, allowing tighter, snugger fits – but still to couple she had to remove hers and lie on it, whilst he still in his, crushed her agreeably from above. Like serpentine Germanic gods, the pair had writhingly creaked and gasped their way to lower-end relief.

The squarish fashionable pink telephone burred. Ute absorbed Ingrid's message – 'Leonore Uff' – one of four possible and the signal for her to ring her British Army contact again.

On the small wooden table-top in the seldom used modern kitchen, she wrapped up her cheque book and a bundle of other covert financial papers inside a plastic bag and secreted them inside a crevice amidst the plumbing at the back of the cupboard under the sink and screwed the laminated plastic back panel back into place.

An unhindered summer sun shone over Hanover's Eichenfelsstrasse and even Ute's doleful face grew more animated as she left the flat above the small branch of the Westdeutsche Landesbank and boarded a tram.

As it glided along by the green trees bordering the Humboldt Park, she remembered how she had met her first lover on a tram in Vienna. Her serious Protestant North German nature had been misled by that frivolous tempo rubato Austrian, though on reflection, evidence of his deceits had been to hand – he had poured flattery and compliments onto other girls too and she had felt no special sense of oneness with him when in company with others.

The Sankt Ursula Platz greeted her like an old acquaintance. She liked the airy modern square with its bashful yet dissentient bronze statue of the virgin saint and the lime trees which agreeably broke up the angular contours of the plate-glass and concrete shopping concourse with its vivid and futuristic logos.

At a pavement café, she sat and drank coffee, ate an open roll with salami tomato and mayonnaise on it and watched life drift by.

As she chewed, she saw two thirteen-year-old schoolgirls larking about with two smarmy and slightly older boys, encouraging them to tussle for a truffle bar. Ute knew well enough where such forwardness and frolicking would end. Even she, who had been shy and conscientious and homely had made mistakes ... though she *was* willing to be loyal now.

On warm nights this summer, Ulrich had also liked it outdoors with himself naked or only in his new pair of navy blue boxer-shorts embroidered with pale blue 'Krückenkreuze' or 'crosses potent'. He would lie on their lubricious and sensual leather suits spread on the ground and enjoy the thrill of her chilly slippery leather mittens delving into his underpants and stroking his swollen testicles and massively engorged cannon, before rotating her beneath him to overcome and conquer her with his bare body. All this had flung them both into poignant spasms. She had never known convulsions like it from anyone else and she believed that they were sent to uniquely enrapture each other. He *was* her heroic scrumptious gorilla ... and yet ... when she had hinted at marriage, he had denounced it as an encumbrance. He wanted her to buy a matching set of 'Krückenkreuze' panties and brassière. That was the extent of his devotion.

From a glass telephone booth, she dialled the barracks near Fassberg for the fifth time in three months. She had the number jotted down in reverse along the edge of her swimming baths' pass.

Ulrich popped other girls too, she knew. Why did he not want to be together only with her? Sometimes by allowing other men to prang her though, she won a dubious revenge.

'Buffs and Blues Regiment.'

'Heda! Ute Schniewind here. May I speak viz ze saycoority offisur?'

'Say again.'

'Ze saycoority offisur, pleese.'

'Just a jiffy, Ma'am.'

She could see herself becoming one of those women who after too long being belittled, suddenly flips over from obedient adoration to callous indifference.

'Guy Woollhead here.' The unruffled fatherly tones stirred an unease in her.

'Hello. Ziss is Ute vunce more.'

'Hullo, my dear.'

Ute thought of Ingrid telling her that the East Germans referred to the West German counter-espionage service as 'The Cuddly Bunny Club', from which she inferred that they were pretty incompetent and slow-witted. Yet Ute, herself inexpert and unastute, was equally unfitted for poker games with lean wolves. Both with Major Woollhead and in Amsterdam, she felt alarmingly amateurish. Stupidly even, she had used her hoped-for married name as a code-name.

'A feeshing boat vill sail out of Killybegs on ze Donegal coast and rendezvous viz an unknown vessel in ze evening of ze sirtius of Owgoost. Ze mating vill ohccur tventy-fife keelometres vest of ze Raslin O'Birne light-tower. You understood?'

'A nasty spectacle. I have it.'

'Vot?'

'I understand,' he confirmed mellifluously.

'Bye-bye.'

'God bless.'

Ute resumed her seat and ordered a second coffee and a Danish apple cake.

Under a colourful optician's awning, a pretty mother enacted a well-feigned look of surprise when her doll-like daughter pointed to a poster of a rabbit wearing glasses. Then she smiled fondly at the toddler. Why could Ute not be happy too?

* * *

Ingrid Axt stopped at a little back-street grocer's in Rome, where a grubby proprietor in baggy trousers rose from a crate and supplied her with the tomatoes bread and bottles of cola she requested.

She passed the garage surrounded by Fiats in varying stages of decomposition and saw urchins shouting or urinating near the Renaissance fountain in the street, before turning into the vestibule of the block of post-war flats where she lived, passing a row of letter-boxes and heavily chained mopeds and climbing the four half-flights of plain marble stairs.

On the second floor, she opened her own solid and firmly locked door and entered. It felt calm and cool and spacious, partly because of the doorless arched openings between rooms and partly because there was not much furniture.

She clipped her toe-nails under the vine-entwined trellis over the balcony and looked out both at other flats with balconies and washing lines and below, where a small idyllic garden with a pool and a nymph conjured a whiff of antique solace.

Michael Rose arrived. She admitted him after a cursory glance through the peep-hole and like one wishing to advertise or imitate an unrestrainable sexual appetite, he at once embraced her in a supposedly hot body ravish and began to fondle her grotesquely.

She shuddered at the clumsiness of his maulings, not because he failed to love her – she was not so naïve as to expect that – but because he ruined the simple physical pleasure which was possible if both participants showed some imagination and responded to the other at the right pace.

Her sparsely furnished but clean bedroom, with its simple soft-mattressed wooden bed and the summer breezes and the city's scents wafting in through the open balcony door, offered a good setting for rumbustious enjoyment – as others had proved – yet Rose was a nightmare.

His behaviour belied an age-old sickness. The specious mastery of his everyday polished political posings, dissolved to reveal a sorry shadow fighting with itself and love eternally eluding him who sought it so frenetically and so perversely. His ego-evinced struggle started with their awkward fall onto the bed in the early evening, five minutes after she had let him in and persisted for hours. Ingrid knew that she was not the origin of his difficulties but only the catalyst of renewal. That he must strive to compel himself to the unobtainable seemed remarkable, as if finer and more estimable achievements were of no consequence.

Straddling her, he looked down at her hard features and sought to titillate her by insult in the hope that fired with temper, she might incite him sufficiently to perform, but unable to be aroused, she could not then be angry if satisfaction did not follow. He tried to burn white candles of love and when they refused to be kindled, turned to black ones of filth. He ransacked dirt hunting vainly for ecstasy, expecting such devices to urge him to victory, though he must have known from earlier sallies that these were faithless promises. The only time she gave a yelp was when he bit her clitoris. He exhibited weakness not longing and on it went interminably. When he noted her patience and interpreted it as intimidation, he flung himself into wild self-reproach and utter humiliation, depths unspeakably vile as he scoured every artifice with wearying frenzy to defeat the arch-enemy of unsuccess.

Such was the hidden misery behind the erudite but gimcrack snideness which he liked to portray to an uninterested world. Michael Rose was the British socialist Member of Parliament for Hevermarsh.

Finally she fell asleep. He drank some of her cognac and cleaned his teeth, spitefully hoping to annoy her Germanic sense of order by squeezing the tooth-paste tube at the top and not at the bottom and spraying froth onto the bathroom mirror.

They met next over rolls and coffee as the sparkling dawn of a crystal clear Italian day edged up over the Umbrian hills.

'I have *some* progress to report regarding the blows befalling the supply lines of out Irish foederati.' He spoke with a well-manicured and effeminate pique.

'Gude,' she said with a hint of sardonic amusement.

'It is being overseen by our Army Intelligence arm. Obviously they have a good informant.'

'Ohbviously.' She subtly echoed his affectation.

'The trouble is, they're out of control. They don't record telephone conversations – nor does others' listening in on them seem to reveal anything – they have no secretaries, no office girls, no computers and their minimal archives contain only cards with rows of undecodable indices and hieroglyphs on them. The man in charge – Colonel Archibald Letheren – calls them his "recondite references", I'm told.'

'It is all in zere heads?'

'Exactly,' he spluttered. 'So even if a Special Branch commander or a senior M.I.6 officer investigates this Robin Hood cohort, he can unearth nothing.'

'Outarrrrageous!' she mimicked the Italians, throwing up her hands in feigned despair.

'It damn well is. Entirely unconstitutional too ... I intend to raise it at the next Parliamentary Defence Sub-Committee meeting and demand a thorough inquiry into these

Byronic reactionaries and their cosy fox-hole. They must be made to answer.'

A faint smile shone on her face, indecipherable to Rose, but legible to one of her own species as a sign of deep contempt.

'Ingrid, I need to "debrief" you again – literally.'

She held him at bay.

Ingrid had been brought up in a village of Dano-Saxon houses – half-timbered with brickwork between the beams – in East Germany. There people had been industrious, subdued and even pious in their daily routine. Life had existed in a pastoral placid landscape with small workshops, like an island in time, still in touch with medieval Germany. Ingrid had begun in a world where innocence was still everyday, but escalated to the opposite extreme. She had started amidst folk who had had their ambition knocked out of them and ended up ensconced by layers of tortuous intrigue.

Ingrid stage-managed Rose. By 'drops' and 'intimate meetings' she traded commands for stolen secrets. Rose saw her as a high priestess in his espoused ideology. He refused to see the pointers to her unstated goals.

She had grown weary of poverty. In East Germany there was no fur, no leather, not even good wool. The clothes were shapeless, the food was monotonous, books were restricted, cars were tinny and dwellings and heating wretchedly inadequate. It was not the rules or the lies which made it unbearable to her feminine mind, but the rubbing of shoulders with proscribed wealth.

A sudden thought came to Rose, its suddenness easily apparent to his controller.

'Four shipments have been lost in succession. It could not be that *we* are disclosing certain facts could it, as part of some broader strategy?'

For a moment she eyed him warily. 'Us? Vee use such Byzantine complexity?' she probed with a straight face.

'It has been known.' He smiled faintly.

'No. Today vee are using a new tvist – straightforvardniss.'

He laughed, a short trial burst of noisy neighing and then as it felt good, a more prolonged demonstration of his wit and character.

She humoured him with the smile one gives to nasty children, but it pleased him well enough.

'No. Vee see into ze problame very seriously, I am telling you. But also vee are about to arrange a new messod ... how vee say ... chain of sayparrat men, so vee eliminate ze black carrot.'

'Bad apple.'

'Don't bozzer pleese, viz blue herrings.'

'Red herrings.'

'Qviet!' She snapped tersely.

Women are elemental and plain and therefore less unsure and less erringly human than men, so long as they remain strictly within the métier ordained for them. Ingrid after a decade of pretences, might have *seemed* to have adapted to complex and unfamiliar territory, but behind the differing superficial personae, her greed and her wish to be unshackled shaped a clear and uncompromising continuity. This desire to accrue money and to be lazy was her innate essence, which from quite early in life had blurred beyond recognition any ideals and slowly blotted out her conscience.

'However,' Rose resumed, 'I had a thought this morning whilst cleaning my teeth ... '

'You must have cleaned zem very surrully.'

' ... a stratagem to outwit this Colonel Letheren ... ' Ingrid stifled a yawn. 'A ruse to foil this titanic web of capitalist conspiracy ... '

'Comm off ze rostrum,' she upbraided him curtly.

He pretended not to have heard her. 'His wife is buried in the British military cemetery outside Benghazi. We could tell him that unless he disgorges to us the name of his spy, or at least keeps his Merry Men off our friends, then we will arrange for her grave to be dug up and her bones desecrated.'

Ingrid thought for thirty seconds. She found Rose's desire to see his own country defeated or flattened or ruined, hard to understand. Even she felt some sympathy and pride for her own people, though she of course was not a real communist.

'You have done your homeverk. I must talk viz my chiefs. You must not sretten him or act peremptorily. Zere are maybe hornets' dens vee know nussing about. But all right ... I ask.'

He semaphored his insistence on a last futile bounce on the bed to round off the session. During this, whilst he kissed her with lips like marsh-mallows, she told him to manipulate a certain colleague into broadcasting and she gave him a new and cleverly-convoluted snippet with which to relight an old right-wing scandal.

Later she showered and dressed in a summery frock and went out to a quiet trattoria, where she ate a plate of oregano-embellished goulash and started on a carafe of cheap vino, which she shared with her boss when he turned up.

This Italian of Ukrainian derivation – a man called Igor Hanusiak – had flabby loose open-pored facial skin, big Slavic ears and a coarse affability which tallied well with his simple-minded but gross notions. His personality disorder was no worse than the average boxer's though. On one finger he wore a ring with a sham stone in it the size of an Oxo cube.

Ingrid told of her visit to Syria and of her offer to find help for al-Uzza, but without explaining that she would be behind the new helpers. She mentioned Rose's call, but without discussing his suggestion of trying to force Colonel Letheren to cease his activities.

Under the guise of wondering whether Rose showed signs of homosexuality, Hanusiak tried to dig into what he and she did together. Ingrid confabulated drolly, saying that he liked to dress up in a panther-skin woman's swim-suit and only then, if she looked suitably frightened, could he manage an erection.

Hanusiak's eyes widened and he began to extrapolate on the obscene possibilities of this fantasy, until he shook with silent laughter.

Ingrid at first looked out at the sage green trees and a red cattle lorry parked in the piazza, then she too laughed, though not as Hanusiak thought, at his inventive humour. No, she disliked him as thoroughly as she disliked Rose and the others in the gang, but it satisfied her conceit to see this former Russian peasant swallowing her lies.

He handed over a sealed envelope containing money, to pay her for her expenses and bribes and often fictitious gossip and after arguing with the waiter about the customary attempt to inflate the bill, she went off to pay her wages into her bank.

* * *

Crossing the motor transport square, Major Woollhead caught sight of the regiment's latest young officer, a fellow who would have made the original wet blanket look dry.

'Lieutenant Arden!'

Arden came up to him and saluted. 'Sir?' His first name was Julian.

'Have you worked out the bearings yet for those target tugs on Friday?'

''Fraid not Sir. Spot of back trouble ... from playing ping-pong yesterday.'

'Not finger trouble?'

'Finger trouble, Sir?'

'As in "getting it out".'

'"Out" Sir? Out of what?'

Woollhead sighed deeply whilst Arden tried to puzzle out this conundrum. 'Nobbing hell, you great pilchard. I want them on my desk by 21.00 hours.'

On the epaulettes of Woollhead's khaki shirt were the crowns of a major and the brass 'R.A.'s of the Royal Artillery. His cap, with the red band of an instructor in gunnery, hid a slightly balding head. His face and body betrayed middle-aged plumpness, but he was still both tough and civilised.

He ascended the railed timber balcony of the prefabricated wooden headquarter building of this light anti-aircraft regiment. The plaque on his office door read, 'Major G. A. Woollhead. Adjutant.'

Inside he removed his cap, lit his pipe and picked up Arrian's *The Campaigns of Alexander*, which he promptly put down again as the telephone jangled.

'Woollhead.'

'Sir, your girlfriend's on the line again,' said the gunner on the switchboard.

'Put her through.'

He switched on the standard issue green enamel desk-lamp and prepared to scribble on a pad. 'Guy Woollhead here.'

He pictured her as someone slightly well built, comely and phlegmatic, but also broody and sorrowful.

At the end, he glanced at his watch, subtracted two minutes and jotted down the time – 15.02 hours on Thursday the twenty-eighth of August, 1975.

Colonel Letheren had christened this woman 'Giraffe Trap', presumably as she enabled him to catch those who stuck their necks out too far.

Woollhead made a call to R.A.F. Wildenrath and booked himself onto a Belfast transport aircraft due to fly to R.A.F. Brize Norton in Oxfordshire that evening.

From his office window, he saw a civilian placing something under the seat in his blue delivery van. He nipped out and strode down the road with its neatly-painted white edging-stones to the red and white boom at the main gate, where he arrived simultaneously with the van.

'Bombardier, look under that driver's seat.'

The driver was dislodged with some difficulty and they found a ten kilogram tin of cheese and two large carving knives.

'I voz taked zem to sharpen.'

The duty sergeant let out a short rattle of laughter, like a machine-gun with a clipped start and finish.

'Summon the cook and interrogate him, Sergeant.'

'Sir! And this chap? In the cooler?'

The Major packed up a few items and drove out of the barracks in his quarter-tonner. The roads were hot and dusty with flat fields of unfenced sugar beet and corn on either side.

As he passed through the little town of Müden, he saw a hat land on his Land Rover's aerial. 'Good gracious.' He stopped to hang it up on some railings.

An elderly man puffed up. 'Danke. Danke schön.'

'Bitte.'

A breeze was blowing up.

This 'Ute Schniewind' had first rung in June and demanded to speak to the 'security officer'. She had told him about this Dutch tug en route from West Africa to Rotterdam, which would anchor in Roaringwater Bay and off-load some small arms. He had felt rather agog, but also that she was in some way straight and trustworthy.

He picked his nose – his secret vice and one which was so pleasurable that at times he could not desist even if for instance, stopped by a red traffic light and aware that other motorists might see him.

Before relaying her call to that swarm of homos and hirelings in Whitehall – with their sceptical smirks, double firsts from Oxford and ethics so bent as to be almost straight again – he had conferred with his C.O. The artillery colonel had fully shared his misgivings and suggested Army Intelligence as an alternative.

Thus he had journeyed to a Georgian country house called Coancott Manor beside Culm Barracks on the Somerset-Devon border. It had large quoins, a well-trimmed croquet lawn, apple trees and a discreet though efficient guard.

Rumbling through Hermannsburg, a woman's nylon headscarf blew under his vehicle. In the mirror he noticed that it did not reappear and that the Hausfrau stood glaring indignantly after him. He chortled. It must have melted onto the exhaust.

In Coancott Manor, he had met Lieutenant-Colonel A. H. Letheren, a man in his fifties with an earthy pith inherited from his Anglo-Saxon forbears. Behind a twinkling protruding left eye, lurked a wisdom which stoically refused to treat in the seditious wiles of diplomacy. Letheren did not bother about what he said, nor whom it offended.

In this retreat, Woollhead had had a fumbling but flawless discourse, as both men sought apt metaphors. Here there lurked no servile attentiveness, no counterfeit concern, no corrosive sophistries. The head of Army Intelligence had listened to the Major's briefing uncondescendingly, jotting down the odd note – a number in Greek or an English phrase penned in Nestorian script – which though all very boy-scoutish, no one could ever unravel.

The tip-off turned out to be genuine, as did the girl's second succinct and timely communication.

Woollhead felt a measure of manly trust and unmarred devotion for Letheren. Things were in good hands.

After this, either Woollhead himself or another major by the name of Gorton were always present in camp, to take her calls.

* * *

Rear-Admiral – or Admiral of the Blue – Eydes-Seymour, sat in his swivel chair of grey leather, behind his desk of battleship-grey steel and contemplated the innate unalterability of human nature.

The cleaning girl with the headscarf knotted round her brow, her lipstick daubed inexpertly round her mouth and her blue legs, had for a few months dressed more smartly, applied her make-up more accurately and tried to be more cheerful he had noticed. But now she had hooked the large fish she had been playing – the wedding had been last week – the chameleon had reverted to its true colours of sullen beer-drinking havoc.

Behind his smooth benign and slightly aristocratic mould, stretched a deep vault lined with dark and light blue electronic maps with tiny blue and red lights on them and around his desk were arrays of telephones and computer screens.

He pressed the pads of his two sets of splayed fingers together and lifted an eyebrow at a W.R.N.S. lass who approached him and saluted a little awkwardly.

'Are you my chauffeuse?' He did not so much have a plum in his mouth as an orchard.

The girl had a pretty figure and something of an impish smile. Her navy uniform with its flat hat and chin-strap suited her well, but a rash of boils on her neck and face had given her a complex. 'Yes Sir. Good evening Sir.'

He glanced up at the digital clock. 'That's G.M.T. It's really morning.'

'Sorry Sir. My meridian must have slipped.' She blushed as she realised that it sounded as if her meridian were an item of underwear.

He gave a restrained smile. 'The sun and the moon revolve around you do they Petty Officer?'

She repressed a squeak of laughter.

As he pulled on his camel-coloured duffle coat and his cap with its rear-admiral's braid, a surge of florid radiance spread over his youthful middle-aged widower's face, the evocation of her touchingly feminine timidity, which hc found so charming in this era of ghastly strident masculine women.

They passed along a drab subterranean tunnel of white-washed concrete, broken at intervals by blue-painted steel scantlings and then via staggered lift shafts and elaborate security checks, they eventually emerged into the dark warm night in the vehicle park of this atom-bomb-proof naval establishment.

They halted at a service station on the M4 motorway. The place was dingy and the choice of food was curried cow-pat or some other oriental sludge. As he selected a roll instead, Eydes-Seymour rasped out, 'Why doesn't this vile hole serve

English food? Where are we? Katmandu? Kuala Lumpur?' The restaurant was cold and nearly empty, it being past two o'clock.

A tender yet euphoric twinge assailed the Admiral as they ate. 'I hear you're engaged to an Anglo-Swedish banker?'

'Yes ... ' She smiled wryly. 'He scoffs food like a pig ... '

'Not like a piggy-banker?'

'He doesn't have a slot in his back.'

'Still, I can see you in your Swedish chalet with its view across a lake ... '

'And he insists on lying in the sun, which I can't tolerate.'

' ... pine interiors, fine Nordic antiques ... '

' ... and all he talks about is making money.'

' ... pewter and silver tableware, impeccable clothes, urbane looks ... '

'He collected me once from the reception at *H.M.S. Naiad* and all he commented upon was the value of that Indian elephant tusk. "I bet that's worth a bob or two," he growled. He didn't ask what the story was behind it.'

' ... and up until the age of sixty, you'll still have that refined look which could be anywhere between twenty and forty.'

She gave a comical shrug and then fiddled with smoothing out her cheese wrapper.

'I shall come to your wedding and let his bloody tyres down.' Eydes-Seymour looked at her downcast eyes for some moments. He saw her frailty, her loneliness and her acute sense of being unloved.

'It all sounds so romantic, Sir ... but truly he does nothing for me.'

He felt pity. 'Why not leave him then? Oh forgive me, my dear. I didn't mean to intrude.'

'No, no Sir. I told you these things ... ' she petered out.

He drank up his tea and they left.

She turned their car off onto a dark rural lane, stopped and looked nervously at her chief.

'Do you want to?' he asked.

She watched his eyes for a few seconds and then nodded.

He almost asked if she were sure, but then remembered that women never waver. All evening he had had a premonition of being led somewhere. In her resentment, she might well allow someone else to have her. If he refused to serve her, would she fly to some saucy welder? He ran a finger round the oval of her quiet face. 'I've never done it in a car. It sounds uncomfortable.'

Suddenly she livened up. 'It's quite easy, Sir. We wind the seats back, put the hand-brake off out of the way and ... '

The overture to all this had been the arrival of an army despatch-rider from Somerset at the Headquarters of Naval Operations some hours before, greeted with the usual 'Stand by to repel boarders' and other remarks born of inter-service rivalry.

His sealed envelope had come from Archibald Letheren, a distant relative of the Admiral's and a man too who had reputedly belonged to a circle of officers, which had planned a military coup in Britain, back in 1967.

In Coancott Manor by five o'clock, Letheren had stood up from his bunk-bed, shaved and in a state of semi-dress, moved through to his office.

A diminutive gas-fire burned, inhabiting the old Orpheus and Eurydice grate. Its fenestrated pieces of baked clay glowed orange as the hissing flames heated them. A long elm refectory table served as a desk and a red angle-poise lamp lit it brightly, whilst in the shadows were oak bookshelves half-filled with dossiers and tomes of reference and drawn heavy green curtains. The dullness was relieved by some gaily coloured plastic paper-clips and a scattering of luminous modern pens. It was tidy but Spartan.

Letheren hitched his braces up onto his shoulders, pulled on an over-sized woolly and spent half an hour engrossed in decrypting a page of Syriac, about an earthquake in Laodicea. Classical antiquity was his life-long hobby.

When the Admiral of the Blue appeared, he rose and greeted his third cousin with an ambience remote from life's everyday frictions.

A corporal bore in a tray with two plates of bacon egg and tomatoes, toast and marmalade and a large pot of tea.

'So Ronald, tuck in,' said Letheren in his soft bass voice, shoving his books to one side. 'What do you think of these Range Rovers?'

'Range Rovers? What makes you ask that?'

'Oh, just that Catharine wants me to buy one. She says she's fed up of jolting about on utilitarian farm vehicles. Yet I wonder if they're not a bit Chelsea, a bit smooth, a bit dog-breeder type?'

'I suspect that's right.'

Whilst Letheren chewed, he surveyed Eydes-Seymour's even unflustered facial topography. 'I've another look-out task at sea I need help with, but without heaving them to this time.' Letheren had bounce and amiability in the creases of his face. It stimulated him to sit and scheme. 'I would like to watch the landward end of it too, but to protect my agent I want you to do it *unseen*.'

'*Unseen*? That means using a sub.,' declared Eydes-Seymour critically.

Letheren sprang up from his semi-circular oak chair, its seat upholstered in holly green leather with brass tacks. 'Tomorrow,' he whispered, 'off north-western Ireland ... Well?'

Eydes-Seymour smiled cryptically. 'It is feasible.'

'Feasible?'

'You're in luck Leatherbags ... as ever. There are *two* boats close enough. There's a diesel-electric boat off County Mayo and a nuclear boat just sailing from the Clyde, bound for the Barents Sea to take part in an exercise with the Norwegians.' His pukkah tones faded, his smile lingered and afterwards broadened. 'Have you heard about the loudspeakers in Norway's coastal defence set-up?'

'No.'

'They're equipped with pre-recorded tapes saying in Russian, "Don't shoot. We surrender."'

After a pause of disbelief, Letheren laughed. He squeaked like an old leaky leather bellows. It was infectious and the Rear-Admiral found himself laughing heartily too.

'Magnificent.'

'Exit the Vikings.'

'Have you any clues about the mystery vessel?'

'None.'

The forehead of the Director of Naval Operations puckered, because the two available boats were very different. Faced with a sophisticated enemy warship, the diesel-electric *Rorqual* would be preferable, for the water was shallow enough there for her to lie on the bottom with her motors off, producing only a very faint heat signal and there she could listen to the arrival's propeller's cavitation signature and compare it to the list of known recordings or if unexpectedly the star guest were some soot-caked old coaster, she could still turn on her motors and come up to periscope depth for a peek. Against all this, the nuclear-powered *Warspite*, though more easily detected because of her heat-generating reactor, had a vastly superior underwater speed and endurance with which to search or follow.

Letheren massaged his chin. 'If it's the C.I.A., it won't be anything high-powered. They daredn't risk using their own ships ... '

'*The C.I.A.*?'

Letheren's walrus face smiled gently. 'Some faction of it. Don't tell me you're surprised ... after their antics in Singapore, French Indo-China, Suez ... not to mention all their bribery to clinch trade cartels and aircraft sales ... the House of Orange, General Tse, the F.L.N., the Peruvian Philippic, the Kennedy shootings ... to name only the better known instances.'

'No, I suppose I shouldn't be, should I?' conceded the Admiral of the Blue, narrowing his eyes again.

'Then again, if this stuff's from the East, I've never known the Ruskies use a submarine or a surface warship. Perhaps they think that you fellows are too good at tracking them?'

He stepped out through the French windows, onto a small balcony with a wrought-ironwork balustrade.

Eydes-Seymour joined him and espied the stars, still used for navigation in his younger days. They shrank as dawn encroached over the eastern hedgerows. After ten minutes spent as on the bridge of a ship, he took his leave and went to send a signal to *Warspite*.

Letheren, through reverie, tried to see something of this girl who called herself Ute Schniewind. Who was she and why had she rung them, he mused? Perhaps she had a nominal reason, but did she also have a conscience to salve? Her upbringing would have included the home-taught German virtues of orderliness docility and scholarliness. Then in the widening sphere of adolescence, she had gleaned a taste for zest and ebullience and crudeness. The unreconciled mix of these had left her unsure if she should submit meekly to life as God gave it or seize it by the throat and force from it all her ambition. He could see her, vacillating with one hundred per cent faith in neither, led by the vision of success and the lure of wealth on the one hand, yet unable to dispel her childhood belief in humility on the other.

With this vague shape of his fortuitous ally, he set off for his farm in northern England under the same blue proscenium arch as those scurrilous woodworms who plotted chaos. He counter-plotted and heaven favoured him, not because he was so good, but because his enemies for their wickedness deserved the fools' torment of defeat.

* * *

A wan sun shone over the white-flecked grey-green waters of a choppy Atlantic. Its orange disc rested on the distant low line of the coast of Ireland, where the white threads of beaches and the grey flecks of promontories were backed by the slight swell of hazy dark blue mountains.

This could be seen to port, as the steel-hulled trawler yawed gently southwards, to the oscillating throb of her diesels. The salt-laden wind occasionally made the East German flag or one of the red pennons snap on the stays and rigging beneath the numerous antennae on the mast-head.

The captain and the radio officer were playing chess in the chart-house, when the helmsman summoned them through to the enclosed bridge. He had spotted a helicopter approaching.

An ungainly Wessex, with Royal Navy insignia, came close and hovered alongside, before tilting its bulbous nose downwards, to slew both upwards and away.

The captain greeted it with a hippopotamine yawn.

# 33

The radio officer displayed a leisurely stock frown of pseudo-concern. 'Just routine Comrade Captain ... or do they know?'

Not only were they playing the Russian national game of chess literally, but also figuratively. Like all acolytes of the late and unlamented Lenin, what you said seldom coincided with what you thought.

Both men's main objective was to sail to the friendly port of Havana, toss back some raw rum and find some juicy whores as quickly as possible. Neither man could care less whether or not the frigging British knew of their doings the previous evening, but they could not openly say so. The rules of the game decreed it so.

The captain gave the retiring helicopter a two-fingered salute.

*   *   *

From her first-class window seat in the TriStar, Ute Steyer saw the illuminated terminal buildings loom up in the dark grey morning. She had come overnight to Damascus – some say the oldest city in the world – on a stolen Dutch passport in the name of Emma Zijp, acquired on one of her many trips to Amsterdam. She had not wanted the last stage of her journey to be traceable, nor did she wish to involve an expert forger – hence the theft.

She fought her way through a seething screeching bunch of boys in the arrivals area, all dressed in assorted tunics and rags and trying to sell her their dubious wares.

A man distinguished by his light grey Western-cut suit, red fez, sandals and sun-glasses approached her.

'Mademoiselle Zijp?'

'Oui.'

'Venez donc, s'il vous plaît.'

He led the way to a patched and pop-riveted old taxi and they rattled off, not down the new asphalt highway to the city, but eastwards into the rising sun and were soon on a track which crossed brown and barren slopes dotted with low thorn bushes.

The car's engine gave skirling howls as it half-bogged and ploughed through the soft rutted undulations and its jolted passenger looked out at the azure blue and the deep brown tedium of the Anti-Lebanon. Behind it, the vehicle trailed a cloud of sand and dust.

Then through the shimmering and hallucinatory air near some dusty orange groves, the tiny desert town of Qira resolved into view, its ochre walls of roughly-hewn ashlars and crude battlements enclosing a clutter of grubby white-washed houses with flat roof-tops.

Hassan al-Uzza awaited his meeting. He dismissed his servant Nahid with a blend of harsh and mellow Arabic hisses.

She lowered her head and said, 'Yes Sayyid.'

He read the note. The last package of arms had made it. That was a relief, because his master in Tripoli – His Excellency the Wazir the ever-devious Mustapha al-Khalali (Order of the Yellow Turban) – was growing restless about the recent failures. He had met him yesterday at a tranquil old Turkish house on the slopes of Salhiye. It was also fortunate for this imminently due Miss Zijp, because he suspected Ingrid Axt of some sort of indirect double-cross and had been contemplating torture for her new envoy if grilling failed.

In a tornado of dust, the taxi lurched through a blurred arch of carved brick and halted in the straw-strewn quadrangular courtyard of a shambolic caravanserai, where a herd of camels from the Nefud stood with coloured saddle-rugs from Baluchistan under their rough leather sumpters. Men with desert-blackened severe faces and gleaming teeth were unloading them amid the static heat and the stench of dung and rotting vegetable matter. A harsh effulgent white sun hung overhead, a mollaqua wailed from a minaret and a boy in a small crimson hat played mournfully on a zummara. The entire scene could have survived unaltered from Old Testament times.

Ute saw fleetingly a father resume thrashing his small son for not having woven enough baskets and a poor lice-infested donkey with a cart, whose back had a huge open sore where an ill-fitting yoke chafed it. It bent its head down sadly, its dull fly-pestered eyes resigned.

She was watched in remorseless silence by the meqba-clad doughy faces of women who stood beside the creaking wheel of a well. Her escort hustled her away, away from the austere and lecherous eyes of merchants and robbers and led her along a crooked narrow alleyway, past some shuttered hovels with overhanging balconies to a stumpy squat door on which they rapped. Nahid, a short girl in a girdled grey robe and a white head-drape opened it. She had a low broad forehead, straight unvarying brows and the eyes of an abused but uninnocent servant. Ute felt frightened.

They led her through a tiny yard with no greenery except for some stunted lemon bushes, down some steps and then by a second door into a small storehouse containing two rows of stone ewers and permeated by the scents of uncertain spices and musty grapefruits. They filed down some tight irregular stairs under a wooden hatch, into a sort of hidden sub-cellar – a secret oubliette – set actually within the ancient wall of the town. It had a thin slit which looked out over the endless desert and from which a knife-edge of bright sunlight clove the little marquetry-inlaid table and the flagged uneven floor before diffusing itself in a white haze.

Hassan al-Uzza shook Ute's moist hand with a malevolent smile. 'Sit down, Miss Zijp.'

She did so, evidently nervous. Outside she could see the sun, a ball of radiance cutting into this lair, where perhaps five millennia before men had concealed stolen silver or plotted a king's overthrow.

Al-Uzza dismissed both his servants and waved a hand at a selection of drinks. He quizzed her a little about her journey.

'Although the last consignment of pearls and peppers we sent abroad appears to have been safely received, I would still like to discuss the possible employment of your organisation.' He spoke English well except that some 'p's sounded a bit like 'b's and an occasional falsetto screech replaced a long 'e'. 'You come well recommended by our common acquaintance, but I am unclear which specific operations you have to your credit.'

'Zat is proof to our skill,' she replied adroitly.

The puckerings of his smile intensified.

'Vot qvontity of stoffs vud you vish to move?'

Ute Steyer's stature was of medium height but broader in the hips and more bosomy than Ingrid's. Her light brown hair had been plaited into a coil in the style of Tyrolean peasant girls, though she was a woman and not a girl.

'Say, five hundred kilograms.'

He studied her edgy and slightly animal air, the smooth white neck, the delectably feminine forearms protruding from the three-quarter sleeves of her dark blue cotton dress patterned with miniature white flowers. Its belt too, emphasised her tantalisingly moulded Western female shape and beneath its knee-length hem were the two well-sculptured legs, not disagreeable as usual to parting, he guessed.

'A price?'

'Sree hundred sousand dollars.' She opened a tin of fizzy orange with a pop. 'If your man Rabbah Eissa take it to Türkei, vee see over its furzer progress.'

A shifty gleam suffused his dark eyes. 'You are unknown in this field. This would be a trial to establish you. Eighty thousand ... on completion.'

Ute's intuition to avoid detailed discussion had been right, not least because Arabs never believe you. If you say you earn a good wage, they assume you are bragging and if you claim a pittance, they imagine you are raking it in.

A faded piece of vellum was the sole adornment on the rough walls, framed in a crude oblong. An exquisite cursive script in gold and pink boldly filled this piece of beige leather, bordered with delicate flowers in pale blue, indigo and umber brown. Ute's eyes looked at it as a distraction from her host's hypnotising stare. She shuffled.

'It is a side from the Hali ibn Said Quoran. Gold leaf and rose ink on hide and decorated with insect dyes ... copied in Edessa the year after Hegira three fifty – about nine sixty in your calendar.' He took a couple of mint chocolate balls from a small mahogany box and tossed them back into his mouth.

She examined it sceptically. 'Vot is it saying?'

'It is the command to the faithful to be merciful to Jews and Christians as brothers in worship of the One True God,' he lied. 'My brother bought it at an auction in Paris.'

'I sink ze bids vur not so eager for zat page.'

This insult, doubting his brethren their strict belief in the Quoran, angered him, but he hid it. He would gratify his lust for vengeance by having her. She was inured to sexual trespass he could see and far less wily and sophisticated than Ingrid.

A yellow butterfly fluttered away as from something offensive and distasteful. It disappeared through the slit, out into the whitening heat.

'Two hundred and seventy sousand,' she intoned.

Modern German women do not rest their feet on the seat opposite them in the tram, they fill in every detail of their tax forms with exemplary precision and they report the number of any vehicle which does not park exactly in its allotted box – all impressively efficient law-abiding and orderly, very Apollonian and serious. Yet come Friday evening and the office party, they metamorphose and become wildly Dionysian. They swill down vodka and in their forthright Teutonic way, demand that the brutish hunk they have been eyeing up for the last week, shag them violently. It is performed on the carpet under the teleprinter console and quite sordidly, yet this disparity between the aesthetic and the unaesthetic seems not to bother them.

'One hundred and fifty thousand,' he shrugged cunningly and drew her reluctant form towards his couch. She sat anxiously beside him. 'How shall we solve this?' He seized her firmly.

'No!'

'One hundred and eighty thousand,' he hissed.

'I don't vish it,' she said listlessly and wondered why she needed it at least twice a day. In the top class of her Realschule, the girls had had an epigram – 'She who needs it, sense she spurns; When it's over, sense returns.' But it was useless to question why, it just was so. You just had to try to grow hard and if men pissed on you, piss back up.

'Two hundred and twenty,' he whispered consolingly in her ear. 'That really is a very good offer.' Al-Uzza laid her down and though troubled, she submitted.

And so her occidental seriousness and his rampant Arabian volatility coalesced briefly in the encircling torpor. She was less adept at the quick couple than Ingrid, less brisk and business-like and Hassan expended more effort this time in pleasing them both. He puffed, agog at her incredible absence of emotion. Then he saw that she too had one pale blue and one yellow eye and felt startled.

Back at the sweltering airport, her escort engaged the scrofulous taxi-driver in an eyeball battle and cursing those suckled on the milk of his besmirched mother, reduced the demanded fare by a half. Still grossly overcharged, Ute paid, suspecting too that her protestingly helpless escort was a party to the swindle.

Then the oily cur who flicked open her passport, noted the dissimilarity between Emma Zijp's visage and her own. Ute snatched it back in a panic, thrust a wad of notes between its pages and handed it over again. 'I hope zat to be in order,' she spoke with a violent tremor.

The money vanished as by the expertise of a conjuror and the passport was returned with a discreetly obsequious grace. 'A la perfection, Mademoiselle.'

With a befitting expression of xenophobia, she crossed the runway and took her seat on the aeroplane.

Again what should have been satisfaction at having survived the dangers and overcome the impediments and struck a most lucrative bargain, was replaced by a lugubrious anguish and a sensation that small snakes were sliding over her skin and spitting venom and again she recognised that her happiness was a myth. Yet how could she right it? Life was not like knitting. You could not simply unravel a few rows if you had made a mistake and reknit them.

As they took off, she saw in front of the port wing, an oasis of alders and walnuts and a tiny town of white sun-baked houses – so picturesque from the air and yet so grim on the ground. In this wilderness, fancies thrived and evaporated from the smallest grains of rumour and all seemed terrifyingly unpredictable.

At Athens airport, the luggage-free traveller went through the transit lounge, where she reverted to the use of her own passport and a separate ticket also issued in her own name, for her flight to Rome.

She would spend the night at Rome with Ingrid and then fly on to Nice the following day – the first day of September and the first day of autumn.

* * *

Eydes-Seymour's old, dark green, C-type Jaguar rumbled along the tortuous eastern shore of Ullswater in the Lake District, the blast from its large-bore exhaust reverberating off the rough stone walls.

Sheep nibbled the baize-like grassy hummocks, Letheren's sheep – theaves and ewes – for he owned a thirteen hundred acre farm here called Esland's Shieling.

The golden spears of Eos shone through a gap in the hills and cleansed and dewy, revealed the reborn earth. Chaos had slunk back into her chasms, there to scowl impotently at the light.

Nearing a hair-pin on the narrow track, he stopped as he met a Land Rover. Out stepped the Colonel in Wellingtons and a pair of capacious dungarees.

'Good morning.'

'Good morning Archibald, you old bugger.'

Letheren perched himself on a lichen-encrusted dry stone wall, where moss and minutely delicate pink flowers sprouted from the joints and the Admiral leant back against his Jaguar's shapely wheel arch.

'Well, any signals from *Warspite*?'

'She never went.'

'Why not?' This was uttered with a flicker of surprise.

'Because Michael Rose M.P. and Junior Defence Minister was "concerned" that we were "neglecting to play our full rôle in N.A.T.O."' Eydes-Seymour strolled across to the netting fence and looked down on the sleepy stone farmhouse with the wisp of wood-smoke drifting up from its chimney. 'He considered it "unjustifiable to allow such wild goose chases to detract from our proper commitments".'

'Buggeration. Did he ask where the tip-off came from?'

'Under the guise of assessing its validity, yes. I said it wasn't my department and I didn't know.'

'Bah!' Letheren's shiny round face seemed subdued. 'You should have told him to ask that German Gauleiter of his, Ingrid Axt,' he fumed.

The Rear-Admiral looked askance. 'Was she in the news earlier in the year ... something to do with those strike-breaking ore trains in South Wales?'

Down by the rippling waters of the lake, a black gelding cantered out of a small spruce plantation, ridden by a blonde-haired girl.

'One freezing January night, two railway shop-stewards crept into the locomotive yards near Port Talbot, drained the coolant off from four diesel-electric goods engines and replaced it with plain water, which froze and cracked the cylinder blocks. They were seen though and later admitted that Miss Axt had agreed to pay them "expenses" proportionate to the number of iron-ore trains cancelled.'

'In Ostmarks?'

'Was she fed to the lions or shot by firing-squad? No. Some ignoble barter was rigged up and she strutted free.' He emitted a rasping sigh. 'God, no wonder these folk think we're degenerate. Where are the men who fought at Maldon and Les Saintes? And those Viking "tings" were good too, where a man was judged by common-sense and with no toad-like lawyers to ferret out technical loop-holes ... '

Eydes-Seymour slapped him on the back. 'Cheer up Leatherbags. I did it nevertheless.'

'Did what?'

'There was a fleet tanker nearby with two choppers on board.'

'Go on.'

Unheralded, the sixteen-hand mount vaulted the wall and stopped beside them, steaming and shimmering. The Arab was an elegant beast and on the gleaming black saddlery sat the pristine form of Catharine Letheren, the Colonel's twenty-year-old daughter, reserved and watchful – like a policewoman but more classy. She wore black leather riding boots and old-fashioned baggy jodhpurs, an off-white Aran sweater and an old misshapen three-quarter length coat, tied loosely with a belt.

'Hullo, Catharine.'

'Good morning, Uncle Ronald.'

'Go on,' urged Letheren, uninterested in their salutations. 'Catharine, go and tell cook to prepare some breakfast for us.'

At a kick, her horse cleared the pig-netting and trotted eagerly down the turfy slope towards the spruce hanger, knowing that this meant rest and grass.

'It would have been tricky to tranship crates at night. Even though there was a moon, it might be obscured by cloud and artificial light creates attention. So we can assume that if it occurred, it occurred before sundown on the thirtieth.

Yesterday morning, one of the helicopters found an East German spy trawler, the *Rosa Luxemburg*, with a speed position and bearing consistent with having been present at your postulated scenario the evening before. Visibility was good and no other shipping was seen. The *Rosa Luxemburg* left Nikolayev in June, passed through the Bosporus, sailed along the North African coast during July and has since been in the Atlantic.'

'Good. That helps a lot.'

They drove their separate vehicles down to the house, a solid long low two-storey affair in a short dead-end valley, surrounded by a kitchen garden, a meadow and a copse of pines. It was called Tan Hall.

They strolled in to a log fire in the kitchen, to tongue-shrivelling tea, soft-boiled eggs and buttered toast.

Letheren, like a medieval Christian knight, sat by the hearth. 'Who told Rose about the *Warspite*?'

'A jumped-up little secretary. She's sour and trendy, eats pumpkin seeds and is coitally active for about twenty-three hours out of every twenty-four. She sticks out like a sore thumb ... strange how simple these things are.'

'It's just age makes it clearer Ronald. Do figs grow on thistles, grapes on thorns?'

* * *

Ute gazed down at the cotton-wool puffs of cloud below her, awe-inspiring and white.

Once landed, she drove her small red Renault out past the palm-tree sentinels of Nice's aérogare and beneath a clear blue sky in the ebbing warmth of early evening, to wend her way across the yellow and brown ravine-scarred coast-line of southern France to her villa.

It stood on an arid hillside, a converted granary purchased only in May, the unflamboyant abode of this female hedonist. In the buff façade, the oak-framed double-glazed windows of toughened glass were flanked by matt leaden blue shutters. Inside were cool stone walls and white-painted rough plaster, dark beams, tiled floors, an oak stairway and plain red and orange drapes rugs and curtains – a bit Dutch-like in its compactness and its atmosphere of deep colours pierced with beams of light.

Ulrich Schniewind in dusky blue leather shorts and flaxen hair – unquestionably sired by Wotan – reclined on the cushions of a wooden sun-lounger near the pool, lithe and beauteous and bronzed. Yet his pose rankled with its blatant conceit. As with his cousin, his mannerisms betrayed something coarse and headstrong and unseemly.

Ute came into view through a row of miniature cypresses, adopted a vaguely loose and seductive gait and helped herself to some apple juice from an outdoor table. She rested a fist on a curvaceous hip. 'So,' she began in her abrasive contralto, 'I've fixed it. We're in with the big boys ... thanks largely to Ingrid's picking the files of her Eastern Bloc heads.'

He sulked with that juvenile half-hostile half-dependent attitude to women, spawned from the need to feel loved combined with a desire to bully. This animosity was the essence of their foreplay. His misogyny sparked a sturdy temper in her and this in turn stirred lascivious torrents in him and their physical challenges and wants splashed and rebounded in the fertile gorge of exhilaration.

She strolled round the pool with unconvincing nonchalance and pretended to enjoy the view out over the knobbly orange-tiled roofs below her of the sleepy hamlet of Hautfort-St.-Gildas and beyond to the dry steep spurs and the blue and chrome wavelets of the glinting Mediterranean. She ambled round behind the stone dovecote and waited beneath its smudged limestone escutcheon, but not only did he fail to stalk her, he gave an artful laugh.

Incensed, she flew round to him and up-ended his sun-lounger into the water, before kicking off her sandals, leaping in after him, locking him round the neck and holding him under.

A furious threshing erupted on the water's surface and only with an immense effort did Ulrich free himself and manage to come up for a breath. As he gasped the air, she splashed water in his eyes and plunged off for the aluminium ladder. Drowning was just something men would have to risk if they were to deserve Ute, that pinnacle of ignescent sexuality.

He scrambled out in pursuit and went to dive on top of her as she lay supine and wet and smiling on the grass, but as he lunged at her womanly form, she rolled quickly over twice, sprang up and cavorted off again, regulating the pace though this time, so that he caught up with her in a thicket.

A wet muscular arm grappled brutishly with her slender waist and his other hand rearranged her sodden clinging clothes. Her wide pelvis made a good spring-board.

After a time the struggles gave way to grunts and the grunts to gasping and that to a deep and intense silence.

They devoured a salad with spring chicken, a delicate cheese sauce and a bottle of Sauternes prepared earlier by Ute's waddling and disapproving local housekeeper.

'How much?'

'Two hundred and twenty thousand dollars for the first consignment,' she replied.

'Cut three ways?'

She nodded unhappily and began to pick at some imaginary thread on her clean skirt. 'If we do it for a year and then get out, perhaps we can retire for good? Drop the drug line as well?'

'It sounds good.'

'In a couple of weeks, we must go to Turkey, to Jihan's Sawmill outside the town of Narli ... close to the Syrian border.'

Her eye fell on the paving-stone, where two days ago she had buried her third bag of Helvetia-headed gold coins. It was neatly done too, without any sign of disturbance or irregularity. They were set in cement under the slab.

She threw back more wine to drown her recurrent sorrows and a second interlude of tumultuous sex followed between this pair of late adolescent Germans.

Then they retired indoors and read and drank coffee, watched some French television and talked a bit about their trip to Turkey in the softly-lit sitting-room.

# CHAPTER ONE.

The stiff silhouette of Artemis's wasp-like form, receded across the hospital yard on a grey and darkening Saturday afternoon at the end of November.

Her lethal curves were the secret fantasy objects of many lecherous males here. Indeed, so classy and enticing did her withheld sexiness seem, that touch scarcely mattered – orgasm could occur on sight.

Simon Collett though, had fallen in love with her. His heart twitched erratically and leaving his trolley, with its load of blue nitrous oxide cylinders and smaller orange cyclo-propane ones, he flew compulsively after his Siren.

Quivering and panting, his panic-contorted face pleaded with her yet again. 'At the Theatre Royal tonight, in Newcastle ... *Das Rheingold* is on. I have two tickets ... would you like to come?'

Her alluring shape halted. She dispensed a supercilious smile to the asphalt. She arched her brows and lowered her lids and savoured the taunt of a bored sigh, yet an echo inside her head of the anguish inside his, unexpectedly disconcerted her.

She usually enjoyed flaunting her sex-appeal and slaying ruthlessly the macho-wolves whom she had induced to leap into the fire and burn their paws, but Collett was an anomaly. He was not one of the sensual jousters, but somehow devout and inscrutable.

Still, the alpha female of the place should not allow a much lower male to come too near. She stifled her unease and with cool emphasis said, 'No, thank you!'

Collett stood still, his pain too awful to voice, his deep belief that this time she must accept, speared.

Sustaining her well-practised demeanour of aloof amusement, she swung round on her heel and strutted briskly away.

She passed through an opening into the basement passageway of the four-storey massif of the main hospital building, a red-brick, late nineteenth-century structure, laced with cast-iron drain-pipes.

The numbed Collett faltered jerkily back to his trolley, as pale and despondent as one close to death.

'Damn,' she whispered to herself, angry that such an idiot could upset her. She told herself that she did not want Collett, nor sex, nor love, nor anything else at present, except to become an actress and rich and soon.

Under the clusters of hissing steam pipes, lagged with asbestos and pitch, she walked uncomfortably before turning into a brick vault where rows of metal lockers stood lop-sidedly on an uneven concrete floor.

In her finely-striped blue and white uniform dress, she opened her locker and tried to evict Collett's lurking but unwanted image from her mind. Her fingers extracted the white hair-grips holding the white hat with the one blue band which denoted a first year student. She removed too the blue belt with its plain silver clasp, which squeezed her narrow waist tightly and together with the starched white pinafore, stowed it away.

Stupid sodding Simon had assailed her five times in ten days.

His tall broad-shouldered physique *was* quite appealing, but his manner ruined everything. Her clitoris might have been stimulated had he behaved with more aplomb and self-confidence. He suffered too from acne, though she supposed that some sex might restore his hormone balance and cure that, but his real failing was his lack of money and connections. For one too, whom rumour said was the daughter of a Scottish laird, she found it demeaning enough to be treading water as a mere nurse, without adding to the humiliation by befriending some menial porter.

Artemis took off her black flat-heeled regulation leather shoes and pulled on a pair of stiff black lustrous semi-high-heeled ladies' leather boots over her black tights.

'God!' she gasped, straightening up and unbelievably catching sight of Simon yet again. He stood noiselessly to one side of her and she felt that he had been reading her thoughts.

'I'm s-sorry Artemis ... but I want to be near you. I can't help it ... everything in me craves to hold you, to cuddle you ... '

No one had wooed her like this before. It was usually the lewd innuendo from unclean lips, easily despised and dismissed. Like a military commander outmanoeuvred by a new enemy weapon, she searched for the required defensive tactic.

She emitted an explosive puff of annoyance and waved him away like an irritating spaniel. 'Stop prowling around after me, because *I* don't want *you*!'

He stared ruefully at her knot of dark brown hair and then at her less lithe and more ungainly movements as she pulled on over the flared cotton nurse's dress, her close-fitting coat of good quality, thick glistening top-side black leather and tightened the belt with a defiant tug. She swung her squarish black oxhide handbag on its long shoulder strap, up onto her left shoulder with a determinedly casual action, slammed and brusquely padlocked her locker and marched off.

Stopping by the door and glancing over her shoulder, across the joyless room to the frozen mask of quaking tragedy, she laughed briefly at his extreme and evident edginess, yet her pleasure in being cruel and untouchable seemed shallow and sinful. 'I'm simply realigning you with reality,' she remarked.

She spun round to exit boldly, but caught her belt-loop on the back edge of the door handle. It jerked her back, veering her round into an undignified collision with the door-post. 'Sod the thing,' she mouthed with an underlying fury, though she seldom swore. She seethed even more as she failed to rip the well-sewn loop free and had to painstakingly disentangle it. An urge to beat up this insolent door welled up in her, but she did not wish Collett to see that he had ruffled her.

Some street lights glowed their initial magenta red in the deep evening gloom of North Shields, as Artemis left the hospital compound via a side-gate and strode down a cobbled lane beside a row of small terraced houses, heading for the nurses' home beneath scudding black clouds.

* * *

Four eyes bulged and swivelled at the window of sister's office on the upstairs gynaecology ward.

Artemis's gait was erect and elegant, like an antelope's by comparison to the local Tyneside girls, whose clumsy graceless movements betrayed their fathers to be miners and shipyard workers. Yet it was not wholly natural. Something rigid or self-conscious lingered there. If she did things with her hands too, she lacked flow and deftness and pliant harmony, for they moved with suddenness and violence. She had ridden horses all her life, but could never excel as a horsewoman because she was not gentle or lissom and even a good horse could not feel concord with her mind.

'The time has come,' announced John Goldstraw, the roguish and chauvinistic obstetrician. 'All we need is a little social lubricant.'

'Not a sexual lubricant?' asked his houseman.

'The same idea,' Goldstraw shrugged, 'facilitates entry and reduces pain.'

'There's a party tonight at the nurses' home ... if she goes.'

'She'll go.'

'What colour underwear do you think she wears?'

'Black. Definitely black.'

'Not white and lacy?'

Goldstraw paused with latent humour in his eye. 'I'll tell you in the morning,' he confided.

The hunter opened the window as the hospital's sex-mascot approached and called down across the wall. 'My beloved, come in.' He beckoned. 'Come in and drink tea with us.'

'Do you mind shutting the window,' snapped the copper-haired Sister Gosling, apparently attending to some paper-work. 'It's freezing in here.' Goldstraw had stuffed this petulant goose plenty of times, but not enough it seemed.

Artemis threw them a brief unblinking glance hinting at scorn, but the womaniser saw her excessive pride and knew its fallibility.

'Her mouth looks a bit twisted and ugly,' said the houseman.

'I could live with it,' muttered Goldstraw. Others' infantry had been shot up, but his tanks would penetrate.

'See you later Artemis, the light of my life,' he called after her with a smile not easy to define.

'I don't think you're quickening her pulse very much.'

'Nonsense. She'll be biting tufts out of her pillow now, waiting for me to arrive.'

'Mrs Hayman needs to be seen, *when* you've a minute,' came Sister's attempted sarcasm.

'Sorry Sister. We were discussing life ... Life with a capital "L".' Sister left and slammed the door.

'Early menopause,' explained Goldstraw, glancing round at the retreating three ex-husband job, who had once even been talking on the telephone whilst he had had it off with her.

'Actually, I'm pretty fed up with these parties,' moaned Nigel the houseman. 'I never meet the right girl.'

'If you can't get laid at a North Shields nurses' party, you need to see someone. They stick to you. You have to scrape them off.'

'But it's not that. There are only tarty cart-horses at these dos. I don't want to screw any old dog.'

Goldstraw rubbed his chin gravely. 'You've had bad experiences. You let them pick you ... then there's no challenge. I agree, I also want to end up with someone who knows how to behave in a restaurant, someone who can speak French ... '

'This lot can't even talk English. This hospital only cultures fat nurses, who when you ask them anything say, "Ah diven nah. Ah've bin an mi breck man". You can only be going there for one end.' Nigel suddenly laughed, 'All this about taste, look at your shoes, two-toned with silver buckles!'

Goldstraw managed a crinkly smile. 'Just piss off, you mixed-up juvenile. I guarantee that within two years, you'll be married to a nurse!'

* * *

Artemis let herself into the huge Victorian mansion which was the nurses' home and climbed the two flights of broad wooden stairs to her attic room.

She made a cup of coffee, placed it on her desk and somehow knocked it over, soaking all her anatomy notes. She fetched a floor-cloth from the kitchen, wiped her chair and mopped up the puddle on the floor.

She considered this mishap with a subdued intensity. Reverses did not happen to her often and she looked up as if to face a mutely present Simon. She spoke aloud. 'Don't you dare try to bewitch me! I'm not having my plans ruined by you, snivelling Collett!'

She stood up, cracked her head on the under-side of some wall-mounted bookshelves and fell back onto her knees, groaning and clutching her head. She let a long venomous curse seep past her lips. She wanted to erupt in a tantrum, but realised it would achieve nothing.

No, the antidote to this was to wound Collett, to make him hate her and so poison himself, to lure him thus to self-destruction whilst she resisted the fatal descent to recklessness. That was how real power battles were fought and won.

So, she would go to this twenty-first party tonight, cast her spell over some docile half-wit such as that bovine surgeon Easton and so taunt Simon beyond endurance.

She would join battle and defeat him.

* * *

Tuneless music throbbed in the commandeered ground-floor rooms and lurid purple and green lights pulsed stroboscopically in this grotto of sadness.

Artemis arrived, slinking down the stairs. A neigh of false laughter came from one group. Artemis ended her silent entry in a small circle, where watery greetings of artificial camaraderie were exchanged.

Goldstraw surveyed above his plastic cup of dilute punch, her icily hard physical loveliness, her pose of pristine conceit and the tautness of her striking facial features.

He slipped into the ring beside her and felt fire flow in his veins. She was sinuous and unblemished. She was potent. She was real woman with life's juices waiting to be unleashed, unlike that dry neurotic bone of a doctor's wife opposite, jerking her head and fiddling with her wooden beads and all the other slags, flaccid sacks debased by armies who had been there before.

Goldstraw nudged her elbow, which she withdrew swiftly. 'I've come to brighten up your evening.'

'Every nurses' home should have one, should it?' she sniffed.

'Do you like my new tie? I'm a fellow of the College of Obstetricians now. You join by bowing and scraping to the august smoothies in London and by doing piles of nugatory research which you present with pompous importance and in such a way as to assure them that you'll be a good boy and not rock the boat and say what a hoax most of medicine is ... '

She cast a glance at the tie. 'A pity it didn't come with some instructions about how to tie it.'

He managed a smile.

Artemis wore a flared black linen dress, very plain but displaying her flowing hips and firm tented breasts nicely. It had the narrowest of lace collars with a red boot-lace bow and then a very wide soft red leather belt. The whole was neat and effective. Black and red suited her – strong stark colours.

He touched it. 'Simple and expensive,' observed Goldstraw, 'Very tasteful.'

She frowned sceptically, knitting her thin but sharply delineated eyebrows. Her cheeks dimpled as she glowered humorously and John wondered if her bottom dimpled too.

To Artemis's other side, someone mentioned a tall porter with short hair which stuck out like a spray, saying that he was part-time and told lots of funny anecdotes.

'Funny?' she queried, 'I haven't seen that side of him.'

'No. I'm sure not. He comes from near Newcastle-under-Lyme.'

'Not Newcastle-under-Lemon?'

She was surprised too, to discover Simon to be a language student. Still, she wished he would come, fall into her trap and be hurt and yet perhaps it was safer for her if he stayed away. Was he watching *Das Rheingold* with an empty seat beside him in the theatre or had he another girl to share his chocolates with or was he lying on his bed having cried himself to sleep over her? A queer impulse that she should leave and try to find him, broke into her psyche. Her stomach felt gelatinous and her legs went numb ... until Goldstraw's elbow touched hers and instead of recoiling this time as if electrocuted, she dangerously sustained the contact.

She could brave the fire and flames and escape unscathed. She would outwit his play for she was Artemis, the goddess of virginity, the moon and the hunt. Every time, like a bird aware of the snare, she would fly. When would this nit Easton appear?

Teresa Fountain, a rhinocerine Negress, stinking of sweat and with her fuzzy hair dyed white and ginger in patches like a salt-and-pepper cat, came sideways through a door and joined the Goldstraw-Artemis ring of about ten people.

'Who's this black whale?' whispered Goldstraw.

'I think her name's "Mountain". She's a health visitor.'

'How many offalburgers and splurges of brown sauce does she eat each day?'

Teresa threw a short hostile glare at Artemis, though she had not overheard her, before pulling a convenient chair into the circle and flopping back into it, so that her orange rubber dress rode up offensively over her massive flabby thighs. Like a Zulu chieftain, she despatched a timid little nurse called Susan Logie to fetch her a plate of sliced turkey and stuffed peppers from the buffet.

Goldstraw touched his cynosure's shoulder. 'She wears a leather belt and a rubber prong.'

Artemis did not resist his intimate closeness. 'What?' she asked.

'She's a communist lesbian slug.'

'How do you know that?'

'She's the one that goes on top. Logie goes underneath.'

Fountain began a tedious egotistical debut about her 'case load' and how underfunded and overworked they were.

Goldstraw jerked his head as if falling asleep.

Logie appeared with the piled plate.

'Good.' Fountain gave a porcine grunt. 'I can fill my hump up here free.'

'You mean your second hump?' asked Artemis witheringly.

The Negress's nostrils twitched, enraged that this honey-jar could make all men buzz, keep its lid on and independently and condescendingly defy her machinations.

'I spent one day out with your lot,' Artemis intoned in her faint Scottish accent. 'After a leisurely breakfast, we set off to see four people. Two were not at home, one in a high-rise flat was inaccessible because of a ferocious and uncircumnavigable dog and in the fourth slum-hole we told a woman how to boil bottles for her baby's milk, which considering it was grubbing about sucking all sorts of filthy things was an utter waste of time.'

Fountain snarled.

'Cynic,' piped Logie.

The consultant's wife sighed and said how sad it was that not everyone could have high moral standards.

'Vo-*mit*!' burst in John Goldstraw, stressing the second syllable as if being sick.

'Is your father a laird?' asked someone nastily and a ripple of mechanical laughter ensued.

'Ha ha, walnut-brains,' flung back the homage-demanding beauty. 'Deluded dingbats.'

John told her a tale. She listened calmly, but then laughed in such a way as he understood her laughter to be at his fishing efforts and not at the story. Incited, he put an arm round her slender waist, only to be vigorously slapped back. He withdrew from this spiteful hussy, planning to give her a vengeance screw sooner or later.

At last the languid Warren Easton came on stage and Artemis started to throw her pearls before this swine.

It swirled like a nightmare in the intermittently purple darkness, with smoke curling and ghouls smirking. Easton's swollen, cowardly and deeply demoralised pink face glowed above his fat torso. He had spindly limbs and small trotter-like extremities.

The depraved and atheistic Fountain tried to coax the slobbish Easton to bed his prestigious admirer, to sully and degrade this sword-crossing beauty, but he was too lethargic, even though it was obvious she would make it easy.

'Say something ... and mind your "p"s and "q"s,' entreated the doctor's wife.

'His "f"s more like it,' mumbled Teresa and belched.

The final player entered, Diane Cain, a micro-biology technician with short-cropped orange hair and a blotchy common face adorned with caterpillars of green eye-make-up and silvery lipstick.

She approached Easton with grotesquely lewd serpentine squirms and brazenly ignored Fountain's flashing eyes, her maddened and everted lips, her sweat-beaded brow and her protruding snout, which twisted like the black muzzle of a wild hog about to root.

Diane wore a very short mini-skirt of imitation brown crocodile skin and a frilly pink blouse, cut very low. A cigarette wafted about between finger nails painted with black varnish.

'Oh Warren, do you find me sexually attractive?' she drawled, giving him a hug with a sugary smile hoisted onto her already scrawny face. 'Most men do.'

This forwardness tantalised Artemis for an instant.

A distant Goldstraw sucked a clementine and smiled happily, as this genital fungus case stole Artemis's catch.

Diane's floppy bedizened body seemed to say, 'Somebody take me. It doesn't matter if I'm asleep, just climb on and take me!'

'Oh Diane, isn't that your boyfriend just coming in?' Her rival tried another desperate lasso and hated herself for such a belittling skirmish. 'Alan, isn't it?'

'He isn't *my* boyfriend.' The sullen snarl whipped back, before her cooing smile reverted for Warren's benefit and she kneaded his turgid balls not too inconspicuously.

Too shocked to continue the combat, Artemis accepted defeat and hung her head in incomprehension and pain.

Easton's luminous face loomed out of the darkness and went past her. Diane's sulky garish face peered at her, sticking her tongue out in a display of infantile triumph, as she towed away her captured Easton.

A green light blinked appropriately in the gloom.

Fountain and her allies pretended to rub their hands and guffaw at this, but their impure minds regretted that Artemis's autonomy had not been broken and ravished in a mire of obscene passion. Once crushed and craven, their malignant benevolence would offer her succour.

'You dwarfs,' said Artemis dourly. Her pale complexion had a dramatic presence in the near darkness.

A small chorus of jeers arose from the scoffers.

She threw her remaining half-cup of wine over an odious tyre-fitter.

The doctor's wife gave a gasp of horror.

'Come on,' Artemis begged, 'Say you're appalled and saddened ... *please* be saddened.'

The obese tyre-fitter tried to grab her with a fat dirt-engrained paw, but she jumped back adroitly. He lunged after her but slid in a pool of vomit and spilt ale and knocked himself unconscious on the corner of a table.

His agile adversary skipped over a selection of discarded cups and bottles and a drunken corpse, swirled round the newel post and ran up the stairs.

She paced back and forth in her unlit room, angry and restless and blaming it all on those unspeakable curs down below. She rarely took pills, but swallowed two aspirins.

She ruminated on those despicable vultures down there and the discrepancy between their golden words of altruism and fraternity and concern and their deeds of enmity. The kings of antiquity would have set them to slave in mines and rightly so. She heard the baying of the ambulance come to collect the lout with the cracked skull. 'Such *caring good* people,' she said to herself, as she took from her window sill a miniature bottle of brandy which a patient had given her and drank a half of it.

She remembered her sodden anatomy notes and in a flare of temper, flung the empty mug onto the floor, where it exploded into fifty pieces.

Then her mood changed to tears and she knew that this evening's mess were all her fault. She knelt and held a cushion to her face and with her elbows on the edge of the bed, implored some kind angel to soothe her.

She alternated again to a loathing of that quasi-aesthetic sham-civilised gang with their masks of snobbery and the transparent plumage of pseudo-philanthropy, all incongruously poised beside envy and crudity and the horrible tokens of barter.

Someone knocked on the door.

'Who is it?' she called in a shrill unsteady voice.

'Me. Your beloved,' replied the wily Goldstraw.

She leapt up from her bed and flung open the door, simmering with rage and intending to inform this obsequious flatterer about the vileness of himself in particular and of everyone else in general, but as the blue-panelled door swung back and she saw his swarthy cheerful mien, her iron feminine resolve took another turn.

He could see her delectable hour-glass outline against the glow of a street lamp beyond the window with its undrawn curtains. He licked his lips and knew why he had come.

'Come in.' A sinister digit beckoned and in he came as if under her control. The door shut. 'Do you want to go to bed with me?' Her voice spoke as if ready to be derisive of his manhood if her dared waver.

'Yes.' Again, had he really said that?

The darkness was suitably intense, yet he could imagine her firm flesh, silky skin and superb shape. Her body would be tense and dynamic for she were not some washed up old sack.

Artemis knew that the fair flowers of her girlhood mind were being metamorphosed into lush and slimy toadstools, but she did not care any more. If abstinence and struggle bore no fruit, then to spite the film producers who would not take her, the gods who would not bless her and imbecilic Collett, she too would spurn affection and self-mastery and goodness, she too would perform acts calculated and defiled. She would show that she could be wanton too and confound the consequences.

He took off his trousers with heavy breathing and she dropped her panties before kneeling on the bed, made alert and ready by the erotic whiff of nihilism.

He was on her. They toppled and he placed loveless kisses on her neck. Their tongues rubbed together and she tasted smoke and whisky.

She drew her legs from underneath her bottom and he remounted her, between those malleable limbs which then folded like steel scissors behind him. He stroked the smooth hard long outer sweep of the thighs and nuzzled his mouth in between her modest breasts. Her skin resembled supple high-grade and ultra-soft sheep's leather.

It is said that the first time a girl sleeps with a man, it is often painful, but Artemis found it not so,

She did not reach orgasm and so after an anti-climactic post-coital pause of relaxation, her strong sinews suddenly turned them both over like a tossed pancake.

Gripping him from above, like some industrial grab and breathing like a furnace bellows, she did all the work and with a force and fervour such that Goldstraw could barely catch his breath. His excitement, whilst immense, was marred by the fear of physical injury to his own vitals, so savage were her exertions and so tight the vice of her smooth rounded knees clamping his flanks.

This time, both were gratified. She exhaled a huge long sigh of relief and then rolled over and lay still.

The brief pleasure evaporated. The sickly odours of semen and the pungent sour smell of vaginal fluid crept into her nose. One hand used her crisp white cotton underskirt and the hem of her black dress to mop up some of these obnoxious liquids from her thighs, but she soon ceased that and gave Goldstraw a forceful shove with her foot.

He just stood up before a second thrust would have pushed him over the edge. He dressed wordlessly and left quietly and apparently unnoticed.

The turmoil which had afflicted her, at last yielded to soberer and humbler thoughts. The self-lessening and unseemly nature of her sortie left her trembling. She seemed to have entered a tunnel where the only lights were behind her.

Her red glazed eyes, protruded uglily in the gloom. Her usually well-toned body sagged limply like a rag-doll's. She put her face into her shaking hands and wept quietly before rolling onto the floor, where she hunched herself up in a semi-prone position, retched and was sick.

* * *

Simon Collett had overcome his pride, submitted to the most ardent emotions and yet still been rebuffed. Yet despite his wounds and weaknesses, he felt a strange composure and a clear simplicity in his head, as if purged of all confusion.

His rented room was on the first floor of a large Victorian terraced house in Jesmond. In front of the two drab sash-windows stood a long ink-stained table on which were spread many of his books and notes from his course at Newcastle University.

He had sat down and tried to translate a piece of Schikaneder, but it had been in vain. He had tried to stave off the incipient luxury of bitterness, as every detail of every unloving encounter with her went round and round and the terrible why of it all racked his aching breast. The only alternative to rancour was further painful love. A leaden numbness had eventually taken hold of him and he had lain on his bed and sobbed until his satiety of misery and hopelessness had drowned him in sleep.

He awoke at midnight on top of his counterpane, still wet from his tears and heard a creaking on the boards of the landing outside his door. His heart took a huge beat and then seemed to stop. Could it be Artemis Boden come to see him?

'Shhhhh! Come on Marlene,' whispered the fellow who rented the garret and who wore gold ear-rings and greased pigtails like a Chinese pirate.

'Sharon!' came the nettled reply.

'Yes yes, of course. Come on sexy Sharon.' The randy youth smoothed over his blunder.

She giggled foolishly. 'Why am I so weak over you?'

'Have you ever considered why all men are so weak over you?' came the deep-throated bass.

She tittered again and after some ghastly saliva-rich smooching, they moved on up the second flight of stairs to his riding pen, having evaded the landlady Mrs Henderson.

Simon was cold, so he put on a woolly, switched on the light and made some cocoa. As he drew the curtains, he could see in the sickly light of a skewed street lamp that snow was falling heavily, even if not settling very well. An early foretaste of winter.

He put on his navy duffle coat and thick leather mittens and went out. He pushed his little Japanese moped out from the tiny back-yard and kick-started it in the alley.

He swung round with a gasp, as in the corner of his eye he saw a girl passing beside a wall of dark bricks in the eerie greyness. Her hair had borne some faint resemblance to his loved one's, but the lass in a dark raincoat and a striped college scarf, was only one of the medical students who lived in the house behind.

He rode out to the coast with his hands almost rigid with the cold. He felt infinitely lonely and as if he were a mere shadow of the true and whole Simon which could have been. He was an empty shell, an abandoned plan, just alive but mostly dead.

He stopped at North Shields, near the nurses' home. The embers of the party still glowed, but as he looked up at the window of the girl he loved, all was darkness. Why would she not take him as she should?

He sat there for an hour and then rode back to Newcastle.

## CHAPTER TWO.

A sprinkling of snow lay frozen to the fences and fields and a distant leaden blue sun shone brightly but coldly, low on the horizon.

Captain Nicholas Letheren lay in the frosty blue blades of grass on the edge of the coppice. The sleeping vegetation exuded no smells and a bird above him wailed its song like a lament.

He took another glance through his Barr and Stroud, army issue, metal binoculars. The three men down in the shallow gully between the sheep-grazed knolls, still stood out against the dull grey waters of Lough Eske, but he could hear neither their voices nor the thuds of their spades cutting the clods.

A white hare stopped close by him, blinked, shivered and hopped off again on its uncertain way.

Letheren gazed downwards once more. It was taking them a long time to dig up their cache, because the unexpectedly early frost had stiffened the soil.

Nicholas had been detached from the 2nd. Lancers for some months. He had forgone the soldierly image, shearing off his hussar-type moustache, allowing his hair to grow untidily and only shaving every third day.

He had spent the night in a derelict windmill nearby, watching an isolated tavern with spiralling brick chimneys, where the excavators had lodged. He had crawled through a hedge into the gravelled car park at three in the morning and tied a transmitting device to the chassis of their old estate car. It had been unnecessary for they had only driven up the side of the pass.

Knowing their purpose, Letheren gave up his vigil and slithered down off his ridge. He walked watchfully to where he had left his rust-red Beetle in a dell between a small rowan copse and a stream. There was no habitation on these bleak slopes and nothing to tempt even a poacher at this time of year.

He drank some tea from a flask and ate a roll, then started the engine with its characteristic throb and drove down from the exposed foothills of the Blue Stack Mountains towards the main road.

The lane dipped between two hoar-frosted bracken hedges. Ahead, the stone tower of the ruined windmill rose silently from the landscape and beneath it, black and white chevrons indicated the sharp left-hand swing.

The Volkswagen hammered round the bend and then with the embankment of the old Donegal Railway on its right, climbed to come level with it.

Behind a sprawling thorn thicket, a petrol engine erupted into life and an archaic tractor lurched unannounced onto the wintry scene, blocking the incline and forcing him to an abrupt stop.

The tractor driver, huddled in a thick coat and women's fur mitts, peered sideways with a bloated morose cottage-loaf face. The tractor too, with its rusty engine coaming, its closely set headlamps like gimlet eyes and its rattling hostility, emanated an air of evil.

Nicholas's heart pounded in his breast, like an eagle trying to batter its way out of a cage.

Knuckles from nowhere rapped on his window. He wound it down with an expression of flabby irritation.

In the mirror, the narrow strip of pot-holed asphalt with the curve and the ditch, looked uninviting for a rapid reverse. Behind the tractor, a small ploughed field with its iron-hard brown furrows and snow-speckled crests, might be too much for the springs and the clearance of this civilian vehicle.

'Ah, 'tis a foin marnin' is it not?' came the lilting and slightly insolent Irish baritone. 'Ken oi airsk yer yer business, good Soir?'

From the corner of his eye, past the cloud of condensing breath and the brown-jacketed trunk of his interrogator, Letheren espied a revolver in the man's farther hand.

Remembering some carpet sample books on the back seat, he said, 'Oi'm a kairpet seerlsmun so oi em, on ma wee ter Letterkenny.' He had been perfecting a Cork or Waterford dialect for some time now and it did not arouse suspicion. 'An' excooce ma flahoolick kooriusness wit' you chancers, but be Holly Mary, what hairv yer troyed tee do?' He felt the sweat trickling down his spine, though he had been frozen to the bone all night.

'Yer nairm, oi'll remoind yer, fur yer gaw tese lairst foo moils?'

A shoot-out was inadvisable and not just politically. Letheren's pistol was loaded and cocked and needed only the safety catch flicking off, but it lay in his inside pocket and he would certainly lose the draw unless he could employ the ruse of searching for documentation.

He extracted his gold cross on its fine chain from under a grubby collar and fingered it. 'Nairt at al',' he snapped sarcastically, though his jumpiness showed through. 'Cunlin McRory.'

The man smiled unpleasantly at his discomfort. 'Cairy on ... an' sey, yer *nairver* noo mey!'

The tractor reversed, snarling as if cheated of its prey.

The Beetle juddered off between the mould-encrusted posts which marked the dismantled level-crossing and past the Stranean Tavern with its ornate brick chimneys and light blue walls. Kneading his chin with its ragged stubble, Nicholas swung his car onto the main Stranorlar road and put his foot down to be sure of his escape.

* * *

Four soldiers sat in a dingy barrack-block at Lisburn, togged up and waiting to go on a surveillance sortie. Three of them were playing Black Maria.

Corporal Bonsall led the knave of clubs, so taking the last trick of that round. 'She was called Meave, doey-eyed and sensual ... and then along comes this Idi Amin ape ... Why the bollocking hell didn't anyone lead a diamond in that hand?'

'You're well rid of her Bonzo. There were no lights on upstairs, no one at home lad. Maybe the downstairs was all right, maybe all right for a squirt ... but nothing else,' concluded Corporal Simms who sat to one side chewing at a cold beef butty, liberally smeared with mustard.

'All Irish women are sluts,' came the rare contribution from the taciturn Sergeant-Major, as he swallowed bites of a dry pancake which looked like an old wash-leather rolled up. 'And when *is* this bleeding patrol moving off?'

'Twenty-five points against me and none for you again eh?' observed Bonsall. 'Your deal I think, Private "I've never played this game before" Norton!'

The boyish private made an awkward conversational entry. 'Is it true, that when gorillas have sex their scrotums turn blue?'

Simms reviewed the self-conscious youth with all the disdain which a twenty-year-old feels for a seventeen-year-old. He noted the longish sideburns and the forwardly sloping face and said drily, 'You should know.'

There were brisk metal-heeled footsteps in the bare corridor beyond, a thump on the door and a bellowing echo. 'Get fell in!'

A freezing sea mist had crept in over West Belfast and occluded the thin crescent moon.

In Wallace Street, the pallid spheres round the small street lamps cast weird tentacles over the grim façades of the small terraced houses, some occupied and others awaiting demolition.

As an infantry platoon, consisting of forty-one men instead of the usual thirty-seven, debussed from its three-tonners and commenced a foot patrol of this sad road with its closed curtains and closed minds, a Land Rover and a one-ton Pig joined them to form the van.

In an alley which ran down beside the sub-post-office, a whore loitered and mistakenly thinking the slow-moving headlights to be those of a customer, she showed herself.

When she saw the army vehicles and soldiers, her fake smile reverted quickly to its habitual sourness, for like all her ilk, she only smiled or was pleasant if it promised an immediate reward. She tried to run off, using that ridiculous dolly gait, hampered also by the fluorescent pink high-heels on the ends of her ungainly legs – legs used more to opening outwards too, than running. Her arms waggled and her shiny plastic mack rustled.

Stumbling, she grabbed the rifle barrel of the first soldier to run up to her. He tried to shake her off as she spat out oaths and kicked his shin. His mates seized her and threw her squirming carcass into the back of the Pig.

They checked her for identification, weapons, drugs and messages and then, as with any unruly Catholic, punished her by dropping her off in a Protestant area of the city – in this case the Shankill Road – where her enemies would beat her up.

They used the same trick of course, vice versa, for Protestants. There was no religious discrimination.

The platoon received the 'all clear' and continued its advance, sections one and two on the left-hand side of the street and section three and the platoon headquarter section on the right. At the far end of Wallace Street only thirty-seven men emerged.

The foursome had slipped into a derelict house and crept quietly up the stairs. Fallen plaster crunched under the soles of their carefully placed D.M.S. boots, as they crossed the floor-boards of what had once been a front bedroom.

Oblique beams from a nearby street lamp cast rhomboids of yellowy phosphorescence onto the peeling, floral-patterned wallpaper on the end wall, depicting it in grey hues.

The Sergeant-Major positioned himself well back from the shattered window and watched Finnie's house directly opposite, beside the little post-office.

The other three settled themselves into a corner and brewed up behind an overturned table. They set out some rations, a new fast-transmitting radio and their weapons and braced themselves for a cold and monotonous night.

They had only an hour to wait before a Commer van drew up with a muted squeal of brakes. Its driver climbed out and looked around unobtrusively in the gloom. Finnie's door opened darkly and swallowed the shadowy newcomer without delay.

A signal was tapped into the radio which described the van, its occupant and her reception. At the touch of a yellow button, the scrambled message went on its way, contracted into a four millisecond pulse.

Simms spoke. 'What *are* we doing here? Two months ago I was in Cyprus and this travel courier from Essex – Sarah Roberts – had taken a liking to me. We'ld sit on the balcony of her flat looking out over the blue and pink Med. as the sun went down, pâté and biscuits and wine on the little table ... and she was a bit interested in ancient coins and inscriptions.

She had a lovely shape and she had that neat lively nature as if she hadn't had it before ... though she had *and* knew how good it was. That's the splendid bit about new girlfriends – when things are still novel and the other half's not wholly predictable and of course the sex to make it all potent and vital. Then a few months later, when you're standing in the supermarket queue on a Friday night or she's vacillating between the strawberry and the raspberry flavour of yoghurt ... then you start wondering if it's worth your while.'

'Do you ever discuss anything else, Simms? All you seem to do, is bang five different women a week and talk about it.'

'Now Sergeant-Major, I never said that Sir. No, that's too many. You can't feel intimate and close then. About four a year is the right number ... yes, one per season, that's just ... '

'Shhhh!' hissed Bonsall on observation go, as the light behind the tightly-drawn Hessian curtains in Finnie's parlour went out and then the woman and a man left the house and drove off.

Bonsall had glimpsed only a faint vision of the woman, but he realised that she had no nose. Instead she had a purplish swelling with two long slits in it and a plasticky twisted mouth. His jaw dropped. 'What happened to her?'

'That's Anne Fogarty, Bonzo-boy.' The Sergeant-Major told the story of the R.E.M.E. squad who had found a rifle en route to the I.R.A. and had drilled a criss-cross of fine vertical holes in the left wall of the breech-block and then sealed the tops of the holes.

'Anne was the first one to fire it. It went off like a grenade. She ought to have died, but only lost her nose and some of her right cheek and jaw.'

A second signal was sent and the remainder of the night was uneventful, until a tardy grey dawn groped its way over the sombre rows of roofs at about eight o'clock.

By eight thirty the surveillance detachment had drunk their tarry cups of tea, eaten their tins of stodgy porridge, packed up their kit and were having a smoke whilst waiting to coalesce with a second infantry patrol, due shortly.

Quite suddenly, an unexplained clanking noise caused them to exchange puzzled glances. They had still not fathomed the source of this racket, when the bucket of a tracked demolition shovel crashed through the end wall of the bedroom.

As falling plaster showered down their necks, they fled down the stairs and into the street, followed by a whoosh of dust as the entire house caved in behind them.

They stood stupidly on the cobbles, eyed by the resentment-centred local women with their devilish catfish-like faces, all waiting for the sub-post-office to open so that they could collect their undeserved wads of social security money.

* * *

On the coast of County Kerry, the foaming Atlantic rollers expended themselves lazily on the singing white sand of a deserted bay. Two gulls wheeled and the wind made the rye grass on the dunes tremble.

Inland from the jagged slate-grey rocks at one end of the cove stood an isolated stone cottage, modernised with new windows and interiors and adjoined by a row of stone stables with bisected brown doors. Around it, in tufty paddocks, horses were grazing.

# 73

Rain clouds shrouded the tops of the distant crags and below, down the dirt road of this mournful peninsula, a speck-like motorbike advanced slowly, heading for the farm.

Aoibheann, the stable lass, was plucking up the last of the fallen apples in one corner of the meadow, so that the horses did not eat too many and get colic.

'Weer's Mr Proyer?' called Danny O'Boyle, pulling his bike onto its stand.

Aoibheann indicated the house.

Eoin Prior came out into the yard. 'Just where have you been the last three days?'

'Oi was invoited up to Clare te shoot, so oi was,' said O'Boyle, looking very pleased with himself.

'You were invited up to Clare to shoot,' repeated Prior slowly and with a sarcastic nod of enlightenment. 'You were invited up to Clare to shoot.' He sucked his teeth and continued to nod. 'You were invited up to Clare to shoot, so you were. Well well.' The soft tones, as of comradely understanding, began to worry O'Boyle and he moved uneasily on his feet. 'So you were invited up to Clare to shoot?' Prior said for about the thirtieth time, as if he really meant, 'You had an appointment with destiny and instead you dared to piss off to Clare.'

'Oi'm sorry Mr Proyer, oi tort te operation was al' set.'

O'Boyle gulped and rested his large tired frame on a post and rail fence beside his overlord and vacantly surveyed the lines of a fifteen-hand sorrel mare with a foal at foot.

'There's been a leak Danny.'

'In te name of Mary, Mutter of God,' Danny crossed himself quickly. 'May te good Lord protect os.'

'Amen,' said Prior wryly. 'Firstly, a vehicle near that tavern on the Killyfergus Brook ... Jim Gawley thought it seemed legitimate, but we've checked its registration plate and it doesn't tally. We now know too, that Finnie's house was being watched last night, when Anne called to pick up Donal Fitzgibbon ready for the trip.'

Unlike many of the I.R.A.'s enomoty, Prior was not too evidently the victim of his own self-lowering activities. A degree of charm and seeming contentment shielded his malignant genius. His horse-rearing interest too and his distance from the atrocities he commissioned, perhaps kept his soul less firmly fettered in the dungeons of joylessness and pain.

O'Boyle on the contrary, looked grey and his face bore those lush furrows of poisoned illusion and deep indifference. His whole life had been a muddle of lies and half-lights and drifting and drink.

'So the jelly can't be taken back in the van. That's exactly what they're waiting for. No, the van returns empty and with the stuff in rucksacks, you can lead Corban's men over the border near Ballynons tomorrow night, crossing the Mourne Beg about a mile downstream from where the Crellán Brook joins it. Then hide out at Mona's Farm until Liam arrives with somc alternative transport.'

O'Boyle, ever happy to let others think – not least because he himself could not – mounted his motorbike again. His eyes narrowed to a leer and he scanned Aoibheann's body, but only to record it for savouring later in fantasy. She was the handmaid of the mighty warlock Eoin and any notions of enervating episodes behind the barn were definitely out.

'God be wit' yer, Mr Proyer.'

'And you too Danny. You might need it.'

He set off on his new errand, riding cockroach-like into the melancholy solitude of the peat-bog and the low gorse, past the one ruined croft with its weed-engulfed rusting farm machinery, before climbing a treeless and heathery cleft and disappearing.

It was Sunday the thirtieth of November and Aoibheann too left half an hour later, to go to mass. As Prior watched her car cross the promontory, electrine sunbeams burst through the clouds and reminded him of the spells of Celtic folk-lore and the misty magic of the clans and he hoped that this new plot against the Saxon invader would bear fruit.

* * *

Sergeant Gourdie and Private Sneddon of the First Battalion the Gordon Highlanders had crawled down to the edge of the Mourne Beg, a stream as wide as a small river but shallow. It marked the border between the Province of Northern Ireland and Eire.

The clear water swirled and eddied smoothly along its boulder-strewn course and in a wide patch of gravel in the shallows near the bank a pair of salmon were going through their mating ritual, burrowing amid the pebbles and turning them over to lay their eggs. The stream was easily fordable here.

The soldiers rose up off their bellies and crept back as the gleam of gilded light falling through the leafless bracken and the bare branches of an occasional tree faded and the pinks and greys of the western sky gave way to dusk and heavier clouds. They followed a faint track, where alternate short and long patches of grass suggested rabbits rather than human usage. They regained a huge flat gritty rock where they had left their equipment and slunk round to the opposite side of it, away from the dubious track.

Here, shielded by ferns and saplings and backed by a copse of firs, they drank tea and then set out on the flat upper surface of the rock their Sterling sub-machine-gun, light-machine-gun, unwrapped chocolate bars, spare magazines and water bottles, so that any item could be found by feel and without noise or mishap.

Their faces were thoroughly blackened, the carrying hooks on their equipment had been taped so as not to rattle, their webbing buckles were daubed matt black and their weapons cocked.

They belonged to 'B' Company which was spread out over about five square miles, because doubt existed about which farm Command had indicated.

The last cerise rays of a peaceful sunset waned, grey clouds swept in and a steady downpour began, as if accompanying the darkness.

They possessed a thermal imager but as water droplets absorb heat rays, the rain rendered it inoperable.

'It never stops raining in this country for more than half an hour at a stretch,' complained Gourdie. 'Or if it does they call it a drought.'

As there was no moon and the clouds obliterated the starlight, the image-intensifying night-sight on the L.M.G. was also useless. The enveloping darkness grew so intense that you could not become accustomed to it and see anything, simply because there was no light by which to see.

They had knelt down to wait. Occasionally, if the wind dropped, they would hear the stream tinkling and gurgling. Rain from the overhead pine needles dripped down onto them.

For six hours no man-made noise was heard. Then, as Gourdie sucked his last piece of mint-cake into nothingness, the distant echoes of a car somewhere across the border penetrated to the concealed infantrymen.

A convent's campanile bell, carried on the wind, had faintly marked the passing of two o'clock, when from somewhere near the stream came a slight sound – something between a clink and a scrape – perhaps the metal arc of a heel striking a stone.

Sneddon's elbow pressed Gourdie's whose reciprocated pressure indicated that he too had heard.

Sneddon's hands reached for the light-machine-gun, but Gourdie's invisible arm restrained him. Firing prematurely would hit no one and only give away their own position and that was unnecessarily sporting.

For one and a half minutes they listened intently, but heard only the even patter of the rain on the evergreen foliage and the mossy ground. Then a twig snapped ... then another, on the opposite side of the rock.

Gourdie took up a grenade, pulled the pin slowly and lobbed it gently the necessary three yards. He dragged Sneddon down with himself behind the stone.

The tossed metal landed with a clunk. Then a vivid orange flash lit up the branches above them and an instant later a muffled bang, unechoed, surrounded them.

A low anguished groan stammered something about help, a second voice gave hellish orders to, 'Get back!' and a third's piercing whimper was swallowed up by the listening night.

Gourdie hurled a second grenade after the stumbling footsteps as they retreated, then Sneddon opened up with the L.M.G. in the direction which the track took towards the stream and emptied two magazines each of twenty rounds.

Shouts and orders could be heard in the distance. A Ferret armoured car started up, a parachute flare burst in the sky and the cow pastures and hedgerows became eerily visible.

* * *

Prior rose, opened the bedroom curtains and saw the first trickles of liquid gold filling the charcoal chasms on the eastern horizon.

The pale light diffused across the room, revealing under the tangle of grubby bed-clothes his niece and mistress Aoibheann Leahy.

With her bluish-framed glasses on and her hair drawn back to a pony-tail, she could look almost pretty, but now without these adornments, even in sleep her face was plain. That was sad, for she had a good figure, dainty arms and a large curvaceous bottom to get hold of. Also she had a nice nature, a smile of reserved knowingness and a lightness and nimbleness of spirit, not darkened or made sullen by primitive tribal jealousies. And she was good in bed, forceful and passionate and in the stables when he interrupted her oiling the saddlery and singing an old Erse folk-song and took her there and then, in her brown rubber boots and old green dress with small orange flowers embroidered round the collar and hem. It was a happy choice that she had come back from Australia and was content to groom her Uncle Eoin's horses and cook for him and sate his other needs, especially as his sow of a wife had recently run off with a rich American hotel owner.

In the kitchen, he filled the kettle and lit the Calor Gas stove. Then out of habit he turned on the radio, not anticipating any item of consequence.

The first sentence of the news shook him. An engagement on the border in the early hours, between the forces of the occupied North and a brigade of Provisional volunteers ... three dead, two wounded and captured, one or two escaped back to the Irish Republic. This was an unbelievable disaster. What *was* happening?

The kettle whistled and he made the tea.

The telephone burred. 'Yes. I've just had the wireless on. Eight o'clock tonight. I'll be there.'

He shook Aoibheann's blanket-decked appetising outline and put her tea on the three-legged stool beside the bed. He kissed her and she opened her eyes silently.

'Aoibheann, I have to leave for Dublin. I'll be home tomorrow. If Conall rings about the filly, say three hundred pounds and don't take less than two-fifty. Bye.'

* * *

Judge Molloy had taken a walk to the centre of Dublin and had a coffee and a whiskey at Bewley's Coffee House by O'Connell Bridge, where he read the first edition of the *Evening Herald.*

'Moider,' he hissed as he tried vainly to tease out clues from the over-dramatised article. 'Buluddy British moider!'

For six months, the I.R.A. had suffered sufficient set-backs for it to be evident that they harboured a rotten apple – or a good apple, depending on how you saw it. They had debated it until they were blue in the face, but were still no nearer to solving it.

Depressed and angry he walked in the direction of Heuston Station, to his favourite bar on the North bank of the Liffey. A lot of senior Republican figures drank there, but it was a Tuesday and rather early and he saw no close acquaintances among the sparse patrons.

He sat on a high stool in the flood of dazzling light from behind the bar, reflected by the bottles and glasses, the tiling of mirrors and the gaudy polished brass. The barman in his black bow-tie and red waistcoat supplied him with a double whiskey of the requested brand – though the bottles were all filled up with the same cheap variety each morning.

Molloy suffered from a heart ailment, which lent a bluey-purple colour to his big ears and lumpy nose.

A girl approached him, attractive and quite strikingly dressed. She loomed out of the smoke like a phoenix in a bright red leather jacket and a shortish black leather skirt, designed to be noticed. She stopped and gave him a forceful smile.

In the distance, the other drinkers vaguely watched, baggy dissipated types – the alimony men – seedy slick divorcees who drove B.M.W.'s.

'Hoi yu, thi venyuce' bin chairnged.'

She had moved from Northern Ireland some years before, but now unleashed the full thickness of her Ballymena accent again. She pretended to cough on the smoke.

'See yer moi dear, tis evanin's meatin'?' He seemed puzzled, but edged a little closer.

Trying to remain a little detached, she blinked her watering eyes and cleared her throat. 'Yoh. It's bin spraird oot naw. Gaw strairt thru te thi wee Ertis Club ahgairnst the sairf ... '

'Whet?' Lust oozed out of him and he advanced a preparatory leg, like a tentacled octopus arm.

'Is yu Mr O'Loghlen?'

'Ne.'

'Whart? Na? Ahrgh ... ' she said, as if her head were in a bucket of water, 'Excyuce mi ... '

'Ech, niver moind. Yer'll hev a loivly dram wit' me, so yer will?' He effused bonhomie like a tarantula.

She smothered her revulsion. 'Ah'd rairther net arl thi sairm. Ah's te be prairsent ... '

'Ne ne. Oi'm te bleim. Oi'm te Uí Failghe Sorcerer an' oi lured yer te moisell.'

'Nu nu. It's may huce guilty. Ah'm thi Antrim Enchantress, en it wairs *ah* who lured *yu*!' Her smile altered to betray the cunning truthfulness of this.

He let out a cackle, hoping exuberantly that he might soon be undoing her brassière and ramming his old stick into her.

Her sharp eyes swung away and settled vacantly on a notice by the bar door.

He clawed a shred of meat from between his discoloured tusks and then heaved the sleazy folds of his face into an eager smile. '"Dun an doras",' he quoted the sign. 'It seece "Cloce te door". Cum te me flat an oi'll tell yer sometin' about te Oirish Gaelic. 'Tis a lufly lyrical tong so it is ... an' me howcekeepor's lift me a deloitful frish salmon mousse – much te much fer moisell.' His eyes were glued to her breasts.

Her planned cheerful smile was gone. 'Ah'm sahry, but it'll kairp mi fram thi kenferunce ... ' She vanished.

Molloy sensed too late, that something peculiar was afoot, some deception or labyrinthine plot.

Moya Laing, originally a Protestant from Northern Ireland, was now a gym mistress in Perthshire, but occasionally she did some unofficial work for an ex-army warrant-officer with an artificial arm. Her instructions had been to approach Molloy unostentatiously, but where Republican sympathisers would see it and to seem to exchange a few private words with him. She would now board a flight back to London and collect the four hundred pounds for her three days' work.

Why had this warrant-officer and former boyfriend wanted her to meet Molloy? Presumably to sow rumours in Dublin that he could be a high-level I.R.A. traitor. And why that? Presumably to protect someone who *was* a high-level traitor.

Molloy left the hostelry at seven-forty and puffed up an incline away from the coloured lights at the centre of the metropolis. In the deeper greys of the peripheral southern quarter, speckled only with small orange street lights and faint curtained oblongs of light, he came to a quiet square.

He closed the wrought-iron front-gate of the Georgian mansion behind him and traversed the small front garden, before ascending the steps between two Grecian urns. The house belonged to a governmental official, one Courtney Byrne, who in spite of his nominally minor position exercised much influence.

In the high-ceilinged study, with replete old bookcases, a dowdy chandelier and brown leather sofas, the banjakst wizards met in their 'fleadh'.

Yet again they wrestled with the idea that they had one or possibly two informants in their ranks. What about Deas, Killeen, Foley, Egan, Sheehan? But there were no new or clear pointers. The clues available seemed equivocal and no pieces of evidence added up to a strong single indicator. Their frayed humours started to show.

Prior spoke. 'Supposing we view it like this. Put aside the traitors for a moment. There is someone in British Intelligence who knows what is happening, who knows why they are running rings round us. If he – or they – can be traced and his network revealed ... ? *We* cannot do this, but certain of our friends perhaps could.'

No one answered immediately. At last some imaginative new territory lay before them. The claustrophobic atmosphere eased.

'Oi tink anyting be foin, so leng es we ken shoit on te British bairsteds,' contributed Pat Doolan, a vitriolic brigade commander.

Mickey Ferris suggested that their communist links be sounded out to see if they could supply them with the necessary bowel capacity.

The predatory convenor thought that the pro-Irish elements of the C.I.A. or a sympathetic U.S. official say, might ask less in return and Prior enjoined that he agreed with this.

They decided who was to buttonhole whom and then left in ones and twos.

Molloy departed, crossing the back lawn with its statue of Artemis the huntress and slipping out through a door in a high stone wall, into a dark alley.

A cat scampered off from behind an oil drum and an unseen youth gave a shrill whistle which contained an ominous note.

Molloy reached the road. Other youths ceased kicking a cola can around. He saw his own shadow lengthen in the glare of each passing street lamp. The night was cold and clear.

Purposeful footsteps pounded jauntily behind him. Blood-lusting shadows grew beside his own as another lamp receded. The spectres seized him. Others converged from grimy crevices, about fifteen all together.

'Listen leds, ye've te rang fella, oi tell yer.' His firmness changed to a plea.

A cudgel slugged him in the neck. A knife slashed his back. They wore sports shoes mostly and denim jackets or other flimsy items for a December night. A chain cut his lip and cheek. The tempo of fists gathered momentum. The orgy was unstoppable once begun, like sex. Blood flowed down his face and coat.

'Bairsted!' came a demonic scream.

Realising he could not placate them, he cowered pathetically on the pavement stones. 'Oi did ne know te crersin' pless ... Oi ... leds ... ' His whimper failed as the callous mob, without remorse or inhibition, finished their deed.

No one would come near until it was all over.

The thugs were safe too. No native politician dared condemn them for fear his house would be stoned, his daughter be beaten up or his business set ablaze.

The mound of flesh did not move. Its blood gargling ended. The troupe of sinful feet moved off, trying to resound with buoyancy, as if no trace of conscience were troubling them.

A Catholic priest, overcoat over his cassock, came by. He knelt and drew the sign of the cross on the clammy bloody forehead with his thumb. Molloy's forlorn face leered even in death. He had had no true friends, no happy companionships and had often judged wrongly to satisfy some vain prejudice. God, what were his faults?

'In the name of the Father, the Son and the Holy Spirit. May almighty God forgive you your sins and bring you to everlasting life. Amen.'

## CHAPTER THREE.

A sultry orange tint broke the grey clouds over Tyneside at eight o'clock the next morning, but not until an hour later did the stronger light filtering through the cotton curtains of Artemis's room rouse her subjugated form.

It was Sunday and the first of ten days of holiday which she had due.

She stood up, a little less sure of herself than the former Artemis, with the primness and crispness diminished. She showered, washed her hair and tied it to hang loosely down her back and then viewed herself critically in the mirror, where happily no puffiness or lassitude or darkened rims round her eyes spoiled her exquisite features.

She dressed in white socks, a thin black woolly and charcoal dungarees with red stitching and two square pockets on the front, again sewn on with red thread. On deliberation, she wound up her hair and transfixed it with a skewer passed through a black leaf-shaped piece of embossed leather.

Passing a cleaning woman, menially mopping up beer and broken glass and picking cigarette stubs out of the kettle, she went down to the basement with her night-dress and bed linen and the black dress soiled by Goldstraw's vile sticky ejaculate and put them in the washing-machine. Returning upstairs, she collected three items of post from the pigeon-holes in the hallway and went to the first-floor communal kitchen to eat a bowl of cereal. She met no one, though twice, male footsteps descending the stairs attested to the success of the party the night before.

She crunched her breakfast thoughtfully. She had made a mistake, but that did not make her a whore. A grown woman with sense and equipoise should be able to put that one disgrace behind her and regain her self-esteem. Yet she sensed a faint though constant intuition, which said that with Simon life would be arduous but happy and that spent without him she would be condemned to some painful lower path. She could choose. Yet the suggestion of compulsion made her stubborn and determined to dig her heels in. She would defy this nonsense. She would *not* run after him. She would *not* repent. It was all rubbish. Her face would be flint.

One of her three letters caught her attention. She tensed and viewed its buff oblong shape and its Manchester postmark. At last, after six months of letter writing, applications, recitals and refusals, here finally the first acceptance she had been promised had come. She permitted herself a modest smile, inserted her little finger under the flap and tore open the envelope.

Her body's substance remained seated but a rubicund flush of fury suffused her face. Then it turned bluish and lastly, deadly white. Elodie Davidson, who had definitely stated that the rôle of Ennis was hers at the end of the audition, now dared to send this impersonal rejection. She 'regretted' that 'due to unforeseen circumstances', she was 'unable' ... so ran the trite meaningless clichés – not even a decent down-to-earth apology.

A superficial calm replaced her fleeting demonic visage and up in her room she tidied up and put on her boots and a bright red nylon cagoule before setting off for her home in south-western Scotland.

She drove an old dark grey Alvis saloon, which dated back to the early fifties. It belonged to her father but he let her use it, though quite illegally for she had never taken a driving test.

With her holdall on the back seat, the sluggish three-litre monster propelled itself along the Coast Road to

Newcastle and from there, using the hilly and exposed Military Road, on through steady rain and a buffeting wind to Carlisle.

Elodie Davidson was a divorcée of about forty, with an artificially flouncy gait, a long skirt and a felt trilby. She was given too, to trendy expressions of endearment and effusive cries of rapture or anguish. She exuded a certain pseudo-elegance, wafting her chic cigarette-holder about with arty nineteen-thirties type gestures and flinging her fur stole round her scrawny crabby neck with neurotic abandon. This show, this mask of flamboyant sensitivity, cloying hypocritical and profoundly pretentious, hid rather poorly her real problems. Behind her sham art, lurked something haggard and grimy.

The film, *The Baked Bean Cicatrix*, due to be shot in some Lancashire television studio, was in keeping with its producer some vacuous avant-garde drivel 'composed' by a 'brilliant thinker' with ten Ph.D.'s in Nothing Very Much, an endless string of women and an alcohol problem. It contained all the in-vogue ultra-liberal 'concepts' of enlightened thought, drenched in explicit filth – because as Davidson had explained, its author 'believed in brutal frankness as a philosophy of life'. And this was not sour grapes. Artemis had recognised this earlier, but her own part had not demanded excessive carousing or undressing – indeed Ennis was the blinkered upper-class dim-wit of the piece – and she had decided to take it for at least it was a start, a chance to rub shoulders with people of influence or who were nearer the right circles.

The windscreen wipers swished the rain off or was it sleet? Inside, the car still had the feel of old-fashioned comfort, with its deep well-worn red leather seats, the walnut dashboard and the thick cream plastic grip on the huge steering-wheel. Artemis used a cushion on the driver's seat to improve her view.

She had one further audition to attend, in a week's time in Berkshire. The typed invitation, in contrast to Davidson's letters, had been courteous and with spring in it as if written by a real human being. It possessed the hallmarks of someone of genuine standing, which indeed Sir Robert Falcus was.

On the higher ground, snow began to settle. The bleak hillsides looked forbidding in their whitening grandeur and a flock of sheep huddled together near a gate, where a farmer was unloading some fodder for them.

The tranquillity and stark beauty around her made her understand the unwisdom of letting Davidson's rudeness and dishonesty upset her, yet she had to ruminate on something to fill the emptiness. The good true white Artemis would have thought of Simon and their future together, but denying this led to the first steps of an existence counterpoised against light and the start of the slide towards darkness and torture. It was an inescapable relief, to be travelling away from North Shields.

Her secondary schooling had been at a private girls' school near Fort Augustus in Scotland, but prior to that she had spent three years at a small preparatory school in Nîmes. France had broadened her mind and made her distinctly élitist, so that she saw the nurses in North Shields for what they were. A few were all right, but most were a sniggering rabble. To avoid debating whether or not Simon too was mindless, she switched back to the Davidson affair and tried to analyse soberly and dispassionately, what she ought to do. She wanted suddenly to extract a civil explanation or if not, hit back. She pictured no one answering Davidson's door and herself breaking in and finding out nasty secrets.

To someone who has never stolen anything or even thought of such a deed, contemplating a break-in is quite scary. Her heart pounded, but she felt also wonderfully alert and concentrated.

The Alvis – which could be described as 'heavy' and 'well-engineered' – battled on through the stinging rain and dirt. She had put too much detergent into the washer bottle, so that each time she fired its jets at the windscreen, temporary rainbows obscured her vision. The car splashed through Dumfries and charged on westwards until it reached Loch Eilan. Here the rain had lessened to a steady downpour and a mist hung over the dark green waters of the loch, an elongated freshwater lake encircled by silent dripping fir trees, where a feeling of eerie enchantment hung in bad weather. The mud-washed car snarled into the track which led to her father's demesne, passing the old Easter Tickell Gatehouse first, before bumping and squelching down the one and a half miles of ill-repaired driveway to end beside Uanrig House, the sole and solitary dwelling on the loch's shores.

Dusk's pall shrouded the house, as with a crunching of stones she came to a halt in the yard behind it. The headlamps' glare on the three brown-grey stone stables died slowly after she switched them off.

By this time, her mind was made up – she would go to Manchester that evening. She would dare whatever awaited. Some sixth sense told her it would all evolve as she had foreseen it. She told herself that it was justified. Her trembling and trepidation made it feel exciting and the excitement made it feel right. Her youthful resilience could withstand one bold adventure into these unknown caverns. Besides, she could not resist the urge to seek revenge.

The house was empty. Her father had journeyed to Calabria with his palette and easel and Sheelagh, the woman who kept house for him, finished at two – or probably earlier if no one was around.

What should she wear? It needed to be protective and also she had heard that materials such as nylon or leather were good because they left no tell-tale fibres. Her father kept several old motorbikes and had once bought some clothing for a vintage rally, but then not gone. She rummaged in his bedroom cupboards and found the pair of leather jodhpurs, well-made from thick shoulder hide, narrow in the calves but otherwise wide and baggy, black, lined and fitted with large square knee-patches, a big round bottom-patch, deep pockets and ankle zips. She had in fact worn them in a play in her last year at school, together with her black riding boots and a longish chemise of bright red silk with a yellow double-headed eagle on it and a black cord at the waist. She had been a Russian count in a stylised October Revolution. She put these trousers on over a pair of knickers and a pair of warm hockey socks and used a length of cord to pull in the waist.

She made some soup by cutting up a chicken breast left in the refrigerator and boiling it with salt, a diced onion and a chopped leek. This she ate with a roll and a cup of tea.

She then brushed the dust off her leather riding boots, polished them vigorously until they gleamed like pitch and pulled them on.

Over her black and red check blouse she put on a black polo-neck woolly. She took her mid-thigh length red cagoule with a black leather belt to go round the middle and keep it from billowing out and a red scarf to partly hide her face. With a pair of thin leather gloves, a pair of fur-lined gauntlets from her father's hoard, her handbag and a flask of tea, she extinguished the house lights and set off.

Levenshulme turned out to be a dreary suburb of Manchester, consisting of Edwardian terraced houses, corner shops, laundrettes, skate-boarding yobbos, immigrants and a pervading air of grubbiness and unrelenting decay.

It had taken her four hours to drive down via Carlisle and the M6 motorway and her watch said ten past ten as she parked in a lifeless back-street. It drizzled too, so she put up the hood of her cagoule before she wound the scarf round her throat and mouth, pulled on the thin pair of ladies' black leather gloves, hitched her handbag onto her shoulder and set out along the narrow, uneven, chip-paper-strewn pavements.

At this time Artemis was not aware of her leather clothing emitting any aggressive overtones, nor was it the *cause* of her psychical shift towards hatred and anger, but being clad in this durable defensive equipage enabled her to feel safe and immune and warm, protected against the elements and physical harm and this in turn made her feel daring, heady, even invincible. So dressed, she *could* be disobedient and spiteful.

Her cheeks glowed, her toes tingled – she was full of a thrilling reined-in impetuosity – as before going on stage.

Number six Ballarat Grove stood in darkness. No one answered the repeated tinkling of the door-bell, audible to the girl on the step. Through the letter-box her peeping eye saw a scattering of letters, their white shapes made vaguely luminous by a shaft of light from the main road, reaching out to this generally ill-lit spot.

She strolled round the block and in the narrow cobbled snicket behind it, bordered by high brick walls, she counted the chimneys to reckon which would correspond to Davidson's house. The door into the tiny back-yard she rattled carefully without result, for it was bolted from behind. The black and red she-devil hoisted the strap of her handbag over her head, so it would not slip off her left shoulder and from it took the pair of large thick black gauntlets and pulled them on over her thinner gloves. She moved a handy dustbin up to the wall and a sodden old oblong of carpet which had been conveniently dumped in the alley, she threw over the broken glass cemented on top of the wall.

No one was about and no overlooking neighbouring window had a light on. The rain too, helped to hide her.

She crouched cautiously on the dustbin and then stood up. She clawed and heaved herself up until she straddled the wall and its jagged rug-draped glass. Later inspection would show a couple of slits in the seat of her cagoule, but the jodhpurs luckily were not penetrated.

Still no one was about. She slid down into the concreted yard and dragged the worn wet carpet down out of view. Removing a gauntlet and holding it against a pane of the kitchen window, she jabbed at it repeatedly with her free elbow – and with gradually increasing force – until the glass cracked. With a tinkle, a few sharp sabres fell inwards. With her thick gloves back on, she used her heavily-padded fingers to tug more curved segments free, until an inserted arm could reach in and undo the catch. With much exertion the intruder raised the lower half of the sash-window and crawled in onto a draining-board. A nail or splinter in the window frame ripped the side of her cagoule and a plate fell to the floor and broke with an ear-splitting crash. Having pivoted round and lowered her feet to the floor, Artemis took a deep breath, closed the window and propped a square bread-board against the shattered pane. After groping her way through a doorway and falling over a pouffe, some postcards on the mantelpiece seen in the dim rays of a street lamp confirmed that it was Davidson's house.

Eventually, up the black velvety stairs, she found one small back bedroom which seemed set out as an office. Artemis drew the curtains and switched on a feeble light. On the walls were some cheap dowdy Burmese prints. Sitting down, the chair creaked, her thick leather trousers creaked and a moth fluttered round the lamp. Keeping on the thinner gloves because of finger-prints, Artemis went through the papers on the desk. A folder labelled *The Baked Bean Cicatrix* spewed out sheets on costumes and ideas for direction *and* a typed cast list. Beside 'Ennis', it had said 'Artemis Boden', but that was crossed out in pencil and the name 'Carolyn French' substituted in Davidson's spidery hand.

After bending two knives, she went in search of a substantial screwdriver and duly forced open the desk's locked drawer, splintering its leading edge. Here the topmost item was a Manilla envelope containing bundles of ten-pound notes. A rough count suggested about a thousand pounds. Artemis placed this inside her handbag. Was it a bribe from Miss French? Although no proof of this existed, Artemis felt convinced that it was the case.

At about midnight she left, closing the front-door behind her and then striding the half-mile to her car. As the long night journey home crept by, she felt tired but pleased. It had not been a criminal deed, but one of legitimate retaliation. It felt good too, to have obtained this redress *secretly*, because in this modern world of double standards, you could not admit to having nasty war-like thoughts against your foes. Everyone would proclaim you to be 'morally disgusting'! Yet if you merely smiled sweetly and waited for fairness to reward you, you would be abused and end up bitter and wrathful. No, the art evidently was to *appear* genteel and to affirm virtuous ideals, whilst in the dark you spiked the tyres of other contestants, triggered the guillotine onto the necks of your opponents and promoted yourself by stealth. This game appealed to Artemis. There seemed to be a delightfully diabolical flavour in enacting passive innocence on the one hand and being an abominable covert avenger on the other. And she enjoyed being solitary and alone too, a self-sufficient and unweakened organism, unlike women who toiled laboriously to achieve their ends through the agency of lumbering husbands. Artemis would play white when others played white, but black if they played black. She would not vacillate and fumble ineffectively in the greys. If anyone crossed her from now on, she would inflict retribution.

At a half past five in the morning, she tumbled into her bed at Uanrig House. After a day of recovery she meant to visit Denise, a past school friend. For one who kept her own counsel as strictly as she, Denise was the closest thing to a friend she had. After this, she would read some Oehlenschläger plays and generally prepare for Sir Robert Falcus's crucial do.

* * *

A twenty-watt light bulb, dangling unadorned on a piece of flex, lit the porter's lodge with a yellowy-brown light.

Simon Collett's feet rested on the rickety coffee-table beneath the uninspiring notice-board and a chipped mug of instant coffee stood on the floor beside his ripped leatherette armchair.

A book rested unread in his lap, whilst his mind grappled with the discovery that love is not about egotistical bliss, but forbearance and suffering.

Miss Irvine, the Matron, entered stiffly and used the telephone to answer her bleep. Collett slowly lowered his unshod feet. As an afterthought on leaving she turned, gave him a standard smile and said, 'Collett, there are some chairs stacked outside the x-ray department. Take them up to the top gallery, will you?'

'Yes, Miss Irvine.'

When she had disappeared along the high-ceilinged cream and blue half-tiled corridor, he noticed a key beside the telephone. She must have laid it down whilst holding the receiver. Its wooden tag read 'Nurses' Home – Master'. He pocketed it and wondered what he should or dare do.

His late-duty shift ended at nine o'clock. The trains were on strike and a fall of snow that morning had made the bus slip on an incline, though the driver had herded everyone to the back and that had put enough weight on the rear-axle for the wheels to grip. It had since snowed more and the journey to Newcastle was not enticing – especially as it was away from Artemis.

Without knowing really what he expected, he plunged down the narrow street, icy cold and hostile, to the fading splendour of the nurses' home. In his pain and loneliness, reason and sense meant little to him.

No one saw him let himself in. He passed a cork-board of rotas and memoranda. Some giggling leaked out through a half-open door. 'But Janet, he was after you!'

'I know,' came the reply and shrieks of merriment followed.

In the dim light of the top landing, he found her door. The cardboard oblong in the brass name-holder read, 'Student Nurse A. O. Boden'.

He knocked and waited.

He admitted himself and closed the door. When she came ... well, either she would go berserk or sit and listen to his plight.

With the light on, the room embraced him as if his presence were legitimate. It was homely and tidy, cosy and scented, with her bed in one corner, a modern beech desk in front of the twelve small panes of the sash-window, a fitted wardrobe, an easy chair and a writing chair. She had added to this a bright rug, several cushions, a poster depicting a Foreign Legionnaire outside his white-painted sand-ringed fort, a couple of cacti, some photographs, an old rag-doll and the varied accoutrements which convert a room into a home with that touch which only women possess.

He sat on the chair – *her* chair – and trembled slightly at his nearness to those objects made sacred by being hers – her hair-clasps, her ruler, her talcum powder. No medieval Christian could have felt more wonder or devotion on seeing the relics of a revered saint. A picture of her on stage as Electra, wearing an Ionian robe and carrying an amphora against her hip, reminded him both of her flawless loveliness and of her unique effect upon him. The simple flowing curves of her body had the same bold and uncluttered appeal as Hellenistic sculpture. Perhaps like Mary of Magdala, if forgiven much, she would in the end love much.

He opened her wardrobe and pressed against his burning face, every garment – every dress, every sock, every brassière – all hallowed through having been worn by her and he replaced each exactly as it had been.

Then he dared to open the desk drawer, curiosity overcoming a sense of sin and baseness and he started to peep at her letters – an official one about not leaving the lids off the jam jars in Ward 2's kitchen, one from a French school friend, one from her father on holiday in Finland – all rather unspecial really, much to his surprise.

Yet as with a barbarian who has begun to plunder and despoil the astonishing temple and let brambles spread over the holy ground, his worldly indifference after a while reverts back not to the initial awe, but to a fascination with the mundane reality of it and a humanity more endearing than the legend. The tangerines in the little woven basket seemed eternally right. The sheaf of physiology notes on the little set of drawers were perfect in their disorder. And Artemis herself, she was so feminine that even the faults of that supremacy were strikingly uncommon.

From her address book he noted her date of birth, her home address and telephone number, her last school in

Scotland. Her invitation to Sir Robert's appeared and from the treble underlining of the date time and place in a thick red felt-tip, he deduced that she would attend. He slipped it into an inside pocket of his anorak. He drew the curtains and dipped into her books, some of which were French and real French books, not school ones.

He wanted to hold her. He took out a uniform dress of striped cotton and clutched it. A lavender sachet fell off its hanger. Its shallow conical pouchings to hold her youthful uppish breasts seemed to tease him. As he hung it up again, he realised at last, from her absent coat and boots and the 'tidied up' feel of the place, that she had gone away and he would not see her tonight.

In the wash-basin alcove behind the wardrobe, he cleaned his teeth with her tooth-brush, washed with her blue soap and grey flannel and then drank juice from her mug. He slept restlessly in her bed, cuddling her deep red, long cotton night-dress as an inadequate substitute for her. Twice dreams of her woke him. Once she was kicking him with a disrespectful and pugnacious complacency. The second time he wrote a love-letter to her and left it on the desk.

> 'O Artemis,
>
> I repeat your name night and day. I cannot forget you for more than a few seconds. I do not understand why it is so, but such it is and so I am vexed by your lack of kindness and encouragement, for I feel I am your template and although God sometimes teases us, He does not do so about these matters.
>
> Yesterday, as my stereo' played Beethoven's sixth symphony, the last movement, the Song of Thanksgiving, I fell into a trance and seemed to be on a mountain, high above the earth and all its kingdoms and epochs were there on the plain, balmy and colourful and

whole. And in amidst it all, you were there too – a black insect, displeasing and defiant and perverted and casting a twisted shade around you because you were not as God wished you to be.

Some days I imagine all the fizz to be leaking out of me, as if I soon might die or live on almost dead. You are so strong and true in every detail in my mind, that it seems as if I have done nothing else in my whole life except love you.

I admire classical romanticism and I believe in its images of good and evil. Love, religion and civilisation are inseparable. You have all three or you have none. When I was small, I had a box of wooden figures – kings, queens, soldiers, princesses, market girls and slaves – and they were solid and straightforward. Cheats, swindlers, liars, they do not exist, they dwindle and are nothing, but enlightened men become one day, as great as God. And you, if you are awry, a bad fairy, destined to become a thief and a killer, then I shall destroy you and not you me, because my faithfulness and my sacrifice are more potent than your cunning and dark determined greed. Love *is* the greatest power.

It is soon Christmas, an attractive time to be sad. I shall write my home address on another piece of paper here, so you can write to me if you wish.

When you first refused, I thought it only an enforced restraint on your part to test my sincerity, a suspension of events to give pause to savour how poignant the delayed but rightful encounter would be. But now I am more sober and more unhappy, because I fear you are hardened and impervious and only some terrible disaster will mend you. How can you so harm yourself, to curb and stunt your nature by such lovelessness?

Last night I slept in your bed. I cried at times and dried my tears on your night-dress. I kissed your pillow instead of you, because you had deserted.

I still hope for you my beloved.

Your Simon.'

He ended it with five wild kisses.

He left early the next morning, taking with him her white Cashmere woollen scarf, wrapped round his neck.

As he closed the door, Staff Nurse Victoria Inall came out of her room next door. She eyed Simon suspiciously and said as they walked down the stairs a few steps apart, 'Excuse me, but I thought Nurse Boden was away? Isn't that her scarf?'

She half-extended a hand to retrieve it, but Simon's knuckles went blue and white as he gripped it with demented firmness and a terrible look filled his eyes.

Victoria changed her mind about tackling this madman and she slowed her pace to drop back from him.

# CHAPTER FOUR.

A white sun rose over the land, alternately scorched and frozen, an ageless waste of untouched peaks, puce and steep and barren.

The poorest of villages hung round the remnants of an ancient aqueduct. Neglected olive trees and boulders dotted the sad valley and a hoarse bustard crowed evocatively in the eternal melancholy.

An old six-wheeler Büssing lorry, covered with an awning of tan-coloured tilt, drew up outside a khan, once a thirteenth-century hospital and the two lemon-faced Kurds who had driven it from North Africa to the Levant climbed down.

They spoke to a man sewing bags who sat surrounded by his wares under a carob-tree, then to an iron-forger who hammered on his anvil in a cramped niche. These shook their heads. They almost ignored the blind beggar who sat patiently, seeming to be selling bottle tops and tatty plastic bags and in inexpressible poverty, yet for a coin he told them where to go.

In the almost levelled ruins of a fifth-century Byzantine basilica, with flowers and lizards in the crevices of its fallen stones, they found a small Cypriot man. He had an oily khaki face and bow-legs – as if used to riding those little Turkish horses – and was eating a leisurely breakfast under a nebk tree. He possessed those heavy eyelids of the Middle East and with hanging lips he sipped mint tea and took varied bites from a circle of powdered bread, green figs and some foul goat cheese. The small segments of his eyes which were visible were bright and crafty. Militiades Samaros was known also as Rabbah Eissa and as Cem Arslan, not to mention other unflattering appellations.

The Kurds showed him a half of a torn Dutch one-hundred-florin note, with Admiral de Ruyter's effigy on it. He produced the matching half and they handed him the lorry's key.

A little later Rabbah Eissa drove out past the dust-coloured hovels and sparse bushes and zig-zagged up a rutted fawn road. Three hours later, having passed some Syrian border guards who had already been squared to wave him through, he descended to Narli, a small forgotten railway town beside the bed of a deep wide wadi, strewn with boulders and cut into the baked wide valley.

The vehicle shuddered up a track between an overgrown olive-press and a poor orange-grove and stopped.

Here two Germans lay on a rock beside a military type estate-wagon. Ulrich Schniewind took over the unwieldy six-wheeled lorry with its obsolete crash-gearbox and lurched off on the few kilometres to Jihan's Sawmill, whilst Ute dropped off the Turkish-Arabic-English-French speaking Greek Cypriot at the railway station.

Ute mulled over her inability to become pregnant, despite taking no precautions ... what word had the English doctor used to describe her condition at the infertility clinic – 'inconceivable', 'unbearable'?

The sawmill was a large compound with stacks of cedar, Aleppo pine, acacia and birch standing to season and sheds containing steam-driven machinery of German origin, dating from the twenties. It had recently been bought out by a West German businessman called Werner Hüttner.

Ulrich and Ute stood and watched as the contents of four pressed-steel crates from the Büssing were packed into the hollowed-out halves of four stout baulks of greenheart, sawn longitudinally. The packages were wrapped in heavy polythene. The edges of the hollowed-out baulk-halves were then smeared with glue before being butt-jointed together with careful realignment of the grain pattern and clamped. Later, when dry, they would be planed again and the ends sawn level, so that the hair-line of the joint would be virtually invisible.

Then on an articulated lorry marked 'Turkish Citrus Fruit Exporters', together with boxes of melons and lemons, they would journey through the Balkans to Bologna, where some fruit would be off-loaded and some tinned tomatoes taken on board. The towing unit would change here for a German one with the registration number KL NE 35 and it would pull the trailer to England. All the export papers and goods invoices were in order and the drivers knew nothing of their concealed cargo. Today was the third of December and this would be the third shipment to follow this route, the others having gone in late September and early November.

Ute, in greeny-blue fashion dungarees, a blue and green chequered blouse and a sea-green anorak, heard the three workmen talking in Turkish.

'I wish I could understand them,' she said.

They dredged the shallows of their not ultra-clever brains for a few glib remarks.

Ulrich had the hiccoughs. 'These deformed hic-gnomes ... we need to hic-know nothing about them.'

'Our German master once told us that German had absorbed some Turkish substantives in the sixteenth century ... but the only one I remember is "Kartoffel". That was their word for "potato" ... though not now.'

'Very useful.' He glanced at the greasy black hair and the evenly-spaced teeth of these gnarled and accursed-looking men. 'Only one being here attracts Ulrich, that bold Franconian knight ... ' He looked at her ravenously.

'Tannhäuser seduced by the Venusberg?'

'Spot on.'

As if still overseeing the operation, she looked ahead and ignored Ulrich, standing with her feet slightly apart, her hands resting casually in her dungaree pockets and keeping her head and feet still, she thrust the centre of her body round in a circle between these antipodes. The effect of this gyration was to call attention to her middle, as if her pelvis was the mid-point of her existence.

Up in the hills at a long-disused marble quarry, Ulrich stripped the old Büssing lorry of identifying marks – plates, engine number and scraps of paper in the cab – and rolled it into a deep vertically-sided sawn and blasted chasm.

In their four-wheel-drive estate-wagon, they set off for the snowy and treeless upland passes. The first night they spent in their thick sleeping-bags near a shattered cistern in a desert of whitened rocks. Frozen grape hyacinths bordered the ledge where they pitched their tent and cooked their gammon and tomatoes and coffee. The second night was in Istanbul, in the five-star Scheherazade Hotel, with a huge en suite bath, vast taps which filled it in no time, solid silver cutlery and service almost good enough for a caliph.

* * *

Two men paid the bouncer on the door and descended the stairs into the dim smoky blue light of the night-club cellar.

A girl with a huge black bow in her black hair, black underwear and suspenders, black stockings and black shiny thigh-boots came up to them trying to make her weary body sway excitingly and her listless eyes sparkle with extravagant delight.

Anastas Zanko, the leader of the duo, loathed these seedy subterranean grottos of champagne and prostitutes with the intensity of a Puritan. The lurid sham of exotic sophistication seemed epitomised by this poor girl, whom he dismissed.

He purchased two orange juices at the lighted cavern of the bar and he and his assistant seated themselves at a back table, in the shadows well away from the lilac stage light where a hard-faced cabaret 'artiste' wailed into a microphone with brazen insincerity, 'Yeahhhh! Ma heart is bleedin' ... ' Honorine Artis, the singer, was accompanied by a brash clamour of organ, guitar, cymbals and drums. At the end of this mediocre cacophony, the expected patter of applause followed.

The pair were K.G.B. men and with their belted trench coats and Homburg hats appeared much as portrayed in third-rate films. Zanko though was unusually garrulous for the breed.

'I remember a case like this four years ago,' he explained, 'No, I tell a lie, five years ago. On a Friday morning ... or was it a Thursday ... ?'

Sozinski, more typical of their circuitous tight-lipped hierarchy, braced himself for the torrent which was *never* interesting, never 'I've cracked it,' or 'I've found a supply of raving Amazons,' or 'I slept with Elke Sommer last night.' No, it was mule stuff, backpacks and drudgery. He nodded dully, resigned as ever to being pinned just out of reach of an alluring and overripe world.

A burst of carnal feline laughter erupted nearby, attempting to drown its own self-disgust. The cigar smoke of her fat admirer, coiled upwards like a charmed snake. Zanko did not interrupt his story to look, for he had seen it all before. He knew all the standard scripts that went with the festering substrates of humanity.

Sir David Penman O.B.E., fifty, portly, sluggish and condescending, had come to Amsterdam for the weekend under obligation. He left the American Hotel in the Leidse Plein and set out in the garish city darkness, where lights of vans and cars, the lighted windows of trams and cafés and the ubiquitous neon signs all shimmered in the rainy blackness of the evening and the shiny puddles of melted slush. He turned down the quieter darker Heren Gracht with its smelly canal, walked over hump-backed bridges, passed the narrow gabled houses and the leafless trees and making sure that he was not being tailed, turned into an alley off Damrak where he would meet his rough and nondescript summoners.

Twenty years before, a Polish tart in Kensington had duped him into dressing up in women's undergarments whilst having sex with her on the floor of her bed-sit. A flash had made him look up, startled in the midst of his exertions, only to be greeted by a second flash. A man with a camera had rushed off through the front-door and the whore Sylvia Cywinska had laughed like a drain, but assured him that all would be well, as long as he assisted her 'friends' with certain services. In exasperation he had kicked her fat bottom, only to be threatened with a beating if he touched her again. Feebly he had allowed himself to become embroiled in small matters and so had come under the Russians' thumb.

Plunging crossly down into the night-club, he too had to fend off two whores, one trying pathetically to look mischievous and the other affecting a sulky tantrum at not being flattered and spoilt.

He joined his hosts and Zanko ordered a further three orange juices and three crab rolls. Their nickname for Penman was 'Treacle Pudding'.

Penman raised his glass. 'What are we celebrating gentlemen? Liver recuperation week?'

Zanko unpocketed a photograph of a man in his mid-twenties and jabbed a nicotine-stained index finger at the cherubic features. It was Nicholas Letheren. He was in the army, in the cavalry, or at least supposed to be. Really though, he was undercover in Southern Ireland.

'Tut tut,' commented Penman as he nosed his orange juice, 'Not on his tank with its guidons fluttering, but doing something nasty and underhand?' He looked at the picture with an unhappy and officious gaze.

The phlegmatic Slav explained to his pompous minion, that he believed Letheren to be using a pseudonym and that as head of the passport section of the Civil Service, he wanted him to discover the details of his duplicate passport.

* * *

A winsome girl left the arc-shaped reading room of the university library and wended her way home with a bag of books and a violin case.

She walked through the nebulous gloom of Hillhead where waddling grey women in grey coats and knitted hats peered at trays of mince and bottles of detergent in a dreary row of shop-fronts, before reaching the more spacious roads of North Kelvinside. Here she turned off onto a row of once grandiose mansions which overlooked the Botanic Gardens.

She met her brother on her doorstep. He had come via Glasgow's circular metro line and a grid of blackened stone tenements.

She looked slightly puzzled. 'Am I late?'

He smiled. 'Five minutes, maybe six.'

She pushed back the cuff of her navy mack and peered at her small gold watch on its narrow black leather strap. 'It's stopped.' She took off her woollen mittens and wound it. 'Actually, that explains quite a few things.'

Innogen's blonde hair had been plaited and the plait coiled in a ring on the back of her head, but a few wisps had defied this means of tethering and they lent a slightly hazy, out of focus look to this diffident upright and unerotic girl.

At the top of the stairs they entered the living-room of her flat. Whilst the twenty-four-year-old Nicholas turned the electric fire on and set out two plates, two forks and two glasses of water on the table, his sister set about preparing a spaghetti dish. A bizarre mixing of the flour and the tomato purée produced a sauce of the most hideous pink. Nicholas for a time forced himself not to laugh, but as they started to eat, odd explosive bursts escaped from him, until eventually he was prostrate on the floor in a rictus.

'Shut up!' said Innogen, bringing her small fists down onto the table and trying to look cross, but he was powerless to stop. After some more minutes she stood up, clutched his ankles and dragged him round the carpet.

'No! My new trousers ... !' Tears rolled down his cheeks. He gasped for air. 'It tastes good ... despite the colour ... delicious ... '

Finally his hysterics ebbed away and he breathed more easily and Innogen, who knelt beside him, permitted a smile to form on her own shy and high-souled features. She held his hands and kissed him.

'When does your ferry sail from Stranraer?'

'Not until this evening.'

'How much longer will you be in Ireland?'

'Only a couple of weeks I hope.'

Innogen was twenty-two, tall and with a sweet-tempered face and a pale delicate skin. Her youthfulness and her unself-conscious grace stirred mildly sensual delights in men, though she would have been very embarrassed had she understood this, for she had no knowledge of the effect a woman's body can have on men.

'What do you do over there?'

'I live in Cork pretending to be a Provençal, whilst being a courier to two of Pappa's spies.'

'What are they like?'

'One's a shrewd but engaging lass down in County Kerry and the other's a fourteen-year-old girl in Newry.'

'Fourteen?'

'It sounds young doesn't it? And in her kilt and tartan tie in the local pipe band she looks beguilingly innocent, but these lasses are more worldly-wise than we are, believe me.'

Cooking had never been Innogen's strong point and the tea-cakes she now toasted ended up half-raw, like sun-bathers who had forgotten to take their shirts off.

As Nicholas departed into the darkening and unfriendly afternoon, snow was settling, driven by a razor-sharp wind.

Her smile of parting seemed haunted, as if tinged by some spectre which even her child-like goodness could not deflect.

She gazed out of the cold window. Nicholas passed out of view, only his footprints remaining in the bluish and faintly iridescent fresh snow. On the opposite side of the road, near the high railings of the Botanic Gardens, a girl in a black coat slipped over.

Innogen expected another visitor that evening, a man she had met only the week before at a party at the Surrey home of Major-General Sir Algernon Fey, where she had partnered her father.

Sir Robert Falcus came punctually, dropped his mack onto a spare chair and said, 'Thank you for seeing me, Miss Letheren.'

She squinted her eyelids slightly, which together with her already full cheeks, formed a smile of encouragement and approachability.

They sat down and he explained that the proposition which he had for her concerned a play entitled *Christina of Bolsena*, written by a classical German playwright called Luise Gottsched. He said that it was set in the late Roman Empire, centred round a contest of good and evil and was named after a girl who later became canonised.

Sir Robert felt unalloyed pleasure as he surveyed her flawless form. Hers was not the ethereal fairy-like enchantment of nineteenth-century German romanticism where the pale beams of moonlight depict an idealised eidolon of womanhood, but a classical and ingenuous solidity, a sublime passivity.

'I have wanted to stage this work for some years, but the difficulty lies with the title rôle. It is *not* a dramatic part – Christina says and does very little – in contrast for example to Xystia, the pagan priestess who tries to lure her to vanity and fateful self-trust.'

Her face, even prettier now that it was serious, adopted a frown. 'This is very flattering Sir Robert, but I can't act.'

He pondered, like the merchant who has found the pearl of great price. Her blouse was of medium blue with a high neck and tiny pink flowers printed on it and her darker blue knee-length skirt was soft and voluminous.

'Have you ever acted?'

'Only at school. A couple of choral parts and then in my final year, Orestes in Euripides' *Electra*.'

'Orestes?'

'It was a girls' school.'

He smiled at his own oversight. 'No matter. Perhaps a part of the contradiction with Christina, is that anyone who is an actress, is *per se* too extrovert.' He considered her hair-style to be aptly Roman and she did not fidget or roll pencils and this bestowed a ring of placid animation round her. 'I would spend time with you as necessary.'

She swallowed apprehensively.

They drank tea with slices of gooseberry tart and cream. Sheets of music lay scattered around and books had been left open, conveying her muddled ways.

'Many drama school pupils today are taught only technique – drawing lessons and such refinements have all gone out of the window – and it results in people with an unsound grasp of the theatral art and who are unable to grow within it. After a brief display of so-called "precocity", they're seen to be horribly sterile.'

Innogen gave a smile of constrained sweetness. 'I can imagine that many theatrical types are poseurs of one sort or another, but *someone* must be suitable.'

As with small children, her sweetness was derived mostly from her not being conscious of her own sweetness.

He had considered one girl endowed with an air of compliant serenity, but she came over as being weak.

'No. You are the right girl.

I know this is a rush, but I'm holding the auditions at my house in Berkshire on the eighth ... What is it today ... the fourth? I had had a translated Danish play in mind, but my preferred alternative is *Christina of Bolsena*, depending upon your acceptance. Could you decide within two days and telephone me?'

'All right. I will.'

He gave her his card, a copy of the script and a list of those he had invited to his selection cocktail party.

Her eye caught a name on this list, Artemis Boden. 'I was at school with her.'

Sir Robert winced. 'Indeed. I only asked her because she sent me an eager sparky letter and a nice photograph.'

'She played Electra.'

'What a coincidence. Are you friends?'

‘No. She was two years below me. She was very impressive as Electra though – strong and vengeful and disdainful. Such parts suit her better than tender ones I think.’

‘She sounds like Xystia.’

Robert Falcus felt happy and unflustered as he drank his second cup of tea. He noted that Innogen, whilst things might amuse her, would seldom aim at humour and again as with small children, he found it hard to predict what she would find funny.

She paid very little attention to general chatter and this had earned her a reputation for being proud. The sort of contrived wit which entertains vulgar folk, she could not comprehend and she detached herself from such circles.

‘”Letheren” is an unusual name?’

‘I believe we’re from Somerset originally.’

Sir Robert’s hope had found its zenith. He took his leave.

As he walked down the bitter icy street, he remembered a character called Ionice in another Gottsched play, *The Siege of Corinth.* Her goodness too is seen only by wise men. The loud-mouthed brassy men with their gilded dirt, are unaware of the camouflaged fine spirit in their midst. The Muses hold their eyes so that they do not see.

Innogen could not ease her consternation about Nicholas, but made some coffee, sat down and opened up the script of *Christina of Bolsena*.

* * *

The village of Athaghis – on the northern edge of County Kildare – consisted of a crooked manor house in a few acres with its own well and peat-bog, a bakery with an original art deco front, a hair-dresser’s, a fishmonger’s where local salmon were smoked and a handful of cottages. The farms were poor and cattle were still driven along the main street, but all the donkeys had been replaced by cars. It was a desolate spot and utterly black at night-time.

A tempest blew over the land and whipped in through the crack of the dark telephone box, where the door would not shut.

Prior stamped his feet. His self-luminous watch hands said six o'clock precisely.

The telephone's jingle made him start. He snatched up the invisible receiver upside-down and spoke into the ear-piece before correcting this mistake.

He exchanged code-words with the caller and listened to her message against a background of yodelling and a tinkling zither, the popping of corks and the smacking of Lederhosen. Evidently she was in some Alpine Gasthof.

'Vee ken see dayfinitely, zat he hez not been issyooed viz enuzzer Breetisch pessport.' Drunken giggling and cumbersome German laughter half-obliterated the farewells.

Prior found his car in the darkness and drove eastwards towards Dublin, stopping on the outskirts at a tavern called The Menagerie. It had rough benches, sawdust on the floor, a stink of stale cigarette smoke and a few rough customers from Dublin's slums.

He approached the bar for a neat whiskey, to warm up his nipped blood.

A plump girl, swanking gold nail-varnish on her long claws, a cheap white fur jacket and a low-cut black dress with gold glitter on it, eyed him up and down. 'Hairv yer te toim?'

'For what?'

'Moin's a gin.'

He ignored her and ordered for himself.

'Shoit,' she spat and turned away.

Prior might have laughed had he not felt so thwarted in his skirmishes with the progeny of Cromwell's squadrons, who were ravaging his troops on every side in a new and drawn-out Drogheda. Then he relented and smiled and spoke to her umbrage-emitting back. 'How could I look down my nose at someone in such a beautiful and lady-like fur jacket?'

She gave a sniff and turned round. 'It's woit wievil, so it is.' The bedizened slattern gave a simpering smile.

'*Weevil*? Don't you mean *weasel*?'

'Ech, crap yersel',' she snarled and strutted off, snagging her white tights on a splinter on the corner of a graffiti-etched bench.

Prior tossed back his whiskey. There was only one thing left to do. He left by a gloomy corridor, where the girl was engaged in selling small red cotton packets of hashish outside the toilets to two youths who scooped up spoonfuls of curry from foil trays whilst they haggled.

As Prior pushed past, he adroitly stole the bulging purse which protruded from her jacket pocket.

He turned southwards to pick up the dark road out to Blessington. In his boyhood, he had travelled occasionally on the old steam tramway which once ran beside it out to see his grandfather, but tonight nothing jogged those young memories.

He parked near some trees down near the reservoir and counted out the girl's money by the car's weak inside light – over three hundred pounds – not bad. He stuffed it in an inside pocket and dropped her empty purse through a drain grating.

At the top of a steep gradient, stood a bungalow with two imitation brass coach lamps illuminating its driveway. This property had been rented by one Edgar C. Nolan, private secretary to the chargé d'affaires at the U.S. Embassy.

The greying, pink-faced, obese and pseudo-jovial Nolan in a loose brown cardigan and floppy orange and yellow check trousers opened the door and peered at the coated shadow on his doorstep.

'Mr Nolan?'

'Yip.'

'Eoin Prior.'

'Mr Prior ... You meant *this* Thursday?'

'Could you spare ten minutes?'

'Yeah sure. Come on in.' In the hallway he tapped the side of his potato-like nose. 'Is it a bit ... ?'

Prior nodded.

'Hold it a mo.'

Nolan went into his lounge and addressed a lanky short-cropped red-head. 'Hey Cherry Pie ... ' he began, 'I guess we diplomats are never off of duty.'

Her pose of languid sophistication disintegrated and she stubbed out her long cigarette with jerky sulky resentment. A flush of anger swept her pasty face as she seized her orange plastic mack and blinked her large green eyes like electric death rays.

'So long Honey Cake,' Nolan tooted sugarily as the vinegary bitch slunk past, wriggling her buttocks at them as if she wished she could spray some of her excrement over these vile males.

The American shut the door. 'Amazin' creatures these women – one minute you're a fiery and fantastic fella and the next you're dog-gone repellent.'

Prior found such a naïve observation hard to answer. 'I suppose she was on heat and excited ... and I interrupted.'

Nolan laughed and ushered his guest through.

'Can she get home all right?'

'Oh yeah. Her automobile's on the sidewalk.' He shook Prior's hand. 'Hi. I'm Ed. Take a seat.'

Prior took off his coat and sat on a sackcloth sofa.

'So it wasn't just happenstance that you sat by me on the train yesterday?'

'No. As I said, I'm an Irish Republican ... there's a problem we need help with.'

The room was dingy, furnished with a drinks' cabinet, two sofas and bookshelves which held a hi-fi system copiously scattered with dials and flashing lights. An incandescent crimson rug and a grey carpet adorned the floor.

Nolan took out two glasses and a bottle of Irish whiskey and placed them on the chromium-plated coffee-table. By an interrogative nod, he inquired if his host wanted a drink.

'Gimme four fingers o' red-eye.' Prior quoted the standard line from saloon scenes in Westerns.

'Then we'll go blow the Pussyfoot's stockade apart, eh pardner?' Nolan smiled grimly and poured.

The host put on some soft music to muffle their dialogue. 'Background noise,' he confided and sat down opposite his guest. 'Well Eoin, tell Uncle Ed about your problem.'

Prior lifted his shot-glass. 'To all sympathetic Americans.'

Nolan raised his tot too. 'Cheers.'

'There's a traitor – or maybe two – in our organisation ... and we think they channel their information to Belfast through an English army officer who lives undercover in the South.'

'Those bison-bouncing Limeys – or should I say *slimies* – are doin' real fine lately.'

Prior managed a smile. 'It's not just coincidence either.'

'Sure. Some bum's nosing into your affairs and I'll bet the carpet-baggers are bribing him ... the Brits do that.'

'The point is Ed, we can't trace the source, so we're trying to find this courier and then work backwards.'

Nolan nodded slowly. 'Any genuwine facts about this cloak-and-dagger hobo?'

'One. His name's said to be "Nicholas Letheren", though searches of governmental registers and flight lists here have all drawn a blank.'

The Yank poured out more liquor and opened a bottle of tonic water. 'So he uses an alias?'

'Probably, but we know he's not using a second British passport.'

'Do you?' Nolan looked impressed. 'Hey! Letheren's a mighty abstruse kind o' name, yeah?'

'I've never heard it before.'

'Well the head coyote in British Army Intelligence is called "Letheren" – Archibald god-dam Letheren.' He paused and Prior watched him. 'This sandpiper could be his son or nephew, yeah?'

'Gosh, if we took him out, it really would torch their testicles.' He raised his glass and Nolan clinked his against it.

The American spoke slowly. 'Do that and the Agency'ld fix you a five-star vacation in California.'

Prior wondered why the United States should dislike this man. 'Why ... '

Suddenly Nolan slapped his fat thigh. 'Gee! I've gotten it. I've gotten the whole grondspindling caboodle!'

Prior waited. Here at last was help – free ready help – from an Anglophobe who had knocked about in the right circles.

Nolan proposed that they made coffee so they moved through to the kitchen. He struggled with the beans and the percolator whilst the Irishman spread blue cheese clumsily onto rye biscuits.

'Now listen my good Irish buddy, there's a sidewinder in Cork, rents a house down by the harbour ... near Cowen's Fish Bar ... name of Etienne Bourachot – pretends to be a Froggy jelly-necker ... swans around with a guide-book and a camera – has this floosie who's a loco antique dealer's daughter and drives a sort of pimp-mobile ... name of Susan Eisenberg from Stillwater, Oklahoma ... ' Edgar paused to pour the coffee and take the cream out of the refrigerator. His precise knowledge of Miss Eisenberg made Prior wonder if she was pretty and that Nolan was envious. 'We know her a little and Christine Buchbinder – our first assistant – met them both one day ... poor Etienne, he slipped up and spoke with this Harrovian twang. Not a Frog. Oh no folks, nowise. Christine's a sharp cookie. He's your lousy stooge.'

Prior let the non-euphemisms pass without demur. Separating Britishness from Continental oiliness was not usually too hard.

Quite abruptly Nolan started to lose his self-control as an alcoholic depression gripped him. Instead of sensibly terminating the interview he allowed himself to ramble.

'Ow!' A violent spasm of pain shot down his back. 'My quack sezz I've a crumbling spine.' They moved back to the sofas and unwisely Edgar poured himself a fourth generous slug. 'I'm mighty pleased you came unofficially. Our new ambassador's pro-British ... but we'll scalp him.' Using the flat of his hand, he warbled Red Indian style, thankfully briefly. 'In Malta back in the fifties, me and a guy called Chuck Adeney were passing the dockyard staff a few bucks to go on strike or to damage British warships ... it was Agency policy then to louse up the British and French colonial authorities ... we shipped arms to the F.L.N. in Algeria too ... They were the days of Eisenhower and Dulles. Great stuff! We guys were big-handed "can-do" men then. We had jumboized programs to get the world right.

Then one night, these Maltese Freedom Fighters held us at gun-point, claimed they knew our real identity and sezz we planned to take over their whale-turd island ... like we tried it with Hong Kong in '45... They sezz if we didn't vamoose in twenty-four god-dam hours, they'ld shoot us. Adeney figured we best skedaddle right on schedule and go take us a break. But I heard years later that these native dweebs were Letheren – then a major – and his jerk pals with a lick of grease-paint on.'

Eoin made an effort to commiserate. 'Ah, very British. Very sly.'

'Shucks! In Cyprus a year later, me and Chuck were drinking in Larnaca one evening and it was some saint's day and all the bars shut at ten. I sezz to Chuck, "Where can we get another drink?" There was some British military police guy near us and he sezz, "Come with me. I'll show you." So he drove us to Nicosia and stopped at this great steel door and I thought, "What the hell's this?" He hammered on it and a little sliding hatch opened and when they saw who we were, they let us in. It was a brothel ... a great horse-shoe bar and little curtained cubicles round the periphery. We sezz we just wanted some bottles of beer and no glasses in case we caught the clap. There was this one German whore, lolling on a couch with her legs wide apart and scratching her crotch ... '

'Sounds tasteful.'

'Well yeah, exactly. She points to Chuck and sezz, "Zat little bald vun ... he can haff me for fife dollars ... zat is viz discount." That's how he gotten his moniker of "Five dollars". The next thing this helluva joint was raided by a British Army police squad. They dragged me off – no god-dam legal right – and slung me in what they called the "slammer". Chuck missed out because he was behind a curtain with some Italian popsy.

The red-cap corporal guy must have been following us. They kicked me out in the morning after they'ld gone through all my pockets and private notes ... twelve limb-atrophying miles from the flat. But again, it was a wind-up by that stuck-up hyena Letheren.' There was a moment's reflection and then suddenly Nolan flared up. 'Fuck the shafting bustards!' He slammed his glass down with such a bang that it was lucky not to break.

'Steady Ed,' said Prior soothingly. 'Your being immensely helpful. This is going to pay them back.' He put a hand briefly on the American's wrist. 'But what passport or I.D. would Nicholas Letheren be using if he's calling himself Bourachot?' He tried to get things back on course

'A French one. Smart, these crap-shooters.'

'How would he come by that?'

'Ever heard of Major Marc Hubert Roubier? Nope?'

'No.'

Nolan eyes were now red and he began to grow nasty. 'Letheren senior and he were in the Spanish Foreign Legion together in the thirties ... '

The discourse ceased. 'Where does Roubier fit into this?'

'Er ... sorry Eoin. He's some garlicky lugworm in the D.S.T. These crumby European clams ... they think we Yanks are just salesmen. They think we have no military or religious or artistic prowess ... Yet they fought on Buster Franco's side in the Civil War! Awful crimery ...

I'm from Maryland originally, but Pop spent some years in Quebec, so I kind o' learned Froggy. In seventy-two I was in southern Belgium, posing as a retired U.S. Army colonel. I'd visited France a couple of times to secure orders for American aircraft corporations – the million dollar persuader here and there to the free-loading chairman of an indecisive airline, if he saw things aright. One day this cool sexy Belgian policewoman raps the door. I open up. A guy with her sezz he's from the immigration bureau ... Monsieur Quellette ... wants to check – oh God, these cardboard swine were French D.S.T. agents ... kidnappers in disguise. They didn't stick around ... but whisked me over the border to Paris. Their interrogation technique's about two centuries behind everybody else's ... a barbarous racket ... They jig-sawed me ... crocodile clips, carborundum, shocks ... They wanted to know if I'd paid some aeronautical engineer to fix the parameters for Concorde's noise tests ... I *had* to tell them, I just *had* to.' He was almost in tears. 'Quellette was Roubier. The Minister of the Interior summoned the U.S. Ambassador in Paris for a pretty ugly moose-size tête-à-tête. Oh boy! They darn near fired me when I got back to Virginia.'

He wailed loudly for some seconds, until Prior touched his hand again and reminded him of his presence.

'Ed, please. This French passport?'

Ed yawned. 'There are extra-official tactics – headless bodies floating down the Seine and such garbage – and there's hearsay that Roubier and Letheren have assisted each other with falsified papers. After all, they're both trying to evade trashy prying governmental outfits on their own sides.'

Prior understood now why Nolan so loathed the British. 'I think I've got it Ed,' he conceded and then added, 'we might be glad of some means to follow young Letheren's vehicle.'

Nolan waved a fat pink fist. 'There are stacks of old E2 transmitter bugs and receiver consoles in the stores. Just leave it to Ed. They're O.K. up to about seven miles I guess – less if it's hilly. The bugs are magnetised but they're prone to droppin' off. It's smartest to wedge 'em or tie 'em.' He gave a huge yawn. 'Lucky you didn't test the water with my boss – oh he's pro-Republican, but between ourselves ... he's gotten an ...

alcohol ... problem.' With this Nolan keeled over sideways and snored.

Prior said, 'Really?' He let himself out.

* * *

Ute and Ulrich had thundered up the Autobahn on his alloy-wheeled black and blue charger, cruising at just under two hundred kilometres per hour. They wore helmets on such arterial roads where police patrols are inevitable. The cold bracing air and blue skies of Germany changed abruptly to a pall of drizzly dampness as they crossed the Dutch border and this grew denser as they neared Amsterdam.

Just short of Utrecht they turned onto a rural track and beside a long featureless dyke, swapped the real number-plate for a false one.

In Amsterdam it is possible to rent hotel rooms by the hour and in the clean post-war suburb of Nieuw Zuid they bought two hours' worth. The nondescript establishment they chose was above a row of shops in the well-to-do Beethoven Straat. The room however was not used for the expected purpose as they had already done that between a thorn hedge and a heap of hardened asphalt at the bottom of the dyke.

Whilst Ulrich showered and put his hands into hot water to thaw them out, Ute went down to the shops and bought eleven boxes, each of one hundred sugar cubes. The numbness eked away from Ulrich's fingers. Regardless of how thick the lining of your motorcycle mittens, the cold always seeped through after ten minutes. It was not so bad for Ute who kept her hands either behind her or round his midriff or occasionally – if on a Sunday afternoon jaunt say – clutching his vitals. In fact once in France, they had shot off the road and into a field because an extra-eager squeeze by her had caused him to swerve.

She set out the sugar lumps in long rows both on the dressing-table and the window sill and slightly spaced from one another. Then whilst she showered, he took from one of the pannier-bags, a well-wrapped half-full bottle of vodka and a glass pipette from a protective tooth-brush holder. The vodka bottle contained a clear, slightly oily liquid. It was an hallucinogenic drug with a butyrophenone structure dissolved in a vinyl jelly percolate. He poured some out into a glass and then with the pipette, carefully released one drop onto each sugar cube.

They sat in their underwear and pullovers, poring over a map of the city, drinking coffee from a flask and reciting the details of their forthcoming foray. They repacked the cubes in their cardboard boxes and brushed any loose granules onto the carpet, before putting on their dark blue suits and black boots again and with wet paper towels, wiping odd streaks of dirt off one another. It rained quite heavily as they rode into the city centre. Ulrich dropped off his pillion rider in Eerste Helmers Straat, a gloomy street with the iron railings of the Wilhelmina Hospital on one side, four-storey turn-of-the-century apartments opposite, tightly parked cars and narrow pavements smeared with dog droppings.

Ute selected the right door-bell button and pressed it. The intercom said, 'Met Jaap,' to which she returned the agreed name of 'Zeke' and the street door clicked open. She climbed the narrow stairs to the top floor.

Jaap Ariëns was a male nurse – one of the floppy wrist brigade. All nurses in Amsterdam came to this Mecca of perverts either because they too were perverts or because they were fleeing from relationships that had gone wrong. In his unclean and ill-aired bolt-hole, he gave her nine thousand

Dutch guilders, which she sat down and counted before handing over three boxes of the sugar lumps. She never let her wary eye wholly leave this forlorn boy, whose face resembling that of a sick monkey, was covered in pustules as if he had blood poisoning and looked to be devoid of human love.

When she had gone, he put on some music to relax by and then took one lump himself. Soon it brought all his friends out of the woodwork, large clockwork beetles, brown and pink or blue and purple, all with lots of friendly furry legs and who danced with whirring noises. His favourite had a body almost as large as a hamburger. Its name was Hendrik.

Ulrich's Honda bike swished through the puddles and the rain, out onto the exposed wind-blown Wester Dok quay beside the Ij. He halted near an orange and white, rust-scarred Belgian lumber coaster and staggered up the gang-plank, lashed by horizontal rain. He dived down steep companionway ladders and duly met Capitaine Marandon in a warm humming engine room, tinged with the smells of nebulised diesel oil and hot ozone. Here, more money and sugar lumps changed hands.

As dusk fell, Ute map-read her way along the cobbled alleys and beside the brick-edged canals, uninterested in the quaint finial-gabled houses reflected in the motionless green water or in the history of prudence and commerce which they represented.

She came to the barge named *Valkenburg* on the dingy though wide Kloveniers Burgwal Kanaal, moored beneath a grim old warehouse.

Oily green water slopped about between the silent hulls and a shudder-provoking unease that concealed plotting eyes were watching you, lurked in the air. The mouldy brick warehouses with their disused beam hoists and faded names stank of dank festering lawlessness, of hidden drug-addicted squatters, of villainous soulless beasts with hearts colder and harder than icicles.

A police car appeared suddenly, so suddenly in fact that Ute spun round and slipped on the wet slimy rounded granite cobbles in her fright, because she thought that for any catch other than herself, this was the sort of place where the police would come only by the van load. But they ignored her, stopped beside another boat and possibly received a note or took a bribe from a briefly seen hand. She turned back to the *Valkenburg* and saw that a leering grotty youth had appeared on deck. He beckoned curtly and led her down a hatchway to a cramped drab timber-clad cabin, lit only by a dirty orangy oil-lamp.

An educated sort of man in a suit and horn-rimmed glasses appeared from behind a curtain and introduced himself as Pieter van Goor. He oozed a distrustful smoothness and his smile seemed tainted in some way. She asked for the name of his company and he most precisely gave the arranged title of 'Odenwald'. She sat down on a side-bench and remarked on his flawless German.

'As a small country of traders, it is a tradition with us to learn other languages,' he explained with that hard niceness which arouses in other men the suspicion of homosexuality.

A squint-eyed greasy grin slipped onto the Dutch boy's morose face and Ute wondered if van Goor were not actually German.

The youth, who needed some dental treatment, departed. Van Goor sat down on the squashed bunk opposite her, pushed an array of empty sauce bottles and dirty crockery to one side on the intervening table and proffered a wad of Deutschmarks in a plastic travel wallet. She reluctantly took her gloves off and counted it. Being correct, she handed him the remaining three boxes of sugar cubes from her blue and yellow nylon rucksack.

He in turn checked the merchandise. He removed the lid of each box and took out one cube. He held it up and inspected it. The drop of liquid had given the sugar a very faint perse-coloured tint, though the amber glow of the oil-lamp when behind it, made each cube look like a small corundum stone.

'Excellent,' he announced as if he were a satisfied gem dealer.

She nodded and started to pull her gloves on.

'You don't by any chance want sex, do you?' It was a passing query.

'No.'

'A thousand Deutschmarks?'

'No.'

'Oh well, a pity. I quite fancied getting my giant pneumatic drill into you.'

'Thanks for the compliment.'

'I remember once at work, a smooth rotund girl – very similar to you, but Danish – I wanted her so much that I pretended I had locked my car keys in my boot and begged her for a lift ... and then raped her ... and she loved it. See how restless the beast is.' He indicated his sex organ pushing at his trouser-flies.

'Not today, all the same.'

'Oh, come on. We're only strange collections of chemicals after all. Think of the extra dosh. It's crazy to allow stupid romantic conventions to deny you ... '

'No!' She stood up to go.

'There's just one other little thing.'

'Yes?' She paused.

'Put the money back on the table.' This was stated with a rigid smile but briskly and in the tone of a command.

She shook her head firmly.

Confronted with this low-born churlishness, he pointed out that there were three boys up on deck who were capable of being exceptionally nasty.

Her one trump card – which van Goor knew nothing of – was that Ulrich was due to pick her up about now. She listened secretly for the sounds of the motorbike. 'If you force the money from me, you may expect a visit from my associates.' She was playing for time, but also did not feel as frightened as logically she ought.

He shrugged. 'The boat isn't mine. It's the same to me if it gets torched.'

The old brass oil-lamp spluttered. Its main function seemed to be to disseminate tiny black sooty floaters and fat specks into the air from its position in the middle of the long narrow table. A bread-knife lay beside it, but it was not pointed and looked extremely blunt.

As she made no move to hand back the Deutschmarks, he said impatiently, 'Look, I take it you wish to leave this city "intact"?' As if to confirm his threat, the sounds of feet scraping on the deck above them and of loitering derisive phrases, filtered down. 'So just give me the bloody stuff!' Van Goor watched her face for a reaction and saw it. His face smirked and turned a stronger pink than before, like a cheap plastic doll's. He edged round the table and trapped her in the confined cul-de-sac on her side of it.

Oh hell! Where was Ulrich?

He made a grab for her rucksack, but she clutched it tightly and during its brief oscillation it knocked the bulbous glass funnel off the lamp and extinguished the flame. This thin glass artefact also broke despite falling a mere few centimetres.

Van Goor swore as semi-darkness invaded their confined shoe-box.

Ute then acted with the suddenness of a cornered animal, so suddenly indeed that she almost surprised herself.

She seized in her right hand the largest piece of the broken chimney, which she could see glinting in the gloom and rammed its razor-like broken edge into the left side of his neck. This manoeuvre was so unexpected, that van Goor made no counter-move. As it sliced deeply into his flesh and his murky blood started to pump out in squirts, he stood there like someone who cannot quite believe what has just happened. The whole masque seemed absurd. Of course she had not just stabbed him in the throat.

He sat down on the food-stained and wine-swilled cushions and felt the warm sticky liquid not only pouring down onto his shirt collar, but coming out in pulsatile spurts which leapt upwards and outwards as if not wanting to sully his suit.

'Dirk!' he managed to shout with some force. 'Help!'

Ute grabbed her rucksack, thrust her way past the collapsing van Goor and with a pounding heart hauled herself up the steep companion-ladder and onto the deck.

At last, the sound of a motorbike!

Six agitated feet shuffled towards the gang-plank to cut off her escape.

'Ulrich!' she screamed, to warn him as he drew up in the shadows by the warehouse.

His headlamp swung round and spotlighted the confused trio of puny spotted Hanks, paltry Dutch microbes in tattered ex-military combat jackets, their thumbs resting pugnaciously in the belt-loops of their jeans. Ulrich dismounted and pulled his idling steed up onto its stand. He advanced slowly toward the enemy-laden barge, bathed in a sickly orange mist from the floodlights of a distant thoroughfare. The supposedly toughest of the three boldly blocked the gang-board, like Horatius holding the bridge over the Tiber. Ulrich approached and then after a stand-off of some seconds, thrust out a high kick at his groin. The weakling flinched and nearly fell sideways into the canal, before retreating to cower with his sibling rabbits at the far edge of the boat. Ute ran round towards her rescuer and sprang across onto the quay. A Dutch woman went past, her eyes firmly down as if she were noticing nothing.

Ulrich retreated ashore warily as Ute urged the bike off its stand and edged it forward. Ulrich leapt on behind her and off they accelerated, swiftly but not as fast as had he driven. She shook badly and as they joined Rokin, nearly collided with one of those yellow articulated trams. She pulled up. Ulrich took over and they headed southwards, where she at least would consider whether or not Amsterdam had become too risky.

* * *

The drifters in Dingle harbour creaked at their cables in the early morning mist. Water slopped against the stone mole but no capstans clanked or windlasses whined. None was preparing for sea, though it was not rough.

Nicholas Letheren had expected one would – perhaps that broad-beamed grey-hulled boat – for Aoibheann had said that one would sail up to Ballycastle in the North with a half-ton of C4 plastic explosive on board, to be rowed ashore at night in a dinghy and hidden in an uncommissioned fibre-glass septic tank on a farm there, buried in the ground.

The sun's shafts had gradually dispersed the blue mist hanging in the wide cauldron-like bay and from his look-out post in a collapsed haystack, a little way back from the headland, Letheren knew that no boat had left since at least two hours before sunrise. A motor-boat had bobbed and tossed as it had entered a little after seven, but that was all.

He heaved himself out of his hidey-hole, replaced the bales and jumped down from beneath the tin roof on stilts, coughing with the dust. He walked up the scarcely discernible track towards the rutted unfenced road where his Beetle stood on the verge.

The gold-tinged bluish hills in the distance were part of a rubric, remote and other-worldly and tranquil, which seemed to be calling his soul this morning.

A stone's throw from his car lay a discarded fizzy drink can, which he had not seen when he left. He viewed it from various angles, ever alert to booby traps, but could see no wires. He threw a stone at it and it rattled away innocuously enough. He examined the under-side of his car too without event, but then hesitated to drive away because things had not developed as Aoibheann had predicted and that was unusual.

He wandered up to some bare beech trees and thought how in summer, it would be a splendid spot for a picnic. In childhood, he and his parents and sisters had been avid picnickers.

He had meant to scan the little town with its jumble of stone cottages and its quayside, but instead a brown Japanese jeep caught his eye, just up the hill and round the bend and suspiciously half-camouflaged by a leafless hedgerow. It looked battered and was adorned with lots of bent tasteless chromium and he felt unpleasantly sure that he had seen it near Cork the day before. As he had swung into a petrol station, it had shot past but then been waiting in a lay-by farther along the road. Had Aoibheann been fed with a widely circulated false rumour, designed to catch spies?

He crept along a rocky gully. Three unshaven mutes sat in the steamed-up bodywork. He crawled on all fours up to the mud-spattered chassis from behind and having good ground clearance, it was possible to slide underneath the vehicle on his back, using his heels to help push himself over the stones and grass. In the oily black engine above him he saw the four leads coming out of the distributor to the spark-plugs. Even with his arms fully extended, he would never reach to cut through these with a knife. Besides he might slip and make a noise. He tried to unscrew the oil drainage bolt, but it was too stiff for his fingers alone. His service pistol lay beside him. He worked the point of his knife carefully through the inside wall of each tyre, one by one, to give them slow punctures.

He felt good as he drove away, imagining the jeep slewing off the road like a crippled war-elephant, yet near Tralee sober unease reared its head again. Aoibheann wished to meet him urgently too. The clues were there to something being amiss. Should he just drive up North and abandon everything? Yet it seemed cowardly to fly from shadows. He must first find out the intents of the enemy camp and Aoibheann could probably answer that.

Eoin Prior had spent the night in his bed, being wordlessly kneaded by the sylph-like Aoibheann, who sucked and stroked and pummelled his middle-aged bulk, slippery with sweat and secretions. This had filled the night except for short pauses of post-climactic rest, for constant renewal was their theme. She seemed more invigorated the more she had, like an avalanche. Six or seven times were usual for them and the next day did not find them sleepy.

Of course he had slept too. He had dreamt he was in a fishing boat, green and hang-dog. He had vomited some lime-coloured bile into a newspaper and flung it overboard, where it had been grabbed by a British sailor in a dinghy bearing an approaching search-party. He had wrung up more greeny stomach residues and talked of piracy and the European Court of Human Rights.

# 131

The dawn found the pair in soporific embrace. Even in sleep he held her shoulders and she his testicles. She woke first at half-light, but did not move.

A year before she had left her work in Wexford with its inert and drunken youth and gone to Australia to seek her fortune in the form of a rich man. She had wanted the trappings of a fashionable house, cars, children, dinner parties and so-called friends – the boringly standard female ambition. She had taken a job as a secretary with a small gold mining company and tried to land the manager, Mr Pile. He bit the bait and she played him well, but mistimed the landing jerk and her line snapped, whereupon he swam off with some brazen American heiress. An Englishman had visited her, who talked of the Isle of Erin, of Eoin Prior, of secret London bank accounts and payment by results.

And until four days since, all had gone smoothly. Now a hunt was on, she had unwittingly passed on false information which was part of a trap and she thought that Declan O'Hagan saw through her.

In the kitchen, she buttered the toast and made coffee with milk boiled in a bent old saucepan. As she drank it, it clung to her teeth like woollen socks. *She* had no grudges against the British. They paid her well. The action on the Mourne Beg alone had earned her twelve thousand pounds. Her savings exceeded thirty-eight thousand now.

Prior was going out.

'I'm popping out too to see Auntie Aoiffe later,' Aoibheann said.

'Well don't bring back any more of her home-made marmalade,' growled Prior, 'It's like poison.'

By afternoon, she had packed her passport, those dull necessary papers, some clothes and a few favourite books and toiletries. She drove off up towards the low hills around

Ballargh Pass, speeding with unusual impatience, sensing the net to be closing and eager to be on safer ground. She would talk to Etienne, make for London where hopefully the British would give her a new name and passport and then fly to the West Indies. Those sunny islands had always fascinated her, though she had never visited them. A little French one, Saint-Barthélemy, which she had read of sounded so balmy and fragrant and remote – like paradise. She would rent a little chalet, take sailing lessons and read romances until some adequately exciting and prosperous man wandered along.

Mist descended and it started to sleet. Her car passed the group of three houses called Killoe and soon after that came the track. A milk bottle beside the stony verge indicated that Etienne had come. She swung off, bumped over a wooden planked bridge across a ravine and passed a ruined shepherd's cottage, of which only four thick and roofless walls remained.

Ahead, a white car beneath a small crag, disconcerted her. The track led to a green pool with a green waterfall and was a dead-end. She pressed on.

Here she had come with her first lover when only fourteen and doted on him as he had fished in vain, happy just to sit beside him and caress his mass of black hair. Then they would go to Auntie Aoiffe's and eat scones beside the peat fire and hold hands – so innocent and so long ago it seemed. A sudden wave of instinct overwhelmed her, peaceful and religious and free and then another followed, doom-laden and fearful. O Mary, Mother of God, pity us our pain!

It appeared, the dusky green lake and the magic waterfall, all shrouded and still and mysterious – and there too stood the rust-red Beetle.

She spoke to Letheren. He said she should go to England at once. They would give her new papers there.

The white car, with its owner in the boot and hijacked by the crew of the sick jeep, moved into view. Men stepped out with machine-guns.

Aoibheann smiled enigmatically, the tears welling from her eyes upstaging the sleet like some insignificant impostor. If not beautiful, the faces of the pair were intensely bright. Letheren's pistol was useless. They were about to run toward a scree-slope, when a burst of automatic fire brought red patches to her arm and his leg.

O'Shea, the leader of the gang, had a fat belly which he used to tell folk was due to a forward-curving spine and not to being overweight. No one ever dared to laugh. His early memories were largely of a waddling mother crossing herself and calling on Saint Patrick to bless the I.R.A.

This coral-skinned mass of meat, forced the injured girl to the ground and raped her. She could not resist effectively with her upper-arm bone shattered, so she drifted off into thoughts of her childhood at Gimmaragh Creek, fresh as a dew-drop and tripping over the lush grass to Cuerff Bay. Her life had run as it had had to run. She had played her erring and ineluctable part.

Unsurprised that it had been bereft of finer feelings, O'Shea finished emptying his sperm sacks and then shot her through the eye with a single shot. But they thought a bullet to be too kind for her English controller, so they tied his feet to the towing-hook of their white Morris Marina and drove it round in circles until he died. Then they slung the bodies into the Beetle, fetched a can of petrol and set fire to it. Its initial puff and crackle broke for a while the soft drone of the waterfall falling into Findagh's Pool.

When the fire waned and the car only smoked, they tried to push it into the lake using Aoibheann's car, but it bogged immovably in a reedy swamp, its tyreless wheels barely covered and its charred human debris still horribly evident.

O'Shea swore copiously as he rammed the Beetle so hard that it broke the second vehicle's transmission and he had to wade back to dry ground through freezing clinging mud. Still, he had shot the long-sought 'Fingal'. He had raped her too, even if only to prove himself to his accomplices. He had also killed a British spy.

He took a bottle out of the car and they all had a swig of alcoholic liquid, wiped their mouths on their sleeves and roared away.

## CHAPTER FIVE.

Uanrig House stood on a flat acre which curved slightly out into Loch Eilan, a silent inland loch about four miles long and one wide and circled with dense hangers of pine trees clinging to hills and crags. The house had been erected in the early nineteenth-century as a hunting lodge and its good proportions and tasteful plainness reflected this date. It was free of the over-ornate confusion and clumsiness of the subsequent late Victorian era. The structure was of stone and built on a four-square plan with four main rooms on each of the two floors, so that from the front its elevation was symmetrical with five identical windows surrounding the central front-door, where two unfluted pillars supported a narrow portico and themselves stood on a huge slab, which was the doorstep. A lawn ran up from the rippling green waters to the untidy and sparse gravel surrounding the house, behind which was a small walled yard with a well and three stables. Undeniably it was a good house and in a most picturesque spot, but for the last nine years little had been done – money and effort were needed. Since the age of one, Artemis had always lived here, so regardless of often being away at boarding-school, it had always been her home and her spirit was very attached to it.

At about midday on Sunday the seventh, Sheelagh, the sandy-haired domestic woman, rattled off from behind the house on her heavy old bicycle. It was really her day off, but the previous day and night had seen exceptional rain even for this region and a prolonged cloudburst had forced her to stay the night. Now that the pelting rain had abated, a howling gale sprang up, whistling through the trees and beating at the windows and causing lots of twigs and small branches to shower down onto the sodden earth. Sheelagh had to dismount and push, leaning into the wind and one gust ripped her billowing plastic mack.

Inside, Artemis was trying on for the second time the dress she had bought in Edinburgh for Sir Robert Falcus's party. She stood in the hallway, surveying herself in the large long oval mirror with the gilt rim, in which you could see your entire form well displayed. The close-fitting knee-length semi-shiny and slightly flared black linen dress had narrow red frills running horizontally around its skirt part at six inch intervals, like a wasp – but red and black instead of yellow and black – and she felt ready to sting. Her hair was pulled tightly back and her ear-rings were pieces of reddy amber mounted in gold. Elodie Davidson had obligingly paid the exorbitant prices.

Most clothes looked good on Artemis, but this outfit reminded her of a girl in a book she had just read entitled *The Binary Ellipsis*, where like the heroine she felt puissant elegant beddable and destined to succeed. She had had enough of being polite and decent and getting nowhere. No longer was she going to be the silly little girl, but a tough hard-nosed one. She was intelligent enough too, to be *effectively* evil.

In her bedroom she packed the dress into her suitcase with tissue paper and care together with shoes and other items and then put on a more everyday black white and red pleated skirt of MacRae tartan, a white cotton blouse and a red cardigan.

She ran downstairs to answer the telephone.

'Dulloch three five four.'

'Miss Artemis Boden?'

Balls! She knew who it was. Earlier in the week, she had deliberately not answered the telephone several times for fear of it being him whom her mind wished to reject. It would be easy enough to prevaricate, to say she would see him next week when she were back in North Shields, yet no ... 'Go away!' By gosh, her voice had been almost a snarl. She slammed the receiver down. The mirror caught her attention again and she saw her face, a piece of rigid ivory, transformed into something lined and ugly. 'Damn!' she muttered. 'Why did I answer the wretched thing? I knew if I did, it would be him and if I didn't it would be somebody else. Leave me alone meddling Collett!'

Trying to fight back her turmoil, she went into the kitchen, cut up a small piece of beef and boiled it, added salt, rosemary, a chopped onion and two diced tomatoes.

As she ate this broth in the sitting-room with a stale roll, a power-failure engulfed the house. The logs of the fire spluttered and a magnified lamina of Artemis's inimitable head neck and shoulders superimposed itself on the wall.

Instead of lighting candles, she made her final preparations to leave in the sitting-room using the warm reddish fire-light. She intended to drive to Carlisle, take the night sleeper down to London, book into a hotel there and spend the next day getting ready for this make-or-break audition. She put on a pair of shimmering black leather thigh-boots which she had bought a year before but then never worn, viewing them as perhaps too showy and provocative. Then she put up the fire-guard, turned all the light switches to their 'off' positions and pulled on her allure-evoking leather coat.

She locked the back-door behind her, put her suitcase and handbag on the back seat of the Alvis and drove slowly out of the yard. The upset caused by Simon's call had worn off and she felt excited, romantic and hopeful.

The ill-maintained track from the house, boggy in patches and encroached upon by undergrowth and saplings, ran beside the loch for four hundred yards and then turned into the forest for a stretch of a mile and a half, passing over a ridge to come out on the main road between New Galloway and Newton

Stewart. As the powerful old car charged towards the low ridge in the failing light of late afternoon, she saw a fallen pine tree barring her path. She scrambled out and stood on the soaking turf, her coat brushing the dripping bracken and eyed this mammoth artefact, utterly blocking the drive. There was an inkling of something supernatural about it, as if it knew it was there for a purpose. Artemis banished this thought, leapt back into the car and succeeded in making the tricky reverse to a clearing where she could turn round.

It entered her mind also, that it would have been more sensible to have let some eminent film producer wiggle his bits inside her in exchange for a decent part instead of letting Goldstraw in for nothing – if that sordid jewelled delusion really had been unavoidable.

By the time she reached the house, she had ejected that fruitless thought too. Planning to ring for a taxi to meet her at the main road and she part-drive part-walk to meet it, she grabbed the telephone but found it dead. Both the electricity wires and the telephone line ran beside the track, so the tree had brought them both down.

An exasperated gasp escaped from her, which suggested a latent virile temper only just below the surface. But anger would not help. Resolve might. Artemis would rise victoriously and break out of this trivial snare by her formidable will-power.

The Easter Tickell Cottage, once used by the ageing groundsman Longwell Ballantyne and which stood at the entrance to the estate, was now empty and without a telephone. The only option therefore seemed to be to employ one of Papa's old motorbikes and by using the bridleway beside the Eilan Burn, to reach either Dulloch village or Castle Douglas and then organise a taxi. She still had twenty-four hours.

The early 1950's Ariel motorcycle which she pushed out into the yard, had been ridden by her before. Occasionally on a dry summer's day, she had tried it out beside the loch or in the woods as a change from her horse. The first two kicks failed to start it because she had forgotten to turn on the fuel cock, but three more made it burst raucously into life.

With her suitcase's contents transferred into the bike's buckle-fastened leather pannier-bags, she was ready to set off again. The clouds had broken up a bit and the effulgent crimson disc of the sun peeped over a high black ridge ahead of her, topped with black pines, its rays giving a tint of enchanted colour to the deep grey sombre chill of a desolate evening.

Artemis did up the top button of her glistening black leather coat, turned the collar up so that it cupped her soft white neck and then twirled her red woollen scarf round its outside and up as far as her nose. She pulled on the gauntlets used in Manchester and sat astride the Ariel on its large black but push-bike-like triangular saddle with large springs under it, sweeping the three-panelled rear of her lustrous coat under the smooth shapely lines of her bottom and glancing at the dials on top of the dark red petrol tank.

She urged the machine off its stand and adjusted the choke on top of the carburettor with a clumsy gloved hand. In shiny black red and chrome it glinted – ready for action.

The sun had gone. She let out the clutch and moved off along the stony shore in the opposite direction to the track. A demonic glow burnt in her features, a clue to something hidden and wayward on the verge of finding an outward expression, a scent of some intoxicating potion, though she knew not what.

Passing a fire-break in the trees, an adder shot out from under a fallen trunk and with large looping movements, bolted into some ferns. The most visible and lingering image about its dubious outline was the vivid orange zig-zag down its back.

In the intensifying gloom – and after covering perhaps half a mile – the headlamp showed up a small five-bar gate in a crumbling stone wall. She dismounted, squelched through the mud around it and shook it savagely, noting the corroded padlock. The rusty chain would not snap, nor the rotting wood break. 'Sod it!' Eventually she managed to lift its other end off the hinges and swing it clear. A short steep uphill section though, through the gate, caused the rear wheel to spin. After a few foot-aided frenzied flailing futile fits, she allowed the motorcycle to roll back to take a run at this obstacle. She revved the engine dropped it into first gear and let the clutch out slowly. It snarled and throbbed and seemed just about to have made it, when a sudden sideways skid, capsized the bike and spewed her off like a broken spider-crab into the thick slimy mud.

Strangely she did not feel anger this time, just disbelief – disbelief that fate could be so stubborn and forceful, even more stubborn and forceful than she, in trying to compel her to veer away from her desired course. In the cindery darkness, she could not see her clothes but could visualise the mess. The shins and knees of her new thigh-boots and the elbows and forearms of her coat were resting in this clayey muck and the hems of her coat and skirt and underskirt too had certainly been dragged in it.

She did not move immediately either. Her thoughts skipped back to another party-cum-interview for a television play last October. A girl called Rachel had contended with her for a small part, a smooth-faced girl with wavy ginger hair and a long pointed nose, rather like a Botticelli portrait. Her every word had been measured, every tinkling laugh calculated and to Artemis this suavity had been evident and nauseating. Yet it *was* neatly executed. It was crawling, but high-class crawling. The insight and judgement of Rachel's responses made it hard to discern, but nothing came from the heart. Everything was designed to massage the glum and narcissistic director's ego. By contrast, Artemis had not hidden her feelings well and so no doubt, had offended this illegitimate quasi-aesthetic snob. Most depressing of all though was that it worked. These diamond-hard arch-bitches like Rachel ingratiated themselves with usable fools and greased their way onto the ladder, whilst the truthful silences of Artemis trod on corns and disqualified her. Rachel had eyed her rival coldly, for she saw that Artemis knew her game. Here was a dangerous foe, not a half-wit able to be pacified by some cooing commiseration.

Artemis abandoned her salaam-like posture and stood up to examine this impasse. There was an alternative way, along the edge of the burn, but there were shallow cross-ditches and thorn bushes and rocks. Yet what had she to lose?

It took a real effort to right the 350 c.c. motorbike. Her lips trembled and her tongue uttered swear words which it had not spoken before. She remounted, kicked it into life, started and stalled it, re-kicked it viciously and her muddy boot flew off the starting lever. She bent low over it and eventually it obeyed her threats and moved off effortfully, for a mass of thick mud clung to the rear wheel making it sluggish and heavy even in first gear. It growled through a few bramble bushes before its unwieldy nature made it refuse to skirt a tiny dell. It tumbled into the hole and she fell with it, into some prickly heather. Her rage was such that she felt ready to explode and would have uprooted trees and smashed fences if only she had had the strength. 'Piss this bloody contraption and piss this mud!' she raved.

The headlamp had gone out. A one-quarter moon burst fitfully through the thinning cloud and she espied the vague form of a low dense thorn bush. A dwarf in this had shoved her into the pit. 'Come out you sodding imp. I don't care if you're in league with Collett. Don't you dare oppose me! I'll fight you all and win. Nothing's going to demean me.' She went to give the bush a maddened kick, but in doing so slithered off an unseen precipice, down into the broad gully where the burn gurgled. Again she was unhurt but had landed in another quagmire and on standing, caught her foot in a creeper and instantly fell flat again.

She started to cry, a mixture of anger and tears, long and unrestrained. 'These things shouldn't happen to me! Why am I blocked like this? Everyone else gets at least something of what they want. I *hate* nursing! I know I ought to have worked harder for my 'A' levels and then I could have gone to university ... but this isn't fair. I'm Artemis, goddess of the moon ... ' she blubbered.

As her sobs grew more spasmodic and hiccoughy, the clouds blew away and revealed a most beautiful, pale blue crescent moon. The despondent girl gazed up at it through the black branches and it gazed back at her, like a saviour or a consoling ally. In front of her, its delicate light caught the swirling surface of the stream and an ash tree as thick as her forearm. She remembered when small and it had been only finger-thick, that the poacher's boy had said it would make a good fishing-rod.

Her chest moved more easily. For a half-hour she lay there entranced and unwilling to move and slowly a warm pleasant sensation crept over her of being able to choose a delightful though evil course. She could become a sorceress. In a quiet way, a dark and deep exhilaration consumed her mind like a calm and long drawn-out orgasm.

She sat up, sitting with her bottom on her heels. The moonlight glinted off the tips of her pointed breasts as they stood out in their smooth leather tents. She folded in her coat flaps over her thighs, seeing as she did so that a thorn had torn a sickle-shaped rent in the red silk lining.

Something irresistible pulled her forwards, something dangerous yet satisfying and she knew that she was crossing the Rubicon. Slightly delirious, she lay face-down onto a large flat boulder and soon felt the heat being sucked out of her breasts and stomach and thighs whilst her nostrils inhaled the acidy peaty damp smells of this patch and her own expensive perfume.

She realised that the small plateau in front of her had been man-made long ago. In the eerie bluish engirding gloom, the moon's rays showed up in the rock face edging the plateau and half-hidden by briars, an even blacker triangle in the black stratum, a just discernible adit to a long-forgotten mine. Her father had said once, that in Roman times veins of lead and silver ore had been worked in this area.

She adjusted her elbows in the wet marshy ground on either side of the mossy slab and rested her chin on her clasped gauntleted hands. Her face shone serenely and wanly. In her spine a new force stirred, euphoric and seemingly benign and it spread through her entire body. Some demon's claws sank slowly into her leather bottom and pinned her there, lovely and unruly and summoning in her mind, shapes inverted and negative and black. Relief seized her as her former ill-fitting white robes were stripped off. With ecstasy, the primeval drug of the ancient stone embraced her – Mother Earth had come to free her from the petty delusions of vanity and from the weaknesses engendered in us by the conflict of good and evil. Artemis babbled brokenly, strange primordial oracles.

'Eostre gesælgu ac cræfte awecce.
Astyre thissum eorthe-fægan sceaf,
On winter-tide.

Gief hiere deoglan coss,
Æt thinum stan on golde and hydum,
        On deopan wealde.
Gegierwe hie gehale mid fyre.
Befæste hie mid sum anrædan cnolle,
        Swa thine cene wode bryde.
Rid behyded niht-gengan,
Wrec ealle cwice lufe,
        Tha ga on se ansundne eard.'

Bubbles floated out of the cave, green and blue and purple. 'I am the Spirit of the Mine, who in your nadir of terrible defeat will win you to my augurs and rescue you and make incantation for your escape – that you may steal and kill and not be found out, flaunt arrogance and taunt mankind and not be felled – yet you shall renounce love, ascribe to it scorn, impute to it failure. Come with me, to the sulphurous nether world, away from the simulacra of light.'

In the deep cave, a red glow, cataclysmic and restless, like the jaws of a smith's forge, burnt dully. An ethereal power, sensed but not seen, coalesced gleefully with her tremulous neat maiden form. Her bowels turned to liquid. Deliciously, rapturously, it enveloped her like smoke invading her eyes and nose and weighing down on her shoulders and spine. No sexual climax took place at this investiture, but her mind was impregnated with forbidden seed.

The nip of the cold stone roused her from her daze and she stood up. A hill fog had obscured the moon. She padded her soiled clothes and recalled the motorcycle disaster. It seemed strangely unimportant now. A wonderful ease had come upon her, a sense of being free at last of human restriction.

A resurrected self-assurance pervaded her movements. She felt different, as if something had occurred in this miry forest to set her on the right path.

* * *

Collett wiped a hole in the condensation on the window as the train swayed and slowed on its approach to the rural halt at Nunley in the blackened undulating Berkshire countryside. It *was* his stop. He fought his way through a jungle of elbows and briefcases and broke out onto the cold empty platform.

As there were no taxis, he had to walk the two miles to Sir Robert Falcus's country estate. He crunched across the gravel past the parked Lancias and Aston Martins and Ferraris and mounted the two steps between the two weather-worn rampant lions which flanked them.

Light and gaiety spilled out into the freezing night air. He showed Artemis's invitation to a haughty craggy butler and explained that he was her boyfriend and that they had agreed to meet here.

Perhaps seventy people stood in the vast reception room and effused vibrancy skittishness and sparkle. A buxom woman, replenishing her plate with cold turkey and gherkins from the buffet, addressed her neighbour. 'Ruth's a superb actress. I wouldn't hear a word against her ... so unfortunate that her last film's been *such* a flop.'

Simon stood near some blue velvet curtains and by the lights of a glittering chandelier, poured himself a goblet of white wine to cover his solitude and as Artemis seemed not to be there, listened to two young B.B.C. assistant producers, who instead of inviting him to join them, ignored him and gossiped in in-vogue style. Their names were Gavin and Adrian.

'I see snivelling Trevor's here,' Gavin remarked with a plasticky sceptical smirk.

'Rooting.'

'But it's not a rooting nose is it – circular and flat? No, thin and nasal – snivelling.'

'A spud.'

'A carrot old boy, not a spud. Do you know what sort of car he drives? No? You had best sit down before I tell you or you'll collapse with laughter. A Fiat!'

'No wonder he's having trouble with the girls.'

'You can imagine the disappointment on their faces.'

Adrian smiled. 'I think he's rooting for a niche on that new Trollope dramatisation. He went out with oenophile Hatch last night and they got hog-pigging drunk.'

'"Hog-whimpering" is the term old boy.'

'He always recovers by the next evening though.'

'As do all we sex maniacs.' Gavin glanced round here at Collett, whom he suspected of eavesdropping despite his apparent concentration on his French bread and Bavarian blue cheese. He looked as if he could be discounted as someone of no importance. 'Who is that tall virgin-looking girl with Fogey Falcus?'

'She's his new "find". No one knew of her before.'

'You mean she's made it without favour-swapping?'

'Favour-swapping? In our circles Gavin? Never heard of it.'

'Perhaps she sleeps with him ... though I can't imagine it somehow.'

'Hard to say.'

'Actually, I can't imagine that the antediluvian Sir Bob would know what to do with anyone really sexy ... but then she isn't *sexy* is she?'

'A bit chaste and pure.'

'Don't be Kindergartenish old boy. They've all had it ... just in some it's less obvious than in others ... all lax old sheaths – none of them's virtuous and new and tight round your prick.'

'Look, Kim's over there with some fat gold-dripping Berber. She's sexy. Who's that Malaysian-like girl with them? She looks as if she's a chromosome or two missing.' He referred to an ugly Persian girl called Miss Shamshag with a narrow vault to her head and large pendulous cheeks, like a pear.

'Don't know. Still, every silver lining has a cloud. God!' he exhaled with leering intensity, 'I want to hot-rod Kim tonight – despite the laxness!' He sucked air in through clenched teeth and flexed his right arm before resuming his habitual air of droll non-enthusiasm. 'How do these Arabs become so confoundedly rich?'

Adrian thought. 'I suppose some have inherited it – but I suspect most of them are crooks.'

'Trevor's moving up to them, complete with a mucous stalactite dangling from the tip of his nose. Let's *slide* across.'

The avant-garde oilers moved off.

Collett turned once more to the long table with its white starched cloth, spread with elaborately decorated fish and fowl dishes, desserts and wines. He poured himself more bubbly. He felt so lonely and could not care a toss if he drank too much.

Like an aberration, the 'chaste' girl stood beside him, a good fairy with her hair in a French plait woven onto the back of her head. Her white linen blouse with its high neck and lace cuffs bore on it a wiry silver neck-chain with a coily Viking-design pendant cross resting on her chest. Her slightly flared skirt was of dark blue suede, interrupted by narrow horizontal rings of dark blue leather. She wore white knee-length socks and neat plain black leather shoes. She embodied something of civilised order. 'Good evening. My name's Innogen. You don't seem to be a part of this frolic?'

'How do you do. Simon. No I'm not. I'm waiting for my girlfriend.'

She smiled with an openness which put him at ease – not the spiky guardedness of the advanced intellectuals here, each with twenty worthless letters after his name. This smile was neither flirtatious nor stand-offish nor looking down and he felt bad about having drunk too much. Why could he not have fallen in love with this beatific entity instead of the obdurate Artemis?

'Who is your girlfriend?'

'Artemis Boden.'

'Ah ... yes.'

'I might as well have gone home to my mother's and lopped her tall pear trees, instead of wasting the day coming here.'

'Perhaps she's hired a giraffe to do it for her?'

'Is your full name Innogen Eione Letheren?'

Her sparse brows tilted inwards in feigned pique. 'Who told you my middle name?'

'I saw it at the top of the doorman's list.'

'My brother and sister have unheard of Greek middle names too. Even my Teddy Bear was called Titus. My father's crackers about classical history.' She spoke in a quiet but clear voice with wide variations of pitch.

'What's his job?'

'He's an army officer, but be a bit discreet here please. This twenty-holiday-a-year bunch are all very anti-military.'

'Envy probably. Theirs is a world of back-stabbing, *After Eight* mints and no *real* toughness.'

For Simon, the pleasure of this dialogue was not the exchange of words, but her prettiness, her quietude and her profoundly human spirit.

Unheralded and unsolicited, a floppy Polish woman called Ekaterina Ouspenskoye, like a camel with humps all round, burst upon them. Her notion of conversation was not of contact between two minds, but a deluge from her of whatever was in her head – a tipper lorry full of sand. 'Oh these vol-au-vents are burnt ... King Alfred trophy my late husband used to say ... going to buy a new sofa ... never bought one before ... unsure what colour ... ' Innogen suppressed a yawn, Simon did not. 'My son ... studied at Oxford ... a lawyer in Surrey now ... his girlfriend's descended from a Norman family, daughter of a vet ... the vet who looks after the Queen's horses actually ... '

Simon butted in angrily. 'Are they happy together or are he and this upper-crust wench at each others' jugulars every night? That doesn't interest you does it? As long as it makes a good story at the bridge club – "Oxford, Oxford, Oxford" –you callous old bag!'

Innogen's gentle unburdened look modulated to one of confused dissociation. She wanted to flee and did so.

The precociously intrusive Ekaterina puffed up her chest with indignation. 'Are you drunk?' she demanded.

'Tipsy. But I'm sad and not able to stomach your avalanche of snobbery.'

She opened her mouth to thunder a broadside, but thought better of it and left in high umbrage.

Her Fatship had robbed him of the unspoilt sweetness of Innogen, whose exalted presence had been healing his cut and bruised heart. As he turned yet again to the Liebfraumilch bottles, an elderly man faced him.

'Her face covered the spectrum from lilac to green and back again. Congratulations. Good therapy for the selfish old harridan. Robert Falcus.'

Simon shook the slightly arthritic hand. 'Simon Collett.'

His long, thoughtful and finely-wrinkled face, emanated sincerity and an avoidance of the elements of glibness and award-seeking in this sea of poisonous fish around him. With his grey hair, his shrewd but merciful eyes and his polymathic integrity, he probed Simon for a few seconds. 'Are you free in a week's time?'

'Free?'

'I'm filming Goethe's *Egmont* in Norroway ... '

'Where?'

'Norway. A couple of fellows have let us down at the last minute – a cup-bearer, a pikeman – nothing spoken and you'll have to lend a hand generally. It's a week's holiday in a way. Well, if you're interested my secretary's over there ... Lynne ... talking to the chap in the van Dyckish beret.'

Alone again, he thought how lovely Norway always appeared in pictures. And might he even meet Artemis on this escapade? It was a crumb off the table of the mighty and yet he was humbly grateful for this opportunity of change.

He moved towards Lynne in her shiny French blue dress with its waist-band of light Palatine purple, to claim his initiation into this bright pool of sex and fame and wealth.

# CHAPTER SIX.

Tynan and O'Driscoll had been unable to see Tan Hall at the foot of Esland's Shieling from the main road on the other side of Ullswater. They had had to take an unwonted hike in order to glimpse it. The long low manor and a short white-washed row of stables – protected against winter storms behind a low hill – appeared well maintained and in apple pie order, but entering the house would be awkward with its thick stone walls, solid oak doors, locked and alarm-rigged ground-floor windows and at least two sheep-dogs. Accordingly they chose the lesser but easier target of the barn.

In the light of a brilliant half-moon they free-wheeled slowly and quietly on their motorbike down the steep track and coasted to a halt six hundred yards short of the house.

The barn was fifteenth-century but reroofed and restored and everything inside had been lined up neatly and squarely. There were two tractors, two Land Rovers, a trailer, a hay-baler, a harrow and a quantity of tools and ropes.

The younger Liverpudlian watched as the older Tynan knotted a cord round a beam and then led it over the edge of a work-bench, where he tied it to the handle of a large paint tin full of petrol. He loosened the lid, but left it in place to prevent the premature escape of fumes. He placed three stubby candles on the floor near it and three on the bench beneath the cord and began to light them. 'We use fucking three for fucking safety,' he explained, 'and when we fucking leave, we close the fucking door, so that some fucking draught don't blow the fuckers out.' He positioned a brick on the floor, so that when the tin fell, one edge would catch it and the tin overturn. He made some final adjustments to the candle positions with an experienced eye, clenched his teeth and stepped back. The cord would take about ten minutes to burn through.

They retreated gingerly to a side-door and were just pulling it to, when two circular headlamps appeared over the ridge.

Catharine had been to an interview that evening in Sheffield and as she bumped down between the iron railings and a hedge of wych-hazel into the farmyard, the orange luminosity of the dashboard clock hands of Pappa's brand new Range Rover, read one thirty-five.

The manner in which the two shapes leapt onto their machine and kick-started it in a panic, left no doubt about their motives. She shifted up to third gear and accelerated.

'Cover the fucking number-plate!' yelled Tynan, letting out the clutch with a jolt. O'Driscoll held the two helmets over it as they bounded forward. They would have reached the temporary shelter of a yew and a hornbeam, had their front wheel not dropped into a hidden rut and they stalled.

The Range Rover's headlamps blinded them like the light of day, obscenities were on their twisted lips and Tynan's foot was poised on the kick-start again, when too late, they saw how near was the snorting bright-eyed bull. O'Driscoll held up a futile arm in the hope of averting catastrophe.

The girl had woken up. She braced herself against the steering-wheel ready for the impact, lurched over the last humps at about twenty-five miles per hour and rammed them broadside on. Above the initial thump and the scraping, she heard the splintering crack of the older man's thigh-bone.

She sat still in the silence for some seconds, before relaxing enough to climb shakily out. The motorcycle was half under her vehicle. In the light of the broken though functioning headlights, she saw that one rider was dead and the other contorted, pain-seared and alabaster white.

The glimmer of flickering lights seen through cracks in the barn doors, led her to investigate. She snuffed out the candles, gently removed the tin of petrol and emptied it into a ditch outside.

The Colonel appeared in disarrayed clothing and armed with a revolver, a long-barrelled pre-war Krag-Jørgensen hunting rifle and his three dogs. He reversed the Range Rover none too gently and relieved the Liverpudlians of their inside pocket contents – name-yielding union cards and scruffy wallets.

In the house, having rung the police and ambulance service, Letheren took his younger daughter's hands. 'You *must* say it was an accident. This mad society compels us to lie. If a simple villain comes before the courts, they may chide him a bit for being clumsy enough to get caught, but if an ordinary chap dares to stand up for what is right ... has the presumption to bash some poor robber on the head ... that they cannot bear. They will not say, "Well done," but be as severe as they possibly can.'

'I understand, Pappa.'

'"Woe unto those who let the guilty go free as heroes and leave the innocent unavenged." Still, cocoa and tell me about Sheffield. Afterwards, I've something to ask you.'

Letheren restoked the dying embers of the kitchen fire and sat on the bench inside the hearth with his arm round his daughter and a forefinger absent-mindedly stroking the fine blonde hairs on the nape of her delicate neck. Periodically he would touch her cheek or ear too. His face shone tonight, softly and more brightly than usual in their small cocoon of fire-light, as the new off-cuts caught hold and flared up. Like small children and wise grown-ups, he had a delightful credulity and a boyish sense of fun, which alternated with more serious thoughts.

Catharine sat there, overshadowed by his immense love. She had never been quick at examinations, but Pappa had said it did not matter. If you were conscientious and honest, all would go well for you. She had left school at nineteen, ill-equipped with certificates. A year in Sweden as an au pair had been novel, but what now?

'This "Arts Co-ordinator" post in Sheffield entailed talking to folk, sorting out programmes, getting leaflets printed and so on ... three of the four interviewees could have done it well enough, but the fourth – a Ceylonese lass with sequin-spangled hair-braids, a counterfeit grin which she imagined passed for being agreeable, a record of stealing credit cards and a pile of planks on her shoulder – they gave her the job. This fat alderman from the panel emerged and with a mix of mincing hand-washing movements and great self-importance, added a fulsome apology to the insult. They would have *liked* to have given the post to each one of us, but felt that ... His face was wreathed in consternation and I think he expected us to applaud this paraded social conscience. "It doesn't matter," said one girl. "Oh, but I'm sure it does," he insisted. "Go to hell!" said the second. What a patronising rank old sack!'

'Well I'm glad you failed. You cannot work for these twisted fake-subservient non-men.'

'But I must find something.'

'Something will turn up. It's strange, but these things have a way of sorting themselves out.' He hugged her.

'They saw your occupation and asked if I'd played with guns when little? I said I'd preferred bows and arrows. They asked if I thought it had encouraged violence?'

Letheren blew out a breath upwards. 'Have you seen the card from Uncle Ronald? He's marrying again next month ... some young W.R.N.S. lass.' He chuckled.

Sergeant Seax and W.P.C. Bagley from the local constabulary turned up and surveyed the arena. Letheren noted their lack of field-craft, Seax swishing through the weeds and Bagley catching her tights on the brambles.

Having reported back on their vehicle's longer wavelength force radio because of the distance, they sat down in the farm's manorial kitchen and shared a pot of tea with the occupants.

'What do you think these fellows were up to Sergeant?' Letheren fished.

Seax tried to convey gravity, but without enough of life's tragedies etched into him to do it well. 'Don't know Sir. Hardly matters though since we can't prosecute corpses.'

'It's still filling in the picture, surely? They must have had a motive.'

'Aren't you even curious?' Catharine prodded also.

'Is there any evidence that they were up to something, Mr Letheren?'

'Evidence? You only have to look at them.'

Seax gave a little laugh. 'I don't think a court today would accept that.'

'I'm sure it wouldn't,' said the Colonel.

Bagley glanced round at the colossal oak beams and the blue quarry tiles, the elm table with the deep blue and cream dishes and mugs on it. Above the huge inglenook hearth hung a battered Danish sword and two small twelfth-century paintings of the Virgin and Child, in reds and golds and blues.

Seax nodded. 'The point here is this; will it be believed that the deceased really drove accidentally under your wheels?' He looked sternly at Catharine, whose back was as straight as a lance.

'I've no idea, Sergeant.'

'You see if relatives of these lads ... or an M.P. even, demands an enquiry and we haven't investigated it, there could be trouble. I have to ask you to leave everything as it is until a scenes-of-crime officer has made a report.'

They all exchanged 'good night's and the Colonel slid to the three bronze bolts on the outer door behind them.

'He knows what's really happened but he's watching his own back. It looks like the police are going to wrack and ruin like everything else,' Letheren sighed. 'Many of the younger officers seem upright and good-natured enough – especially considering the material they have to deal with – but you rise apparently by keeping clear of disputes and sitting on fashionable committees. That sergeant was a career-conscious crocodile, a politically-nosed fixer, indistinguishable from the felons ... except that the felons wear *Magic Roundabout* tee-shirts.'

This time the fire had gone out irretrievably, so father and daughter retired into the cosier nursery and sat on the small pink-cushioned chairs.

'Would you go to London tomorrow and watch a man called Michael Rose?'

'If you wish.'

'Someone called Ingrid Axt is flying in to Heathrow tomorrow afternoon. They might meet up.'

'Who's she?'

'His string-puller.'

'Are they behind this business tonight?'

'Not directly, but they're in league with these evil swine.'

'It's a bit hard that we have to do our own police work, isn't it?'

'When the socialists came to power in the mid-sixties, they forbade any surveillance of M.P.'s without the Prime

Minister's personal permission. So M.I.5 had to drop their watching of many active communists in high places ... and the police didn't want to be involved because of the risk of being set up or accused of political bias. Besides, they aren't very proficient at it. Surveillance to them means sitting in cars with a selection of Beethoven tapes.'

'Beethoven? I shouldn't think they listen to Beethoven do they? And how shall I do it?'

The lamp threw an arc of semi-brightness at their feet and in the shadows, faded wooden blocks painted in dull leaden blue, a porcelain-faced doll and wooden tigers and elephants and palm trees stood in a static row on a long side-cupboard. When small, Nicholas and Innogen and Catharine had sat at the ink-stained table with their French governess and a generation before, he and his brother Hereward and a different governess had sat there too.

'I shall tell you how it's done Catharine,' he said, 'but we had better sleep for a few hours first.'

* * *

Michael Rose sat on one of the long side seats of the London Underground train, swaying slightly under the harsh white light of the fluorescent lighting and unaware that he was being watched from the far end of the carriage, as it rattled along in its deep burrow.

Some way behind him on the escalator at Green Park Station, the girl removed her headscarf and turned her two-way mack to have the dark side outside.

Outside, it rained and was dark as she followed the Member of Parliament for Hevermarsh, threading his way through a traffic jam under the noses of growling red buses and dark-interiored taxis.

He turned into a five-star hotel off Park Lane. His shadow went past and waited under a canopy, her sharp eyes noticing a traffic warden accept a bribe from the driver of a Bentley, who had just parked on double yellow lines.

An ugly clergyman, a stuffed owl in a dog-collar with a silver pectoral cross visible between the lapels of his half-open coat, stopped and asked her something. It took her some seconds before she understood that he had mistaken her for a prostitute. She blushed, unsure whether to be angry or to laugh.

Turning away from him, her eye caught the thirty-year-old Ingrid Axt in a brown trench coat, marching up the steps into the hotel, with her dark hair tied back in an untidy knot.

A further minute elapsed before Catharine too ascended the green marble steps, passed through the automatic glass doors and traversed the thickly carpeted reception foyer, to find Rose and Axt well-separated in the sumptuous, though thinly patronised coffee lounge.

Catharine bought a cup of tea at the bar and crossed over to a small window table, where she took off her navy mack, sat down on a light oak Windsor chair and pretended to be absorbed stirring her tea or studying the artificial ferns and cheese plants.

Reflected in the plate-glass window, she saw Rose lolling back behind a burgeoning plant trough, consuming a milk-shake and a ham roll and browsing in a London guide which he had taken from his pocket. He wore a mauve suede jacket and had a bald pate and a dapper beard. His cheeks were shiny and swollen, as if he had mumps or his mouth were packed full of handkerchieves, assisting his permanently amused sneer.

Axt had perched herself on a bar stool and crossed her imaginedly beautiful legs. She flipped nonchalantly through a woman's magazine and sipped a liqueur. A birthmark on the side of her neck, which looked like an acid burn or an erosion, had not lessened her Germanic assertiveness, nor softened something animal and vulgar in her.

Catharine Letheren, more practical and earth-near and doughty than her sister Innogen, added more unwanted sugar to her tea with a calmness as yet undented by the sombre terrors of this depraved city.

Ingrid strode over towards the ladies' toilets, flinging her magazine down on a coffee-table as she went. Rose sauntered up to the bar and ordered a second milk-shake.

Catharine grasped what was happening. She slipped her mack on and held the strap of her tan-coloured handbag tightly. She would not have a better chance than this. Silently she plucked up the abandoned London guide and then the discarded magazine from the adjacent table, before heading towards the doors.

'Oi!' bellowed Rose, his supercilious half-smile absent for once.

The girl was already through the first set of doors and she quickly reached the pavement and ran. She was a good runner, but not so good as the panic-stricken Rose. After thirty paces, he grabbed her collar. She spun round, hooked a leg behind his and giving him an unexpected shove, despatched him deftly into a filthy gutter. She hopped onto the platform of a passing bus.

An hour later, Rose was still shaking with a mixture of fury and fright. As an M.P. it had been decreed that he should have immunity from these prowling security buggers. Even if they had originally been tailing Ingrid, they ought still to have backed off when they had seen *him*! No regard for the law, these swaggering Fascists!

* * *

The Colonel watched the farrier, bent over and hot-shoeing a gelding called Hamlet. The maid came across the yard and told him he was wanted on the telephone.

The administrator from the War Graves' Commission soon dropped his tone of debonair and well-trained commiseration and reverted to a cooler droller key, when he registered Letheren's abruptness. The grave of Anne Letheren, née Saddler, in the British military cemetery outside Benghazi, had been dug up and the bones scattered for dogs to gnaw.

Archibald Helios Letheren had been born in 1918. At the age of seventeen, he had left school and joined the Spanish Foreign Legion as a private soldier, so coming to spend four years in Morocco and enduring the iron-hard discipline of this force. All childish mirages were quickly beaten out of you in the first weeks of training. Some of the tribes in the interior were cunning and tenacious fighters and only the hardiest of troops could stand against them. They had marched too with Franco in the Civil War, routing the new republican government with its liberal undermining of the traditions of Spanish life. And he had added Spanish and Arabic to his already fluent French Latin and Greek. He had deserted in 1939 and joined the British Army as a subaltern. With his fluent Arabic he had been drafted initially to 'Y Service', a radio interception unit begun in 1928 and based in Cairo and then been briefly attached to the Cairo Cavalry Brigade shortly before it became the Seventh Armoured Division. Subsequently he had taken part in the Ethiopian campaign as 2 I.C. of a recce squadron of rather antiquated armoured cars and then been diverted to the Intelligence Staff in Cairo before embarking in 1943 for Italy.

The Royal Navy was unquestionably the most professional and competent navy in the world at that time, but not so the British Army. The officer corps in particular contained a significant number of wasters and fops – men without conviction or daring, passion or belief – a shockingly poor contrast beside their French and German counterparts. The N.C.O.'s were an improvement, salty steady men with some pride and ability at drill and improvisation. They made the army cohesive and rugged and imperturbable, but even so there were plenty of impertinent fellows around and discipline and loyalty were not all they ought to have been.

Marriage had diverted Letheren's frustrat ion for a time, until he discovered a phalanx of sturdier officers, generally more senior, who were not so sugar-coated and useless and frightful and he had joined their cabal.

From 1958 to 1966, he had been posted in Libya with the British troops and the military instructors allocated to train King Idris's fledgeling force. These years had been agreeable, surrounded by military men and doing intelligence work at which he was quite inventive. Nicholas had been at private school but Anne had travelled with him and he had furthered his hobby of classical antiquity. The two girls had also been there for the first two years, looked after by a maidservant called Nagi, before leaving for a small private school named L'Ecole Sainte-Lucie in Toulon.

Letheren had often sat with some of those surly and hard-to-fathom natives, taken them a sack of grain, drunk apple tea with them, heard how in the old days they had walked five hundred kilometres to Tripoli to find work and gradually they had told him things and given him ancient finds – coins, potsherds, an ivory hair-pin. If you especially wanted something, you had to keep visiting them and mention everything except that, then after a few weeks they would slip it into your bag. But to admire it openly was compelling and ill-mannered – the idea of the Evil Eye resting on a coveted possession being the bringer of bad luck. Amateur American and German archaeologists blundered around brandishing cheque books and were ignored, much to their baffled annoyance.

In 1966 Anne caught yellow fever on a trip to Senegal and died. And now her poor bones had been desecrated. Well well, God would give the men who did such deeds bloody ends.

Since Qaddafi's coup, on Independence Day and other such 'festivals', stage-managed bouts of mock-spontaneous revolutionary fervour had been laid on. The Italian colonial buildings – the only decent pieces of architecture in the country – were often singled out for destruction as being symbolic of the abhorred imperialist past on such occasions. This cemetery near Benghazi – neatly set out with pink-flowering oleanders and pistachio trees – had had a part of its wall torn down on a previous day of jubilation, but a New Zealand construction firm working nearby, had rebuilt it a week later. Some local officials had tried to excuse the vandalism by referring to a new law forbidding walls above a certain height. This time though only one grave had been disturbed and in truth, all these orders came from close to the top.

As he sat in his study, holding a glass of Armagnac in his right hand and a photograph of Anne and himself outside an army bivouac in his left, Catharine returned, rather dishevelled and travel-weary having spent the night on a sleeper from Euston to Penrith, which had had no empty bunks on it.

She called out to cook, to produce some poached eggs on toast for her and a cup of tea and then went upstairs to give her father the two envelopes which had been in the guide and the magazine.

'What are these?'

'I'm not sure.'

He opened them gently, looked surprised and smiled broadly. 'I fancy you've stolen their reports and instructions.'

He held up his brandy glass. ‘A toast. To my brave aide-de-camp.’ He sniffed the yellowish-brown liquid, sipped it and rolled it around his mouth for a time, before perusing the two pages, one in a tall angular hand and the other small and round.

‘So blatant ... not even micro-dots ... Of course this stuff doesn’t surprise us – we know fairly well what they’re up to ... but so open ... They can scarcely even be bothered to disguise their plans.’

He thought of the switchboard lass in Downing Street – the only employee there who was not ex-Oxford or LSE – who kept them informed of the dishonourable corruptions at the centre of government.

*   *   *

The Colonel, too astute to let anger ruffle him, entered the portal of a massive white stone building off Pall Mall. A lift with folding lattice doors, took him up to the fifth floor.

The bored receptionist who was rummaging in the emergency make-up box, hurriedly hid her lipstick and tried to grasp the caller’s question. Despite her smart skirt and blouse, her stock secular phrases, agitated conduct and disgruntled and ill-controlled facial expressions made him suspect her of having a violent sexual relationship with a vicious man, a consciously grimy and reckless affair which she could not resist.

An older woman with half-moon glasses and who deployed formal correctness to hide her low opinion of her bosses, led him to a newly-painted plasterboard sanctum, well-lit by long windows and full of filing cabinets, sapele-veneered laminated desks and tubular chairs. These items were part and parcel of that surrealistic nightmare of pin-striped ayatollahs with their specious affability and obscure power-play games.

Mr Zuckermann had greying longish well-groomed hair and a light grey suit, which with its elasticated trouser waist-band and the jacket's negligible lapels, would have more suited a man in his twenties than his forties. His face conformed to that large-nosed falsely professional type of man, clever to a degree and readily able to express the appropriate emotion, yet too unemphatic for comfort.

Letheren would have preferred talk of foxes and horses, seasons and crops, maidens and sunrises, of the tale at the ford of a fight with stave and splent, but he sat with pinched eyelids and listened to this debonair mister fix-it describe the Benghazi episode in a set of strange alien words, language wholly devoid of any pithy Saxon sentiment. He reckoned that these War Grave Commission men were under instructions not to make a fuss and upset the Libyans, but that question was adroitly avoided by this pretender, this false shepherd.

'The situation is exceptional, Sir,' he said, uttering the 'Sir' as if it were spelt 'c-u-r'.

'"Exceptional" is not the word,' retorted Letheren.

Had they been to the scene? Had they inspected the terrain? It appeared not. They had 'reports'. They were 'anxious not to inflame the situation'. They were 'urging caution'. Letheren despised these folk who worked solely in offices, like priests at an altar with no god. Also, he could pin nothing down. It was like trying to get hold of jelly. A pirate ship you could board and run all the buccaneers through with your sword, but these florid-featured puffs with their fastidiously obnoxious civility were a suffocating and endless mesh.

'Enough.' The Colonel's voice refused to rave and disappointment at this anti-climax showed in the face of the public relations knave. 'Do you know what the difference is between yourself and a camel, Mr Zuckermann? Well, a bunch of Arabs can at least get a camel started.' Yet the Colonel had his revenge because shallow men, despite their capacity for intrigue behind their banality, are very limited in their range of thoughts and unable to escape from fixed ideas. They imagine their cleverness to be gigantism, yet they miss a lot of adult depths and perspectives. This thought compensated Letheren to a degree for not being able to take this squirt out the back and kick his smarmy face in.

At home, Catharine had slept all morning and in the afternoon she read until interrupted.

An army quarter-tonner had driven up and from it stepped Brigadier Noël Salway. He wore combat trousers, boots, puttees, a green army-issue woolly and a staple belt and he thwacked his calf with a swagger stick. He was a tall and very charming man, one who even if he found a conversation dull, would never let it show – though back with his armoured brigade of course, he would bellow and curse.

After introducing himself to Catharine, he asked her if her father were at home?

'No. He's gone to London for the day.'

'Ah ... pity that ... Though on second thoughts, it might be preferable if I tell you and you relay it to your father.'

They sat down in the kitchen.

Catharine felt clear-headed and peculiarly untouched as the intaglio unfolded, but after the Brigadier had left, a sense of inertia rather than sadness seized her. She did not know whether the worst aspect of it was losing her brother, the manner of his death or the effect it might have on her father. If it made her feel gaunt and sapped, what might it do to him?

Her father was not less fond of his daughters than of his son, yet Nicholas was a sort of extension of his spirit in a way that the girls were not. There had been no favouritism, in fact the boy had perhaps been more strictly treated because the deeper love meant deeper concern for his good upbringing. Letheren had not wanted his son to join the army either. Nicholas himself had wished that.

She saw his tough thoughtful face. Would it turn to tears or petrification when she passed on the Brigadier's message? She would try to master herself, ready for the telling.

## CHAPTER SEVEN.

Artemis was returning to North Shields and had stopped at a petrol station near Carlisle. Her breath condensed and mingled with the freezing mist on this cold winter's morning.

As she stood squeezing the filler hose's trigger, she watched a cocky young grease-smeared mechanic giving some lip to a remonstrating businessman, dissatisfied with his car's repairs. 'Look mate, are you some sort of prat? When I say ... ' Duly his eyes fell on Artemis's lustrous curves and took on a ghoulish shine. Her body and its cleavages had lit up his bloodhound instincts.

She responded initially with a look of desultory boredom, but then maliciously changed it to a provocative smile.

He drifted over, watching her pulchritudinous face with its immaculate skin, its broad cheeks and eyes a little widely spaced – a loveliness blemished only by the cold bituminous gleam in her eyes. 'Everything in order with your old TA21 then?'

She smiled back with knowing amusement. 'Is it really the Alvis which appeals to you?'

'Well, one has to start somewhere.'

'Why not just say, "Do you want it?"'

His face blanched and he wiped his grubby paws on some cotton-waste. He could not believe his luck – such a superb beauty! 'My office in the back of the workshop?' He jabbed a thumb over his shoulder and his eyes narrowed with macho anticipation.

Her smile, whilst still amused, cooled. 'You must be joking.' She felt an abhorrence of all these low 'zip-club' men and women who practised this routine.

The mechanic looked both surprised and angry. He followed her confirmatory nose-wrinkling. 'You pissing bitch,' fell from his oily cheated lips.

She shrugged and went into the kiosk, where a jittery youth was shaking a tin of pastilles like a set of castanets. Her way to the newspaper racks was barred by a woman inspecting a cheap furry bunny. 'Isn't he *lovely*?' she cooed.

'We don't need that rubbish.' Her husband spoke as though being throttled.

'I was only looking!' she snapped back tartly.

This vignette seemed to sum up marriage and as Artemis leaned between them to choose a magazine, she thought how she despised men for under-using their powers and letting women abuse them almost unopposed.

In front of Artemis at the till, the jerky youth was paying for a child's Badminton racquet whilst talking to himself and making erratic movements, such that the serving girl cocked her eyebrows.

Out in the forecourt he began shouting excitedly and started swatting his silver Capri with the racquet. He pranced around his car with its chequered tape, absent radiator grille, Colonel Bogey horn and wheels set out on spacers.

Two policemen strolled across from their parked patrol car.

'Oh man,' drawled the prematurely aged and haggard face, 'it won't take off.'

'A common problem with cars, Sir.'

'It's these creepy red spiders clogging the air inlets.' He lashed out at more imaginary beasties.

The policemen could guess that he had taken a drug, but drugs were not common in this area, especially L.S.D. psilocybin and the rarer hallucinogens.

The boy's legs quaked. He fell down and writhed in a slow semi-convulsion. 'Mind the yellow trees. I spent yesterday converting my car to a jet and now ... ' One policeman squatted on his heels and examined the lad's arms for the tell-tale pimiento dots or purple bruises, indicating venipuncture sites. He found only an inky 'I am mad' tattoo. Then the squirming features vomited copiously, inhaled some of it and turned blue.

'Heavens,' groaned the constable.

'Mouth to mouth's out for a start,' muttered the sergeant.

The busy-body woman with the furry bunny, emerged from the shop and informed everyone that she was a nurse and so began the unaesthetic charade of trying to revive an utterly dead corpse. The policemen helped half-heartedly, seeing that this was a mere melodramatic waste of time and Artemis, grimacing to herself, climbed into the Alvis and left this embarrassing pantomime with its assembling spectators.

Beside the petrol station stood a modern self-service restaurant with obeche tables, copper and red glass lamps and a fawn carpet and Artemis sat here with a glass of orange juice, a bowl of cock-a-leekie soup and a soft bap, flicking through her magazine.

She only glanced at the pictures, until an article about a Japanese bank clerk in Italy caught her interest. This girl had separately killed six men with pistols daggers or ju-jitsu chops, before eventually dying in a shoot-out with the Carabinieri. Artemis studied the spade-toothed face with its pinched eyes and angular cheek bones, surmounting the bony sinewy body dressed in a black leather skirt and a black tee-shirt with red Japanese pictograms on it, apparently reading, 'Death to Men'. She remembered too that earlier in the year, during the Baader-Meinhof trial, it had been reported how one of those girls – trained in Jordan – had slipped past the guards at the villa of a rich industrial magnate by posing as his daughter, carrying inside an enormous bouquet of roses a sub-machine-gun with which she had then slain five people in bloody havoc. These girls fascinated Artemis by their extreme bravery and their refusal to compromise with what they hated. When the restraining female anchors snap, they do so totally and unlike cowardly men, these girls then become wholly uninhibited.

Artemis detested – not men like the Japanese girl, nor capitalists like Ulrike Meinhof – but poverty and failure.

Innogen stood at the pay desk with her set breakfast of tea, bacon and egg and a roll. 'One pound ten,' snarled the languishing cashier.

'It says eighty-five pence on that placard.'

'I can't just ring up that. I have to ring up each thing separate.'

'Well, that's all right, so long as the sum comes to eighty-five pence.'

The slob gave a moan and repeated her piece about entering the items separately, as if talking to someone from the G stream of the local comprehensive. Innogen gave a lop-sided smile and paid the higher price without further argument. 'I am useless, am I not?' she said wryly.

The girl, after Innogen had gone, drooled to the next customer, 'Ain't some people thick?'

'Hullo Artemis,' came Innogen's flat low voice, rising humorously at the end.

'Well well. What a surprise.'

She joined her. 'Strangely enough, I tried to ring you last week. The school gave me your number.'

'What about?'

'The audition at Robert Falcus's.'

'Oh yes?'

'Just to urge you to come. There are fifteen girls' parts in his latest staging – Phrygian dancers, Roman slaves, Greek maidservants – and he's keen on original talent. You'ld have certainly been offered a small part.'

Artemis smiled sweetly. 'Have you a part?'

'Yes.' Innogen looked down at her plate.

'Aha! The angels are on your side.'

Innogen knitted her brows. An astringent aroma of fresh coffee drifted across from the hissing copper coffee urn. 'I met your boyfriend.'

Artemis wore a black canvas anorak with an inside cord which tightened it at the waist and her newly-laundered kilt. This kilt was of hunting MacRae or Sheriffmuir tartan, which is mostly black and red with just a fine white line in it and belongs to the Loch Alsh region, where her maternal grandfather had hailed from.

'Boyfriend?'

'Simon, isn't it?' Innogen seemed bemused.

Artemis smiled again, though as she had not yet found the love-letter in her room at North Shields, she could not quite piece the jig-saw together. 'Oh him ... Did he land a part?'

Innogen became agitated. 'Not in the play ... but something in a film, I believe.'

Artemis felt the salt in the wound. Outwardly she smiled for all *nice* English people smile, no matter how many knives are being thrust between their ribs, yet inwardly she stood on the brink of an abyss. The intolerable taunt was that *she* who so wanted to be an actress, could not be one, whilst all those around her could. And she was not going to creep or beg or grovel, but she would sodding well reverse all this somehow. To scowl, to kick Innogen's shin, to fumblingly dash that flower pot into her perfect bloody face, would only demonstrate weakness. Also, in these ordinary clothes, she still felt frail and human and vulnerable. She continued to smile.

Innogen looked inquisitively into Artemis's red probing eyes, which behind the exaggerated smile, spoke of nurtured anger. She seemed to show pain at the unspontaneous spite she saw there, a whipped-up rejoicing in future harm. She recalled thinking that Simon had seemed to be in need of love. 'Simon didn't look very happy,' she blurted out.

Artemis's smile turned even whiter. Her gleaming eyes shot icy thunderbolts and her thin lips went white too. 'He deserves no pity.'

Innogen, perplexed by these irksome wicked undercurrents, stood up half-stuttering an excuse. Her chair caught in another chair behind her and she sat down involuntarily on the floor, before getting to her feet again and leaving.

Artemis allowed herself a sneer of malevolent hauteur as she saw the discomfiture she had inflicted. Like the Japanese bank teller, she had passed the point of no return. She would plunge wildly and delightfully into the blazing battle – for she was at war with Simon and Innogen and everyone else. The ecstasy of a conscienceless struggle with weaklings bound and hampered by conscience, would end in their ruin and eclipse. The extreme hubris of Artemis had determined it so.

As Innogen drove off in a clumsy and battered long-wheelbase Land Rover, she wondered at first if Artemis had had an embittered mother who had brought her up to be hard and anti-male, but on reconsideration she thought the signs suggested not so much a wariness or dislike of men, but an impassioned and vicious love of her own ambition. As a low-loader rumbled past her, a brief exposure like a fading dream showed her both Miss Boden's grievous nakedness but also her susceptibility for the rôle of champion in some fearful coup d'éclat.

Since the night of the débâcle by the Eilan Burn, Artemis had been reviewing the idea of a robbery. She had paced about rehearsing each phase meticulously in her mind, for she saw the possible location. She would focus on one aspect or detail for an hour or so, as an artist planning a major canvas makes sketches of each section, until his final blue-print becomes unalterably fixed.

In the Alvis's boot lay boxes of clothes, tools, ropes – everything which might conceivably be needed.

In North Shields, Artemis worked a late duty in the casualty department from one o'clock to nine o'clock.

The next day, Thursday the eleventh of December, she was again down for a late duty, so early in the morning she drove into Newcastle and parked just off the main Northumberland Street.

Simon bobbed along in the river of Christmas shoppers in Fenwick's department store. The evening before whilst bent over a book of elementary Norwegian, a wasp had come out of hibernation and stung him on the lip, making it sore and red.

He had purchased a bobble-hat, a bright blue and white ski jacket and a pair of padded trousers for his forthcoming sally to Scandinavia.

Just as he was inspecting a set of four type-metal German knights in the toy section, Artemis accidentally ran into him. 'Hello,' he said.

She looked shocked at first, but soon regained her aplomb and smiled with narrowed eyelids at his swollen lower lip and the red crease down the side of his face, from sleeping on a wrinkled pillow. 'Hallooo,' she replied in a slow droll bass.

'You needn't worry. I shan't ask you out anymore.'

'What a pity.'

Simon did not seem to be quite so terrified of her today, yet in spite of his remark, he was still infatuated with her and felt it would be the most natural thing in the world to put his arms round her shoulders and narrow waist.

'I'm looking for a present for my nephew. He's grown out of chasing the hens round the farmyard. It's all crusaders and mercenary companies of archers these days.'

'How old is he?' she asked.

'Seven. But they live in Ecuador, so it has to be something small.'

She gave him a serious look of appraisal, surprised to discover that he had a more human and talkative side. 'To think you had the cheek to sleep in my bed.'

'But without you. I took your white scarf too.'

She shrugged.

He glanced across at the cafeteria entrance nearby. 'Would you take elevenses with me? Or would you care for a greasy chop?'

'No thank you. I don't want you to kiss me.'

He wanted her more than ever. Like Pope Leo outside Rome, he hoped to tame Attila, but part of his problem in suing for someone like Artemis, was that he had no sense of being manly nor any idea that he might be physically attractive to women and so he did not push himself in the way that such women like.

She saw his timid introspective hope flare up again and revived her queasy French courtesan demeanour to counter it or to force him to show his feathers.

He saw again that vain look, derisive of faithful little bores like him. 'It's hard being in love with someone who treats you like dirt.'

'Then stop loving me.'

'I wish I'd never met you. You're too strong ... '

With a contemptuous little snort, she cut him dead and stalked off – the honey bee revelling in collecting her nectar from only the thorniest and most exotic of plants, searching for a *real* man in a hippodrome where biter stallions toss their manes and foam at the nostrils.

He watched her knot of dark hair and her slender neck and sinuous body as they glided away with cool defiance, until swallowed by the sea of shuffling people.

Artemis deposited her carrier-bags of things purchased so far, in her car. She motored up Westgate Hill to a large motorcycle dealer's and went upstairs to the clothing rooms.

Having met Innogen and Simon, both of whom seemed to be in the ascent, Artemis felt again the intolerable shame of her own unsuccess, as if she were being secretly ridiculed. Yet as she fingered the row of one-piece leather suits, a feeling crept over her that such clothing offered not only protection against physical harm, but also that subtly it stated her position as one opposed to these *virtuous* entities. The strongly menacing flavour of black leather made it a becoming costume for a sorceress – suitably immodest and ultra-sexy and ultra-tough.

Women's leather coats were very popular at that time. Perhaps two out of three of her Tyneside nursing colleagues had one, but mostly the leather was skimpily clipped and of drab tatty under-side or second layer cuts, all very rough and shoddy. But Artemis's leather coat – which was now at the dry cleaner and repairer's – with its raglan sleeves, shoulder yoke, neatly sewn inturned seams, well-fitting close bodice half and slightly flared lower half and good grade of thick hide, was vastly more classy and stylish.

At the motorcyclists' shop, apart from a number of accessories, she found the principal item she sought. Again, it was of excellent quality and manufacture, a perfect fit and had that luring black sheen. Of course it was wildly extravagant, but Artemis never looked at price labels – indeed the assistant seemed pleased to be rid of this lavishly high-grade article, which had hung misstocked on his rail for over a year, waiting for the right buyer.

* * *

On Friday, Artemis was on an early shift in casualty. A hail storm at lunch-time kept most potential punters away, but a drunk on a trolley interspersed his puking with bursts of slurred song and invitations to Nurse Boden to 'climb aboard'.

'Bottle it mate,' said Charge Nurse Ayre, 'or else I'll give you an injection of ether into your bum and that'll give you something to sing about.'

His timing was unlucky. Nursing Officer Heather Brodie peered round the curtain. 'A word with you please, Mr Ayre.'

Her plump digit summoned him to a quiet recess. 'Mr Ayre, it is a basic human right of every patient to be treated with dignity.'

In his dark trousers and white uniform jacket, he stood there like a waiter taking an order from a cretin. The sounds of vomit splashing onto the marble floor came from the drunk's cubicle.

'You can't make a silk purse from a sow's ear.'

'It is inexcusable to speak so. We're professionally accountable.'

He detested this overused word 'professional' which actually meant to make a vow before an altar and to commit your life to some path. This woman he decided needed a check-up from the neck up.

'You're incompetent, that's your trouble.'

'And your trouble Miss Brodie, is that you are frustrated. May I suggest a course of sex for you? I would prescribe a loading dose of five times a day for the first month.'

'I suppose you think that's a clever way of being insubordinate, since I can't very well report such a remark? But for your information, I do have a significant relationship with a man. I've been with him for three months now.'

'Meaningful. By the way, I saw your article in the *Nursing Chronicle* saying that the S.R.N. course should be extended to four years and given 'academic status' – *four years* to learn how to tie a bandage or make a bed! And no doubt every simple term redefined in essays of thousands of confusing words ... "What is pain?" ... '

'Pain is you, Mr Ayre. Do you know why I leave my office and come round to see my departments?'

'To drink tea? To prevent yourself from getting chairsores?'

Artemis, too far down in the pecking order to be involved in this locking of horns, mopped the floor of the nearby plaster room and eavesdropped on Ayre's wind up.

Unlike most nurses there, she wore an underskirt so that her body and underwear could not be perceived through her uniform dress, by even the most x-ray of male eyes. Whilst a little old-fashioned, this was consistent with her neat prim turn-out. Her starched pinafore ties hung straight down behind her – all very regular and stand to attention and hands off. Her whole beautiful form was both stiff yet lithe, active yet unswerving, giving the male patients something to live for. She speeded up their hearts in contrast to such frumps as Heather Brodie, who clumped round in one of the new white shapeless sacks which were coming in, cheap and curveless and unfeminine, epitomising the new era of informality – cheeky banter with the doctors and a quick maul in the linen room, the buck passed for every chaotic scenario and the wards a shambles of vacuum cleaners and lolling patients.

Artemis showed a new patient into the treatment room. A teenager with dyed platinum curls and the gaudy plumage of a coppery metallic sleeveless mini-dress, an orange blouse and brown tights patterned with small rabbits entered bearing a lovely gurgling baby.

'What can we do for you?' asked Dr Easton, thinking that a mega-dose of anti-fungal cream was a likely bet.

'He's banged the back of his head.'

'You're going to be a head-banger are you?' Easton tickled the six-monther, who purred and smiled back.

The story sounded weak. He had no bruise on his occiput and had not been sick or unconscious.

'He seems perfectly all right. Go home, keep an eye on him and come back if he's sick or becomes drowsy or you're not happy for any reason.'

'Ain't got a car.'

'Well ring for a taxi or an ambulance.'

'Ain't got a 'phone.'

Easton made a soft gargling noise.

'I thought you had mother and baby observation rooms on the children's ward?'

'What did you say? Your boyfriend's kicked you out and you're looking for bed and breakfast?'

Artemis's head nodded minimally with approval.

'I'll sue you two,' snarled the girl.

Easton shrugged expansively and beat out a rhythm on his desk with a tendon hammer.

She upped the stakes. 'I'll tell me Mam!'

No one seemed worried.

She stood up and tore her blouse's sleeve on the sharp corner of an x-ray viewing box. 'Fuck!'

'This way out,' said Nurse Boden cheerfully, pleased for once not to have to pander to a liar with no sense of worth or decency.

'Did you see her address?' inquired Artemis on her return. 'It's The Flat, Walker Road. Now I could understand *the* palace or *the* manor, but not *the* flat.'

'Perhaps it's THE Flat, i.e. the one to go to when you need certain services.'

'Of course, she'll probably bash its brains out when she's home, just to make trouble for you.'

'I'm making careful notes. I'm familiar now with folk who just don't care about the consequences of their actions. Giving people too much kills the fight in them ... turns them into grey lumps of plasticine.'

The clock hands had turned three and her shift ended. Mr Ayre let her go.

She walked briskly down a dark passageway behind the boiler-house chimney and the grimy old laundry and came to a two-storey building at the back of the compound. It had once been the workhouse, but now housed stores and mushrooming offices.

In the large finance office, which occupied a half of the upper floor, she produced her November pay-slip. Deductions were always too large and when you queried them, you were bumped from pillar to post by young men with a certain bumptious servility, who were seemingly employed specifically to fail at organising bun-fights in bakeries.

But today Artemis radiated indulgent understanding, as she really focused once more on the antiquated safe at the back of the room with its ornate brass keyhole and its huge key hanging on the ring on the belt of the bewhiskered Dickensian treasurer, Mr Sneyd.

On leaving, she paused on the landing. It was deserted. She opened the fire-exit door by pushing its drop bar and then wedged back its catch with a wood-screw taken from a selection of items in her handbag. This jammed the withdrawn bolt firmly in its mortise. A piece of folded cardboard under the door's lower edge made it stick when closed.

Back in her room in the nurses' home, she sat in the armchair for a few minutes. Everything had been prepared. The sites had all been visited, her car packed with every conceivable tool, piece of spare clothing and snack – and even contingency items for if it went wrong. She drew the curtains and undressed, set her travelling alarm clock for ten thirty and with some delay, sank into sleep.

* * *

Collett had tidied up his rented room and was struggling out through the doorway with two bulging bags.

'Oi!' called the garret lodger, bounding downstairs, 'Did you squash my pewter tankard flat last night, after we had that drink?'

'No Terry. You did. You were explaining how soft pewter is.'

'Oh ... Well why didn't you bleeding well stop me?'

A door flew open and Mrs Henderson appeared, curlers in and a broom at the ready, held like a halberd in the 'at ease' position. 'You, Terry Telfer, stuffed my cushion covers with those fatty chips, you lout. I want you out by tomorrow, you hear?'

'Your daughter Violet thinks I'm rather cute,' he retorted with a smirk suggesting he had had her.

'She would, the silly girl. Out by tomorrow you Seaham rascal.' The broom angled itself ominously.

Simon shuffled past. 'Have a good Christmas, Mrs Henderson. See you in the New Year.'

The bus from Newcastle Central Station turned off the riverside road just short of North Shields and rumbled in the darkness through a vast acreage of abandoned coal staithes and rusting railway sidings to Whitehill Point and the Tyne Commission Quay, from where the ferry would sail across the North Sea to Bergen.

Up on a deserted deck, high above the choppy black water, an icy wind rolled in a thin freezing mist. On the southern shore of the river, large arc lights lit the wharves and silhouetted the gaunt jibs of cranes and the eerie superstructures and funnels of cargo ships.

Artemis's face appeared to him, intensified and unlovely and distant. She had not been too good for him, but not good enough. Yet love is like war, you give your all, fresh and sharp, only once. Another time, the red-hot zeal is tempered.

Down in the cafeteria he bought a plate of beef Stroganoff. The boat was less than a quarter full and most of those passengers seemed to have retired to their cabins, but amongst the handful of diners he spotted Kim and Adrian.

'Hi there!' Adrian greeted him like a long-lost chum, though they had not exchanged a single word at the party. 'This is a Scandinavian speciality,' he indicated his food, 'prawn and tomato rolls with a succulent sauce made from haddock livers.' He ended this sentence with a kiss and threw the fingers of one hand away from his mouth.

Kim in her expensive black fur jacket looked houri-like nubile and slightly sticky. She said nothing but her eyes dispensed a long stare at the clumsily boyish but more manly newcomer. She turned over a water glass and shared their bottle of wine with him.

'We were discussing the importance of only accepting rôles in films where you agree with the underlying theme of the script,' Adrian said.

'Oh I agree absolutely. For instance, I could never dream of playing the part of a white South African,' Kim replied, missing the point and mimicking the modern intelligentsia with their distorted lights. Her photogenic and intensely sexy mould became a disaster when she opened her mouth. A ghastly regional accent which Simon could not place, twanged out over a seemingly swollen tongue and uttered banalities as if the sole object of her education had been to expunge from her brain every vestige of original thought.

Simon's ankle met hers. He sustained the contact and she pressed firmly back.

The absence of lights outside the long windows and a slow rhythmical pitching motion, made him realise that they had sailed and left the shelter of the River Tyne.

His testicles felt massively swollen and in need of urgent decompression. He decided to have her if he could and stuff Artemis and affection.

Oblivious to Kim's having already selected her gladiator, Adrian pointed down at his trousers. 'Kim, my love, the fence is weak and the beast is restless.'

As at the party, Simon found it very startling that men and women should exchange such explicit innuendoes.

Kim gave Adrian a hard chin-in-the-air dismissal. 'You men ... '

'I know, we're ninety-nine per cent sexual leeches.'

'Wrong. One hundred per cent.'

It seems so to you, thought Simon, because truer men avoid you.

She rose and went to the ladies', rocking her retreating pelvis with an exaggerated tilt for the benefit of Simon's visual antennae.

'"If I like a woman, I don't let her go until I've had her all three ways",' Adrian cited. 'Kennedy said that. I wish I'd thought of it though, for it sums up my attitude exactly.'

It took Simon some moments to work out the stomach-turning meaning of this statement too.

'I intend to jump up and down on Kim tonight. She's quite a tasty iced-bun according to Gavin ... a bit gooey but no smell of rotten fish. My leaving card is love bites round the labia.'

The analogy that pretty girls were like iced-buns was quite accurate thought Simon – sweet on the outside, stodgy on the inside and a tendency to go stale very quickly. He wondered though if he had misread Kim's signals, but just then she reappeared, approaching from behind the rakish Adrian and holding up the tag of her cabin key, so that only Simon could read the number – 114. She exuded a noisy yawn and excused herself for an 'early night'.

The two men both had a coffee, each waiting in his own mind for Kim to prepare herself. Simon told how he had played ten-pence-in-the-slot miniature snooker in the reception hall on the quayside with another player as bad as himself and they had kept getting all the balls stuck round the cushions and had had to tip the table to liven it up again.

Adrian, with a Florentine smirk, told how on parking there, he had scraped a Daimler, but moved before anyone had noticed. This reminded Simon of his father's premiss, that when *you* bumped someone else's car, you paid them £130, but when they bumped yours, you never saw any money.

He excused himself, crossed the rolling and empty ship's lounge and plunged down a giddying flight of stairs. He tapped on the blank grey door of cabin 114.

'Who is it?' the door said gruffly.

'Simon.'

It opened and drank him.

She wore a *very* short white short-sleeved dress with a golden girdle and a golden neck-chain bearing a large pendant with primitive snakes engraved on its golden surface. His eyes rolled down her body and up again – her opulence and vanity and obscenity attracted predators as blood lures sharks. She leant past him to turn the lock, brushing his arm briefly with her neat breasts as she did so. He held her wrists by her sides, she tilted her head backwards and he kissed her under the chin on her long slender neck. Her skin had a very smooth fine babyish texture.

She knocked off the light switch and the cramped box with its inky blue port-hole, tiny folding table, bunks and her luggage vanished.

He clutched her in an iron embrace. They rubbed noses. How he wanted to ravish her. Someone knocked on the door – twice. 'Hello?' she murmured as if heavy with sleep.

'It's Adrian,' came an urgent voice.

'Who?'

'ADRIAN! I *need* to see you!'

'In the morning,' she yawned.

'*Now*!' The door rattled. 'Kim!'

They heard muffled curses before he gave up. They kissed, not out of fondness but because it was a part of the feverishly tight clasp and this – through his feeling her pubis and she his rock hard penis – energised their sexual capacitors to maximum load. They were spring-boards for each other's libidos, lamp-posts to urinate against, necessary staging posts in what Kim euphemistically referred to as 'healthy active emotions'.

She entered that dissociated state, which is the ultimate sign of feminine surrender and leaving behind them a trail of clothes, they edged wordlessly through the darkness, which concealed her Greek nymph smile as she led him to tumble into the lower bunk in a welter of arms and legs.

'Is it safe?'

'Safe?'

'Yes, safe?'

'Christ, you don't think I'ld let you do it if I wasn't on the pill, do you?'

The silky firm naked breasts, her raven hair, her upturned little nose and her curving hips were so overwhelmingly stimulating that he reached orgasm before they had even managed to couple. A half-pint of spermatic fluid flooded out, giving him a glorious sense of release and relaxation, which he had needed for months.

'God! Couldn't you wait?' she asked crossly.

But her fantasy-inducing shape and his high physiological end pressures, meant there was plenty more where that had come from – seemingly gallons of it. It happened again and again and again and it felt so pleasant and so good – like being an eastern king.

At eleven o'clock she pulled on her blue dressing-gown, turned on the over-bed light and they sat up and made cups of tea with her plug-in travel jug.

When she mentioned Adrian, Simon had to force his face to stay straight. He wanted to laugh hysterically at his worldly triumph. 'From my flat in Knightsbridge,' she said, handing him a plastic cup and a slice of fruit cake, 'I can see a statue on a high pedestal and by it most evenings, an awful hag of a prostitute hangs out – she goes and squats in the park every few minutes, so she must have some infection which makes her want to wee frequently ... well, I've seen Adrian pick her up twice in his swish G.T.I. ... just imagine such a houndy dribbling pus and urine over the plush upholstery. God! I would never let him near me.'

Simon drank four glasses of water.

They climbed the ladder to the upper bunk, as the lower one was awash with sticky discharges and as their ship ploughed across the black North Sea, they mingled sleep with intermittent renewals of excruciating relief – bouncing bouts, expelling great flows of effluent.

'Giddy up,' she said.

'Gee-up. Canter,' he replied.

'No. Gallop.'

* * *

The alarm's pinging awoke her. She was at once alert and if slightly nervous, sure of what she had to do – like an actress waiting to go on stage. The acronycal darkness outside affected her soul, spurring it on to do what the light of day would never allow.

She took a soapy perfumed bath. She went to the toilet – important before dressing up in her latest acquisition, because of the difficulty in pulling this suit on and off – and after a cheese bun and a cup of tea in her room, unlocked the wooden travelling-chest where her pernicious new attire lay stored.

She put on standard white cotton panties and a pair of black tights, with a sprinkling of talcum powder inside. Then came a new light-weight under-bodice with a built-in brassière, elbow-length evening-dress black kid gloves and a thin white polo-neck cotton sweater on top of these. Next she hauled on red woollen school hockey socks, black fleecy school knickers and after these the plain black lady's motorcycle suit bought the day before. From its thick dorsal-cut hide emanated that sour smell of newly-tanned leather, the acidy tang of the birch bark juices used in the leather-making process. It was stiff and unsupple, being as yet virtually unworn. It had sturdy zips at the ankles and wrists, down the front and on the various pockets and it had oval elbow-patches, large square knee ones and a big round one on the bottom. It had too straight legs, not ones bent at the knees as is often the case with racing suits and its lining was of strong black cotton. It fitted very snugly. She had to draw each leg on slowly and struggle to heave it up over her shoulders. It felt a little heavy and restrictive. She could walk well enough in it, but running would be impeded and any quick movement would be less nimble and less agile than in more ordinary clothes. On a dummy run the previous evening she had pushed the driving seat of the Alvis back a notch, because a tightness round the knees made it difficult to bend her legs too far back.

Her well-polished riding boots and a three inch deep solid non-adjustable black leather belt with an ornate bronze clasp, hooked tightly round the narrow waist of her sleek 34-22-36 inch figure, completed her new outfit.

She examined herself in the long wardrobe mirror, tense and terrifying, very tough and very enchanting, scintillating and shiny and shimmering – Artemis, virgin goddess of the moon and the hunt, ready to avenge herself on her tormentors. Her mind grew calm and tractable and a proud evil glimmer settled in her extremely hard yet exquisitely mercurial eyes. As a were-wolverine, she would suffer no longer the lowly moiety of being a student nurse in North Shields. She had read enough of *other* bitches who had clawed their way up to sit in châteaux in the South of France with piles of loot in the bank.

With a voluminous nylon mack on to hide her jump-suit, she put out her light and listened. Some footsteps faded and a door closed. All was still and she left the building unseen as the chimes of midnight rang out over the freezing sleeping town. All nurses' homes claimed to have a prowler – it suggested the inmates lacked sex-appeal if you did not have one – but he too was not around. Her car lay round a corner in a side-street, hidden from the home by a high hedge.

As she drove the eight miles up into Northumberland to the former mining hamlet of Lyseter, a wispy icy fog crept inland from the coast, coming in waves of varying density.

Approaching by way of a country lane, Artemis turned off three-quarters of a mile before the cluster of houses, onto a forestry track and halted on a side-spur of this, under a canopy of indistinct branches and edged by an unploughed cabbage field. She used only the side-lights to crawl into this lair, inspected by her for ditches and obstacles the day before. She tugged on the old ratchet hand-brake. With her mack removed, she knelt down to change the number-plates for some false ones, made in Ayr and under a pseudonym. Again the procedure with torch and screwdriver had been practised in advance. The light of a waxing silvery half-moon filtered weakly through the nebulous haze.

She drew over her head an item called a 'motorcyclist's tube'. It was simply a knitted open-ended black sleeve to keep the neck warm, but it fitted neatly over the polo-neck of her jumper and she adjusted its upper edge to be just below her nose. Her loosely tied sheaf of dark hair she eased through it to hang down her back. She zipped her suit up the last few inches to the collar – outside the lower part of the 'tube' – to where a small cross-strap with a press-stud snapped to to secure the collar ends together. With a black woollen bobbleless hat on too, only a three inch horizontal slit containing her eyes remained. Spare keys were zipped into a thigh pocket, her heavy black leather handbag with its load of maps and torches and tools was slung onto her shoulder and a new pair of soft black gauntlets were tugged on over the thinner evening gloves.

Artemis's insect-shaped body stood ready and ruthless and perhaps in her watchful eyes there lurked an ominous half-grin of satisfaction.

As she started to move off through the silent trees, a long thin unseen greenish sap-filled branch whipped her chest. She bent it back and forth and eventually tore it free from the base of a sapling to take with her. An owl hooted.

Twice whilst she advanced along the grass verge cars passed her, but the warning of their headlights probing the ionosphere gave her easily enough time to lie down in some weeds or crouch behind a bush.

The hole in the hedge appeared. She crept through it to where the eerie ruins of White Briar Manor stood in a lake of nettles and rosebay.

She had learned from her earlier escapades that nylon tore and that coats and skirts tended to be impractical. Her leather suit solved these problems and made her feel inviolable. Dirt and bricks might soil or scrape *it* but not *her*. And this mattered, for women are more concerned than men about their bodies remaining clean and unharmed.

Her boots swished softly through some dock leaves growing in the doorless portal of the gaunt gutted shell of the manor and then scraped up the rickety stairs, where she had to feel with her foot to avoid the missing stair-tread.

From an upstairs window here, she should be able to see across a meadow to a pair of modern bungalows on the edge of the village, one of which belonged to Mr Sneyd the hospital treasurer. It had not been hard to find his address, for 'Sneyd' being an unusual name, had taken up only two entries in the telephone directory. This was her look-out post, to see that no lights were on in his home.

Standing by the shattered casement window, she heard a dog growl directly below and peering down she saw with surprise in the thin pall of moonlight, that some scurvy gipsies had arrived since her reconnaissance.

The dog barked again, four times. A feeble light came on inside the tinkers' caravan.

'Sod it!' Artemis moved quietly yet angrily back towards the stairs. Her foot went through a rotten board, but she withdrew it without difficulty and moved quickly down the creaky collapsing stairway.

Outside, before she could regain the road, the flea-infested mongrel darted round the house, launched itself at her and clenched its jaws onto her right calf.

It had selected a poor spot for its attack, for her boots consisted of a thick resilient outer hide and an inner layer of soft skimmed calf-leather. Inside this lay the leather of her suit, its lining, hockey sock and tights. So, despite causing discomfort and bruising, it had no chance of penetrat ing these strata and tearing her flesh.

She fell down into a sideways kneeling position and looped the strong doubled strap of her handbag round the animal's neck, crossed her hands over and heaved with all the exceptional strength she could muster. Cur-like slaverings and half-strangled voracious snarls ensued and its extended claws scratched ineffectively at her boot. After two minutes its jaw fell limply open and after another minute, Artemis let its lifeless body sink back into the weeds.

As she rose, three figures loomed indistinctly round the corner of the house. She retrieved her supple four-foot long finger-thick branch.

A denser mist suddenly obliterated the weak moonlight and the black apparition, with the two taut breasts pointing forward like cannons, faded.

Feeling hyper-alert but surprisingly pure protected and unfearful, she gripped the young branch like a jockey whip. Strangely it did not seem absurd to be taking on three men. Anyway, she could not squeal for help. She had chosen darkness and that meant that no good deity would come to her rescue.

Hitching her handbag over her head, this female demon crept quietly in the velvety blackness to outflank them. She waited behind a giant overgrown laburnum bush for the instant to strike.

Their legs just made a faint brushing sound in the tall weeds as they moved carefully in line abreast. A flailing thwack from her lash hit the face of the largest figure and – by extraordinary luck – slashed his eyeball. He fell slowly to his knees clutching this injured organ, whilst Artemis shot through the invisible entrance of the manor and stood just inside the door of the dining-room.

The remaining two raced in after her, lured towards the gaping hole in the middle of the floor. One shadow scuttled past her and as she had hoped, slithered into the abyss. A deafening roar filled the room, as firstly his chin caught a nail-adorned joist and then he slumped down into the water-logged debris-filled cellar.

The last musketeer cast around frantically, as if in combat with some formless and unearthly sprite. Neither moved. Then a faint ray of luminosity flickered in through the shrubbery and died. She saw for an instant his outstretched hands by fingers laden with two or three gold rings twinkling on each. She attempted to dart past him, but he grabbed her slippery arm. They sat down abruptly on the floor and some cinders which had spilled out of the iron grate crunched under her wriggling kicking body. She managed to loosen his grip enough to squirm free and then to elude his spidery groping hands.

She fled through the French window opening and tripped over the stump of a stone baluster whilst pursuing hands fumbled to wrestle with her again, but she rolled rapidly over, leapt up, ran ten yards and hit the strands of a thigh-high wire and netting fence. Her momentum caused her to somersault over it and she landed in a revetment of briars. She extracted herself from this by rolling repeatedly and backwards further into them and so flattening a path through them for a few feet before she stood up and waded through the lessening depth of this sea of spikes which clawed her and clung to her legs.

Her last pursuer, when he detected her position and attempted to follow, became wholly entangled in this mass of barbs and snares. They ripped his trousers and scratched his legs and hands savagely. Artemis heard his muffled foul outpourings of purple barbarian rage as she strode off into the black hole of the neighbouring mist-enveloped meadow. Not only had her own superbly tough leather not been easy to puncture or tear, but the spikes had tended to glide off its smooth surface whereas they had caught readily in the weft of the third gipsy's clothing and bleeding and in tatters, he was forced to abandon the chase.

He returned to the first gipsy who wailed faintly, 'Jacky, somemut's 'appened to me eye.'

In the middle of her isolated void, Artemis came to a bank of steep lush grass and deliberately slid down it on her bottom and back to clean off any ashes or dirt from the struggle on the floor. She also wiped her boots carefully in the dew-laden nettles. Far from discouraged in her purpose, the battle had heightened her daring. Like a heady wine it made her sure of her own invincibility. No inconsequential ragamuffins were going to stop Artemis Boden. And it was marvellous to be *doing* something, not just talking or thinking or fiddling with words. Great men and women *did* things, unlike writers and T.V. personalities and other such benumbed and sterile and over-abluted self-abusers.

Coming to a fence she straddled it and feeling her way through a garden in a thickening blanket of fog, she found a bungalow and circled it cautiously. The door number confirmed it to be Sneyd's. No dogs lived here.

Most conveniently, a small sitting-room window stood fractionally ajar. Lifting this, with her feet on the sill and clinging to the cross-piece, she inserted an arm downwards and opened the larger window.

With a pair of hiking socks over her boots to avoid making marks on the carpets, she slithered stealthily into the house, where with a shielded pen-torch, her gauntlets removed and a furiously thumping heart, she moved round the darkness-flooded rooms like a diver in a sunken ship.

Mrs Sneyd snored with a strange sucking sound. On her husband's bedside-table were some cheap souvenirs from Majorca-type holidays, but no keys. But, on the Ottoman at the foot of the bed, were his clothes and on his trouser belt she discovered his ring of keys with the gigantic safe key on it. She detached these with care, ducking at one point as Mr Sneyd gave a vast earthquake-like quavering snort and turned over. During her exit, Artemis pulled the windows to. She gave white Briar Manor a wide berth and returned to her car.

Visibility was about a hundred yards as she drove back into North Shields, where she parked the car on a piece of wasteland behind a public house. The street lamps had gone off and under the veil of grey mist, all was as silent as the grave. The watch on the passenger seat read two thirty-five.

With a coil of rope in a black plastic carrier-bag, she stepped through a hole in a broken fence of old railway sleepers and slid down into the disused railway cutting. She picked her way for almost half a mile along what had been one of the numerous colliery lines running down to coal wharves on the Tyne, passing under a road bridge and wading through a litter of burnt-out cookers, worn tyres, ruptured mattresses, lengths of rusted steel wire, lumps of broken masonry and elbow-high stinging nettles.

The temperature had just dipped below zero, to judge by the dew's beginning to freeze. The hours ahead were the ones where both morale and physical readiness sink to their lowest ebb – a phenomenon utilised by the military in dawn raids.

The cutting had flattened out. On one side a brick wall topped with barbed-wire loomed up. This was the bottom end of the hospital compound.

Her rope had a large steel boat-hook tied onto one end. Artemis flung it upwards and it caught firmly in the wire first time. She had also tied big knots in it at intervals to help her climb up, as her feminine arms were not strong and her boots very shiny and slippery. Even so, it made her sweat, before she reached the top and lay sprawled across the crushed coils, regaining her breath.

She dropped down onto a slime-coated old operating table and surveyed the dark administration block. If all this excited her, it was not easy. Next she had to scale the rusty iron fire-escape rungs embedded in the side of the workhouse. As the lowest rung was at head height, she had to heave herself up by her arms, whilst her suit's knee-patches chafed and slipped on the abrasive brickwork. Eventually she succeeded and scrambled up to the small steel platform and shoved open the fire-exit door whose catch she had wedged back that afternoon, throwing away the screw and the piece of folded cardboard used for that purpose.

Again she put on the over-socks and removed her gauntlets. One of Sneyd's keys opened the main door to the finance office and thus she arrived at last, in front of the museum-piece safe.

* * *

Innogen dreamt.

A man plucked a twig from a small bush and planted it. He wore a blue robe and round his neck hung a chain of hammered gold links. From it hung an ornate circle of embossed solid gold, beaten and chased with a primitive emblem of the sun. His youthful countenance bore a cheerful solemnity. The twig flourished and became a sapling, surrounded with flowing streams and small flowering plants, like courtiers round a child king. The sapling grew into a strong and sturdy tree decked in dark green leaves, where birds of every hue and size perched amid its lustrous globes of succulent fruit and sang and chirped happily, basking in the fragrant scent and golden light. And in a hazier grey distance she espied too, a barren sad landscape with ill-tended and lifeless shrubs, gnarled and stunted and there roamed men shouting, 'Destroy,' as they saw the striking youthful-faced man stepping forth and his tree in its fertile patch, where all life could receive succour under its intense verdure. They gave choking growls and hurled axes and spears from inside their prison, a black isohedral hexagon of unbreachable walls. The sweat of desperation coursed down the gullies between the massed lush toadstool excrescences on their brutish brows. Unable to relinquish their ways of gruesome cynical anarchy, they shaped at cost of further affliction to themselves, a poisoned lance. It struck the blue-robed holy man in the eye. Their lumpy desecrated throats croaked and jeered, but their target seemed not fatally hurt. He withdrew the lance and though blind in one eye, waved to him a sensual maiden in a black tunic. She knelt and he touched her hair with his great gold disc. 'You are my instrument of recompense.' She walked with precocious fearlessness towards the dungeon of those prolific beasts who knew no remorse or felicity, who craved to erase the pieces of concealed true gold, but who could not for wisdom paralysed them in proportion to their swelling malice. The black maiden, austere and serpent-like wove a wand over their grotesquely ugly Nibelung forms and many of them perished in green gore, their moiling binding them as in a sea of tar. The upright priest waved the tunic-clad sylph back towards his balmy plot, but she refused. The benign stoical face of the priest transformed subtly to that of Innogen's father and the sylph's sharp figure became Artemis Boden.

Innogen awoke. She reached for the bedside lamp's switch and its cosy glow assuaged the nightmares of this hour. A small photograph of her young mother looked at her in faded greys amid bleached and thumb-worn patches, like the head of a worn coin. What redolent visions had she had?

She padded through her Glasgow flat in her bed-socks and night-gown to the scullery and boiled some milk. Unable to sleep again immediately, she sat at the table and browsed through a hagiography of Saint Christina of Bolsena.

* * *

The beam of the pen-torch probed all around it, but the safe appeared to have no wiring for alarms. The great key opened it. On the top shelf were a row of ledgers and a petty cash box, on the lower shelf five piles of cheque books and wallets with the sheaves of paper cataloguing the ins and outs of each account. The hospital's five accounts were lettered 'A' 'B' 'C' 'D' and 'E'. 'A', the fund for building and repairs had the most money in it, a little over £23,000. Artemis tore out the last cheque from the lowest cheque book for the account and placed it meticulously in a cumbersome old manual typewriter. Beside 'Pay' she typed 'V. Inall' and in the decimal boxes, 'Two Two Three Two Two' for the pounds and '10' for the pence. She placed it in an envelope with a piece of card to stiffen it and put it in the inside zip pocket of her handbag together with a letter from Sneyd's desk which bore his signature. She replaced everything as it had been, locked the safe, locked the office door and latched the fire-escape door properly as she departed.

A few snow-flakes fell lazily as she threw the rope and hook down from the wall and lowered herself by knees elbows and fingers before dropping into the cutting. She dragged the rope with her for some way and then abandoned it amid the wilderness of refuse.

Back at Lyseter, she returned Mr Sneyd's keys to their place on his trouser belt. She took the trouble too on leaving, to brush the window sill, to set the catches so that they fell to as the window bumped shut and to wipe the ledge and even the paving-stones beneath it with the removed hiking socks.

In her car, she quickly ate a roll and a bar of peppermint chocolate and drank a bottle of apple juice. She had achieved her aim, but it had already turned five o'clock and she felt weary and exhausted. The bone-chilling hour, the curling heat-sapping sea vapours and the cooling sweat too inside her own evil outfit, made her begin to feel cold. She ought to go home, yet a need to do something destructively orgiastic flared up in her like an addict craving his drug. Simon's love-letter flitted through her mind. If she had not chosen this new course, perhaps she would have yielded to him by now, her nose nuzzling up to him and imbibing the special tangs of his sweat and semen. But had she had a choice? It seemed impossible that she should surrender to such a weak imbecilic male. She tensed her thighs and arched her back – in her pure unadulterated leather, she could resist him without effort. Aware of the lubricious hard threatening gleam of her suit and boots and gauntlets again, waves of potency, of almost supernatural self-belief, swept through her. She wanted violence against someone who had slighted her ... against those scum gipsies!

From a petrol can in the boot, she filled up her apple juice bottle and with an old rag from the tool-box, constructed a rude Molotov cocktail. Amongst the camping kit she had packed she found some matches.

The Alvis backed out into the lane and then with its engine off, rolled down the hill to stop near the hole in the hedge. Artemis slunk through it and round White Briar Manor. She crouched down to light the rag. The flame glared intensely in the mufflingly dense charcoal night. It crashed through the glass window of the caravan. Artemis ran back and knelt behind a tree stump. She saw the reflection of the flame in a second window, as it ran along the floor like liquid metal poured from a furnace. Those sullen curs did not rush out. They did not scream. Were they in even?

The fire-ball spread spectacularly, a welcome change to the eternal dreary darkness of this long night. Dripping burning plastic dropped from the combustible chrome-embellished four-wheeled trailer. The springing flames rose higher and higher and licked the black branches above them. With a breath-taking passion, it stimulated Artemis's clitoris. Sparks flew and twigs crackled and the flickering red light lit up her stark scintillating leather-encased body with an angry crimson shine. Her orgasm was spontaneous. She did not deliberately stimulate herself. The merest rub of her underwear triggered it. The ripples of muscular contraction went up through her female channels, rhythmic waves of agonising ecstasy and freedom, which for about a minute threw her stiffened body into gasps and rictuses.

She was still aware of their waning delight as she strode to her car, started it and roared off. That rapturous pulsation made the night complete. She breathed with deep satisfaction.

The glorious blue and magenta eruption had lingered before her eyes, even whilst on a concealed farm track she swapped back the number-plates, put her miserably mortal nylon mack back on and removed her knitted hat.

Artemis fell into her bed in the nurses' home, just before the early-shift nurses started waking up and moving about.

* * *

Kim and Adrian in fashionable winter coats scarves and mufflers were on deck, leaning on the railings between two stacks of life-rafts.

Kim looked down at the rust-streaked blue plates of the ship's hull and at the widening trail of the bow wave and the myriad air bubbles from it forming the lighter green echelons in the darker green sea.

Adrian looked furtively at Kim and wondered if her bright deep eyes and taut hyper-feminine movements could be attributed wholly to a good night's sleep. There was nothing frumpish here, no dowdy flabby walrus which had wallowed like a deflated barrage balloon on its ice-floe all night. No, this animal ran on juices other than sleep. Of course, she made a big thing about jogging every morning, but that was only a publicity stunt. She took a daily sauna too and perfumed oil baths, yet Adrian felt convinced that her tone and vibrancy owed more to certain other invigorating balms being pumped into her.

'I do hope my sister's giving Saracen his extra vitamins and cod-liver oil,' she said, referring to her horse, but in a slightly peeved tone as if subliminally aware of Adrian's nasty thoughts.

All these rich girls with their horses were, as far as Adrian was concerned, a pain in the saddle. He glanced at his pink and grey space-age watch. 'Midday,' he said. 'We can dine soon.' Oats for dessert, he wondered? But she was sending no signals. He had somehow missed the boat.

Simon appeared, sporting a certain easy buoyancy and wiping the salt off his glasses. He glowed and bounced and gone was that adolescent nervousness which he had displayed the night before.

Adrian's suspicions deepened. Again he eyed Kim obliquely, as if to ask whether she were responsible for this transformation, but she merely threw him a surly look and gave nothing away.

She was cold with Simon too, but he was not surprised. He understood from both her legs-apart proficiency and her sex-conscious everyday manner, that she often took an over-inflated male bicycle inner-tube to bed for a one night Tour de France and punctured it and chafed it to shreds and that she was hardly likely to swap simpering intimations about it the next day. Still, that did not matter, she had served her purpose.

A middle-aged Norwegian stopped close by them and peered out over the starboard quarter. He pointed to a faint grey line. 'Norway.' He spoke in a slightly liquidy English. 'I can smell the pine trees.' He began taking deep breaths, as if suffering from an attack of asthma.

Simon gazed at the misty and indistinct line and felt that something special awaited him here, almost – as with the man thinking he could smell the aroma of the pines – as if the rocks and the trolls and the waterfalls were his second home.

In the cafeteria again, the threesome ate bowls of a rather greasy dish of boiled cream and flour, to whittle away the last hours of this tedious crossing.

Adrian asked Kim if she had worked under Sir Robert before, enunciating the words 'worked under' with a hint of ambiguity. The sex-centred Kim, quick to pick up sensual allusions if nothing else, stared at him belligerently.

Simon had had enough of their touchiness and back-biting and clever badinage. Excluding his stint in bed with Kim, he had passed his time on board reading Norwegian notices and brochures and thumbing in his pocket dictionary every minute or so. As his two colleagues continued their veiled jousting, he noted the word 'drikk' on the menu and recognised it as an example of simple assimilation. Assimilation is when the first of two dissimilar consonants changes to become the same as the second and in the tenth century in Old Norse, such shifts had been widespread. Hence English 'drink' equates with Norwegian 'drikk'. From his textbooks on German philology, Simon already knew much about patterns of phonetic and orthographical change, but even so, he was retaining the detail, the grammar, the vocabulary and the idioms of Norwegian quite well. He had been here before. Things which are intended for you, you grasp easily and things which are not meant to be, you make no progress with.

* * *

Artemis did know that her semblance of undesigned simplicity kindled sensual hunger in men. She understood men's lechery uncommonly well and if when fourteen on first discovering this she had been mildly shocked, that had long since changed to a thorough appreciation of the subtleties of her own terrestrial magnetism. Hers was not the slit-eyed smile of the whore who would secure lovers, but the open-eyed coquetry of vanity, entertained by seeing men *try* to catch her. The paradox of such an allure though was that she must constantly rebut. Had she started to yield, her tantalising magic would vanish. Yet she had grown weary too of those bold boisterous creatures round her with their sly knavish grins. Also, too much choice and habitual rejection had led her to be dissatisfied, to want something unusual or strange. Some thought her inability to be close to anyone would make her into one of those girls who suddenly marries a Polynesian fisherman say – someone whom everyone else can see to be totally unsuitable. Sick of excess adulation, she would fall for one who was too severe. Her classical beauty had served her ill, made her self-obsessed and consequently the task of finding a good man and of being content with cabbage soup and of baking cakes with her children, had become impossibly hard.

As Goldstraw watched her, he thought that her proud femininity *should* make her vulnerable and he could not understand why it did not. She must have some need to ease her pelvic congestion. The signs of her new substitute criminality had not yet started to show.

It was the official hospital Christmas party – not a beer and screw affair, but sherry and Cantal cheese with evening dress or lounge suits at the very least. The medical staff, senior nurses and higher administrators were present and a 'cross-section' of humbler staff which just happened to include Student Nurse Boden, for no male employee there did not know who she was or could avoid wet spots inside his trousers on seeing her ravishing shape.

'The first time your good looks have ever been spoilt?' John Goldstraw asked, referring to a slight bruise under Artemis's right eye. She had hit herself when tripping over a discarded palliasse in the railway cutting.

'If you'll excuse *me*,' said Heather Brodie, 'I can see I'm intruding into a private conversation!' She stumped off, jealous of Artemis receiving all the flattery.

'These lesbian pillock nursing officers ... they contribute nothing. All they do is attend "seminally creative workshops" ... ' The thought crossed his mind that if Artemis were to be present then they would be 'seminally creative' in all senses. 'The old matron always knew exactly what everyone was up to, could be found when you wanted her and yet didn't interfere unnecessarily ... '

'Brodie always gives us precisely the holidays and placements we don't want, as if she's bent on crushing the last ounce of individuality out of everyone.' Brodie wanted those under her to creep and stage one of such creeping was to not disclose by their manner that they saw through her. 'Perhaps we should beat her round the head with some plaster cutters.'

'Did you see the letter in the local newspaper from that midwife here with the fat legs? She signed herself "Aerona Taylor, *Lactation Consultant*". It's delusional beyond belief.'

'Especially given that with breast-feeding, you either can or you can't. What's she actually doing?'

Goldstraw stood there in a slightly tight navy evening dress with a light blue bow-tie poking out from his stiff white shirt collar. Artemis wore a long skirt of dark blue and red MacLachlan tartan, a white silk blouse and a jabot with her silky hair drawn up into a soft flat top-knot.

She felt a certain Platonic bond with Goldstraw, because they both had realistic minds. His having mastered her once though annoyed her deeply, even though she acted as if it were of no consequence. She did know however, that it would not happen a second time.

Sister Gosling latched onto them, squelching a chicken leg between her neighing horsey teeth. Her midi-skirt had a huge vulgar rear slit in it, almost showing her bum and her blotchy lumpy legs would have been better off inside a long dress. She showed them some holiday photographs of herself and two colleagues in Uglyslavia. They were seen cavorting on a beach with some pot-bellied tattooed middle-aged slobs and piggy-backing on them in the water with their underwear showing.

'Who are these?' asked Goldstraw, his face creased in painful distaste.

'Oh, just some plumbers we met,' said Sister Gosling casually. 'We all got drunk and had a good time together.'

'What fun,' remarked Artemis to herself. She saw in one of the pictures, that Gosling wore a badly cut and terribly tight yellow top with sweat stains round the armpits. 'What's that blouse made of?'

'Acrylic. Something invented in this century – so you won't have heard of it.'

'No spare material in it, is there?'

'It's *meant* to be tight,' affirmed Gosling.

'It looks as if it's made of bubble-gum.'

The nurses' nickname for the lithe pale-limbed Artemis was 'Prudy', a title which might have suited more of them a decade before. Then nurses had mostly been more proper and had hoped to marry someone a bit respectable. Now the younger ones were very sloppy and down market.

Artemis had come late to the party, having been on late duty again in casualty. In the morning, she had risen after only three hours of sleep, practised Sneyd's signature about eighty times, thoroughly destroying these efforts afterwards and then forged a good likeness of it on the cheque with gloved hands. She had gone into Newcastle to pay it in to an account which she had opened on the Thursday at the large Barclay's Bank there, chosen both for opening on Saturday mornings and for its impersonal size. The account had been in the name of Victoria Inall and was a so-called 'Gold Plus' one. Artemis had secretly redubbed it her 'Gold Minus' deposit.

Goldstraw related the tale of a woman in the labour ward with a trendy husband in rainbow braces, sandals and beard, who had wanted to take their placenta home, fry it and eat it. He was an infectious raconteur and Artemis let herself laugh.

'*I* think we need to be more *sensitive*,' insisted Jeanette Gosling, reiterating again that over-used word, so that it jarred in Goldstraw's brain. 'Laughing at these things seems all very childish to me. Mankind needs to share experiences.' Her insolent freckled face jerked about angrily. 'Tell me John, what took you to Gibraltar?' She sidled up to him.

He edged fractionally away. 'A BAC 1-11, I think it was.'

She just managed to swallow this snub. 'Yes, I saw that coming.'

'Yes, I did too – along the runway.'

Gosling turned a livid pink. 'Damn you!' She disengaged herself by moving one pace backwards and then gave his face a resounding slap.

Goldstraw stood there and received this rocket manfully – as one does on such occasions – whilst nearby groups turned to look on with interest disguised as incomprehension.

Jeanette whirled away in a cloud of figurative dust. She lent herself regularly to debauchery of the worst kind and dared not look at herself squarely for fear of the terrible scornful colours she would see. Yet strangely, she feared being pilloried more than she feared the feelings of guilt or restlessness inside herself.

Against his own judgement, Goldstraw tried to seduce Artemis, but this horse would not run tonight. His soft and unmalicious heart twinkled in his eyes. 'My sweetest, I think you've a false impression of me ... ' He took her wrist.

She snatched her arm away and whispered with a taunting smile, 'I don't want to go to bed with you again. You were one of the most unexciting I've ever known.' She danced off to the buffet.

On returning from Scotland, Artemis had found Victoria Inall to be away on three weeks compassionate leave because her mother was dying. She had also found the master key left by Simon, which had made things easier. Borrowing some documents to prove identity, she had opened the account with Barclay's, wearing gloves for every piece of paper she touched and even wearing a pair of Victoria's glasses in the bank to give an element of disguise. She had intercepted the new cheque book this morning in Victoria's pigeon-hole, so all she now had to do was to wait for three days for clearance, arrange to withdraw virtually all the money in cash and then when the storm broke, there would be only an abandoned bank account with its untraceable forger owner. She would deposit the money in building societies in false names and keep the books hidden somewhere in Uanrig House.

Artemis was easily the most eye-catching figure at the party. Nothing could diminish her stature or her beauty. Most beautiful and striking women owe something of their attraction to the flow and deftness and precision of their physical movements. Their thoughts converge wholly and simply on the reality in hand, without discordant splits or stultifying doubts and this is reflected in their lithe sweeps of harmonic motion.

Artemis had easy and irresistible movements too, which were evidence of her single-mindedness, but they were abrupt rather than graceful – an outward manifestation of extreme resolution. True, no cross-currents impaired her strength, but her moods, fixed by her own selfish epicentres rather than the circumstances around her, were sometimes inapt.

Yet the salivating knaves advancing on her now were not wise enough to see the ugly enigma growing inside her or its clues in her behaviour. For a time they stood watching her from behind, both the entirety of her perfect body, but also the broad flat strip at the top of the female bottom which especially lures men. She swung round, her arms crossed and one hand holding a wine glass. Her arch smile still lurked round the wry mouth line in that pale Helen of Troy face. They talked eagerly, each keen to be witty in front of this classical Galatea and to shag her with such force if the chance came, that the air would be thick with the smell of burning rubber. Uniquely unassailable, she thought of her own glorious warrior-like leather and conversely how she loathed these grey-suited termites, so lacking in colour and pageantry.

Goldstraw afar off, thought he saw in her an increased delight in playing the innocent retiring little girl with this crew, but which sins made it so poignantly and teasingly pleasant, he could not guess. Also, if he could not catch her, he was sure that these pimply little operating theatre technicians could not – boys punching the air as they tried to show off and play with their loveless brisking virility. These pustules made inane risqué remarks to impress, but grown-up people had heard it all before and so ignored such stuff.

Goldstraw targeted Elspeth, a radiographer in an apple-green satin trouser-suit. He had had her several times about a year ago, when she had still been a trainee. She was yet another tart full of righteous ideals about anti-racism and social equality and yet the night she had passed her exams, three different men had screwed her in the toilets – he knew because he was one of them. Since then though, she had controlled herself. She had stalked an air-headed surgeon and had accepted that being bored out of her mind and sacrificing a varied sex life, formed the price of eventually becoming a consultant's wife, with the children at private school, the big house, the Volvo estate and the four-by-four and of course the status and the snobbery and the income. Goldstraw had watched her gradually execute this frightening ambush. She did not *love* her feeble-minded fiancé and such calculation gave Goldstraw the shudders. As he chatted shrewdly to her and discreetly rubbed her thigh, she giggled languidly. Her other half was away at an *important* meeting, so perhaps she could do as she liked tonight and lie her way out of it later. These sort of girls were all boringly the same he thought, but then perhaps they felt the same about men. He saw the bright green light of submission come on in this voluptuous hot-house polecat and followed her out at a distance.

Artemis gave a yawn and left for the nurses' home.

All was quiet as she sponged her leather get-up lightly with soap and water and then dried it with an old towel. There were a few steaks of dirt, superficial scratches and a big brown rust mark inside one thigh from a girder supporting the fire-escape platform, but no serious damage. After drying it for a time on the radiator, she packed it neatly away in her travelling-box.

In the silence she became aware of her own conscience. She had lost a proportion of her enlightenment. A subtle coarsening had crept over her attitudes, something dark and vicious and cynical. When she had come here four months before, she had been cheerful and industrious and eager to make people think well of her. But either these malcontents and scroungers whom she worked with or the lack of an encouraging opening in drama, had destroyed these pleasing virtues. The integrity and obscure sense of fun gleaned from her father and the shyness learnt from her mother, were dissolving and she could not prevent it.

Her tummy gurgled audibly.

Twenty-two thousand pounds at that time would buy a good detached house outside London. Such a sum would make her independent for a few years, during which she could make her next move or perform her next crime.

This evening she had heard an anaesthetist moaning about being up half the previous night for an eye operation on some stinking gipsy, whose remaining family had all perished in a blaze in their caravan later that night. No one had mentioned arson.

Artemis remembered her acts with a resurgent thrill, truculent and wayward and daring. She was pleased she had repelled the sex monster Goldstraw too. Yet had she let herself be Simon's, all these other dangers and battles would not have existed. In his thrall, letting him take pleasure in her, eating with him, kissing and letting him put his penis in ... 'No!' she squealed, angry with herself for being weak enough to allow herself to even think of him. She flung herself onto the bed and buried her head in the pillow to stop herself from screaming.

Romantic fiction always depicted the man pursuing the woman and she eventually surrendering. In reality though, that seldom happened. Women arranged things. They worked out the parameters and knew with lightning speed what they wanted, whilst the men faffed and wavered, still wondering if they should not dip their toes in some other pool. Why then was Simon in command and not she? Why? Drat it and burn it in hell!

Her hand rummaged in a drawer for some sleeping tablets, which she had once taken from a drug trolley. The two tiny green pills shook in her palm. No, she must not start this folly. She swilled them all down the wash-basin's plug-hole.

She had gone too far. She could not and would not recant. She must bear the darkness, however painful and intense.

Was there any acceptable solution to this dilemma? She wanted to plan other sorties in her impregnable black leather and out there in the purging purifying night, feel the illusion of being cleansed as by the water of some astringent bitter well. Those wild potions reduced all wisdom to nought and soothed for a time the surging restiveness within her.

Was there no way out of this cleft other than death or madness? Was there no legitimate reason for doing these dark deeds? 'Somebody hear me!'

## CHAPTER EIGHT.

Catharine had been wrong. Archibald Letheren did not take his son's death so badly.

He trod down the steep hill of nibbled grass, as the shimmering unadorned orange balloon of the sun sank behind Helvellyn. A pair of lapwings flew up from the valley, as if querying the creeping freezing greyness. Somewhere in the distance a man's voice sang pleasantly.

Where he joined the stony track beside the bubbling gill, a small stone sanctuary stood, used occasionally as a sheep pen but said once to have been a Saxon chapel. 'Hoc est enim Corpus meum'. Letheren could see them kneeling, their hearts as uncluttered as the rugged unplastered walls. Those men had *known* not *thought.* Nicholas was away, bedighted with Anne and Hereward and God. On he strode, down the track towards the lights of the farm. As the Spanish proverb said, both begetting children and losing them opens up the heart. Letheren had seen much today.

Nicholas had always been good-natured. When small, if Innogen had been smacked for being naughty and cried, he would set up a wail too and comfort her. He would not secretly enjoy others' misfortune. His feelings were gentle and his mirth unsullied. He had been happy at school where he was not very good, happy in the army, happy even playing the oboe very badly. Thinking this over made Letheren himself feel mediocre and poor in contrast to his son, self-centred and uninnocent. When six or seven, nothing had delighted his son so much as helping to rake up mown thistles and burn them or painting gate-posts or stacking fire-wood and not just for ten minutes but for hours on end. No distant holiday or expensive toy could compete with such pleasures. And as he had grown up, he had always remained pleasingly open – not for him the debonair suits, intense looks and assumed opinions of the tailor's dummies who thought they were somebody. The cycles of centuries had moulded us therever for burning thistles, eating meat-balls and mashed turnip and family peacefulness and not for galling office work, suave colleagues and scheming secretaries. Nicholas had hated grey suits as if emblematic of that perilous half-world.

As a boy he had liked picnics too, of which the family had gone on many, especially when in England and Cyprus and on one of these when about five years old, Nicholas he remembered had asked that when they died, they could all be buried in the same place, so as still to be together.

But Letheren had had other thoughts too on his cold frosty hike. He had realised that he ought to have resigned some years before, but without Anne and frightened of being lonely, he had carried on. He should have retired though, because the chasm between the good world which he had envisaged and been taught about in his youth and the bad world of modern impatience and avarice was unbridgeable. He should have withdrawn to his books. The notion of a corporate worth sustaining a national order had all but disappeared. People asked, 'What was it all about?' They wanted no duties, no obligations. An example of this was the two hundred and twenty or so active terrorists in Northern Ireland. Militarily no difficulty existed. They could have been taken out in one night and in the days when the direction of British affairs had been in the hands of men with a deeper sense of principle than legal details and the fear of a clamorous rabble, there would have been no hesitation. Yet hamstrung and misrepresented and ridiculed by boastful demagogues, his only wise course was to seal his lips and fall back upon individual virtue. If you loved what was good, you wanted to defend it by fighting what was bad. But it seemed that many did not love goodness, indeed wished to see it harmed. The tide was against him. Popular opinion did not care any more. There were too many wolves now and the real shepherds had fled. He was hopelessly outnumbered. He could only make a last act of defiance even, if an outside agency took his side.

So he ate his dinner with his daughters like Job, with a simple view of things. All the pieces fitted together at last and were consistent. Yet if he accepted his own bereft slot as an anachronism and was reconciled fatalistically to the death of his son, the tables had turned in another way. Whereas before he had always led and his children – who had been brought up strictly never to lie, never to steal and always to obey – had followed, now as he became meeker and more pliant they experienced a surge of determination. Catharine especially, as they all sat and ate braised lamb and mint sauce with potatoes and Brussels sprouts off their best Wedgwood Florentine plates, thought that one last effort to settle some scores was right. They had a duty, not to be stupid, but to pursue any existing chances.

Innogen thought of her dream of Miss Boden, of her seeress-like premonition that this woman would be an instrument of retribution. There she had seen either dreadful ambition incited by imagination or dreadful imagination incited by ambition. Elegance and charm seem partly to excuse a laxity of morals where sexual frivolities are in question, but increase culpability where murder and robbery are the crimes, the capability for which Innogen had seen in Artemis. An erroneous belief in their own personality sometimes misleads beautiful women and here an erroneous belief in her own ability to be intelligently villainous held sway. She had the advantage though of being unknown within the epicyclic circles of the intelligence services and of leaving the Letherens free to establish alibis for themselves. As the cheese and biscuits went round, Innogen felt that this was not the moment to tell of these things. Perhaps the drowsier hour before bedtime would be better.

Catharine was interested in a scrap of paper from Tynan's grubby purse, bearing the number '010-49-511-81102' and the line '1900 hours – central European time' and transferred from lethargy to action, she stated her intention to go to Hanover.

* * *

'Ingrid, my full blossomed flower,' oozed Sir David in a rather peeved voice, 'must you sit cross-legged over there like an old-fashioned tailor? Or perhaps a more apt simile in your elegant case my dearest, would be of one practising yoga or meditating on the beauty of a falling snow-flake?'

Ingrid arose with cold grace and Sir David smiled encouragingly to her. 'Come and sit by the fire, my darling. I would like to talk to you.'

She traversed the room emitting the silence of one who is dutifully complying with one's host's foolish wishes for civility's sake, but finds it all tiresome in the extreme.

'No no,' urged Sir David in a whisper as she reclined into the grey leather armchair, 'Over here! Sit beside me on the sofa.'

She moved and sat stiffly next to him. 'Vot is it you vont?'

Penman's Mayfair apartment consisted principally of a large room of about fifty-five feet by twenty-five, which ran from front to back of a seven-storey block on the top floor. It had panoramic windows at either end which at the front opened onto a terrace with boxed plants and miniature trees and from here were views in the middle distance one way to Grosvenor Square and the other to Oxford Street. Everything in the spacious room spoke of dull quality and anaemic expense. The sitting-room section of this long evergreen-carpeted expanse contained a live-flame gas-fire with mock lumps of asbestos coal, a cream marble surround and two table-high marble statues of classical figures on either side of it. In front of it lay a polar bear rug, a large coffee-table of hard mottled grey limestone inlaid with rose quartz and blue jade and an armchair and two sofas in silvery-grey leather. The walls were white and above polished pine cross-beams lay a sloping clerestoried ceiling with large perspex roof-lights. Some artificial ivy climbed a trellis.

Sir David surveyed this woman – her dark hair, her tall slender and subtly sexy body, her touch of lewdity ... but there was always something to criticise with anyone. She would be company and a suitable adjunct to his luxurious and pampered life-style and besides, he believed he detected in himself a certain attachment to her.

He recognised however that a furtherance of his effusive and unappreciated courtesy would not make her more malleable and so he would try another tack.

'Look Ingrid, I'm going to be straight with you. Firstly, I want to be with you and I want to marry you. Secondly,' he brushed a piece of cotton thread from his dark grey waistcoat, 'you are too good for these low enterprises which you are involved in ... this ridiculous "men with their coat collars turned up" brigade. You're too intelligent to deceive yourself. This covert support for the nuclear disarmers here for example, enticing those who can see gain in it for themselves to make specious moral arguments in its favour or duping the naïve to direct all their own grudges to this issue and blame Western imperialism for their own personal failings – it's absurd. I know you don't stand shrieking with the smelly mob, you do it by bribing men with sex or money or blackmail over dinners in five-star hotels, but that does not make it any less objectionable – in fact because you're clear-sighted enough to see it all, you're *more* guilty of mischief-making.'

Ingrid wore a soft cream blouse and over it a sleeveless pinafore dress of Burgundy red suede. 'Have you feenished?'

'No.' He rested his left arm round her shoulders and she stiffened but stayed seated. 'You don't believe in socialism. You know that Europe is too fond of effervescence and history and polemic to ever accept such humdrum conformity ... '

'Time vill show. If you are corrupted and seduced, zen ze fault is yours for being villing to be corrupted and seduced,' she answered coldly.

'"Evil be unto him who evil thinks."'

'Oh shut up!'

'No I won't shut up,' he retorted proudly. 'For your own good I intend to go on.' He sipped his brandy but put it down as she stood up and drew his fat hand.

'Come into ze bed,' she said.

He discreetly licked his taut upper lip.

In the bedroom she stood on the tiger-skin rug and wearily peeled off her clothes. She liked the stuffed head of the rug, for it always smiled. She lay under the quilt and waited for him to fumble with and drop a portion of his clothing. Eventually this butt of lard called Penman embraced her mawkishly.

'As I was saying, you don't want to acknowledge the falsehoods in your own life, but you must know they're there. You're anything but dim and you can undoubtedly see that supporting all this wickedly intentioned concern-hawking injures you and prevents you from being the happy and contented woman you could be. Oh your discipline, your concentration, your mental faculties are masterful ... but misapplied. Where do they lead?' The seriousness with which he now spoke, after a year of exaggerated niceness and unearned consideration which she had inwardly despised, surprised her.

There was a certain amount of unstylish frigging around under the quilt.

'But vot about you? You serve us because you are so in love viz cumfortable leeving and gourmet food, zat you are prepared to betray ze sing you say you have belief in. You are neizzer vun sing nor ze uzzer.' She fiddled with his penis. 'It shows too in ze sex, zat is vy I brought you to bed. Your orgarn is like a floppy empty pea-pod. It is smaller zen my leetlest toe. If you loved me, you vud screw me easily. If you hated me, you vud too. But no, just nussing.'

His face flushed and his hand made a quick flurried sally to his genitals to try and liven them up. 'We have the qualities in us to be greater, to turn or hearts to wiser objectives instead of wasting time on games which don't succeed.'

'Vee cannot change. You are a fat faffing doughnut and I am a machinating German spy. It is too late to change our vays, far too late.'

He sighed and half-swamped her with his blubber-ringed torso. 'This is so depressingly pessimistic.'

'Vee are fixed. Vee are vot vee are. I tell you, some of ze men I lie viz, some of zese steel vurkers for exemple, zay can pump out a geyser of burning seed-cells and boiling foaming juice and forse it up in a fountain into my vumanly coils ... '

'It sounds as if they're peeing.'

' ... for hours on end, but you ... a few dirty dribbles zat fall into ze sheet? Like Churchill said to Attlee, you are a sheep in vulf's clohsing. Flopped virtue and flopped evil, ze lust valve opened just a leetle ... '

Although she did not let it show, he had touched her conscience and worried her. She felt ugly and paralysed and remembered her handbag on the chaise longue in the entrance hall. In it was a cyanide pill, easily dropped into his wine. Then if she rinsed the glass well after this instant-death electuary had done its work, there would be no trace. Even if she were suspected, she could say he must have done it himself in despair after she had rejected his offer of marriage. 'Stop looking at me David. Gott, get on viz it!' She tried to look unflappable.

'Don't damage yourself further. Have the courage to trust me. You will feel naked at first, but then comes another power after the arts and artifices, greater than the acumen you ... We could marry ... change our names ... run away ... ?' He squinted his eyes in pain as he saw that she had been taught and honed to be able to win men and not be hurt. He averted his head sharply and uncertainly, as he saw that his debased morality could never overcome her steadfastness and training. 'I cannot believe you. You must be human!'

She smiled a smile which contained many things, sweetness, victory, scorn, liking, dislike and perhaps even remorse. 'I am not ze free vuman I may seem. I hated ze smug arrogance and hedonism of ze Vest, its leeberal licence, its misalliance of freedom and faiselessness, but now I vont it. I used it at first only as a ruse, zo viz pleasure as it demonstrated so vell all your foibles and veaknesses. I sort it all vice. Now I see its value also.'

She left him there, lost in feeble indecision. She dressed and put on her brown leather trench coat, white fur hat and high brown leather laced German boots, arming her feminine cynosure physique and making ready to leave.

She fought down a pricking conscience, angry with herself for allowing this pompous British establishment figure to affect her. No passion or fear should make her weak or unable to contend with men-folk, yet she saw that paradoxically she had thus become a slave to the fetters of cunning and lies. 'You are as bad as zat apattetic Michael Rose.'

'I thought he was homosexual?'

'He doesn't know vot he is.'

'Do you know what you are?'

'Yes, of course ... vell, perhaps not. Perhaps none of us knows.'

*  *  *

It had gone midday when Artemis awoke on the Sunday, this lie-in compensating finally for her lack of sleep on the Friday night.

After a bath she breakfasted in the spacious kitchen where someone had left a radio on. A newscaster's meticulously neutral tone promised her an 'update on the situation in Karachi'. She sprang up and jabbed the 'off' button. She did not want such extraneous distractions as the 'situation in Karachi' to confuse her and blind her to seeing her own course. Artemis wished to concentrate her essence, not dilute it.

Back in her room she could not hit on the right thing to do. Reading nugatory nursing textbooks full of undigested boring facts was out. A part-read thriller had lost its interest, sparking off no original perspectives. A trivial crossword seemed an even worse way of dissipating her time. She visualised Simon's timorous form and clasped her hands together in supplication. 'A donkey, a donkey, my kingdom for a donkey!' With a whoop of laughter, she flopped back onto her bed.

She knew what she really wanted – to begin planning her next strike, the next assault in her campaign to rule and accrue riches.

Without warning, a searing pain spread up the left side of her face and invaded her whole temple and eye with an agonising and burning feeling. She held her head and pressed it against the cold wall until numb in places, but the pain would not abate. She banged the chair against the desk with indescribable ferocity. It eased a little.

Deciding to pop down to the sitting-room to browse through the Sunday papers and see if anything gave her the germ of an idea, she opened her door and found a man there with a crooked knuckle ready to knock.

He was in his fifties, of middle build and physically in good shape. His face, which had that recondite warmth about it of people who are genuinely tough, gave her an enquiring yet friendly smile. 'Miss Boden? My name's Letheren. I'm Innogen's father.'

She shrugged and waved him in. The pain round her eye subsided abruptly.

'Thank you.' He sat on the edge of the bed and she in the armchair with her legs stretched before her and crossed at the ankles. Her dainty fingers peeled an orange – those fingers which so many had dreamed of tickling their genitals as they caroused with her in a hayloft.

'Hats off to your parents,' he said, 'Artemis Oenone Boden – two Greek names. We only had the courage to give Innogen a Greek middle name.'

Artemis judged him to be a strange mixture of shyness and shrewdness.

He watched the fire-cracker with her overweening pride and her fierce intolerance of a menial existence. Behind the show of callous indifference, he saw that she felt bitter and thwarted and angry. She had slept badly too, he thought.

His eyes looked into hers and she looked into his. She less often looked at people when she spoke these days, but here was an exception. As when small, her wide eyes tracked him unblinkingly. Here was someone intriguing, someone perhaps whom she needed.

'In Shakespeare's *The Tempest*, there are two characters called Prospero and Caliban ... '

'I know. Caliban is the twisted imp, who is bound to the good Prospero by his wickedness.'

Her clothes today were really her shabbiest – a blue serge skirt with a single box-pleat at the front, an old white school blouse and a greeny-yellow cardigan – yet her superb physical loveliness still shone through and rescued her.

He looked at her again and she looked back.

'Am I Caliban and you Prospero?'

'Perhaps.'

She nodded. 'All right.'

'My guelder rose – pretty flowers and poisonous berries?'

'Ta galérienne.'

He smiled. 'If you wish it so.'

When Letheren spoke of history or a military encounter, he would speak slowly, sampling the esoteric art of choosing apt and colourful words, but here in this hard and obscure realm of spirit, it was a question of waiting for the words to come.

Artemis slipped a segment of orange into her mouth. It was against her nature to capitulate to anyone, yet as she thought this, a latent throbbing began in her temple once more and the searing ache threatened to resurface like a blow-lamp playing on her eye.

'I walked along an old railway embankment recently and came upon this twisted apple tree. I could just reach this one misshapen apple with a couple of maggots peering out of it and yet, it was the sweetest and tastiest apple I've had in years. Things are not always as they appear.'

'Do you wish me to perform forays which are ... criminal?'

'Technically criminal. Apple trees often grow beside railways, perhaps because folk throw their cores out of the windows.

I think you will find a sort of unique delight in these tasks. You will make a lot of money – which I understand might matter to you – and the guilt, if there is any, will be mine. Whilst you serve me, a sort of bulwark will I hope protect you and at the end – in a month's time say – there will be a chance for you to annul all your earlier wrongs and begin to lead a right life.'

He had said his piece. Now he would discover whether he and Innogen had made some wild mistake or whether their insight was accurate.

Her coolness waned. She saw that she could not fight on all fronts and win. A pact here might give victory in her other battles. This was the answer to her prayer. Here she could yield, because it was in secret. She went into the recess behind the wardrobe and washed her sticky hands. The paralysing stinging in her head passed off wholly as she resolved to submit.

She sat beside him on the bed and took his warm hands in hers. A sense of unwearied relief swept through her. She felt pliant and acquiescent. The traits in her twenty-year-old face of a more worldly-worn and tartly sarcastic thirty-year-old which had set in lately, faded and the rare loveliness and extraordinary piquancy of her youth shone afresh. Like the priestess of an evil god, the one who has defied love, the needs she had forced into abeyance burst out. The alert sentinel of self-control fled. She threw her face against his chest and put her arms round his body and clung to him for some minutes.

His manly face surveyed the top of her head. He kissed it and put his arms very gently round this five-year-old's shoulders. The sharp fragrance of her Chloé perfume wafted up into his nose and ousted the earlier rose and bergamot scent of the cushions and clothes. He had seen the indefatigable and ruthless will in her to carry out the deeds necessary to achieve her desired aims and he cherished this as one sign of a higher mind. Where angels feared to tread, Artemis would not hold back, but there was no hypocrisy in her and if led by his right intents all should go well.

He stroked her smooth back and neck and shoulders. 'You're a bold girl Artemis. When we're young, extremes seem good. Wildness is the more potent for usual strictness, revelry for customary denial. We go too far. It takes time to learn to love, but it will come. Don't be too hard with yourself.'

'Mr Letheren, most girls who go out with a boy these days, tell him they love him on their second outing.'

'Do they? Dear oh dear.' He chortled softly.

'It is so soppy.'

She lifted her head up and he saw a tear or two on her lashes. 'Do you want to tell me who he was?'

She almost sobbed, but not quite. She looked down again. 'No, not yet.'

His inscrutably benign face focused briefly on her shapely calf muscles and ankles as she stood up. 'Shall we have a cup of tea and then drive up into Northumberland?'

'All right.' She straightened out her skirt and cardigan over the firm curves of her superlative body. She dried her face. Almost no flaw or blemish marred her ignipotent feminine figure, except that the spirit of lovelessness, if in retreat, was not wholly evicted.

* * *

Catharine knew that of the telephone number 010-49-511-81102, the 010 signified international, the 49 West Germany and by working through the international code sub-sections in the front of a British telephone directory that 511 stood for Hanover. She also knew that a West German telephone directory for a given region is sub-divided into towns. Thus she could look up Hanover and go through all the numbers until she found 81102, assuming it was not ex-directory. This highly laborious route appeared necessary because you can give directory enquiries a name and ask for their number, but not vice versa. Hanover, said the encyclopaedia, had 460,000 inhabitants. That meant perhaps 130,000 telephones.

Her plane left Newcastle early on Sunday morning and en route she drank tea and ate a squadgy mince and onion pasty, which was like trying to eat a hot-water-bottle in that wherever you bit it the filling migrated away from you.

The taxi from the airport dropped her in the Ernst-August-Platz, in front of Hanover's main railway station. She walked away from the station and into the town centre. A thick layer of white snow clung to the steeply-gabled roofs of the older buildings with their mustardy-coloured rendering and brown window-boxes, whilst piles of greying slush edged the pavements. The simple neat signs, the beautifully clean and modern shop windows and the well-cared for civic amenities were indicative of both orderliness and stylishness, but being a Sunday, it was very dead.

In a cobbled side alley called Hollengasse and under the arches of a cream-painted building with grey-glossed quoins and red and white diagonally striped shutters, she found the entrance to a small hotel – the Hotel Columbus. A waistcoated fat man wedged behind the reception desk, attended to his accounts. A lovely smell of wax polish hung in the air and there was a large array of silk anemones.

Catharine tried her schoolgirl German. 'Bitte, haben Sie ein Einzelzimmer für zwei Nächte?'

Her room was high-ceilinged with a net-curtained window, but dull in spite of the modern furniture. The atmosphere felt lonely and friendless, though at least she could see a telephone and a local directory.

Going down the columns of Hanover's telephone numbers and checking each five figure number with a leading '8', it took her two and a bit hours to scan the hundred and six pages which preceded the entry of 81102. It read: – Steyer U.H. Eichenfelsstrasse 11A.

Catharine dialled the number and listened to the interrupted buzz for about two minutes. No one answered. She used the coffee-making equipment set out on the desk and drank coffee with a cheese sandwich from her luggage. She rang 81102 again and waited for a full three minutes this time. She rang the reception desk and ordered a taxi.

With her blonde hair tied back, her erect youthful stature, her fur-lined boots, navy leather mack and knitted white scarf and mittens, Catharine could well have been a native. She alighted from the taxi outside Eichenfelsstrasse 35, the number she had specified. Deserted and still, the fifteen-year-old suburb looked remarkably drab, especially by the innovative and well-executed standards of German town planning. Despite the good order and cleanliness of the concrete cycle racks and the yellow litter bins poking up through the trodden snow, the six long blocks of glass and lintels seemed very characterless. A flight of concrete steps between a bank and a sports shop bore the numbers 11A 11B 11C and 11D and at its top were four doors, all dead and faceless and alike. A bell button beside 11A's teak veneered door carried an illumined slot with the name 'Ute Steyer'. She could hear the bell chime inside, as she pressed it five times.

Sweat moistened her blouse collar as she tried to feed her cheque card round the edge of the door and ease the latch back, but German doors and locks are superior to English ones and she could not manage it. Because of the airport security checks too, she had not brought her father's massive bunches of skeleton keys. The unwashed landing window looked out over some railway yards and directly beneath her stood a flat truck with a container on it, bearing the red and white angled monogram, 'DLR'.

Back in the street an orange snow-plough scraped past and a lone man walked his Dachshund. To pass time until darkness fell, Catharine crossed to a side-street which tailed off into football pitches and light industrial premises. Here the grey footprints were fewer as were the grey tyre ruts and their spatterings in the off-white snow. She came to a rough café where youths played table-football earnestly or quaffed light lager with deep manly gasps.

They overheard her buying a bowl of soup at the shabby counter. One Egon Etler came and sat opposite her, eager to show off his English, although some spoil-sport played an accordion and drowned him out with song.

'Are you Eenglisch?'

She smiled faintly.

'Germany is impressing you, yes?'

'Yes.'

'Everysing is vurking and clean and in goot repair?'

'That is true.'

'And ze farms and ze forests?'

'Yes, very pretty. And the chalets and the geraniums are so picturesque.'

'But vee are needing more directing, less traitors, more ... challenging?'

'I don't know.' She gave a discouraging sigh. 'I've spent only a little time here.'

'Hitler voz a great man. He had ze goot ideas.' He held up a finger to his lips. 'Ze sohsialists vish to destroy all zat is loyal and binded. Zat is vy zay vont ze immigrants and making ze vurst rubbish Schutt-peoples here to multiplies.'

Catharine had finished her soup and roll. Her smile, a little distant though not wholly unfriendly, peered into his sly eyes. 'He ought to have chosen more upright advisors.'

'I have a Luftwaffe long-range Kondor peeloht's ooniform – it is very vunderful. It has ze lezzer trousers,' he added significantly.

She raised her brows.

'Do you sink me a little strange, peeraps?'

'Do you enjoy wearing leather trousers?'

'And wot is wrrrongg viz lezzer trousers?' He seemed stung and this response was a trifle aggressive.

'Oh, nothing, nothing!' She shrugged with a hint of theatricality.

'Vill you come and drinking coffee viz me in my flet?'

'No, thank you.'

'Vy not?'

'I don't like coffee.'

'Ach! You are a untypisch Eenglisch gurl. Come viz. Pleese.'

'No.'

'But vy not?'

'Because I don't want to.'

His smiling over her shoulder made her turn. She caught sight of a serving girl in a black Dirndl with a full skirt part and a tight bodice part pulled together under her swollen padded breasts by a red string, threaded like a shoe-lace. Under it she wore a synthetic frilly short-sleeved white blouse. With the fingers of one hand bunched together and pointing upwards, she jerked them up and down between but slightly in front of her legs, implying Egon's sex organ and the English girl's vagina. With a lewd sneer on her face, she resumed her attention of the table-football players.

Egon leant closer to Catharine. 'Ven I am taking holiday in Spanien, I fock ze Eenglisch gurls all ze time. I fock zem all ze day and all ze night. Zat is all zay vont – focking.'

He seized her forearm, but she sprang up and prised him off so violently, that he fell backwards onto the floor, to delayed jeers of mockery from his watching associates in the background.

Darkness had arrived and with it, a lazy fall of fresh snow. Hanover no doubt had classy quarters, where well-educated couples after dinner sat with their sons and daughters and played string quartets together, but Eichenfelsstrasse was not one of them. It was dreary and even spooky. If only Nicholas could be with her or even befuddled Innogen, it would be much less frightening.

Still no one answered 11A's door.

At the end of the block stood a children's playground where the slides and swings were coated with a phosphorescent icing of unsullied frozen snow. Luckily there were no lights close to this desolate enclave and no one was about. She popped a barley sugar sweet into her mouth and looked up at the temporary tower of scaffolding which stood here at the end of the long three-storey oblong. It was icy and slippery and it swayed slightly as she clung to its cross-pieces and trunnions, hooking her arms round the poles for a safer grip. Half-way up she paused.

Behind her, a local passenger train rattled over numerous points, threading its way past the wagon sidings and spilling out light from its windows to make the rails gleam like bars of platinum in an ocean of black treacle. The icy air bit into her face and neck and knees and hands.

The twenty-year-old Miss Letheren was not readily frightened by physical dangers, but was by the thought of discovery, of blue lights and green Polizei uniforms. She used to run in the eight hundred and eighty yards for Norfolk, often played tennis, rode in cross-country equestrian events on and off and had done some canoeing and abseiling and so was fairly fit and not given to fear of injury. Against this, she was very uncosmopolitan. She found little pleasure in flitting in and out of foreign countries and this combined with the illegality of her present actions, made it scary.

On she went to the top of the tower, there to scramble across the end parapet into the lead-lined gully which ran along the back edge of the roof.

* * *

Artemis drove the Range Rover and the Colonel read the Ordnance Survey map. Short of the peaceful rural town of Rothbury in the hillier western reaches of Northumberland, they pulled off down a frosty lane, hemmed in by small juniper trees. On foot they followed a footpath through some woodland, crossed a disused railway line and after climbing over several stiles, descended a slope into the deeply cut meandering River Coquet, edged by fallen twigs and wilted weeds and the other strange jumble of hibernating winter.

Their boots squelched in sodden muddy mulch.

The Colonel was dressed eccentrically in baggy breeches and long socks, old leather hiking boots, a sleeveless brown jacket over his jersey and a battered fishing hat.

They tight-rope walked across a fallen tree to an islet with thickish vegetation on it. 'Deadman's Eit,' whispered Letheren, peering at his map. He abruptly pressed her down so that they both stooped and could see a stretch of green river beneath a bowing willow branch. 'An otter.' He pointed to some concentric ripples.

'I didn't see anything.'

'Never mind.' They straightened up and found a fallen mouldy bough to sit on. 'Have you heard of David Penman O.B.E.?'

'No.'

'*Sir* David – he's very fond of the "Sir" – owns the finest collection of gold moidores and ducats in Europe I'm told ... though some Texan has a larger one, as you might expect.'

She still wore the well-worn serge skirt, her ordinary knee-length boots, a couple of woollies and a sea-green three-quarter length mack of rubberised canvas plus a pair of everyday black leather gloves.

'Keep still,' he whispered in her ear. She waited until he guided her gaze. 'See – a red squirrel.' He pointed at the shy creature, eyeing them from above. She adjusted her handbag noisily. 'Shhhh!' he reproved her.

He remembered seeing her as Electra three years before. Then her modesty and self-consciousness had made her sweeter and softer. Once whilst his company had been flushing out a village in Spain, he had been shot in the leg. In hospital a young nurse in a long blue uniform dress with a starched white apron which had had shoulder straps crossing over on her narrow back had tended him. She had been touchingly shy and had once dared a timid look up from under her downcast eyes and then blushed when he had winked. Her pale face and dark hair had shared some resemblance with the younger Artemis. Now though, like a gooseberry, she had grown tough-skinned and sour. She did not mope and wait and hope, but with a woman's fury and cruelty and a degree of masculine stamina, tackled everyone she suspected of being against her.

'Penman is a permanent undersecretary in the Home Office. He is a pompous man but has a knack of seeming to possess some presence. I suppose I mean he habitually looks down his nose.' Their eyes probed one another. 'He serves clandestine coteries of tyrants in waiting. To inveigle yourself into his company – in order to organise his despatch – there is an auction tomorrow evening in London of medieval Hispanic maps and coins and instruments.' Some binding Mithridatic force entwined them. He kissed her softly on the cheek as he would his daughters and gripped her left hand between both of his. 'He *should* be there. He is yours if you so desire.' A kingfisher paused near them.

'Goodness. We are lucky today.'

'My wishes converge with your needs and because mine are just, you may compel that which is usually forbidden. Many have sought in vain to be wicked without detriment to their beauty or quick wit. It is given to you to negotiate this impasse, upon the condition that you remain a weapon of my revenge. *That* is what shields you from destruction and makes the impossible possible.'

Had she been a ward sister or had a husband who was not the one she wanted, she could have made others' lives a misery and thereby made a statement about her own dissatisfactions. But as a student nurse, no one would stand for it. So, things had to happen in secret, her legitimate limitations be exceeded in the dark. 'I may with impunity slay and steal from the immoral men whom you name?'

'Yes.'

Some black swans with red beaks swam by, before as dusk crept over the land, they wound their way back to the vehicle in the cold eerie stillness, pierced at one point by the shrill tin-whistle-like sound of another kingfisher.

She yielded mentally. It felt good and soon like lovers, it almost did not matter which one of them gave voice to each thought, for they were so unified in intent that their lines were interchangeable.

Thc trees held abstract phantom-like shapes for Artemis, who recited silently to herself her litany. 'I am Artemis the virgin huntress, who gleams resplendent in leather in the darkness and conquers at will. I am Artemis, goddess of the moon and none shall obstruct my will.'

She turned the Range Rover's ignition key and switched on its lights. At the old-fashioned 'Halt' sign at a cross-roads, with the tiny red reflectors imbedded in its maroon ringed triangle, they stopped and viewed the skewed signpost in the twilight and the light of their headlamps. 'That way,' said Letheren, 'Nether Lashburn and Scotsgap.'

They drove down the narrow roads of rugged lovely Northumbria. As they passed through a flooded dip under a narrow stone bridge, his fingers outlined the triangles of her small feminine shoulder blades and then settled on the lower slopes of her neck with a gentle roughness, for he knew that she lacked human contact and tenderness. Not even her father embraced her as affectionately as Letheren these days.

At the nurses' home she stepped out and Letheren climbed across and drove off.

A skulking youth drew his breath so hard at the sight of her, that his entire cigarette burnt up in one puff. She turned away from this unpleasing loiterer and strode up to the door of the nurses' home.

Artemis felt delightfully relaxed as she took off her boots and mack and lay on her bed. Like Hercules she would wield the club and kill *his* vile foes.

The desk-lamp threw a pool of light onto the patterned rug, leaving the upper part of the room in semi-darkness.

Outside, someone began hitting a dustbin lid with a hammer. There was an old woman who lived in one of the houses which backed onto the nurses' home, who began drinking each afternoon and continued until she collapsed late at night. She would sometimes scream about the nurses being fodder for sex-craving men or at other times talk about men in riding pinks and jack-boots. She wore awful dresses and thick woollen stockings and blamed her ill-health on her smoking – not her drinking. Bang bang bang. 'You snooty toffee-nosed whore nurses, I count all the men creeping in and out! You disgusting sluts! And I've seen that one creeping in and out in her iniquitous black leather.' Bang bang bang.

Artemis with her hands interlocked behind her head, put her tongue between her lips and blew a raspberry.

Artemis had become Artemis the Immutable. No uncertainties lingered any more. Again, it all slotted together. Today and tomorrow were her days off this week. She would drive to London in the morning, attend the auction and see if she could seduce Penman. 'Lex talionus' – the law of retaliation, the inevitable tooth for a tooth. It all felt intended. It would redress the corrupt barbarity and impure conceits of this fat civil servant. She could see him. She could see how it would all take shape. She would kill him and steal his gold.

*  *  *

Over the back parapet she could easily spot the 'DLR' container in the darkness below, just because the other wagons on the track nearest to her in the cutting, were tank wagons and open wagons. From this Catharine knew which of the slanting dormer windows belonged to Steyer's flat.

She paddled all the way back along the slush-filled gully to the scaffolding tower, lifted up a short ladder from its top platform and carried it horizontally and slowly and noiselessly to the window she wished to enter. Lying flat on it as it lay flat on the snow-covered forty-five degree roof tiles, her toes on the fifth rung supported her abreast of the window she wished to break in through.

It was necessary to return to the scaffolding tower yet again *and* climb part way down it, to where she recalled seeing some tools on a platform of planks. Back on the ladder, with the edge of a fat cold chisel inserted under the lower rim of the window and with its top end wrapped up in her scarf, she tapped it softly with the lump hammer, using to cover the noise another passing train. It snowed more heavily. With the chisel about an inch in under the leading edge, the brass pin on which the securing stay was fastened snapped, enabling the window to swivel freely on its central pivot.

She placed the tools in the rain-water gully and then tackled the very difficult manoeuvre of climbing in backwards through the window.

It was seven o'clock by the time she dropped down onto the floor of the tiny bedroom, an hour almost since moving into the children's playground at the end of the block.

She shut the window, drew the blind and turned on the light. The room had a double mattress on the floor with a quilt and some pillows and three cardboard boxes tied up with green string. A poky store-room contained a small chest freezer with some frozen pizzas, loaves and berries in it and a few stacks of old books. The bathroom again had a tooth-brush, some soap and bottles of hair shampoo and a couple of towels, but not a lot. She went down the spiral wooden staircase and bolted the front-door from inside. In the sitting-room she found no carpet but a coffee-table with a light pink telephone on it, number 81102 and two armchairs, one with a few clothes dumped in it and lastly the kitchen revealed a packet of muesli, a pair of scissors, several mugs and a couple of plates. This modern, good quality German rabbit hutch was a quarter-furnished. Someone did stay here, but not on a regular basis. There had been no attempt to make it feel homely – no flowers, no pictures, the curtains were too long or badly hung and there were no complete sets of crockery or cutlery. This seemed consistent with the notion of its being a hide-away for such pitiful shadows as those who want everything rotten to flourish and everything good and fair to be crushed.

Catharine Letheren had closed all the blinds and curtains and switched on all the lights. She removed her coat and shook off all the loose ice crystals and water, noted that it had torn along the seam under one armpit and hung it up in front of a fan heater, which she turned on to dry it off. The scarf used to muffle the chisel lay lost somewhere on the roof. Her knees had been grazed on the parapet coping stones and were slightly bloodied, whilst her stiff boots were scratched and scored here and there and water had seeped in round the welt and made her socks wet. She wrung these out and hung them up too, with her sopping dirty gloves in front of the heater and started to suck yet another lump of barley sugar.

The sounds of gun-fire and shouting could be heard faintly on the neighbour's television, interspersed with bass chords. She took a pair of screwed up old gloves from the depths of her handbag and began to poke about.

A town hall circular letter gave the owner to be Fräulein Ute H. Steyer and her date of birth as May the fourth, 1944. It occurred to the investigating Catharine that that might well fit Ingrid Axt for age, but some old school exercise books of Ute's in the store-room did not have the same angular spiky handwriting as the page of instructions intended for Rose had had.

There was a large dust-covered tome of organic chemistry with the name in it of one Dr Christopher Roden of Iserkirchgasse 2, Swabing, München. Some pages in it were well-thumbed and some passages high-lighted. She found a library card for the Heugel Pharmazeutik Bibliothek and a children's story book with red covers and a faded pink spine and crumbs which fell out of one page, perhaps from a 1950's afternoon tea. She would take some of this with her. There was a pair of men's shoes, size 48 and a pair of socks and jeans. In one of the pockets was a letter. It had an Austrian post-code and was addressed to Ulrich Schniewind, Bergweg 3, Wilsattel, A-4011 Österreich. The signature read 'Andrea' and it might have been a love-letter. It too went into the strong plastic bag she had unfolded.

She spent a dreary hour flipping through books spine-upwards to see if anything fell out, rooting in the rubbish bin, down the sides of the armchairs, inside the zipped cushion covers and a hundred other places without success. The floors were concrete with tiles glued to them, so there were no loose floor-boards to be discovered. She employed a solitary screwdriver to remove the bath panel and the panels over the main down pipes – for German buildings have no external pipe-work because of the cold winters. Eventually, in the cupboard under the sink, a back panel which presumably hid more plumbing, seemed to have brass fixing screws with rather shiny scratched heads and worn slots. Here she found substance, a plastic bag full of cheque books and documents to reward her for her risks. Briefly they were the papers for two separate accounts, both with the Unterwalden Kreditbank's Luzern branch and in the names of Nicole Frédérique le Saige and Uwe Bauss. Also here were three passport-sized photographs of an unknown woman who looked thirtyish.

Catharine washed her hands face and knees and cleaned her boots with a pair of Ute's pyjama trousers, retied her hair and dressed up tidily, ready to leave. She turned everything off and closed the main door behind her.

In her dull room in the Hotel Columbus a little after ten, she hid her bag of treasure under the wardrobe plinth and soon fell asleep in the over-soft bed. So ended her long bleak Sunday, played out in a nebulous world, devoid of agreeable humanity.

Early on Monday morning, she climbed the steps up to platform five of Hanover's large railway station and caught an express to Basel in company with hordes of teenagers going on skiing holidays.

Inside the carriage's green and aluminium interior, Catharine sat surrounded by the leg-pulling, harshly-voiced show-off boys and girls in their fashion-conscious and showily-coloured ski-wear. She listened for a time to their language, then looked out at the white countryside with its peeping villages and dense forests. On her lap, rested her dog-eared unlined handbag of thick orangy-tan leather with its heavy brass buckle on the flap and brass rings to hold the shoulder strap and a faint bas-relief motif of a spear-wielding Achilles embossed into its front and on the rack opposite her lay her small suitcase. In both of these were the results of her detective work.

In the vast concourse of Basel Station, she ate lunch in the grandiose vaulted *fin de siècle* restaurant and bought a ticket for Bern, again using cash and collecting enough Swiss coins to telephone England.

'Hello Pappa. Catharine. Some progress. I'm at Basel Centralbahnhof and on my way to Bern. Home tomorrow night hopefully.' Peep peep peep. 'All my love. Bye.'

* * *

The West End hairdresser had shorn Artemis's locks to the latest vogue short style. Firm and silky and almost black, it just revealed her single pearl ear-rings and the lower halves of her ears and at the back of her neck it tapered to a stop an inch short of her collar. Her full below-knee skirt of thin stiff shiny cotton was black with a few forks of red lightning on it. The bright red silk blouse had simple buttoned cuffs and from under its plain collar, a long single string of pearls hung down over her chest. Her legs wore plain black tights and ended in a pair of high-heeled pointed black leather Italian shoes, eminently plain and elegant and somehow epitomising vicious femininity, as if designed to kick the rear end of any erring male. Their metal heels rang out with an assertive clarity. Both Artemis and her clothes were exactly right for this auction – classy and sexy, but not vulgar or brash.

The venue had once been the ballroom of a large Stuart mansion in W.C.1. The stucco pseudo-half-pillars, the ceiling's plaster mouldings and other remnants of stylised baroque finery betrayed this. Rows of chairs were lined up on the slightly springy wooden floor and at the front, near the well-lit dais, were the alarm-rigged show-cases where the manuscripts and old monies were displayed alongside their lot numbers.

'Ah, Sir David,' she heard someone say to Penman, 'has King Harold's personal jester found you yet?'

'What are his qualifications – just so as I know what level to talk to him on?'

Penman glanced down at a selection of fussy gold coins, set out on an imitation panther skin under the glass. 'That E.F. franc there from Hainault and the French écu d'or are not bad.'

'What date's the French one?'

'1270? Thereabouts.'

Affable remarks and concealed questions were being exchanged by the company, who with the exception of two women in dark dresses, were men in genuinely well-tailored suits – personable fellows, mostly wealthy, well-educated and with unsnobbish notions about art and antiques.

Many men adjusted their stances to secretly watch the Atalanta-like poise of Artemis, as she pretended to study a renovated globe. They admired her beauty, tinged as it was with hauteur harshness and high-handedness. With a pointed toe she described a small pattern on the floor with beauty's artifice – *un rond de jambes* – whilst her mind delved into the slyness of her own intent. A woman's sexiness indicates her need and so men know when they may attack, but Artemis could circumvent this rule, as her needs could be sated elsewhere. A row of men, like birds on a telegraph wire waiting to migrate, scanned from behind her narrowed sculptured shape, which looked as if up until today it had worn only fiercely constricting Victorian lingerie. They bounced their sexual ids on their mental trampolines. Men feel sickened if they indulge in dirty fantasies about good girls, but about bad girls it is less harmful. Thus Artemis caused much agitation, her potently erotic mould being the source of many doting oneirisms and frustrated penile stiffenings. And most infuriatingly of all, she moved with agile steps – more suggestive than graceful – and seemed so outstandingly self-possessed as if she knew she were taunting the onlookers. She appeared to be expressing her defiance physically, like a sensual ballerina who refused to be caught and made to do the splits. The watchers' eyes told of reined in roars of rage, as from trapped bulls, whilst Artemis glanced at them like pinioned worms with her steady clear eyes and proleptically icy manner. 'It's cold this evening,' said someone.

David Penman had sat down on the front row and as the surrounding seats began to be occupied, so that she could sit beside him without it being too obvious, Artemis did so with discreet ostentation.

With ill-concealed frenzy, Penman padded his pockets for his glasses and prodded himself in the eye in the process of putting them on too quickly, for he had seen her desire-igniting shape as she swept her skirt beneath her bottom and sat down. Without moving his head he could savour hazily her fine dark hair, her long slender neck and the delicate contours of her arms and breasts.

She pretended not to register the activity of this latest obscene ogler and made her watchful eyes follow the auctioneer as he climbed onto his podium. She substituted her usual smile of lop-sided reflection on the stupidity of others, for her dimpled and gloating one. It softened the forceful line of her mouth.

'Ladies and Gentlemen, good evening. On behalf of Jones and Jones, I welcome you to the auction of the late Comte d'Orange's renowned collection. Lot number one is on page two of your brochures and is the map of the southern Baltic, drawn in coloured inks in about 1460 by Suzanne ter Schelde in Antwerp. It is on canvas and measures approximately thirty-two centimetres by fifty-one. At this time, the Dutch were emerging as the foremost cartographers and in this particularly well-preserved specimen, you will note the use of ... '

Artemis had taken a small note-pad and a pen from her handbag, knowing that her simple appealing movements were being watched minutely. She pulled her longish skirt over her crossed legs and tried to write with a pen which she knew to be empty.

'Allow me.' A solid gold pen was proffered before her.

'Thank you.' She feigned surprise and by subtly willing it, oozed more coy sexiness from her combatant body.

Penman had short stumpy legs, a fat midriff and folds of rosy flesh round his big cheeks, viciously-tenored little eyes and lush hooded eyelids. His face emitted a ruddy arrogance, at once offensive to men, yet conversely, often peculiarly attractive to women. Like many older men, he vainly imagined himself to possess that mixture of charm and sympathy which can be captivating to young women, though his real bait was his money. He chose his girls to be impressive, as others choose flashy cars and therein lay his failure to find a good wife, though as a half-homosexual this may have been deliberate.

He bid for a Sp anish double excelente and a Scottish twenty pound piece of James the Fourth's reign. He secured the latter for a little over £3,000.

She savoured an unsmiling smile, as she patiently played the civilised girl, thinking that everyone else in these power-ridden circles believed like her that polite behaviour was a mere charade. Recourse would be needed to force and murder and bribery to actually win.

As the hammer fell on the last lot amidst the rustlings of impatience, she closed her pad and handed the pen back with a simple smile, carefully not overdone.

'Thank you.'

'Not at all.' He searched quickly for a sequel. 'David Penman. How do you do?'

She shook his hand briefly and said, 'Denise Stoneley,' pronouncing it 'de-neece' and not 'de-neeze'.

'I didn't see you bid.'

'No, I'm a part-time journalist for *Le Monde.* You missed your Anjou florin Mr Penman ... '

'David, s'il vous plaît.' He absorbed her lethal image – she was one of the very top flight of women.

She had to prevent an awkward pause. 'Minted in Florence did he say? 1250?'

'They're so very rare and if two people both want it, the price just spirals.' He shrugged as if life had other consolations. 'Only earthly treasures. A thief tried to break in to my flat last month, but luckily I had just had these new infra-red beam alarms fitted ... you know, if the ray's interrupted it triggers the bell.'

'It's so shocking, all this crime?'

'Do you have a special period of interest, Denise?'

She mused with an ambiguous smile, 'The high Middle Ages?'

He could not decide if this could really be an offer. 'Does that include me?'

She gave him an enigmatic smile as they stood up, a definite signal that she was ready to flirt. 'It might do.' She bent to pick up her bag, hung it on her shoulder then casting her eyes away from him, gazed elsewhere as if assessing alternative possibilities.

'Would you like to come to my flat?'

She spun her head back to face him again and realigned her eyes on his nose. After seeming to weigh the offer for four or five seconds, she accepted. 'That would be nice.'

Penman led off but tripped on a chair leg and fell onto his knees. His magnifying glass fell out of a pocket and broke.

'Dear oh dear.' He righted himself and tried to make light of it. 'See what an effect you're having upon me, you enchantress.'

Artemis smiled her actress's urbane feminine beam and aware that her tantalising form had burnt itself onto the retinae of at least a dozen men here, moved loftily towards the cloakroom with airy dismissal.

When her magnetised victim caught up with her, he regaled her with hints of his idle and indulgence-seeking whims, whilst she did up the buttons and belt of her beautifully renovated black leather coat.

'I saw a raven on my kitchen window sill this morning. It was an omen of meeting you, I fancy,' she proposed.

'Undoubtedly. It means fortune and good luck.'

'I thought it betokened beheading?'

He laughed doubtfully.

Whilst waiting beside a row of pegs in the now empty basement room for him to adjust his coat and scarf, she unexpectedly clutched his trousers where his short marrow hung down underneath his pot. He gasped. She advanced and pressed her pointed breasts against his breast.

His hands coiled round behind her and each one grabbed one of the tense hemispheres of her firm broad bottom, but her muscles contracted to India rubber hardness, so that his claspers could not pinch up a ripple to clutch, but slipped off.

'David ... do you ... do you want to be untrousered?' She had been sent to tempt and torture him.

'Do you need to ask?'

She felt no seed pod as she pushed her pelvis forward against his. 'Where is it?'

'It's exotic. It only flowers when the moment's ripe.'

'It doesn't exfoliate each winter?'

'No. It's a French bread stick when I want it to be.'

'I hope the baker didn't forget the yeast.'

'No. He didn't.'

'Then let's go.'

He ambled out, eagerly looking forward to a night of tempestuous frolicking with this deity-sired filly.

In the multi-storey car park, four yobbos were kicking a football about and bouncing it off cars. They easily out-stared Penman and might have harassed him had not Artemis's stronger eye fire-power cowed them and they slunk off.

'The police are never where they should be,' cursed the civil servant feebly, when locked safely inside his car.

'Why don't you go and beat them up?' She let the water out of him.

'That's not my way.'

'For you are happy to nourish violence or at least to obstruct those who fight it?'

'I *like* your sarcasm. It's the sign of a bad woman and I *like* bad women.' He pressed his shoulder against her glistening black arm.

'Good. I am a priestess of Chaos and Darkness and I only admit bad men.'

They nudged their way out into the evening traffic of the capital and the girl took in all her surroundings. The seats were semi-reclining bucket seats and the vehicle felt hard and aggressive and not at all suited to the weakly decadent Penman.

'What sort of car is this David?'

'A Porsche 911S,' he said as if it were nothing, but felt secretly flattered. 'Do you like it?'

'Very much. It doesn't suit you though.'

'Why not?' He seemed nettled for he was proud of his new bright red German sports car with its chromium window borders and black and polished steel wheels. Its smooth unbulbous unugly shape at that time was still quite lean and unusual – the opposite pole to the flashy American influences.

'There's a cottage at the far end of my father's estate and a man lives there with a few pigs and a few cherry trees and he drives the school bus and delivers the post in the village and plays in the kirk band. He looks a wee bit like a frog, but he's a contented man. One year he had a bumper crop of cherries and made some extra money and with it he bought this hideous silvery-green suit. "Och," he said, "sae fause." He knew he had made a mistake and tried to be what he was not.'

'He sounds like a tedious little peasant.'

'Quite the contrary,' she asserted firmly, 'it's you who's the boring and lost little nonentity.'

Penman took a deep breath. 'Denise, you're afflicted from what in modern parlance is called a "sense of humour breakdown" ... You think you're some crazy prophetess, but you're not. You're just vicious.'

'Well, if you want to screw me, you'll have to put up with it. Anyway, what do you suppose all the other high-class whores you pick up think? I'm sure it shows on their faces, even if they purse their lips.'

He swallowed. He could have pulled up and booted her out, but decided to bounce on her first and then return her nastiness. 'And if this Porsche represents such a foolish excrescence on my poor life, why are *you* interested in it?'

'Because it *would* suit me.'

He dimly realised that this might be true. The black facia and steering-wheel, carpet and mats and the blue and red tartan upholstered seats and door panels, as well as its shape and power, were suited to her extreme beauty and devilry.

In a back-street near Grosvenor Square, forced to reverse by a badly placed rubbish skip, he crashed into a concrete bollard. He did not even bother to climb out and look at the damage, nor kick up a stink with the hirer of the skip, but just lamely accepted it.

After being sworn at by a van driver, they turned into a bare ferro-concrete basement car park with a ramp and an automatic door. The Porsche's brakes squeaked and echoed in the exhaust-tinged air. Its occupants climbed out.

'I might buy a personalised number-plate.'

'Wait another two years and you could buy T-W-one-T.'

In the lift up to his Mayfair penthouse flat, she blew her nose on a white lace-edged hanky to prevent him from kissing her, but instead he fumbled with her underneath. 'What sign of the zodiac are you under?'

'Aries,' she said wearily, whilst he pushed her coat and skirt ineffectively up into her vulva. This was true. Her birthday was the sixth of April. Aries meant great ambitions and a wild temper, an able speaker and an independent mind. And this Ram, this study in darkness, now possessed a well-assessed contempt for Penman. Such a hatable being did not deserve to exist.

She hit his hands and pushed him away. He gave her a very twisted smile of resentment for this chastening and prepared to maul her all night in revenge, fiddle with her and insist she let him poke things in and out of all her various orifices.

Inside his flat he entered the number to cancel the alarm. She hung up her coat, moved through into the long main room, unlocked the sliding door and walked out onto the small roof terrace with its dimly visible plants set in wooden boxes. She leant on the concrete and wrought-iron railings and peered down into the hectic canyon below, where a shuffling board-game of white and red vehicle lights was in progress. An occasional toot or a shout echoed in this gorge of cool and garish night.

Penman materialised at her elbow and handed her a glass of Beaune, laced with a little brandy. He related tales of his successful share purchases – Anholt-Stern, S.L.S. and Kleve Auto – he had at least doubled his money on each of them in the last twelve months. She reluctantly permitted him a kiss of departure on her cheek, before he went inside to prepare a light supper for them.

She wiped the kiss off with a hanky and threw her drink out over the narrow street, recalling with pain her father's worsening hard-up state. The shares he bought, were always the wrong ones. Last summer he had sold his last lot – some Canadian nickel mine ones – at a quarter of the price he had paid, to clear some debts. Uanrig Estate surrounded the northern half of Loch Eilan and covered an area of just over five square miles, but with the exception of two tiny fields it was all pine trees, often on difficult terrain and with no proper access to the tracts North of the house. So only a modest amount of lumber could be felled and replanted from time to time and then there were just three cottages and a handful of fishing permits. Most Scottish estates had much more income from fishing and shooting, from livestock rearing, from buildings to let out to craft projects or small tourist enterprises or to rent as accommodation, but not their lonely Uanrig. The last of their other property – two houses in Bridge of Allan – had been sold a year ago and they were slowly but surely going under. Therefore her father had told her last summer, that she must take a job and provide herself with at least a small income whilst she awaited her chance in the film world. Artemis loved the seclusion of Loch Eilan though and had begun to plan not only the renovation of the house, but the reconstruction of the main track, a new forestry track, the clearing of some trees for a home farm, a pair of new cottages, fences and its general regeneration into a spruce and well-kept noblewoman's abode. It would be for her father and herself – the new Lady of Eilan – and the money would be supplied by such fat turncoats as

Penman, lumps of meritless eating breathing sleeping walking meat. She felt such disregard lately for the great worthless morass – barring a few exceptions – that to rob or murder such treacherous slobs seemed scarcely a wrong at all.

'Denise, my fair flower of the forest, the soup is ready.'

Yet was it right to kill this man? Were there no other ways to fight the political villainies of the age? Her friend Denise was at a teacher training college near Worcester run by a cohort of zealous Trotskyites. The students had to write 'reflective logs' on their teaching practice and cram them with profound sociological drivel. If you did not and were more straightforward, they failed you. So to pass you had to surrender your integrity and independence, which the wicked petty dictators relished. Denise had dubbed them 'despotic slime-balls' but as they painted everything in colours of 'doing good' and had allies on every committee, it was nigh impossible to oppose their regime.

Now though was not the moment for dreaming of being Lady Artemis, with her fine stone Scottish homestead, her expensive clothes and cars, her leather and her gold hidden in the old mines under the ridge.

She glided inside, locked the catch on the sliding door and walked over the polar bear rug in front of the marble-ringed gas-fire. She sat on one of the grey leather sofas and leaned forward over the soup bowl nearest her on the coffee-table.

'David, could I have some bread please?'

'But of course.' He put down his spoon after only one mouthful and disappeared off into the kitchen.

She had stolen some chloral hydrate from the hospital and taking it out of her handbag, she poured some from its brown glass bottle into his soup and stirred it gently in, it being miscible. The usual dose to induce sleep is a half or one gram. She added about ten grams.

Penman returned with a plate of bisected cob rolls, a dish of garlic butter and a knife.

As he sat down she placed her hands on either side of his head and kissed his crumpled nose, following it with a sweetly acidy smile which hid her unpleasant thoughts. Mr Letheren's habitual discipline and steady mores would ensure that he never slipped into senile dotage, laxness or silliness as this fool would do – if she did not intervene and kill him.

'So, my black and red shark, I hope you will soon cover me all over with kisses ... to atone for your churlishness in the lift when we came up.'

'I thresh a little, my little fisher. You have to wade ashore with me under your arm, but ... '

He broke off eating his soup and with his little fingers bent daintily backwards, massaged her breasts. 'I hope you're a girl who *needs* sex?'

'Aha!'

'There is so much more tumultuous fun in those, than in girls who just give it to oblige.'

'Sad to say ... but finish your soup first or we'll have an accident.' She kicked off her shoes and pulled her obscenely lethal legs up under her bottom.

He broke off again to tickle her tummy and blow softly into her hair and ear and to simply admire her pallid skin and beauteous eyes.

'Soup.' She stood up and moved round the room with a subtly sinister slowness of motion. The gas-fire's flames curled and flickered and a number of lamps on cabinets and bookcases glowed an orangy-yellow through their shades. She examined a hung plate with a dragoon on a grey charger on it and a copper etching of the bay and broken breakwater and Bradda Head from Port Erin. She passed a spherical white vase of spiky orange dried flowers and then tilted her head sideways to read the titles of various books, some of whose colourful spines were in tooled Spanish leather – split horse-hides dressed and tanned.

He stood up and ripped off his crested tie. He kicked off his shoes and advanced towards her. He endeavoured to speak to her in a caring tone, but when she ignored him, amazingly this paper tiger at last grew irritated at her persistent intransigence. 'What *is* the matter?'

'I'm Denise, that's what's the matter and I don't like rotten civil servants.' She waltzed off round the room. 'God, you're so racked by doubts.'

'Don't you *ever* wonder what is the right course of action?'

'No!' If others had perished in such games, the Spirit of the Mine would uphold her.

'Do you have no compassion, no sprinklings of affection?'

'No. I feel only indifference, complete indifference.'

'Denise!' He rushed at her, cornered her and tried to undo her skirt, clutching at her madly. 'I want you. I'm going to rape you ... ' She pulled him down onto the floor and they lay there together. 'I want the icing on my cake now.'

'I don't like icing, especially the liquid variety.'

'Your shallow heart and trivial pride ... '

'Am I going to melt like snow under your hot sun?' She laughed and held him round his middle.

'For heaven's sake girl! Let me get it out.'

'No no no no no no no! Not yet. I'll find it soon, if it's *big* enough to find,' she hissed into his ear.'

He could not work out the swings of her game. Was her mood just very volatile or was she acting? How could he tame her? He found himself unable to repress a yawn.

'Bedtime,' announced Artemis. 'I shall have a quick wash and then put on a pair of your pyjamas.'

She sprang up and went into the bathroom where she ran a tap and made splashing noises for a time. She reappeared and saw him still lying on the carpet and yawning again. She entered another door and sat on his bed after closing the wooden-slatted blind over the double-glazed window. The stuffed head of the tiger-skin rug smiled.

She picked up a magazine from half a dozen which lay on the bedside-table. It was headed *The Thespian* and whose bland pasty face should be on the cover but Innogen's? Was this paltry sop really going to become an actress, with her thoughtful brow, her small and undemonstrative movements and her knee-length white school socks? The article inside connected to this picture, barely mentioned Miss Letheren though, but discussed Robert Falcus's choice of Gottsched's *Christina of Bolsena* as opposed to the Oehlenschläger piece he had considered earlier. After a half-hour Artemis went out to the main room to view her prey.

By now Sir David lay in a snoring heap on the sagey green carpet. The chloral hydrate had lulled him into a semi-comatose state – as she knew it would from reading up the effects of overdosage in a pharmacopoeia. Her main worry had been the taste of the mixture, for in testing it earlier in different drinks, she had been able to detect its acerbic tang.

But could it be so easy?

She took her gloves from the pockets of her coat, hung up in the entrance lobby and slid the two solid bolts on the main door. From her handbag she pulled out a coiled bicycle brake-cable. She unwound this and fed it gently under his fat walrus neck. Then looping the ends round her gloved hands, she pulled with a steady but considerable strength. He moved slightly and made gargling noises, but offered no real resistance. His face grew a dusky dark violet and swelled up and his neck bled a little where the wire abraded the creased old skin. It came to her that an injection of insulin under the tongue – a site which might not even be noticed at autopsy – might have been neater.

Artemis took a tea-towel from the narrow but magnificently fitted kitchen, moistened one end of it and adding some drops of detergent, firmly wiped everything she could recall having touched with her fingers. Then still feeling hungry, she ate a bowl of tinned cherries with some single cream and drank some water.

His wallet contained £330 in notes which alone represented four months' salary for a student nurse. She ripped up the photograph Letheren had given her of Penman, switched on the waste-disposal unit and swilled the finely-torn fragments down the sink into it.

The main room had five doors off one of its long sides, interspersed with pastel water-colour paintings. They led to the bedroom, the entrance hall, a store-room, a bathroom and the kitchen.

In the rear part of the spacious sitting-room were solid walnut bookcases and a polished desk with a table-lamp on it with a modern conical orange shade.

Unlocking the top desk drawer with one of his keys, she found another £800 in cash. This was what it was all about. A miniature ten-drawered cherry and sandalwood coin cabinet stood on one of the bookshelves. She unlocked this too. There were around four hundred gold coins and two hundred silver or bronze ones, but as well as the Venetian and Mantuan double ducats, the English angels and the francs d'or from Flanders –

all so difficult to dispose of because of their rarity – there were a good number of commoner eighteenth and nineteenth-century pieces, sold readily in moderate quantities without exciting suspicion. In order to keep all the descriptive cardboard discs, she put the whole diminutive chest of velvet-lined drawers into a soft red leather holdall from the store-room.

Next she glanced at Penman's rows of historical, numismatic and literary books. They were mostly hardbacks and well cared for – *Coins of Cnidus*, *The Sheep on the Wall*, *Babylonic Scripts from Uruk* – and some French books too – *Guillaume le conquérant*, and *Le rouge et le noir* and *Le chien des Baskerville*. Then her vertically-tilted eyes spotted *The Siege of Corinth* by L. Gottsched which she took to read later. On the sofa she flicked through a picture atlas of Greek mythology pausing to read a note on Athena. Athena had no mother. She was the daughter of Zeus alone – sprung from his brain – and so was pure unadulterated Zeus. Artemis wondered if similarly she was pure unadulterated Letheren, sprung from his thought?

She stared at the flabby and unlovable head of the sacrificed Penman and with a fervour for the seer who had sent her, reviled his greying mask. 'You hated Archibald Letheren and his salty old-fashioned truths didn't you, as all liars and hoaxers hate honest men? You sold weed-killer as medicine, exacerbating society's ailments under the guise of curing them. You wished to multiply the bad and harass the good. You were eristic in dispute, wanting victory not truth. You were a lackey to those who would delight in our country being humiliated and defeated militarily, because of their perverse desire to denigrate whatever is decent. And in particular you rigged up the Mephistophelean ruin of Sir Hildreth Buckley, who refused to bow to your ignoble and traitorous demands and tried to untangle your horrible web.'

She knelt down and prodded the cooling nose and cheeks gently with the butter knife. His brow and eyelids bore a rash she noticed of tiny reddish-purple spots or petechiae. These owed their presence to his being strangled. They were a sign known as 'Tardieu spots' after the French police surgeon who first described them.

'Then you laid evidence to frame him and at the same time arranged articles in the press praising and exaggerating his excellent character, in devilish readiness to enhance the later "shocking exposé". Then the axe fell. As "loyal servants" you were all "stunned" at his "duplicity". You "reappraised" his contributions in this "new light". M.I.5 investigated him and the Fur-Hats in their embassy rubbed their hands with satisfaction and tossed back a few celebratory hunting vodkas.' Her thoughts were a transposition from Letheren's mind. The quiet fury was Artemis's alone. The knife tested the squashy dead eyes. 'So the stalwart's demise was well arranged, you had your O.B.E. ... and nobody cared. It was your hour. But the avenging furies do remember and through one man and his insuperable hidden assassin, the wheel has turned.'

An increasing agitation welled up inside her. She made some cocoa and only with an effort desisted from smashing up the kitchen.

There was a French Bible too on the shelves – in red soft cordovan goatskin leather she remembered – and fetching it she opened it at random and read aloud, standing on the rug as if treading the boards. '"Wisdom says, guard yourself against the woman who entices so compellingly. Ah, look out of the window – there goes a stupid boy, to the corner where she stands as the twilight fades and the night comes on. In her whore's clothes and with her sly plans, restless and unbridled, she kisses him and says in her insolent swagger, 'I have been to the temple today and made good offerings. But so it is good I have found you. I have laid bright Egyptian coverings on my bed and sprinkled them with aloe juice and perfumes. Come, let us enjoy love's tumbles, bask in love's whirlwinds until dawn.' Her allure conquers him. Her silky lips lead him like an ox to the slaughter. He does not understand that it is about life and death. The way to her house goes to death. Remember this, my son."'

It seemed an admirable description of this evening and it pleased her to think that she was an irresistible trap for these faceless amoral upper-crust parasites.

She dragged the corpse by its bloated ankles into the store-room and dumped it amid umbrellas, flower pots, tinned food and cases of wine. 'There we are David, banished to eternal oblivion, because you lost the only battle which really matters – love and hate – they are the greatest powers and you could manage neither.' She shook her head. The grey anonymity of collectivism – a hiding place for those spivs who fear to be judged alone – tiny souls in a tiny civilisation.

Artemis felt an odd sensation of every detail and quirk and nuance of life seeming almost excessively real. Everything had its place and fitted as it was bound to do. Everything was strong and significant if you were living life as you were supposed to be living it. It felt both exquisitely frail and overflowingly thrilling to be doing this – the ephemeral delights of a butterfly having broken out of its sleeping chrysalis. Yet these alive and untouchable and goddess-like sentiments seemed to bring with them the danger of unrestrained recklessness. True these came most easily and delightfully to her when dressed up in her impenetrably tough black leather suit. When in it, it seemed she could rise above all the constraints and penalties of mundane mortal flesh. Yet even now ... she felt irrationally maddened and savage and wanton. It occurred to her that had she been on this errand solely on her own account, she would have mutilated Penman terribly and swept everything crashing onto the floor, but under Letheren's augury and perhaps because of her likelihood of success without a final come-upance, she fought to remain stable and balanced and resisted the compelling urges to wayward excess. Even she wished to show an exactitude and precision in her new work.

And so, governing her surges of intolerance and actually savouring the avoidance of anything gratuitous, she went to the toilet in the bathroom with its Greek bordered tiles and its shelf of womanly perfumed soaps and salts and ointments and performed other tidying up acts with decorum and accuracy and scrupulousness. This was quite an achievement, for soulless criminals generally – such as the Baader-Meinhof species say – have to wreck everything in sight and smear their bodily fluids over the scene whilst they spit out epithets which reflect their political persuasions.

The entrance-chimes rang. A swiftly sobered Artemis placed her handbag and the heavy holdall near to the main door ready to leave. She put her coat on and did up its buttons and belt methodically. She glanced through the peep-hole just as a key grated in the lock. Heavens! She ducked down in case the lens worked both ways. A frustrated fist banged ineffectively on the solid door. Who might Penman have given a key to? Baffled footsteps receded.

Artemis turned off the lights and the fire, checked the peep-hole's arc of vision carefully and when satisfied that the coast was clear, drew back the bolts and left, quickly pulling the door shut behind her. As she moved past two sad-looking potted palms, the lift bell pinged. She nipped through a door into the stair-well and peered back furtively through its round port-hole window.

Elaine Amos, a statistician at the Bank of England and Penman's daughter, had returned from Belgium two days earlier than planned. She had a pseudo-precision about her, a lank figure with an indecisive air, dark hair held back in a pony-tail and a clever but spiritless face. She had tiny floppy breasts, like trouser pockets turned inside out and was the sadist playgirl to one of her father's chiefs – rubber belts, trussing him up, tickling him with feathers, flailing him with chains ... Thinking she must have made some silly mistake, she depressed the bell again. Again she tried her key ... and surprisingly this time the door opened.

Artemis had walked out of the tinted glass portico and about fifty yards along North Audley Street, when she heard an horrendous screaming erupt from up above. The capital's traffic had slackened to a mere torrent by now – approaching midnight – so she skipped diagonally across the road and into an expensive bar with green awnings over its ground-floor windows and there amid its plush copper and bleached oak decor, she strolled across the Brinton carpet, ordered a mocha coffee and sat down by the neo-Georgian windows, looking back in the direction from which she had come.

The altering patterns of lights generated by the cars and buildings in the dark night was commonplace, but the discordant klaxons stirred something in her mind. Then the pulsing blue lights arrived and they awoke a deeper pleasure inside her lower body. The delight was much accentuated by the element of secrecy. She had caused all this and no one would find out. Only Miss Boden and her Prospero knew.

This time her orgasm began slowly, hovering uncertainly with latent ecstasy on the brink for some minutes as if pleasantly teasing her. Slowly and poignantly it started, deep and long-lasting, finer and more relaxed than before, stronger and gentler and stronger still, each contraction starting so reluctantly but ending in violent crescendos. She made the effort to sit still and look unruffled. This warm rhythmical delight – tingling and radiant – seemed to spread all over her, giving her a raging sense of well-being. She had never known anything like it. Luckily it was near to closing time and no one sat nearby or studied her.

She paid the waiter and went out into the damp cold night. She crossed back over and passed the flats in her leather coat and gloves and shoes, carrying her black handbag and the red holdall. The blue lights of an ambulance and two police cars sustained her internal waves but at a reduced level of intensity. Harsh crackles of radio transmission burst out of a policewoman's radio. Artemis was not ant-police like the infernal Rose and his breed – quite the contrary – but it was just sad that so often they were straight-jacketed by misguided laws into defending traitors gays and other assorted and corrupted vermin.

Her private ecstasies made her dizzy. She walked out into Park Lane and then along this the short distance to the underground twenty-four hour car park, where her ancient Alvis waited.

The pattern was familiar. An all night drive with a stop on the motorway, a few hours sleep and then her casualty duty starting at lunch-time. But she was making money and gaining a sexual independence from men. And yet she wished she could have been dressed wholly in leather. She felt wet below, from vaginal or sex gland secretions. From here onwards, it would happen only and always in her black leather – of that she was sure.

## CHAPTER NINE.

The peripheral streets of Hanover were covered in a layer of compacted snow. Ulrich had to steer his heavy motorbike carefully and with his feet down, sliding them along the ground.

On the dismal stairway outside Eichenfelsstrasse 11A, he registered mild surprise when his key only rotated once in the lock and not twice. The lavish ransacking inside scared him. Were anti-terrorist or anti-drug KRIPO officers lurking in ambush?

The snapped stay-pin of the bedroom roof-light and the inexpert clumsiness of the search allowed him to relax a little, but he improvised a string of obscene sophisms when he saw that the hiding place under the sink had been exposed and the vital bank papers stolen. He had neither duplicates not proof that he was Uwe Bauss – especially since he was not. The cheque books and letters had been the evidence. The bulk of his savings were in that account too, unlike Ute who had spent hers or Ingrid who kept hers salted away probably in Italy. Could the girls be guilty of perfidy, singly or together?

Peering out onto the roof he espied the ladder, the soaking scarf and the tools in the rain-water trough and these seemed to confirm the genuineness of the break-in. But who? He hurled the coffee-table across the sitting-room with such force that it knocked a hole in a plywood partition. His initial response, the restraining of a half-bucketful of diarrhoea from running down his leg, was replaced by anger. Who had dared to steal his fortune? Double fuck and raping apes!!!

He took a shower, slipped over and in a rage smashed the plastic door.

He made coffee and cogitated.

Ulrich had never been cut out for the pharmaceutical industry. Such men had thick-lensed glasses and rounded shoulders, they studied the details of their pension policies and checked their car tyre pressures every Saturday morning.

A year ago to the day, at the Christmas party at Heugel Pharmazeutik's Munich laboratories, he and pharmacology had parted company.

In that sterile glass and dark brick palace, in the imposing high foyer where the tall plastic Christmas tree with its white candle-shaped lights had stood, he had rashly tried to seduce Frau Doktorin Professor Elisabeth Sommerlath. Wine had loosened his tongue. He had begun to wink at her, brush against her and breathe kirsch fumes over her. She was thirty, blonde, pretty, very German and immaculately presented, but very self-disciplined and clever too. The Director of the Research Division, a talented musician and the authoress of books on the art of the minnesingers, she had asked him, 'What is your opinion of the Niebuhr regulations on testing compounds for teratogenicity?' He had replied that there were two salient points. Firstly it was imperative to abide by them for legal reasons and secondly they were a useless waste of time. She had led him through a darkened laboratory, where he had imagined they would partake of some slurred extra-seasonal merriment underneath a retort bench, but no. She delivered a corrective lecture to him on his poor and shoddy work. He had recklessly tried to embrace her, been beckoned further to a glass-panelled office where the fluorescent lights had been turned on and here she had sacked him. Behind her desk, for once without her spotless white coat on but a prim blouse with a high ruff and an expensive and well-cut skirt, she had folded her hands beautifully together on the unstained blotter and formally curtailed his appointment there from that instant.

As he had gathered up his belongings up in the empty and darkened fourth-floor offices, his prospects had seemed to consist of three months' severance money, bad references and no chemical serendipity with which to brighten or lubricate his future. Then there had flashed through his mind a discussion he had heard about a discarded trial substance which had inadvertently turned out to be highly hallucinogenic. Forgetting for a while his detestation of his pernickety goose-stepping over-thorough and abstract-minded colleagues, he had started searching through a row of filing cabinets. The three groupings of folders had corresponded to the company's three areas of interest – pink codices were for antibiotics, blue codices for hypnotics and black codices for diuretics. He had eventually located and stolen the required file – Codex Blue EF31A.

He had been living in a hospital flat then with Ute, who was working as a nurse at the Sankt Johann Klinik. They had sat up all one night, assembling the glassware and the steel pressure vessel, adjusting temperatures, measuring out reagents and purifying and testing the resultant liquid. With this first batch of their new drug, they had journeyed to Amsterdam to sell incognito, this sample lot as L.S.D. Its effects, though discernibly different from L.S.D., were apparently both vivid and euphoric. Then Ingrid had sprung onto the scene with better underworld contacts and thus the possibility of higher prices and a wider market. It had so come about that after his rift with Heugel Pharmazeutik, he had found his true métier in crime. The misfit had become the freebooter.

Reverting to the upset present, he felt deeply worried about what might have been found here. Could the addresses of their three separate homes have been compromised? He must act quickly against those he felt convinced were behind this intimidating burglary.

Ulrich redressed in his well-worn blue leather motorcycle suit, with its taloned eagle badge on the left upper-arm. The mirror reflected his tall broad-shouldered muscular physique with its short fair hair and its appeal to prowess-seeking females. At twenty-seven he had both the ripened allure of youth and enough knowledge of life to have worked out what was going on where women were involved. He wore plenty of woollies and underwear underneath his blue leather swaddling and in his boots and tight-cuffed gauntlets and helmet, he prepared to set off.

The Autobahnen would be free of ice and despite the haze of vaporised slush thrown up by the lorries, he reckoned he could reach Amsterdam by about nine that evening. He chewed some stale rolls with jam and bits of cheese with the mould cut off and swallowed two more cups of strong percolated coffee.

He departed to engage Werner Hüttner's Dutch drug ring, which seemed rationally to be the only likely culprit to have inflicted this disruption. He had once met up with Hüttner's daughter and afterwards found his first plastic charge card to be missing from his wallet. Anyway, he had no intention of giving anyone the benefit of any doubts.

The scent of action brought him alive. His German soul itched for the contest. Tonight would see the encounter of a fearless German Adonis with a collection of Dutch water rats and morbid queers. Off he roared like a tornado – a Hercules versus the tuberculese.

* * *

They ascended the stone steps of Hanover Opera House's broad base. The box-office had two returned tickets for the back row of the dress circle. A doorman dressed like a Prussian general opened a glass door for them and they climbed the red-carpeted stairs, edged with the autographed photographs of famous soprani and conductors who had performed there.

Ute and Ingrid leant on the brass rail behind the back row and gazed out over the sea of blue velvet seats, to the blue and gold fluted proscenium pillars and the stage curtain with its scene of the Greek Muses dancing.

Men in evening dress stood in small clusters discussing music or local politics, whilst their womenfolk with their elaborate hair-styles, fur jackets and rows of pearls, gossiped together.

Ute enjoyed the presence of others, even if not directly participating. Watching their expressions and mannerisms made her feel less lonely and more human. One man she could see had an elastic face which covered a whole spectrum of emotions in phase with the dialogue of his circle.

'I think we should quit this drug business,' remarked Ingrid. 'Dangerous subterfuges are developing in Amsterdam and there's also a risk that my bosses in Normannenstrasse might soon have some feedback about my movements there.'

Ute concurred. 'I've a sixth sense that something's not right with these arms shipments as well. When this fifth one's been delivered, I suggest we pack up that too and retire.'

'We might even sell our knowledge of al-Uzza's maze to the C.I.A. as a last act?'

'The difficulty is that Ulrich wants more.'

'It's two against one. We just have to talk to him. But I have enough. There's no point in carrying on and ending up with a stomach full of lead. I bought a cottage last month in a valley in northern Portugal. It's a bit remote, but perhaps wise for a couple of years. Don't tell Ulrich please.'

'I won't Ingrid.'

The girls were right. Each of the trio had about two million Deutschmarks. It made sense to wind up their modus operandi and cover their tracks.

The orchestra was tuning up. The girls took their seats and opened a box of dark chocolates. Between the three of them, they had made eighty trips to Amsterdam Copenhagen and Hamburg. The lights dimmed. A hush spread over the audience. The high notes of the first violins and a flute opened the overture.

* * *

In Amsterdam's red light district, in the old part of the city, was a club called 'L'Ovale Bleu'. It had originally been a lair for male 'gays' and been known as 'The Pink Triangle Club', but the police had so enjoyed doing it over at regular intervals that the owner, Herr Vermeulen, decided to turn to the less trouble-generating female homosexuals.

Ulrich parked and locked his helmet in the bike's top-box, in the chilly night air beside the narrow dead-end canal spur in the Oude Zijds Achterburg Wal. All sorts of flotsam floated in the slimy water and many garish neon lights and signs were reflected in it. He strolled past some of the sixteenth-century pinched houses and descended a flight of steps to the cellar entrance of the club with its illumined blue oval sign and title.

The girl on the door, Anne, in a denim pinafore dress with dungaree-like metal fasteners for the shoulder straps, a red tee-shirt under it and red tights, explained in German, that men were only admitted in female attire. 'I have a special appointment to meet Herr Vermeulen here,' he explained. Anne shrugged and let him pass in his wet blue leather suit, rather like a North Sea diver or Superman without his scarlet cape.

This grotto contained a bar, alcoves, side-sofas and coffee-tables and a sparse clientele. Whereas male homos. usually emanate a seedy flamboyance to try to demonstrate that their tawdry lives really are colourful and satisfying, the women equivalents are generally very quiet and apathetic. They eat pumpkin seeds, are against nuclear war and wear smiles which say, 'It isn't our fault we're so nice.' Two women were kissing, Dutch girls with intelligence and good education, but so lacking in self-esteem spirit and sense of adventure that perversity had intervened and shipwrecked the promise of their earlier years.

A notice-board in the passage which led to the toilets hung festooned with cryptic invitations, pamphlets about the rights of lesbians and advertisements for equipment and steroid preparations. A door located here led into the kitchen and a store-room. Ulrich slipped through this. He nipped past an opening behind the bar, unseen by the two serving girls and crept up the very steep and winding stairs. Ingrid had once explained that if you went up these to the very top, you came to an attic office. The door to this attic was shut. He entered. No one was there, though he had hoped to find Vermeulen. He tugged at a trap-door in the ceiling and an aluminium ladder unfolded. He trod cautiously up into a small roof-space, where on all fours you could crawl along a catwalk of planks, over two houses which had no access to this cramped triangular apex, to arrive at a fourth, where again you could climb down. Ingrid had said that the K.G.B. occasionally paid Vermeulen and his estranged wife, who owned the other house, to use this ingenious facility for surreptitious meetings with high-ranking informers. The second house was a brothel.

He closed the first trap-door behind him. The catch clicked to. Without a torch he fumbled forwards, clouting his head on a low cross-beam at one point, which he had to squirm snake-like beneath. He did not so much find the second trap-door as fall through it. With a splintering and ripping sound and a cloud of plaster dust, he ended up on top of a couple in one of Katrijn Vermeulen-Polder's brothel beds.

The whore scrambled free and in only a grubby brassière pouted indignantly at this intrusion. The English computer programmer struggled on the listing collapsed bed with a sore shoulder. 'By George,' he growled across the fusty room at Ulrich, who was brushing fragments of lath from his hair, 'You've got a cheek, bursting in here like this.'

'I am sorree,' said Ulrich. 'Is zat vy you were getting so very verked up?' He laughed humourlessly at his crude joke.

The Dutch tart glowered. 'Just what the hell are you doing?'

'Bloody Krauts, barging in everywhere,' added the fellow who given himself the pseudonym Piers Haws.

Ulrich threatened him with two fingers. 'Be qviet or I kick you to hell.' The Englishman shrank back and Ulrich grinned unpleasantly.

The whore – now with a loose robe on – gave a derisory vulgar rectangular-mouthed cackle and picked up a long leather whip.

The visitor seized it and snapped it in two before bowing out under the low lintel and closing the skewed little door behind him. He moved warily down the narrow crumbling stairs, which were extraordinarily gloomy and smelt of cat urine. At the bottom, to the accompaniment of creaking beds, he opened the door of the old parlour.

Here he found Vrouw Vermeulen-Polder, scratching her pussy which sat there stuporosed like a hedgehog. The room had peeling brown and cream paint and a sickly yellow light bulb hanging unadorned at its centre, whilst a red one glowed on the other side of the curtains. The woman's eyes were slittish and her face tinged puce – her mother had been Javanese. She actually lived in a nice three-storey house in Stadionweg, but this was her place of work. She showed surprise at Ulrich's presence, but assuming she had perhaps left the outer door unlocked and that he had just walked in, put on the greasy understanding smile of her type.

He imitated her queasy smile by way of reply, turned the key in the lock, partly unzipped the front of his suit and inserted a hand into an inside pocket. 'I have something for you, Frau Vermeulen-Polder.'

Her smile grew puzzled, wary, alarmed.

The dagger was long and sharply pointed and Ulrich's steely look seemed avidly earnest. The dagger had arabesque scroll-work on the hilt.

'Scream and you're dead, you yellow sow.' His terrible face and his savage simian grip of the knife almost petrified her. She terminated a deep gasp as the dagger's tip pressed against her breast and his left hand seized a hank of her greying hair. 'This will go between your ribs and cut open a lung or pierce your heart if you lie to me,' he growled with conviction, for he meant it – indeed he intended to kill her anyway.

'Wer sind Sie?' Her German was competent enough, even under stress.

'I am an associate of the dark-haired lass who supplies your husband with a certain hallucinogenic drug.'

'I don't have anything to do with that side of matters. Truly I don't. Has he swindled you? I know where he is. Please, please don't kill me. I will help you. He has swindled me too.'

'I want to know where Werner Hüttner lives.'

'My God, I don't know. No one knows that ... but my husband would know how to contact him.'

'Where is he?'

'In "The Bare Facts", across the canal – almost opposite.'

The dagger entered her bosom with a swift forceful thrust. It squelched initially and then advanced with a gritty feel, as though in hard clay. Air bubbles spattered the oozing blood for a short distance. She attempted no self-defence or scream, but with something akin to Eastern fatalism in her dark eyes, she sank onto her knees. He released her hair and she fell forwards, convulsed twice like a dying and badly manipulated marionette and then lay still, whilst her thick blood seeped out onto the threadbare carpet.

In her handbag he found about eight thousand guilders – the night's takings so far – which he pocketed. He washed his face and hands briefly in a cracked corner basin as well as the dagger and then used the towel to quickly wipe over his dirt-spattered suit and boots. Animal-like, he gobbled up a wedge of dry fig cake and swilled down some milk from a carton. He moved the key to the other side of the parlour door and locked it behind him, taking the key to throw into the canal. He slammed the main door behind him too, with its two pink boobs painted on it and as he strode away, he saw a prospective client approaching that same knocking-shop door to rap hopefully on the knocker.

* * *

*King Ynyr* was about a minor dark-age British monarch. A decent effort had even been made with the scenery, which was a change from the current vogue of a few science fiction silvery trapezoids and although musically it fell short of being a work of genius, it did avoid any cloying or stereotyped constructions. It contained too the essential requirement for any masterpiece of art, namely it drew its dramatic strength from a contest of good and evil.

With the entrance of Princess Uxflæd, a Saxon noblewoman, the piece took on an air of sublimity. The flaxen-haired soft-voiced contralto imparted to it a demure serenity and a fairy-tale-like grace, as she stood there in her white dress pinched at the waist by a blue band with a silver snood. Her timbre of benign intercession and the mellow tones of a kindly spirit affected Ute.

Ingrid's arm and hand rested on the arm-rest between them. Ute put her own hand on top of Ingrid's. Ingrid rotated her hand and they gently intertwined their fingers for a few minutes, before Ingrid disengaged. They were dissimilar twins, but having been brought up separately, it was not easy to feel a wholly sisterly relationship.

Their father, Gottlob Lenz, had been killed in Italy before their birth in 1944 and their mother, Viktoria Reh, had died in Berlin when the girls were both one, crushed by a Tiger tank they were told, though it had probably been a Red Army T34.

In the chaos of defeat they had become split. One, Heinrichina Lenz, had been adopted by a Lutheran pastor's family on the North German Plain, the old-fashioned 'Heinrichina' abbreviated to 'Heike', and 'Ute' added in front of it and her surname changed to that of her adopters. The other, Sieglinde Lenz, ended up in an orphanage in East Germany. The name 'Sieglinde' with its unacceptable Nazi and Wagnerian overtones, had been altered to 'Stephanie'.

The Priestess of Eostre was on stage, an Angle whom King Ynyr had made a bargain with to enable him to capture and wed Uxflæd. She wore a black dress and declaimed in her piercing soprano voice, whilst three Celtic goblins in glossy black tutus and camisoles and tights danced with fleshy sly lasciviousness as they slew a pen and her cygnets as a sacrifice. The man beside Ute, adjusted his binoculars and muttered to himself about the Priestess's underwear, visible through her belted black dress of knee-length diaphanous netting.

Stephanie Lenz had spent her childhood in the orphanage in Griez in Thuringia, a white summer palace in the Early Classicist style, used also partly as a museum. The children had lived in the former servants' rooms on the second floor, taken lessons in the library and the orangery and eaten in the banqueting hall. They had played in the English pleasure gardens and gone down to the River Estler to learn to swim. In her teens Stephanie had started to solve the riddles imposed by communist rule. It became clear that everyone knew that everything bright and inspiring came out of individual effort and not out of the decrees of petty committees, even though no one said so. With that silent sagacity, born of a lonely and unaffectionate childhood, she had calculated judiciously that some time devoted to sports meetings and sitting on the front rows at rallies, might lead to a few privileges. In fact in her younger days, she had had some sympathy for the Marxist ideals. The East German middle-level communist leaders were sincere if of limited vision and indeed Germany was the one country where with its philosophical straight and dutiful people and rooted in those historic German qualities, socialism might just have had a chance of succeeding. But gradually a more selfish and mercenary instinct replaced her youthful altruism. She worked hard to pass her end-of-school examinations and managed to join the police force in Magdeburg. Two years went by and then one night in plain clothes, acting as an *agent provocateur* in a district of the city known for its prostitutes, a Catholic priest had approached her and asked for the customary favours. Before magistrates he had claimed to be going to preach the gospel to these poor degraded women, but laughter had drowned him out. With the Catholic church as a prime enemy, there had been great satisfaction in Party circles about this case and it received extensive publicity. Stephanie became a temporary celebrity and was introduced to local chairmen and jubilant ideologists in the communist camp, but above all this, they gave her the critical promotion to officer rank within the Volkspolizei. With that had come the freedom to travel around the beautiful German countryside, with red roofs dotted amongst the trees and the warm dry balmy sun of summer. She had had the money too for a glass of wine or a coffee wherever she went and the authority to obtain, for example, good seats at the open air playhouse at Schloss Stolpen near Dresden. At about this time too, she had begun to learn that over the fence in West Germany, folk possessed powerful Mercedes convertibles, splendid yachts and luxurious clothes and that they took intoxicating holidays all over the world and pursued any number of studies and hobbies. She was twenty-four when she first had sex and swiftly found out how enticing it was. She used her tall sensual figure to inveigle herself into her chief's favours. She let him into her knickers, she played her cards with rare skill – and duly he arranged her transfer to the V.f.K. – East German Military Intelligence.

Her plans were set, to be sent to the West, to accrue money there and then to desert. She had come to the West by 'escaping' across the border strapped underneath a passenger train – the sniffer dogs were held back from her at the crossing point – and so she was granted bona fide citizenship of the Federal Republic under the name of Ingrid Axt and a passport. She had taken a secretarial job for a while and then moved to Rome. She was therefore a so-called 'illegal' agent, that is one who mixes with the populace and has no official posting, as opposed to a 'legal' agent who works out of an embassy or trade delegation in some nominal capacity. Having long since established who she really was, once in West Germany, it was not hard to trace her sister to the Sankt Johann Klinik in Munich.

* * *

A saxophonist parped his way up and down a broken chromatic scale and the guitarist thrummed with a mechanical coolness. Girls in green dresses behind the bar poured pink drinks into wine glasses and Vermeulen sat at a table with his new blood-sucking girlfriend. He made occasional philosophical witticisms which she tried to pretend that she found funny, though really she did not even understand them.

Standing behind Vermeulen and gorging a cheese roll, Ulrich pulled agonised faces to the girl at the old sugar-daddy's attempts to be humorous. Ulrich had great confidence in his he-man's physique and its ability to turn many a young female heart to jelly and he believed that men had much larger hands of cards to play than women. Only too late in the day do such males realise their delusion. As the girl ignored him so pointedly, he took it as a sign of success. It meant she was annoyed with herself for fancying him. She uncrossed and recrossed her legs stiffly, blinked the lilac shutters of her eyelids and stared firmly in another direct ion. Ulrich laughed.

Two motorcyclists pushed their way to the bar, parting the jaded crowd. 'We want two coffees!' said one of them aggressively.

'Well you're not getting them here,' the barman said out of the side of his mouth, whilst he cut a sandwich.

'Look mate, we're thirsty.'

'There's a canal out there.'

'If we don't get these coffees inside one minute, I'm coming round there and making them myself.'

The barman raised minimally his huge meat knife. 'Come on then. Come and fetch this coffee.'

The youths kicked at the bar with their heavy boots. 'We're going to wait for you tonight mush. We'll be outside when you leave.'

'All right, but I'll have this cleaver with me.'

The displeasing yobbos left scowling.

Vermeulen's girl went out to the toilets, waggling her mini-skirted hips and disease-suggesting legs. Ulrich followed and in a dingy back corridor, grabbed her in a breath-crushing delirium-inducing embrace. He led her out into a tiny yard, where behind a pile of tottering crates, he reckoned he had time to rake her before Vermeulen came searching.

The music and the drone of voices seemed very distant and in the curtain-filtered glow from an upstairs window, the piece of concrete they stood upon gleamed white. He pushed his hands up under her mini-mini-skirt and jerked her dirty panties down. She drew down his long zip and inserted her slim hand to extract his elongated prickly cactus. By standing on a couple of loose bricks to elevate herself and with his long muscular leather-covered arms clasping her tightly – one round her slender waist and the other under her bottom – they began. She lifted her legs and locked them round the back of his thighs.

She gasped and tried to free herself as her eyes caught sight of two suede shoes behind Ulrich's boots, for though she frequently let these coarse passions swamp her, some vestige of modesty made her want to keep it secret. In the company of a choice male she would succumb to unreserved frenzy and any low perversity, yet to society in general she wished to appear free of lust. As Ulrich resolved to turn the contents of her pelvis to a pulverised pulp, like a good electric food-mixer, she tried to evince signs of dislike and non-participation and finally to resist.

'Keep still wench,' growled Ulrich, adjusting an unsatisfactory position. He pinned her more firmly against the crates.

'They're wet and filthy. Let me go!' She tugged and fought with futility. 'This is rape.'

Vermeulen announced himself. 'Ingeborg, I do believe you're enjoying it.'

Ulrich crossed the brink just as Vermeulen spoke and ruined it for him. He packed away his howitzer and some of its gooey mess inside his leather suit and dismissed the girl, who tried to make tears of stolen ecstasy sound like sobs of molested innocence.

'Good evening, Herr Vermeulen. It is really you I wished to see.'

'Indeed?'

'Yes. I'm a partner of the tall girl who delivers the boxes of "Aurum" to you.' 'Aurum' was one of the street names for their drug.

'I see.'

'Well I hope you do see, because I *need* to meet Herr Hüttner tonight.'

Detecting Ulrich's urgency and hostility, Vermeulen decided it was wise to be civil. 'How do I know who you are?'

'I'm speaking German am I not? I can describe our courier minutely and I know about the sugar lumps.'

'That proves nothing.'

Unable to stop it, Vermeulen saw him rapidly unsheathe the dagger from inside his open leather suit and press the point against his fat belly.

'I can send a message for you to Hüttner, but I don't know where he lives – really I don't.'

Ulrich had convinced himself that Hüttner knew too much. Not only did he buy a portion of their drug output, but they had contacted him too about using his sawmill in Turkey. He knew quite a few of their details and had a hold over them which he was misusing and Ulrich had determined to pin him down and obliterate him. 'Who *does*?'

The point pressed steadily harder against the Dutch abdomen. It broke Vermeulen's skin. 'Ow!' He could not think up a lie in his fright, so he had to tell the truth. 'A girl called Janneke van de Est knows. Take the main road up to Den Helder and about three or four kilometres before Den Helder is a hamlet called De Kooi. Three hundred metres before it and just before the major junction where the road to Sneek and Leeuwarden turns off, is a grassy track on the right which leads to the Noord Hollandsch Kanaal and Juffrouw van de Est lives there in the old sluice-gate-keeper's cottage. For God's sake, move your blasted knife away!'

In desperation, he shoved Ulrich's dagger wildly to one side, even though it cut his shirt and scored his skin superficially. He head-butted the taller and stronger man ineffectively and set off an avalanche of unstable beer crates down onto them both.

Ulrich battled his way through the tumbling boxes and catching sight of Vermeulen's cringing timorous back, lunged his long dagger deeply into it a few centimetres to the side of the spine and below the ribs yet above the pelvis, the spot where it might hit the right-hand kidney and its major vessels. The brief squeal and gasp from the loser, were followed by a hellish laugh from the victor. Ulrich zipped up his front, took Vermeulen's diary from his jacket's inside pocket and strode off back through 'The Bare Facts' and around the terminus of the canal on the slippery cobbles to his machine.

In this murky cavernous world of vice, no crime, no scream, no murder is of interest unless it actually involves your own body or your own money. As a rule no one called the police and the police were happy not to be called. But when Vrouw Vermeulen-Polder's girls had not been able to rouse her or open the door, they had smelt something fishy, forced the door and found her dead body, yellow and purple in a dingy blood-stained heap, like a discarded pile of soiled blankets. They registered very little in the way of shock, but it was a bit inconvenient that they would have to find a new employer and that that night's earnings had been curtailed – they had gone through her handbag and drawers to no avail. With weary resignation, they had concluded that they had no choice but to summon the detested police.

It was foggy and drizzling as a van and a car drew up and seven officers climbed leisurely out, despite the flashing blue lights. They studiedly paid no heed to the twisted glares of hatred and the odd insanely screamed obscenity, but whilst they were still knocking on the brothel door, a Caribbean ape hurled itself at one of their number. Inadvertently he hit his head on a cast-iron post and slumped unconsciously to the ground, as the attacked officer stepped adroitly to one side. His associates started to accuse the police of brutality.

'If he dies, we'll sue you for a million florins!' someone snarled, his rosy muzzle twisted in caustic contempt.

Behind this commotion, Ulrich was busily pulling on his helmet and leather mittens and pushing his bike off its stand in as low profile a manner as possible.

Amongst the whores at the door, some of them with droopy naked breasts, the one who had been flagellating the computer expert strode brazenly out and prodded one of the policemen on the shoulder. 'That's the bloke who knifed Mrs Vermeulen-Polder.'

'Just a minute,' came the unhassled reply, 'We're dealing with another incident first.'

But the slag-heap was keen that she and her chums should not be accused or even temporarily arrested. 'He's pissing well going to push off and you're just letting him!'

The policeman removed his glasses as if this would help him to hear better.

Ulrich was indeed just engaging first gear and weaving out between some railings with bicycles heavily chained to them and a car.

'Oi! You! Stop!'

Like the Black Knight in the tales of old, Ulrich felt a sinister and ruthless temerity swell up inside him. He would kill a hundred measly weasly Dutch if need be. In his mirror, he saw the police car doing a hurried five point turn. Its klaxon started up. He roared down some side alleys to come out on Damrak, from where he tore along the Prins Hendrik Kade, manoeuvring skillfully in and out of the busy traffic of late evening. The animosity between Dutchmen and Germans meant that Ulrich's German number-plate spurred the Dutch police on a touch more, whilst reciprocally he felt a much lower regard for them than had they been say, French police. He thundered out along the Haarlemmer Weg to the A10.

As he shot down the ramp into the Coen Tunnel, there were two patrol cars some way behind him struggling to push past the heavy night-life traffic. As the tunnel began to climb again from its burrow under the Ij, Ulrich amidst the echoing din and rows of red lights saw two flashing blue beacons at the top of the ramp. He tucked himself in behind an articulated lorry and bent low over the petrol tank. As the blue lights reappeared round the edge of the high trans-continental trailer, he rocketed out and past this lumbering shield and slewed off down the first slip-road, which led him into the new and half-built suburb of Oostzaan. Skidding on some wet grit and realising that he could not hold himself on a sharp S-bend, he shot deliberately off the unkerbed asphalt, through a flimsy wicker fence which demarcated some allotments and ploughed through empty furrows and rows of bamboo canes and came to rest upright and unharmed. With his engine and lights off, he sat on his saddle and waited.

He did not wait long. The squawking crows arrived. Three cars and two motorbikes congregated on a low dyke and probed the cabbageless plots with their headlamps until they picked him out.

Transfixed by searchlights, he leapt frantically onto his kick-start and bounded forwards. 'You filth-filled Dutch pustules!' he shouted angrily inside his helmet. He passed gingerly through a screen of small bushes, out onto a wide plateau of bulldozed wasteland.

The police vehicles kept to the two slightly elevated roads which embraced this low-lying basin, spacing themselves out slowly and turning their engines off after each repositioning so as to be able to hear the growls of the unlit motorbike.

Ulrich knew that the Dutch Panzer divisions were outflanking him and with Semitic cunning were refusing to chase him into this boggy triangle, but were cordoning him off in this semi-reclaimed and treacherous mire. Yet this spectre of impending danger, only heightened his thrilling and reckless zeal. He flung his helmet away. Like a spastic gorilla, he seized the handle-bar grips of his bike with his gloved paws and its main frame and engine between his big thighs and revving madly, he lurched out across the flat uneven mud on his S.S. suicide mission. 'Sieg Heil!' In the few metres in front of him, dimly seen in dark grey hues, caterpillar markings, vast clods and huge churned-up ruts made by the tyres of heavy earth-moving equipment kept appearing. The ugly silhouettes of concrete blocks of flats under construction were vaguely discernible and looming closer. More sirens wailed and blue lights blinked, all controlled by hook-nosed pacifists.

He slid to a halt in front of a shallow and recently excavated ditch with a trickle of water in its bottom. The sides were well bevelled, but the earth looked suspiciously soft and water-laden.

He built up the power to a screaming crescendo before moving forward into the water-course, but despite the howling flailing propulsive force, the bike just sank in up to its axle in seconds. Why was Ute not here to help him? German women were supposed to be strong and loyal. The enraged and captured monster gave a last shriek of defiant wild fury and then, the mud up to the top of its back wheel, it choked and died.

Ulrich slithered and stumbled through the sucking mud. He ran clumsily with weighted boots the last half-kilometre to the edge of the mammoth building site. He scaled a temporary wooden fence. He jumped over trenches, scrambled over half-constructed reinforced concrete walls, until in the shadow of a scaffold-enveloped monolith, he saw the beckoning black hole of a huge and half-finished manhole. Its sides were held up with sheet piling, supported by wooden cross-props. He swung himself down on these and entered a one and a half metre diameter new sewerage pipe. He could see nothing at all, but he counted five hundred crawling paces on his knees and then he sat crosswise with his legs spanning the shallow puddle of ice, which lay congealed in the pipe's curved cold bottom. Here he would wait and listen and regain his breath.

*   *   *

The unmelodramatic sincerity of *King Ynyr* had reawakened in Ute a nostalgic school-days' wish to study medievalism, especially the myriad bishopric states and grand duchies and margravedoms of Germany and Italy with their minor courts, artisans' guilds and pageantry, but her return to Eichenfelsstrasse gave her a soberingly rude shock.

The first bolt of the visual mayhem gave way to the even more worrying implications that someone was on to them. Ingrid paled, the play's lingering images of delicate and untrite truth instantly ejected and forgotten. Who was responsible for this sabotage?

Ute, tossing away the theme of love's mystical shores as delusory and unreal, snatched up Ulrich's letter which commanded her to meet him in Amsterdam. It said he was following up the most likely trail and eliminating the culprits.

'A pestilence be on them,' mumbled Ingrid. This, she noted, was an amateur job. They need not flee over-quickly, though certainly the time had come to tidy up, sell up, pack up and vanish in an orderly way.

* * *

Ulrich slept for perhaps two hours before the numbing cold of his catacomb-like hide-out penetrated his thick underwear and woollies and leather and he awoke shivering violently. Leather is not wholly waterproof and under his suit's saturated mud-soaked legs, some dampness had seeped through.

He crept shakily and unseeingly along this lightless shaft, until the dimmest of shadows hazily described a cuboid box ahead, its square of meagre light betokening a second manhole. He stood up and padded the concrete walls until he found some steel rungs embedded in the concrete. He climbed slowly up and peered over the coaming. Nothing stirred. Through the rolled shrouds of icy mist, this humbled German crawled warily and insect-like. He crawled across a hundred metres of freezing stiffening ooze, dotted with stacks of bricks and heaps of gravel, silent cement mixers and small deep-rutted puddles with thin films of ice on them. By an oil drum he saw the foot of a ladder.

Up he went, up into an eerie tangle of scaffolding. On the planks at second-floor level he allowed himself a pee, but a breeze blew most of it back down the outside of his leathers and boots. His teeth chattered.

The planks joined a concrete walkway and he came to three flats with curtains up, indicating that they were occupied. A luminous digital clock on a stereo-system in one read 02.05. Chilled to the core and without food or drink, he had to break in to one of them.

A kitchen window lock had not been properly engaged. He wiggled it and it opened. He slid dirtily inside and shut it again. His eyes probed the gloom and he opened his front zip to withdraw his still bloody knife. A baby cried. He stood breathlessly still. A girl's voice spoke softly in baby-Dutch. He heard enthusiastic sucking noises, gurgles and burps and through the crack behind an open door he could just trace the outline of a mother sitting up in bed, breast-feeding a bundle of clothes. A mobile of cardboard stars and moons on wire loops hung over a small crib. He must not cause her to scream. He removed his gloves slowly.

As he knocked on the light in the confined little bedroom, he fell rather theatrically onto one knee and held up his clasped hands. The baby looked up momentarily from its target in the opened night-dress.

'Please don't scream,' he begged. 'Please don't. I promise not to hurt you if you don't give me away.'

Her mouth opened, but his words disarmed her alarm in the nick of time. Though poor and rather lowly, she knew German from her mother. Ulrich thought that she looked vulnerable and easily cheated and he felt sorry for her. An air of sad and forlorn patience in her being moved him almost to believe that he could love her.

She gazed at the clay-plastered and shaking apparition. 'What do you want?'

He produced Katrijn Vermeulen-Polder's wad of takings. 'You may have this in payment, but I need a very hot bath, food and a change of clothes.'

'The police came at about one o'clock, searching for you.' Her baby wrinkled its brow, closed its eyes and resumed its feed.

'Where's the telephone?'

'It's not been connected yet.'

Ulrich undressed in the middle of the tiled kitchen floor, trying to limit the mess he made.

Insisting that she stayed where he could see her, he ran a bath and lay in the scalding water for a full half-hour. He felt less ill at the end of this, but still weary and enervated.

In a jacket and trousers of her former boyfriend's, terribly tight and with wrists and ankles showing, he ate slice after slice of bread with circles of sausage or squares of cheese on them and drank four cups of hot coffee. He saw the key to her D.A.F. elastic band car.

'I have to ask you to come with me, so that you don't give me away, but I'll give you more money and I promise that after three or four hours you can drive home again unharmed.'

'What have you done?'

'I knifed a drug-pedlar in Amsterdam.'

The girl half-trusted him, indeed she had even started to feel sorry for him too. He sat on the sofa and watched her clean up some of his mud marks and nearly dozed off.

At five o'clock, hand in hand, they walked out to her parked car. Ulrich carried the baby and was careful not to sneeze on it. Such company gave him excellent cover.

Inside, the car rattled and vibrated, like being inside a drum. It rolled through the grey haze around Alkmaar and proceeded northwards towards Den Helder. Beside the road, the Noord Hollandsch Kanaal ran elevated in a broad dyke, so that as by some optical trick boats sailed along above the level of the flat green meadows. The houses and barns for the most part were of that inverted boat hull design with white walls and green doors and red roofs and with tidy gardens and farmyards around them.

The baby seemed contented to be held by Ulrich and he, rather belatedly, felt that he ought to settle down with Ute and sire their own tots to bounce on his knee.

They missed the turn before De Kooi and as the road swung round beside a sandy and shingly beach, they slowed to turn. A fisherman's boy and his sister were pushing a rowing-boat down past a wooden groyne and into the turbulent grey bay, so treacherous to the land-lubber's eye.

They found the grassy track and parked. Ulrich took the car keys, but promised to be no more than half an hour.

Up on the dyke and beside the man-made waterway, the whitewashed sluice-keeper's cabin came into view with its rickety sooty stove-pipe. The visitor marched up the steps to the one-roomed cottage. A cutting wind from the North Sea went through his trousers as if he had none on. He passed an axe and a block with a heap of newly-split birch logs and a scattering of splinters. The sluice gates, matt black and in their heavy frames of slime-streaked grooved iron girders, were visible beyond the farther lock.

Through a small clathrate leaded window, he saw an oil-lamp of iron and copper and two candlesticks on a dark unpolished elm table, a large cast-iron stove, a sofa, a bed, a speckled rug and in the even clear grey Dutch light, a girl preparing quails for herself and a boyfriend who had gone out. He knocked at the squat door.

Like most Dutch girls, she was rather sexless and masculine-minded, but she wore jeans and a sloppy sweater and thought herself attractive.

'Janneke van de Est?'

'Who are you?'

'A friend of Herr Hüttner's.'

'A name?'

'Moritz.'

'Come in. I'm plucking some quails for spatchcocking for lunch. Come and talk whilst I carry on.' She closed the door softly but firmly and with an over-friendly smile led him like a bear into her trap.

Janneke was a politics student and her German was marvellously correct.

On a side-table with an enamel-tiled splashback, she removed a ground-glass stopper from a clear glass bottle. 'This is apricot oil, which I smear over the fowls before cooking.' She held the bottle of clear colourless and slightly oily liquid under his nose for him to smell.

Deceived, he bent forward to sniff it, whereupon she dashed some of it into his eyes.

Some of the concentrated hydrochloric acid slopped onto her jeans and some ran down onto her fingers. She rushed to the sink and rinsed her hands vigorously. The spots spilt on her trousers were fizzing and burning and turning the blue denim brown.

Janneke had recognised him as being the tall German sought in connection with the murder of the Vermeulens. This news item had been broadcast on the radio that morning.

Ulrich screamed tremulously. He fell over four times as he struggled to rush out and fling himself into the canal.

Janneke waited until he unseeingly tried to heave himself up onto the tow-path, when she cracked his skull with the blunt edge of the axe and watched his unconscious body sink back into the icy water. With a barge-pole she steered the dead floating shape to a side basin where in the submerged shell of a sunken car, she enmeshed it to decompose unseen.

The girl in the D.A.F. waited uncertainly for a time, before using her spare keys to drive back to Oostzaan.

* * *

Ute sat in the wide first-class window seat, sipping orange juice.

She picked up a discarded French magazine, edited it appeared to appeal to women who adjudicated themselves by the amount of male flattery they received. Yet in her broodiness, Ute was at last beginning to understand those temperamental and moody women who are obsessed about being *really* loved. Being popped was not enough. If you did not demand consideration too, you became doleful. She had had sufficient of Ulrich telling her that she was a restriction on his free spirit. She would make him choose. And if he refused to terminate their superfluous continuation of their criminal deeds too, she would leave him anyway. She had been soft for long enough. It was time to be firm.

Her hair was divided into two plaits. She had on a white blouse and a sleeveless pullover, cobalt blue baggy trousers and black boots and so externally she looked quite pretty, yet inside her head she felt that beetles were gnawing away and destroying her true persona.

The plane glided down over the neatly ordered red-roofed villages of Holland, over rectangular fields and long strips of water, straight roads and counterweight-lifted bridges and then the runways of Schipol.

After school in Hermannsburg she had gone to France as an au pair girl, then worked in a bookshop there and lastly as an auxiliary nurse, always with one or two affairs with older men going on in the wings. In 1972 she had moved to Munich to begin a proper training in nursing at the Sankt Johann Klinik. Its solid four-storey building had been erected in 1938 as an S.S. barracks, but in 1945, a nursing order of nuns fleeing westwards had found it and deciding that the original occupants were not going to be back for a while, set themselves up there. The main x-ray screening room had once been the commandant's office and a huge moulded plaster eagle with its talons clutching a swastika adorned one wall, though its original black red and gold colours had been painted over. Whilst Ute herself could like or dislike individuals but not nationalities, the Bavarians she found, were very different. She remembered well an elderly blonde-haired Valkyrie-like sister draining the pus from a large boil on the back of the neck of a British airman. She stabbed it with a lancet and squeezed it and scraped it with a long surgical spoon, trying her damnedest to hurt him and all the time repeating, 'Ze Eenglisch is soaft,' over and over again. But the airman had gritted his teeth and been equally determined to hold out in this conflict of wills.

One evening Ulrich had knocked on her door. They were cousins by adoption and he had heard that she was in Munich from his mother. They had occasionally met as small children at funerals and similar celebrations. Her liquidy suggestive movements, for once to a man younger than herself, had cut short all the usual protocols and they had been at it unhindered within fifteen minutes of meeting.

They were both dissatisfied with their lots and they had talked much about their hopes and dreams and ideals. They attended a number of motorcycle rallies, went to two Neo-Nazi meetings which were disappointingly lacking in credibility and toured Italy for a month that summer on his bike with their camping kit piled high on the back. But the exhilarations of touring, of sex, of camping and of cooking on the edge of a wood by night wore off. They bewailed their pittance-like incomes. They attempted a bank robbery in a small French town, but had to flee empty-handed. If Ulrich went away for a week on behalf of his pharmaceutical employers, she could not be faithful. The stiff white uniform dress with its red cross looked clean and clinical enough to her, but the hunky housemen seemed to know what she was and that she could not resist. Neither did her kisses transform Ulrich from a toad into a prince. She knew that he kept jumping on other girls too. They needed ever more daring schemes to keep their illusions alive. Then he had been kicked out of his job and they had started synthesising EF31A in her flat at night.

She passed through passport control at 16.10 hours. Ulrich had said he would meet her in the arrivals area at around 17.00. By 19.00 she had asked at the airport information desk if there were any messages. She pored over the local newspapers on the bookstalls, but such stabbings and chases as Ulrich had been involved in were so commonplace in Amsterdam, that they were not reported unless they contained some novel ingredient.

She took the newly-built and little used line in to Amsterdam Zuid and from this pristine concrete station with its subway and bicycle racks, caught a number five tram into the older brick-built centre. Here she would spend the night in a hotel and if Ulrich did not appear tomorrow, return to Nice.

## CHAPTER TEN.

Artemis spent Tuesday in casualty. Her absence from North Shields on the Monday to murder Penman should not have been obvious to anyone.

The duty surgeon for casualty on Tuesday was a chap from Barbados, who was not only manually maldexterous in such arts as stitching and reducing fractures, but he appeared unable to form a proper spacio-temporal visualisation of the task in hand. He could not adapt theory and learning to the presenting problem. The nursing staff were left pulling blue-white smiles as they tried to urge the patients to have faith in this fellow, despite the unsettling indications to the contrary. Since only two of the thirty folk in the waiting area though had anything wrong with them, the scope for disaster was fairly limited.

Artemis spent most of her time castigating the embryonic juvenile delinquents who were running haywire and their fat frowzy brainless mothers, who instead of instilling some behaviour into their rampaging offspring, displayed indulgence-seeking grins and prattled with one another about how to fiddle this or that concession out of the Social Security office.

She made a discreet telephone call to Barclay's Bank, claiming to be Victoria Inall, ascertained that the £22,322 and 10p. had been credited to her and asked them if they could arrange for her to withdraw £22,250 in cash the following morning. They undertook to have it ready for her.

In her tea-break, she went to see Heather Brodie and remarkably found her not in a committee meeting, available and even pleasant. The motive for this agreeableness was the hope that she could use Artemis as a launching pad or a bait in later man-trapping sallies. She looked up from drafting an advertisement for a nursing tutor – 'Making a Healthier Tyneside' it began. 'If you would like to maximise your personal development in a caring situation and join a team dedicated to ... '

'Miss Brodie, I had a telephone call from my father's housekeeper this morning, to say he has been taken seriously ill.'

'I'm sorry to hear that Nurse Boden. What with?'

'I'm afraid that isn't clear at the moment. I did wonder ... is it possible to take some more leave at short notice?'

'Let's see, you've had nine days so far this year. How much would you like?'

'Four days?'

'Very well. No one else is on holiday at this time of year, so there's no difficulty. When you return, you'll be on Ward 4.'

'I'm most grateful.'

They exchanged wily smiles of parting as if both had gained by underhand inducement.

On Wednesday morning Artemis appeared at the bank, presented the made-out cheque with a gloved hand, re-signed it on the back when requested to and was handed stacks of notes which she packed into Penman's compact red nappa leather holdall.

She walked down Grey Street to Newcastle's Central Station in the motionless but icy cold air and caught a train to York. York had the advantage of being well away from her usual beats and housing a Porsche dealer and three coin dealers.

Victoria Inall's papers had already been returned with meticulous care to their original home and the nurses' home master key had mysteriously reappeared in matron's office. At

York, the finely torn-up paraphernalia relating to the bogus bank account were dumped in a station litter bin.

Even by lunch-time in this Middle Ages walled city, the freezing icy air still clung to everything. In an evenly drab sky, a small crimson sun glowed like a weak fire-ball. Artemis ate steak and chips and tomatoes in a restaurant, removing her coat and gloves.

The classier coin dealer with his spotted bow-tie, offered her £2,700 for the forty-five gold coins she had brought with her – the commoner sovereigns and guineas from Penman's collection. Happily he proposed cash, of course to keep the purchase off the books and thus evade paying the Value Added Tax on their later sale. Artemis accepted.

Outside the Porsche show-room, a lank gooey dyed-blonde was demonstrating a pale yellow Lotus Elan to a bespectacled executive. Nearby stood a Porsche 911S, which had been resprayed in a semi-matt black, even plainer and less flashy than Sir David's – appealingly non-appealing, subtly snazzy in a low-key way, raw and basic, the exact opposite of 'stylish' luxury cars. The window surrounds were black too. Here was a sly and understated car and if now they are commonplace and passé, in 1975 they were still rare in Britain. This specimen was three years old and cost £5,000.

The manager skidded out. They took a test drive, firstly with him behind the wheel and then her, out into the flat frozen countryside, to Stamford Bridge and back.

She had dressed in a hurry that day and was not quite her prim brusque self, with an old blue and black dress and a cardigan on under her leather coat and boots and no perfume. None the less, the manager's concentration and attentiveness were faultless, even if this was to be only a picnic without sandwiches.

The seats were cupped and narrow and with high backs, like the pilots' seats in fighter aircraft. They held you closely in soft and very pale blue leather.

She persuaded him to reduce the price as there was no part-exchange and again, all the notes she intended to pay with would provide the chance for another spot of tax evasion.

Seated in her new car, she left York, stopping after a time to adjust the seat, set the mirrors and play with the instruments. The steering-wheel seemed small, especially as the Alvis's steering-wheel was so large – like driving a lorry. The driving position was not so far reclined as in many sports cars. The facia and carpets were black as in Sir David's, but the upholstery and mats were pale blue and the steering-wheel white. The 2.34 litre engine, the hard suspension and the cramped driving compartment, again made it feel like a combat aircraft, particularly after the lumbering spacious Alvis. Perhaps the oddest feature to her were the pedals which being pivoted under the floor instead of in the bulkhead, seemed to roll backwards towards the heel when depressed and not slide away toe-wards as with most vehicles.

Heading up the A1, she practised a burst of power as she overtook a coach – the roar of the rear-mounted engine sounding like the marine diesel of a speed boat – and then on a stretch of dual carriageway she cruised for two minutes at 130 miles per hour, before reverting to soberer and more legal speeds. Speed and power gave her a small kick of pleasure, but they did not have the same fascination for her that they have for a certain type of macho and image-conscious male. She had faith in herself without recourse to such appendages, though she did enjoy the knowledge that these latest extravagances could be hers. The unpampered control and the slightly rigid handling also suited the masculine element in her temperament.

Via the A66 over the snow-sprinkled Pennines, she crossed over to the West.

Just before five o'clock, she stopped at a general store in the little village of Eastriggs just off the A75. The bell tinkled as she pushed open the door and entered the old-fashioned counter-service shop, crammed with soups and cereals and sacks of vegetables. The long-faced dour owner in his brown smock did not look up from his restocking activities.

'Do you think I might be served,' asked Artemis after about a minute.

'Och, don't lose your rag lassie.' He tucked his pencil back behind his car.

The customer took a deep breath. 'May I have a bread roll, a banana and a yoghurt?'

'Bananas in December? Dee youce ken where this is lassie? It's nee doon in London.' It was more his abrasive manner which gave offence than his words.

She left, slamming the door so hard that the long glass pane fell out of it and broke with a dreadful clatter on the pavement.

Mr McGurk shot out and hurled fluent lowland Scottish abuse after her, but she coolly ignored him and drove off in her wicked black arrow.

A little further on at a small roundabout, a builder's pick-up darted in and forced her to brake sharply. The road was very quiet and so there was no excuse for this cheekiness. She tooted and received a waggled two fingers in exchange. She was often accused of being aggressive because she was awkward with people who were insolent or unpunctual, yet she had learnt this in France and did not feel it wrong. In Britain people accepted delays, bad service and shoddy workmanship too meekly, whereas abroad folk would shout and wave sticks and register their displeasure. 'You shagging fuck-rags,' she mouthed.

An hour later the 911S was nosing its way down the bumpy track to Loch Eilan, with its rock hard springing jolting her about. This dark isolated lair seemed a perfect base for secret raids. Lights were on in Uanrig House.

Donald Aeneas Boden in his mid-fifties, was a sort of genteel duffer, a man who was kindly but not the sharpest knife in the box. His life appeared to contain no rancour or unpleasantness, as if the modern revolution had passed him by. Like the playwright Holberg, he seemed convinced of everyone's inherent good nature, for even Holberg's bad characters give the impression that they are only pretending to be nasty. He had been a bit quicker when younger and when his wife had been alive and they had done things to provide their minds with new impulses, but in the nine years since her death he had rather stagnated.

He had spent most of the day at his easel by the long windows in the drab drawing-room, their faded pink curtains swept back and tied with braided and tasselled ropes. His canvas depicted some Moorish boys playing on the quayside of a North African harbour, with colourful tunics and bright eyes and a background of sailing ships and forts shimmering in the heat. He was a gifted neo-classical artist, but it was a style which aroused little contemporary interest by comparison with the more affected and outlandish schools of the turn of the century.

As dusk fell, he drank lemon juice and ate minestrone soup and bread whilst he listened to a television documentary on Torquato Tasso's *Gerusalemme Liberata*, with a napkin tucked into his collar. At the end of it, the reverberations of an unfamiliar vehicle's exhaust drew him to the window.

Still with the dealer's wax polish and turpentine glinting on it in the outdoor light in the yard, the 911S looked slim and expensive. His daughter too looked so lovely and this blackbird suited her well. She took a red bag from the front boot and came in from the stable-yard through the utility room back-door and into the kitchen. Here he peeled off her coat for her and quite oblivious to her attitude of cool collectedness, embraced her with love in his heart, hugging her gently and oscillating from side to side as he held her head against his and kissed her short hair and temple and ear.

Artemis was surprised to find how sweet and becalming this could be, like some food she had needed but not known she had needed. In a deeply depraved and profane morass, about which it was so easy to be negative and cynical, her father and Mr Letheren were like two rocks of good sense and sanity, pointing towards the thoughts which quicken human existence.

Upstairs she put on a pair of very thick socks, which she used around the house like slippers and in them slid up and down the polished oak boards of the landing a few times, as if reverting to her childhood in her father's proximity.

As the evening progressed he detected a degree of laxness in her physical movements, a slight looseness of limb in her mode of locomotion and something less strict and rigid in her attitudes, which suggested to him that some sexual shark had taken her to bed. Had the shark also bought the sports car for her?

She bathed because her skin felt greasy from the hours of travel and was disturbed to find a small cluster of tiny pigmented pedunculated outpouchings in front of one armpit, marring her perfect body.

He saw her descend the lacquered oak-panelled and galleried three-stage staircase and the legend of Poppaea Sabina, haughty and vain and scheming, crossed his mind. She passed three of his paintings and the large oval mirror with the gilt rim. One was of the ruined pillars of an Egyptian temple with rushes growing in the sand and a white moon shining in an ominous sky. The second had as a backdrop, a huge yellow sun in an orange sky topping the black silhouettes of a jagged mountain chain and in the desert foreground, Philip baptising the Ethiopian envoy. The third displayed a little girl standing on a ruined fortress wall with yellow celandine growing on it, the sea beyond and in the hazy distance, another Cycladic islet. It had a title, *Artemis on her fourth birthday*. There had been no evidence of exceptional beauty then.

Throwing more pine logs into the iron fire-basket, he made the fire up and they sat on the dowdy old blue leather sofa with cups of milky coffee and slices of apple tart and custard.

It is the nature of fatherly love not to press a daughter with, 'How's your job?' 'Have you a boyfriend?' or 'Where's the car come from?' Donald Boden waited and in due course she told him. With her legs pulled up under her, she let him cuddle her as she told how her efforts to begin an acting career had all fallen on stony ground, but that she had accepted now that it was meant to be so. Besides, something else had landed in her lap.

'I saw the old Ariel in the stable there, thick with mud. I hosed it down and gave it a run – actually it goes better than before.'

'Then there's been a boy ... Simon ... who fell in love with me ... but I rejected him. Do you think I was wrong to do that?'

Her father chewed for a moment. 'If you had loved him, you would have followed him anywhere. As you did not love him, you were free to choose.'

Yet had she really loved him or wanted to, but drowned its seeds in her selfish pride? Was this the horse-shoe nail, whose want had caused the entire empire to collapse? But if so, it could not stem from one refusal, that had just been the eruption of a long-dormant abscess.

'Did Mama have a relative who had all sorts of sessile growths on her skin?'

Charlotte Louise Sloss-Eyles had been the daughter of a family doctor up near Pitlochry. There being no one of the right class to marry her locally, her father had tried to press her onto his newly-qualified assistant, one Dr Sword. Tickets for the Hunt Ball appeared, sometimes they were locked out so that they had to throw gravel up at the windows, until Dr Sword had fled, saying he wanted to take up surgery. On a trip to Hampshire Charlotte had met Donald Boden, a poor and idle romantic in her father's eyes who sploshed paint about on canvases, but in love, she had married him despite being ostracised by her family. For a year they had wandered around Italy, living cheaply, him painting pictures which no one wanted to buy and being very much in love, like a sandboy with a sandgirl. On their return they had rented a flat in Highland Road in Edinburgh.

'I remember the night you were born. We took a bus most of the way to the maternity hospital and a taxi just the last few yards – because we were hard up yet in those days it was the expected thing, to arrive by taxi – daft isn't it looking back? Now the midwife had these most unfortunate tiny fleshy outgrowths over her neck and forearms, poor girl ... You could see that she had a dreadful complex about it. Well, we discovered that she was a third cousin of your mother's and I believe there had been another member of the family afflicted with it. It had a German eponym ... von Recklinghausen's disease I think. Have you met someone with it?'

'No,' she said.

'We were so thrilled to have you, because we'd both married a bit late in life you see. Then of course, a few months later, Mama's eccentric uncle died and left this house and everything else to us.'

They cuddled one another idly as the fire-light danced on the walls.

'How are the finances faring?'

'I've a four hundred pound overdraft and I've used up everything else. I'm on my beam-ends. I keep hoping that something will turn up ... but I shall have to move soon I suppose – though I shall miss it here. All the decor and furnishings were chosen by your mother.'

Artemis knew that things were bad. Last summer she had sold her horse to go on holiday to Greece with Denise without asking Papa to pay. She broke free and ran upstairs, reappearing with the red leather holdall. Kneeling on the carpet, she began to count out £10,000, stacking it in blocks each of a thousand like toy money.

Donald's mouth dropped open. 'My child! Where is all this come from?'

'Don't worry Papa. It's not illegal ... but don't say it came from me. I'm not allowed to say what I'm doing, but I will explain it to you one day.' She glanced up at his expression of consternation, pummelled him and gave him a kiss. 'Come on, look pleased. It's all right. And it is what we need after all. More should come, then I can give up nursing and we can do up the house and go away on holidays together ... ?' She smiled wanly at him and he managed to smile back. 'If tomorrow you could take me to the station, then I can travel to North Shields and retrieve the Alvis and some things I need. On Friday I have to go away for the day.'

'To see a man?'

'Yes, but not in the way you mean.'

He thought she was hiding something, but he hugged her once more and they went to bed.

Donald lay awake. In one way, the promised shower of gold opened up the chance of a new lease of life. He could repair the house and overcome its 1950-ish time shackles and travel more. Artemis could attend drama lessons, live in London or Paris, mix with brighter people and perhaps escape the dullness of an otherwise humdrum future. Yet if this affluence had been won by wickedness and so carried a curse, they would be far better off without it.

The alarm clock ticked away beside his darkly awake features.

He thought of the damp ceiling in the yellow bedroom and the need to reroof the house. He began designing in his mind a new and properly concreted entrance out beside the Easter Tickell Gatehouse with steel box-girder posts and a decent gate. He saw lorries tipping road-stone to improve the softest and boggiest patches of the track and men clearing back the woodland and undergrowth for some yards on either side of it, new windows appearing and the stables being repointed and redoored and refloored. Then he fought down these unwise fancies and got up to empty his bladder.

Passing her door, he heard the jarring scraping sound of grinding teeth. He went in and saw her asleep on her front. Her facial musculature seemed unnaturally tense, even demonic. Her teeth grated together insufficiently hard to damage themselves, but enough to reveal a mind in conflict with itself. He knelt beside her small quaint sagging old four-poster and held her hand.

Then she babbled a sequence of riddle-like words. 'You are Artemis ... my unexpurgated nymph ... Soon you will erase Helios and Collett ... and ... ' Then as if the exsiccatory side of her nature which had tortured her were gone, she sighed and smiled coyly. A benign influence asserted itself and a more tractable and happy, ductile and docile spirit took over.

Donald kissed her hair infinitely softly, then went back to his own bed and wept silently.

* * *

The local choir in red cassocks and white surplices sang the unaccompanied chorus *Brother thou art gone before* from Sullivan's *The Martyr of Antioch*. The coffin with Nicholas's remains in it, finished with by the forensic pathologists in Ireland and England, rested in front of the large gold altar cross and candles in the squat stone Catholic church.

Behind the small knot of family, were a dozen uniformed men from the 2nd. Lancers, who not being Catholic by persuasion omitted to cross themselves at the appropriate places.

The bearers had to tread carefully outside, because of the packed snow along the paths. A hyperbolic ridge of snow had drifted against one edge of the new unpolished headstone. It read, 'Nicholas Xenocrates Letheren 1951-1975'.

Thick clouds, a sharp wind and a hint of further snow jointly tried to hurry the people behind the holly hedge. The corpulent priest in his white lace-fringed alb and red and gold embroidered stole peered down through his gold-rimmed half-moon spectacles at his book of offices and quoted from Ecclesiastes. '"Like a man caught in a net, is he who lives in evil times. The good are robbed and slain and no one bothers."' Behind him loomed the grey-white fells, timelessly and silently impinging themselves on this mortal scene.

The Colonel's face throughout was disengaged and sun-like, grave but happy. All was definitely in the hand of a wise and ever-nearer creator.

Later at home, alone with his daughters and eating fillet steak, mashed potatoes and salted beans, he felt a continuation of that tranquil detachment which lately attended him often.

Catharine, who had only just made it home for the burial service, told the tale of her journey to Germany.

They were three unlikely conspirators, not bent zealously on some absolute tactic, but rather content to be blown as the winds of fate decided. Despite their seriousness, Letheren sensed too an element of children at play in their attitudes. For him, toys and games and fantasies had always been more magical and enthralling than the obligatory pull of the real world. To him, reality was a fraud, a tiresome projection of imperfect men. True reality was a subjective surrender not to bogus facts, but to a wise imagination.

The signature on a photostatted copy of a letter to her bank in Luzern, when compared to her school exercise books, proved Nicole le Saige to be Ute Steyer. Uwe Bauss could be a heteronym for Ulrich Schniewind too, they thought. The statements for both accounts showed credits to each both in the form of deposited cash and in three large transfers from a numbered account with the Zürich branch of the Cairo and Khartoum Bank. Whilst le Saige had withdrawn most of her money, Bauss had not. She had 81,000 Deutschmarks, Bauss over one and half million.

Letheren felt a little bit blessed. Whatever Catharine did, brought results and Innogen's suggestion that he proposition Artemis Boden, had placed in his hands an instrument of rare obscurity and unexpected strength.

In Bern Catharine had forged cheque signatures and transferred le Saige's and Bauss's money to a new account in her father's name.

'I found these photographs too, in the flat,' she said.

*      *      *

The old enamelled thermometer in the yard read thirteen degrees Fahrenheit, that is minus eleven degrees Celsius.

Artemis had the Porsche's engine idling and she was using kettles of hot water and a scraper to clear the ice from its windows.

Inside, her father cooked bacon and eggs and read yesterday's newspaper. 'Land prices in Scotland are rising fast. Folk here are even boasting about the sums they have paid for tiny farms – at least Englishmen are.' Beside the bacon he added two slices of black pudding and the Scottish kind, made with cereal instead of suet mixed with the pigs' blood. Not only was this less greasy than the English variety, but it came out a bit crisper and crunchier. With a fried egg, a tatty-scone, a slice of dry bread and a cup of tea it was heaven.

He had deduced that his daughter was leaving on some clandestine and possibly unlawful mission. As they drank their second cups of tea and ate toast and marmalade, he half-wanted to tackle her about it, but some invisible genie held him back.

Artemis took out a box of clothes and maps and a picnic basket and put them on the narrow bench seat in the back of the car, before going to change.

She reappeared in a new pair of thick black motorcycle dungarees bought the day before in Carlisle, some riding boots which zipped up on the inside and the black canvas anorak with a draw-string at the waist and whose lower hem came down to the outer point of the curve of her hips. It was a size too large and had two pullovers inside it, so that she looked a bit over-padded and not quite so sexy as usual.

Donald looked dumbfounded as he had somehow expected her to be going on an indoor get-together. Her immaculately cleaned and polished leather boots and trousers he sensed were a little ominous, especially when added to her strict and forceful demeanour. It all carried overtones of hubris, of military correctness and an overweening rigidity. It seemed to him to be a blatant assertion of an unbridled and possibly wicked intent. The only other girl he had seen in a black leather outfit was the daughter of an old friend he played chess with from time to time. Hers though had been a thinner, looser, two-piece fashion garment intended to convey confidence and sexiness, but as that particular wearer had worn tinted spectacles and been highly nervous, its effect instead of enhancing an image of force and self-belief, had been merely to draw attention to her pitiful neuroses. Yet Artemis's attire though daunting was somehow correct. It embodied an image of physical action and hinted subtly at the disrespect she felt for the forces by which good men guided and controlled women. The loveless and nemesis-incurring state which arose from this however, still lay hidden deep down. Most erring women vacillate. They wish to feel loved and so – though no temptation is stronger than pride – they periodically have to lay aside their loathings and sue fickly for affection under dubious sobriquets. Yet here stood an almost over-real and ultimate expression of consistent waywardness and even in this semi-leather-apparelled state, she epitomised that unyielding stance.

But even the obdurate Artemis could not stop a half-cautionary yet half-fatherly hug from blessing her tenderly, as she pulled the half-unzipped zip up over the burnt orange polo-neck woolly underneath it up to her throat. With her gloves and her woolly hat in her left hand and her keys in her right, she took her leave. 'I'll be back tonight.'

It was a quarter past seven.

At about ten o'clock as she sped across the flat boggy moor towards Loch Linnhe, rutted with streams and lochans, bleak and wind-swept and below a clear arching sky, Goldstraw came to her mind and the night he had used her sexiness to fire his libido and undam his life-freeing juices. She had been just more coal for the furnace. He was said to suffer moods of deep depression at times – good! Women were being avenged on him for his using them without compromising his own demands. Her difficulty now though was not Goldstraw and that club, but her father, Simon and Mr Letheren. These were the men who were guiding her by their irresistible powers, indeed who seemed to have her like a puppet between them, a creature who had lost all self-determination. One day she would break free. Dared she consider killing them? Was that what the Spirit of the Mine ultimately wanted her for? It seemed too hideous even for her. Such a renunciation of kindness surely would spell her end. They had her trapped. Her leather might defend her physically from blows and barbs and mud, but it could not ward off love. She sensed a silent presence listening to her. What was she then, just an aberration shaped by their wills? Confound it! Why did these intangible forces just not kill her and be done with it? 'Why taunt me like a boy playing with a spider?' She shouted, 'Answer!'

There was a bang. The vehicle juddered violently. It slewed as if to veer off the causeway and into the bog, but then spun round and shot along the road backwards, so that the amazed girl watched the asphalt strip rush out from underneath her.

The Porsche came to rest at the edge of the icy road. Artemis had felt helpless but unafraid. Spitting out a swear word, she walked round her vehicle and was surprised to discover that the only damage appeared to be a shredded front tyre.

The road was utterly deserted. She took her gauntlets from the back seat and lifted out the spare wheel, the wheel brace and the jack. She paused and gave the chewed-up tyre a kick with the toe of her riding boot. This event she deemed to be an assertion by her ruling spirits of their unbounded power. They refused to injure her, yet they compelled her to do what they had predetermined at every turn. 'Why should I have to demean myself changing this oily wheel? Why can't I forbid it? Show yourselves! Fix this tyre!' Nothing happened. The tyre did not spontaneously repair itself. She had no choice but to humbly kneel down on the black ice and heave at the wheel brace to loosen the tight air-spanner-tightened nuts. 'Move!' she gasped. If women in general have a poor idea of levers and fulcrums and couples, Artemis was quite practical. She bashed the brace with a large rock to begin loosening the toughest nuts, worked out the necessary sequence of actions and completed the task.

Not only was the temperature still minus six, but a strong North wind added to the freezing conditions. Despite struggling with the wheel and having on extra knickers and woollies, she still felt cold. She peeled her anorak off and pulled on an extra red woolly over the orange polo-neck one.

She turned the Porsche round and resumed her journey, pausing at Ballachulish for some hot tea and some buns from her basket. It had snowed a lot here.

The message from her uneven quarrel with the extracorporeal seemed to be, that all would go well as long as she did not try to deviate from the way mapped out for her. She must resign herself to this, then she would seem to be invincible. Only when she opposed it would defeat chasten her and make her yield to that which was truly omnipotent. Yet her humiliations always happened away from the eyes of men – as the Spirit of the Mine had promised. Nature might look down on her with an insulting grace when alone, but to other men and women she would appear to be beyond mortal limitation and she liked that.

She drove past her old school on the approach to Fort Augustus and at the agreed meeting point, near the southern tip of Loch Ness, she saw Letheren's blue Land Rover. Down near the inlet which led into the Caledonian Canal, her master was talking to a man scraping an upturned boat, whilst across Glen Albyn stood a squarish stone kirk, a house built of granite blocks with white fretted barge-boards, a modern bungalow and a row of tarpaulined motor cruisers, all backed by a steep drop of Douglas firs canopied with snow. It looked so typically Scottish. Farther out on the far side of the loch, she saw a patchy white scar of rock below the serried trunks of mixed birches, where once she and some fellow schoolgirls had picnicked. It was mirrored too in the still shallows of the water.

Standing beside her black car, she gave a peep on the horn. Mr Letheren turned and waved and she waved back. He ended his chat and then strode up over the rattling grey pebbles towards her. He smiled. 'Follow me.'

They drove in tandem along Glen Moriston, parallel to its frothing burn in the boulder-filled gorge, but hemmed in by its spruce trees. As the snow beside the narrow road grew deeper and deeper, Letheren stopped where they could leave her car in a large camping lay-by. 'It's best we go on in just the Land Rover,' he remarked. 'At least we have four-wheel-drive then. You drive.'

The utilitarian, short-wheelbase, mid-blue cross-country vehicle was a far cry from her sleek 911S, with its high dashboard, clumsy pedals, almost non-existent suspension and the large diameter steering-wheel, reminiscent once more of the Alvis.

They continued westwards into the wilder and more desolate Glen Shiel. Here the scenery opened out. In the distance were the Five Sisters, sharply pointed bluey-white peaks, roughly pyramidal with their ageless tips scalloped on one side like cowls beneath a faintly blue-tinted heaven. They were white on their sun-facing sides and greyey-navy on their shadowy sides. Their rock-gashed snowy slopes ran down to the flat broad marshy alluvial plain, where frozen water channels cracked the dazzling icy white snow of this lovely lonely landscape.

'No hitches with Penman?'

'No,' she said peremptorily before mellowing. 'Except that the cycle brake-cable was too fine. It cut into him and made him bleed – rather messy. A clothes-line would have been preferable.'

'Judging from the newspapers, his flat was pretty sumptuous.'

'I suppose so, but it was only a flat. In that patch though, it would cost goodness knows what. '

'He stage-managed the doing up of all those large London terraced houses in the late sixties, for re-housing the "under-privileged" you know. I suppose they had gone a bit down inside, but all those iron baths and grand old fittings were flung out and cardboard partitions put in. A nephew of mine worked for some plumbers on them in his summer holiday. He said the new baths were so light, that you could carry five on your shoulder at once. If as you fitted one, you dropped your hammer into it and cracked it, you just threw it out and plonked in another. The architect would call, take up a few floor-boards and say, "These four joists are rotten. Replace them." The builders would nod and then when he had gone, simply nail the boards back down.' Letheren laughed. 'What scoundrels! Then there was a "repair fund", so that when the new tenants moved in and everything fell to pieces, more men were paid to come round with glue and sticky tape and patch it all up. And of course it was no one's money, so no one cared. What frigging madness. Country houses were demolished in their hundreds too at the same time and it was not only the socialists, Macmillan's lot had been sanctioning the flattening of magnificent terraces to make room for tower blocks which their speculating friends wished to erect.'

Outside the Land Rover lay an ocean of untainted snow. It hung even on the solitary broken fence and on the odd grey hooked rock, sticking up like a carious tooth. In the distance, other mountains of a deeper blue overlapped and merged behind the Five Sisters. The whiteness of winter and a deep stirring silence gripped the land.

He told her to pull off the road and stop beside a lone ruined croft.

They ate cheese butties and drank cups of tea, before getting out of the vehicle. The girl pulled on a pair of light grey fur-lined leather mittens and a red bobble-hat, for she recalled somewhere hearing that much heat is lost through the head. 'If your feet are cold, put a hat on,' was the motto.

Letheren wore a pair of sage green combat trousers, army 'ammo' boots and puttees, two or three worn-out army woollies and an old grey jacket with a toggle missing. They made a strange pair, yet his profound simplicity and strong heart filled him with an irresistible light and bound her to him by forces she could not fathom. Her clothing had initially surprised him, but he saw that it tallied with her conspicuously defiant attitudes and he had asked her to wear something practical and protective. Not for her the shapeless bundle of faded green army fatigues. The shorter hair too looked combat-ready.

'Your kit looks in order – not to run in or swim in, to wash or dry out – for your next operation is a one night affair, a slow cautious advance against a static target. There's no mingling with crowds or being seen except by men who know you're the enemy, so its striking and indiscreet character shouldn't matter.'

This was she reflected, merely her semi-leather outfit. Without her full gleaming equipagc, she would feel like a knight without his chain-mail. And her armour and shield and pennons made her feel braver. 'Morale and daring depend on bold dress.'

'Definitely! The right uniforms and colours are vital. Identity-negating costumes which you don't feel happy in are a handicap in battle. No, this stuff suits you.' He took her hands. 'Artemis, it is marvellous that you are not tarred with this crisis in confidence which has smitten so many in this country lately. It makes me even surer that we are well-paired.'

The river was to the North of the road, but they strode out into the flat awe-inspiring expanse of humpy sparkling crystalline snow to the South. Under it their feet felt the springy invisible heather. Artemis carried a cheap archery target and a green rubber poncho and Letheren a wooden box.

'I hope your bold spirit leads you to victory in these current deeds and that afterwards, you can progress to a happy and long life.'

She nodded thoughtfully.

'You're going to assault a castle. It's well defended both with physical obstacles and electronically, but there should be considerable riches there. Firstly though, I want us to spend some time with the Browning 9mm. semi-automatic pistol.' There was something Boy-Scoutish yet also everyday in his attitude.

After half a mile, they halted in a depression where a deep blue stream cut its way through the ice and here and there a tuft of golden marsh grass stuck up through the snow along the edges of the burn. On a single meagre tree, stunted and brittle and leafless like a deprived dwarf, Letheren fixed the target. Icicles hung from the sparse boughs and snow stuck to its wens and twigs and filled in the cracks of its black bark.

They spread out the poncho and knelt on it and he opened the wooden box. 'I shall metamorphose for an hour or two, into an N.C.O. small arms instructor. So your attention please, Miss Boden. Gloves off.'

He extracted the pistol and held it in the palm of his left hand. 'This is the Browning 9mm. pistol. It is the "Ordinary" version, having a non-adjustable fixed notch rear-sight. It is on the whole reliable and robust. It isn't a rifle, so understand that you are only likely to hit anyone with it up to a range of a few yards – regardless of what happens in American films. Also it's a low velocity weapon, so that whilst a hit should disable, it might not kill.'

He took it to pieces and reassembled it and watched her do it four times. They practised the drills of range safety, charging the magazine, loading, cocking, operating the safety catch and unloading.

The half-gloss black weapon itself she thought looked unattractive, but the short parabola-nosed bullets in their brass cartridge cases were compact and nicely rounded. She had very much wanted a firearm, because the risk of being overpowered by one or more strong men could only be countered by such a device. If she made an error, if stealth failed, only this could save her and deter the unthinkable – Artemis's capture by brutes.

Eventually in their hollow, they turned to face the concentrically-ringed target. 'Position one. Sideways on. Feet apart. Left hand in the small of the back. Head looking to the right along the outstretched right arm. Right arm just slightly crooked. Close your left eye. Look along the sights. Take aim.'

Having demonstrated the position, he set her in the anatomically correct stance, like a window-dresser adjusting a dummy.

'Right, now for real. With a magazine of five rounds, load.' He handed her a magazine and keeping the weapon pointing in the direction of the target but downwards, she inserted it. 'Take aim.' She cocked the pistol and took aim. 'In your own time, fire five rounds at the target.'

After the shots were fired, she unloaded the magazine, checked that the firing chamber was empty and put the weapon down, still pointing down the range. As the afternoon progressed, his unbarked commands would gradually instill into her the established sequence of drill and drill matters if you are not to have accidents or make silly mistakes.

They inspected the target. She had scored one hit on the outer ring and four misses. 'That's good,' observed Letheren, 'because it teaches you that it is not so easy.'

After eight more series of five shots, he had improved her gr oupings a little, partly by getting her to aim at a point six inches below the bull's-eye to compensate for the upward kick. He had little squares of blue red and white sticky paper with which to cover up the holes in the target after each firing. They tried the position facing the target, but not the unofficer-like toad-like two-handed squatting position. They covered jams and stoppages, fired two groups with the silencer on and lastly fired two groups at three yards instead of five and the much improved groupings underlined the point about accuracy increasing as range decreased and ended the session on a more encouraging note, as he had intended.

'Unload. Port arms for inspection.'

She held the weapon up and pulled back the breech-mechanism and he ensured that the barrel was empty.

She had fired a hundred and forty rounds. He produced a cleaning kit, some gun oil and a supply of so-called 'four by two' which was a roll of cotton oblongs to be used with the pull-through. They went rigorously over the parts to be scoured clean and the parts to be oiled.

Packing everything back into the wooden box, he counted like a quartermaster. 'One pistol. Ten magazines – their springs sometimes fail. Ten boxes each of one hundred rounds of ammunition. Silencer. Two tins of gun oil. Roll of cotton cleaning gauze. Cleaning kit.

Don't shoot from the hip – you'll miss, even if John Wayne doesn't. Don't shoot without taking aim unless it's at point-blank range. If you're not in danger keep at least two loaded magazines on you, but separate from the weapon. If you are in danger, load a magazine, cock the weapon and apply the safety catch. If you do have to use it, always remember, *reload*.

In 1947, in Jerusalem, a corporal in my company saw an Arab toss a grenade into a café used by Europeans. He scrambled up onto a roof after him and they exchanged some shots, but missed each other. The corporal gave chase, but the fellow dropped down into a teeming suq and he lost him. So he thought that was that. But later in the day he wandered up this alleyway, turned a corner and found himself face to face with the villain. Now to swing a sub-machine-gun off your shoulder and fire it takes between one and two seconds and so having his pistol just thrust into his belt, the Arab easily beat the corporal to the draw. But when he pulled the trigger, it just went "click". So remember, *reload*.'

They folded up the rubber poncho they had spread their kit on and headed back to the Land Rover. Letheren's hands were rosy and warm, but Artemis's were frozen and numb and even putting her gloves back on had no immediate effect. The military tenor of the afternoon though had been an enjoyable change.

The Colonel turned on the vehicle's engine and heater, but after three hours it took ages before it produced any warmth. He massaged her thin bony white fingers for her and then she clutched her plastic tea cup and slowly life seeped back into them. They ate half-chickens and bread rolls and foil-wrapped cheeses, followed by cherries in chocolate blancmange.

'"Artemis" is eponymus with a Lacedæmonian goddess called "Orthia". She danced with the oreads and punished those who perverted truth. At her altar in Sparta, boys were whipped. "Orthia" means "the straight one".'

'And am I straight?'

He inhaled deeply. 'You can be, if you listen to your instincts and do what they tell you.'

'Do you think I shall manage that?'

He rocked his head uncertainly. 'Everything comes to her who knows how to wait.' His arm lay lightly across her shoulders and she felt submissive, so willing to acquiesce to whatever he said. 'Your objective is Drumairth Castle. It is difficult because it is heavily protected and also it is at the end of a long dead-end road, so if the alarm is raised, you could be trapped. But a lot of money is due to change hands there.

Should you have to flee and go into hiding, go to ... Aberystwyth shall we say and be at the railway station ticket office at midday each day until I meet you? We can arrange your passage to France or even South America if need be and we've enough money and false documents to help you.'

She passively absorbed all his points like an obedient novice.

'This Porsche of yours is an unusual and interest-arousing vehicle.'

'I can change the plates on it.'

'Even so, there can't be many of them around. If it was seen, it wouldn't be too hard to trace. How about swapping with this Land Rover for the raid? It's four-wheel-drive too which is important as the terrain's wild and wet and marshy and amongst crofters and foresters, they're pretty ubiquitous – no one will pay any attention to it.

We're going back into Glen Moriston now. It'll be dark soon. We'll hide our vehicle there and move up through a hanger of trees to a house which belongs to an old friend of mine. He has set up a number of counter-intruder devices – beams we have to crawl under, trip wires you must feel for with a stick and then secure without altering the tension in them before cutting the other end ... We're going firstly to try to penetrate the outer fence and secondly to break into his ground-floor office in the flat white building.'

'How to become an élite agent in one day.'

'Many non-military Walter Mitty type nutters are obsessed with so-called "élite" troops – their toughness, reaction times, survival skills and so forth – but they overlook one of the most fundamental qualities – patience. To lie under a hedgerow for nine hours in the rain without a cup of tea or a newspaper is pretty testing.'

Artemis's cheeks dimpled. 'Everything comes to him who knows how to wait.' She suddenly hoped at some point soon to have sex with this man, but she hid the thought.

'First item, wire-cutters ... '

'What happens if I *do* trigger something?'

'My friend knows we're coming.'

'No, I meant at Drumairth Castle?'

'You mustn't. That's why we're practising. This acquaintance whom we shall meet later tonight will talk to us about the commonest commercially available gadgets, supply us with special paper which shows up infra-red beams without interrupting them and so on.'

The girl found it bizarrely electrifying. It helped to obliterate any thought of Simon. A stillness started to suffuse her well-schooled pose, a calmness far removed from her nurse and doctor colleagues who rushed about like wasps in bottles. How far had she come from her days as a silly spoilt schoolgirl, when she and her companions had occasionally travelled up through these glens to Fort William or the Isles?

* * *

Donald Boden had been into Castle Douglas, paid fourteen bills in cash and then split the remainder of Artemis's unexpected donation into his various thirsty accounts such that none received more than £900. Such smallish amounts he trusted would not incur any undue attention.

At home he spent the afternoon wielding a large axe and halving some of the sawn pine logs so that they could dry out. This should really have been done last summer. As he stacked them in the stable used for fire-wood, wearing an old pair of overalls with an iron-shaped burn mark on the thigh, a logging contractor called and they discussed clearing the ground for six yards on either side of the long driveway.

Walking back towards Uanrig with the loch on his right and the house ahead of him, he saw beyond them to the North, the ridge above the Eilan Burn from which the estate took its name. The shiny waters of the loch and the velvety trees near to him were both a deep forest green, but the trees on the low ridge were smoky blue. Charcoal grey rock faces and screes scarred it in places and wisps of mist floated past, giving its rime-bearded countenance an air of primeval mystery. The second element of the word 'Uanrig', 'rig' – a variant of the more usual 'rigg' but with the final consonant elided – had come from the Old Norse noun 'hrygga' meaning 'ridge'. The first particle though, 'uan' was harder and more obscure. It could have come from the Gaelic substantive 'uamh' or its archaic locative form 'uáim', meaning 'cave' or 'den'. It could also have been derived from the Old English 'wonn' or the Old Norse 'vanr', prefixes meaning 'gloomy' or 'bad', though the shift of the 'v' or 'w' to 'u' would be an irregular and corrupt progression.

Behind this 'bad-hill' or 'cave-hill', were other bullet-headed outcrops of harsh grey rock, wet and mossy and treeless, like cancers bursting through the soft smooth concave slopes on the far side.

Sheelagh had come and gone.

In Artemis's bedroom, he sat on her dowdy small four-poster for a time, holding a photograph of her sitting on a camel in Egypt. On the large table by the window were other photographs, hair-grips, pens, letters and then he found the rest of the money and the gold coins.

It was almost three in the morning when the Land Rover woke him. He had dozed off on the sofa, with a glass of Cockburn's port, some Stilton and some cream crackers standing half-eaten on a side-table.

She came into the utility room, unzipped her riding boots and yet still pulled them off with the boot-jack. She padded through the dark kitchen and on into the hallway where she ran into the unseen arms of her father. They fell over clumsily and came to rest with him on his back on the Moroccan rug and her on top of his supine form.

'Are you all right?' he asked.

'Of course, Papa,' she answered curtly and without an endearment.

'I do love you Artemis.' Having children is a great antidote to egocentricity. Only then do we want someone else's good more than our own.

'Stop worrying. I've been crawling around in the snow a lot. The knees of these dungarees are still wet.' She tried to get up, but he held her tightly. 'Let go.' They got onto their knees. 'Feel them. They're not like leather any more, but floppy and soggy like rubber.'

They went through to the sitting-room where the light was on.

'I would feel happier if I knew what you were up to.' He peered into the loveless fissures of her eye-sockets, but her stubborn cold pride resisted him. 'Are you sure you shouldn't marry Simon?'

'NO!' He grabbed her but she struggled to free herself from his grasp, trying to prise his chest away from hers. He let her go and she strode dismissively away to drink water and then go to bed.

She halted on the middle third of the staircase and looked down at his distressed face. 'I have a unique chance before me and I'm *not* going to waste it.' His features did not alter. 'Trust me for heaven's sake! I'm sensible enough not to interfere or complain about your liaison with Paula Gordon, so be even-handed enough to reciprocate. We're going to solve our troubles. A revived life awaits us.' Still he looked fretful. 'How about bloody well backing me?'

After some moments of watching his perplexed face grow older and sadder, she sighed despairingly and marched off to bed.

* * *

In the Lake District, the snow was melting.

In the yard at Esland's Shieling a sulky subsiding off-white soufflé, criss-crossed by pairs of water-filled grey ruts proved it, as did the pitter-pattering of water droplets off the unguttered roof edges of the barn.

Catharine, crossing the yard, saw a sheep up on the hillside with its hind legs caught in a netting fence. She let herself through the five bar gate in the wire-topped stone wall and waded up the steep white hill to where the animal lay ensnared in a surplus strand of coiled wire, not properly tidied up after some fencing repairs. It was a Blackface and it looked so twitchy that Catharine thought it might have lost the will to live, but on being freed it skipped off in search of the flock.

Lifting her head to follow its gambol, an artificial blue object on the ridge above her caught her eye, like a blip on a photograph, but when she tried to pick it up again it had vanished. Puzzled and suspicious, she plodded on up through the heavy wet snow, puffing as she reached the crest.

On the shallow far side of this mini-arête, an early morning mist had retreated some way down the slope and now seemed to be penned in behind a drear stone wall.

Heading for this wall was a figure who wore a sizeable thick medium blue anorak over darker overalls. He had half-walked and half-slithered, but as he turned on reaching the wall and caught sight of the girl heading towards him, he showed signs of uncomfortable surprise.

His navy overalls vaguely resembled a police riot suit and he had a pair of binoculars slung round his neck. As the gap closed and she saw him more clearly, she thought that he looked a decent enough fellow – with a tall sprinter-like physique and a moustache – but his embarrassment was intense.

'May I ask what you are doing here?' asked the lass in her long navy waxed-canvas jacket and rubber boots.

'May I first ask who you are, Ma'am?'

'I'm Miss Letheren, the landowner's daughter.'

'I'm a police officer,' he admitted. 'Constable T. C. Holgate, Cumberland Constabulary, number 555. Carlisle Sub-Division.' He padded his pockets and found his warrant, which Catharine inspected briefly.

'Thank you Constable.' She set off, retracing his deep footprints of arrival. They led over the spur of a hill before dropping down to a small tarn, where a well-polished dark green Humber Sceptre stood parked on a dead-end track. Catharine walked round the tarn's frozen surface, edged by a ring of snow-coated rocks and knocked on the steamed-up windows of the car.

A broad man in his fifties climbed out with measured impatience. He wore a mohair overcoat and a dark graphite suit, a white shirt and a maroon tie with college escutcheons or regimental emblems on it. This impeccably tailored conservative dress was of Savile Row quality. His face tended to gourmet-like plumpness and his attitude smacked of the pedantic and the supercilious. His portentousness and command sprang not from goodness, but from his being a complex and uncertain quantity. He had the facility to disconcert.

Within an instant of eyeing Catharine he had upset her deeply, because his sceptically bland features made it clear just how scathing and dismissive was his regard for girls. Girls impinged on nothing in his world and counted for nothing. Catharine, who was not generally touchy or quick to take offence, averted her head and walked away with burning cheeks. There had been no point in asking either of these men what they were doing, since the only thing they could be doing was watching Tan Hall.

On the main track to the farm she stopped the old blue caterpillar tractor, which was towing a trailer loaded with hay bales. Keith, the driver, was a blithe town-born fellow, not given to those strange sulky moods which afflict many country folk and which town-dwellers can never interpret. A deep-seated anger had taken possession of her and it led her to do something which afterwards she would find very surprising and which was quite out of character for someone so passive. She told Keith to unhook the trailer in a tiny passing place and that done, she clambered up onto the tractor and set off, starting with a violent jolt. She had not driven it before, but knew it to be steered by the two brake-levers. She could not change gear and had to stop and let Keith demonstrate. Again the tractor lurched off, banging and making erratic movements. It clattered along the track. It turned hard right up a narrow side spur to the tarn, ascending this steep incline with consummate ease. As it tipped over a ridge, they met a track with a gentler gradient and here she found the searched-for grey furrows of the Sceptre. Catharine, filled with dark distress, saw Holgate and her more pompous foe in consultation at the far end of the white crater of the tarn.

Too late they realised what she intended to do. Holgate had been protesting his disquiet to the fat man and radioing for a more senior officer, when helplessly he saw the four ton tractor bash into the Sceptre and with its immane strength and ample grip, push the overpowered car effortlessly out onto the thin sprinkling of dissolving sugar-like snow on the tarn. The layer of ice beneath it cracked. The car floated for a moment on its own tectonic plate, which then tilted. Its load slid off into the shallows. The doomed hulk settled in a submerged position, except for its boot which remained above the surface.

Holgate ran up, looking very bewildered. 'What *are* you doing?'

'My father will want proof that you've been here.'

Holgate said no more. He believed that both Catharine and the Whitehall oaf knew a lot more about the real game in progress, than the drivel he had been told.

His charge deigned to stroll over. His look of disdain for the girl had increased rather than diminished. It seemed to say that this childish tantrum-like act, unclever and unsubtle as it was, was exactly what one might expect from a female.

Holgate said, 'I think you've put us in a most invidious position Mr Potts.' This bloater could vanish into the anonymity of some nameless department in London and leave the Cumberland Constabulary to explain itself. Miss Letheren, he felt, was really quite homely right-minded and uncapricious, whereas Mr Potts came from a sub-species whose highly devious thought processes and palpable sliminess made him a dangerous and untrustworthy ally. He would take no action against Miss Letheren.

The tractor growled and pivoted round with one track stationary, before clattering off down the hill.

In the yard Catharine tripped as she jumped off it, fell flat in the slush, picked herself up and ran indoors. She threw off her wet outer clothes and bounded upstairs unseen, to hide in a forgotten attic room and burst out crying. What next? Did these swine never give up? Would she be arrested or imprisoned?

She fell asleep in the rocking-chair and dreamt that she was skating on the tarn in an anorak and skirt and that the reptilian Mr Potts fell through the ice as he moved towards her, but still a huge eye remained above the surface and it watched her. She awoke but felt delirious. Should she flee the country? She thought of the rare condition she suffered from, whereby she possessed only tiny breasts, no pubic or axillary hair, no internal female organs and only a rudimentary vagina. She might be statuesque and winsome, but she could look forward to no family of her own. And Pappa had gone to Scotland to train this Boden girl for some new débâcle before heading directly for Germany. Then into this frightening half-world of distorted time, Innogen's voice spoke softly, 'Catharine, you were quite right to use the heavy tractor as you did. They're worried men out there and it serves them right.'

Catharine woke up again.

The room contained an unwanted table and some shelves on which many mahogany boxes and dust-powdered archaeological artefacts were sleepily displayed. They called it the 'Cyrene Room'.

Catharine had been a number of times with her father to ancient Cyrene, whilst in Libya, now inland and at the top of the second escarpment. Just kicking around in the sand in between the ruins, you could pick up forty coins in a day – tiny little verdigris-spoiled bronze blobs or splendid silver tetradrachmae with large-beaked Ptolemaic eagles on them. As Alcman said, 'The sea glittered like an expanse of gold coins'.

She emptied out the coin box and covered a table with hundreds of them. There were small Byzantine ones with a Greek letter on to represent a numeral, thick encrusted Phoenician ones, pre-Hellenistic ones from the North African Pentapolis with wheel motifs or dolphins on, an odd Athenian owl and a couple of Jewish shekels from the time of the Herods.

There were small oil-lamps, votive offering jugs and figurines of shoddy workmanship, baked clay fish-net weights, beads of blue and red which would adorn when all else was ochre and dusty and sand-coloured and a large lump of blackened silver shaped like a bowl on its outside and which her father thought might have been someone's money, melted down when the city of Apollonia had been burned. Seen in a museum these items would be dull, but when you had helped find them they felt more intimate, as did the people who had owned them. She remembered that the oil-lamps each had their hook on the side, so that when hung up the last few drops of oil would not run out through the spout and be wasted.

There was a ring, a small delicate one of thin twisted gold with a deep blue hemispherical stone the size of a ladybird. The stone had a line of gold glitter through it, perhaps a vein of pyrites. Innogen had found it near the necropolis at Cyrene one day. It had been raining and only the stone stood out on a rubbish heap beside a trench where some classicists had been digging. At first her sister had thought it to be just a bead of water. Catharine slid it onto her little finger.

Well-packed in another box were two narrow-necked wine jugs – their best treasures. An excavator had dug a water channel through some ancient graves. Most had been plundered in antiquity, but one set at a peculiar angle had been left undisturbed. The Department of Antiquities man had come along and taken a quantity of stuff, but appeared not to know that at that date there was an ante-room before the main burial chamber. The Colonel had found the steps down, dug around for the bones – the wooden chest had long since perished – and at the head and feet had stood these two wine jugs.

Catharine wanted to marry and settle in a little town in the Border Country – such as Hawick where her mother had come from – called 'Hoyk' by the locals and where 'one' is 'yun' and 'two' is 'tway'. She did not desire a life of educational masochism and career-chasing – fretting and troubling her mind – but just to marry a farmer or whatever, cuddle her childer, bake bread, tend the geese and the vegetable patch and make jam for the church bazaar. Unlike most modern women, she would have been quite content with such a life, but as she could not bear children and the fact that such a life belonged to a vanishing world, her future was very unclear.

She rocked the rocking-chair and fell asleep again.

At seven in the evening, the maid found her and woke her. 'There's some stew for you downstairs, Miss.'

'Er ... thank you.' She removed the ring, shivered and went downstairs to eat beside the kitchen fire.

The cook and the farm hands had already left for their own homes, the stable girl who lived in had gone to stay with a 'friend' and the maid with her dynamic personality and ridiculous ear-rings, though also usually resident, had left to visit her parents.

As Catharine chewed her stew at the heavy and well-scored elm table, an instinct told her that something would happen that night. If Nicholas or Pappa had been there, they would have set up pyro-technic trip-wires and perhaps taken up hidden positions outside.

The outside doors, set in walls two and a half feet thick, were of inch and a half oak with bolts and locks and wrought-iron drop-bars on the inside. The ground-floor windows also had internal oak shutters with drop-bars and two had fixed outside bars too. So when all these defences were in place, even a medieval riot mob equipped with anything less than a battering-ram, would have found it hard to force an entry.

Catharine went round making the house as secure as possible, before sitting in the kitchen and reading by fire-light one of Innogen's books about early court dances. The discussion of pavans and bourrées, cebells and minuets reminded her of school dancing lessons with the courtier-like Mr Foy. She drank tea and ate a Napoleon flaky-pastry cake. A loaded shot-gun hung balanced and broken over the arm of a chair. She felt half-safe, calmly prepared to wait and see what would happen, as if she knew that some good spirits were with her.

At about midnight, she remembered that somewhere in the house was a four-bore elk-hunting gun with an infra-red night-sight. Because of the shutters, no one outside the house could know which downstairs room she was in and by going upstairs without turning any lights on, she hoped still to keep her whereabouts secret. In the dark, in a rarely frequented cupboard, she ferreted around and amidst the cascade of junk which fell out found the gun. In the kitchen again, she detached the rather clumsy and primitive night-sight and found some new batteries for it. Kneeling with it on her carved wooden bed by a first-floor window, it picked up a power line and a couple of bloated globular sheep against the cold lifeless zero-emission background.

She played patience with a pack of French cards.

At two o'clock, one of her intermittent sweeps with this infra-red sight, made from the first-floor sitting-room window, picked up in the black void two science-fiction-like images of human forms. Their transmuted and patchy pale green shapes – trailing comets' tails of fading light when they moved – advanced with clearly human gaits. Probably they would try to enter here, through the balcony's French windows. On this side of the sixteenth-century fortified manor lay a small formal lawn with hedges cut into cubes and pyramids. Here too, a hefty cast-iron drain-pipe ran down from the guttering past the end of the stone balcony.

For stealth Catharine had on only her socks. She tripped downstairs to fetch the shot-gun and some spare cartridges.

Had one of these limpets half-scaled the wall yet?

Upstairs again, she peeped through the crack between the not quite closed double doors of the sitting-room. She watched a vague black shadow on the balcony for a while, mistakenly thinking it to be of human form. Then something moved. Someone was there and giving their slow and expert attention to the windows. But what would he do once inside?

If she blasted him, she could see herself before a wigged and indignant prosecutor. 'You did not ring the police Miss Letheren? I put it to you that you *wished* to murder him, that your father's abominable deeds had to be kept hidden from decent men at all costs? I put it to you, that you considered it a *necessary* slaughter?'

She jumped as a minute light went on. The intruder was inside. He knelt by a small plain chest of drawers. An infinitesimal squeak attended his opening of the bottom drawer. The pin-point light flickered again, like a diminutive sparkler. In the intense shadow, a half-imagined face and hands could be perceived. The hands placed something in the drawer. The visitor departed. The window closed with a soft grating sound.

In the kitchen, she tossed yet more logs into the fire and drank a cup of thick cocoa. After a time she crept upstairs with a torch and opened the drawer. The uppermost item was a buff folder with a crimson band down its middle. Beneath it were half-used candles, some photocopies of articles about Phoenician and Greek alphabets and some old Christmas cards.

Seen in the more satisfactory light of the blazing logs, the papers in the buff folder – each headed with the sequence 'D.I.S./74R18A' – reported a naval incursion inside East German territorial waters. The destroyer *H.M.S. Bristol*, had nominally sailed on a showing-the-flag visit to Stockholm, to let all those tall blonde sex-mad Swedish girls swarm up her sides, but en route at dead of night, she had crept in a blacked-out red-alert state up to the Island of Rügen to test the Warsaw

Pact's defences. She had come to within one and a half nautical miles of the light at Thiessow without any hostile radars locking onto her. The A.D.F. beacon had been on at the Wusterhusen military airfield to guide a returning Russian 'Bear' bomber home and they had picked up traffic from police radios in Stralsund too. Nothing had suggested suspicion or abnormal activity.

She dozed for a couple of hours until half past five, then waking with a jolt, rattled the ashes through the bars of the grate and put on more logs for the eighth time. She turned on the lights, opened up the shutters and set gammon and egg to sizzle in the frying-pan.

The salty bacon and the cup of tea tasted good together. Headlamps shone in the black yard outside – Percy the shepherd she presumed. The worn bronze knocker rapped its back-plate.

Catharine put down her knife and fork and stood up. In the yard stood a white car with an unilluminated blue light on its roof. 'The file,' came her sister's voice, 'Burn it.'

'All right,' she answered nobody.

The red laidly-worm stretched itself along the curling lower edge, before a woof of yellow and blue consumed it sheet by sheet, the black layers of ash falling away in turn.

She opened the door and saw four men. Two were police officers and quite senior too, to judge by the silver badges on their epaulettes, the silver braid on their caps and the way in which they clasped their removed leather gloves in one hand and thwacked them into the palm of the opposite hand like gentry.

'Are you the lady of the house, Miss?'

'Yes.'

'I have a search warrant here, to enable us to look over your premises.

'I know.' Her tone was stern and cool.

The Assistant Chief Constable looked mildly surprised. The overcoated shadows behind him showed no obvious reaction.

The foursome entered, wiping their shoes with demonstrative courtesy on the large oakum mat. The flames in the hearth shone on the cold faces of the mute non-uniformed men and on Catharine's warm soft pale face. Her eye scanned the stone slabs in front of the fire, to ensure that no fragments of the planted documents had escaped in a half-burnt state.

'These gentlemen from London do not have the authority to search by themselves and so we have to escort them.'

She asked to see the policemen's warrants and wrote down their names and numbers and the time on a sheet of writing paper. 'And the names of these men?'

'I suppose you are entitled to know that – Mr Horace Cavendish and his deputy Mr Anthony Thomas.'

'Thank you, Chief Constable. If you would all like to come with me, I will lead you to what you were hoping to *stumble* upon.' Seeing their oldest shepherd in the yard, Catharine opened the door and summoned him in. 'Percy, take off your boots and follow us.'

Upstairs she bent down and opened the drawer, illumined by the weak light of the small bulbs in the brass chandelier.

'Search if you will, gentlemen.'

One of the non-uniformed men took an inaudible but visible deep breath. The policemen looked at him for a decision, but Cavendish turned wordlessly away and gazed out of the French windows.

'Well, I suppose you'll be going now, yes?' said Catharine. 'After all, you're not likely to want to discuss this fiasco in front of me.' It was tartly sarcastic.

Percy inspected his fob-watch. He had been a railway guard on the old Penrith to Cockermouth line and any delay to his daily routine upset him greatly. 'New brooms sweep cleaner than old brooms,' he declared irrationally.

Catharine closed one eye tightly and opened the other widely. She wagged a forefinger at the foiled Cavendish, like a blunt sword. 'You people were being watched last night. I suppose for your outfit to survive though, you have to serve the modern trends?'

Thomas gave the remotest hint of an insubordinate smirk, whilst Cavendish tottered for an instant as though he would overbalance.

As the callers left, the bemused police officers put on their caps, which each touched in turn as he said his stilted, 'Morning Ma'am.'

* * *

The sea had only the slightest swell. Its surface was oily and smooth and green, like liquid glass. The fog was of even density and visibility down to less than half a cable. The two men in the lobster boat *Fiona*, waited helplessly as criminals in the dock await a judge's verdict. The one with the sleepy cunning about his eyes listened to the other talk about his days in the navy. ' ... and on this cruiser we had this fucking C.P.O., who for every meaningless oversight made you throw darts at the dartboard and then deducted pay according to how badly you had scored.'

Then it was there. Edging through the penetrable wall of mist, black and massive and hidden from heaven's arch, the enormous submarine floated close by like a sightless leviathan. Russian military equipment was as a rule, monstrous and clumsy and ugly in comparison to the weapons of the N.A.T.O.

countries and this colossus was no exception. Its breadth rather than its length impressed the men in the cockle-shell, its hull seeming disproportionately and inelegantly large to the stern fin and the unattractively streamlined dwarf conning-tower, which stood out like a boil on a whale.

The midget-like lobster boat's diesel spluttered rudely in the enshrouding haze. Her side bumped into the convex outer casing of the submersible, just as a hatch opened in the base of the conning-tower and out tumbled sailors, some clutching rifles and others with the stanchions and ropes with which to erect the dismantlable hand-rail down the curving upper surface of the hull to the water's edge.

Submarines carry no flag or pennant number. Naval men can by the outline of one though, determine her class and then by minor alterations and dents in it try to decide which particular member she is – an art known by the pseudo-scientific term of 'dentology'. Ian Leith knew that as well as the Royal Navy base at Gare Loch on this coast, that torpedo firing ranges existed in Loch Fyne and up in the Minch and that all these were often used by American and French boats as well as British ones. He had never before though seen a Russian submarine. This eastern Titan he had initially thought might be a Juliett class cruise-missile type, but its sheer size made him dismiss that notion.

Without a word or a greeting, he and a group of Baltic coast sailors helped the man with five waterproof suitcases to scramble over the *Fiona's* gunwale.

The sailors vanished. The black island nudged past, a patch of frothy turbulence at its stern indicating the slow revolutions of its propeller. As the fog and the water jointly absorbed it, it took on for a moment a dull glaucous colour in a mercury sea under a white hazy nimbus and something forlorn and sad about its existence hung in the unsleeping air. As with people who lie, a whiff of worthlessness and doom followed it.

The *Fiona* was alone again, cocooned in the blind eerie silence.

* * *

Drumairth Castle stood on the Mull of Móry, the southern tip of a seven mile rocky finger of land off the West Coast of Scotland and in the County of Argyllshire.

The blue short-wheelbase Land Rover had halted on the single-track pot-holed road which ran down this flat sad spur of iron-grey basalt. The snow on it had begun to melt and then frozen again, so it had a drab sunken appearance with holes in it like Emmental cheese, through which patches of brown broom and gorse and low outcrops of grey squared columnar rock stuck up. To the West was the lack-lustre blue-grey sea and on the East, the small River Ayrth – broadened out into a marsh – lay frozen with tufts of yellow salt-grass poking through the ice here and there.

The temperature was minus three and there was almost no wind. The sea rose and fell minimally with unusual calm and Artemis wound her window down and looked out beyond the flat brown water-smoothed chain of inshore islets, which lay under a pale blue sky streaked with the merest smears of cloud, to the scarred dark blue outline of the Island of Jura across the sound.

Artemis had been up since long before dawn. She had been in Glasgow before nine o'clock ready for the shops to open and bought a long list of tools, snow-chains, a shovel, a fire extinguisher, two long lengths of red braided nylon rope, torches, batteries, rubber boots in black and white, a cheap white rubber cagoule and a green nylon one from a camping specialist's, a tripod and a terrestrial telescope with a magnification of twenty, boxes of yellow cubes for lighting fires and heating water and food, a thick sleeping-bag and large scale maps. All this she had crammed into the rear of the hard-topped Land Rover.

After consulting one of these undirtied maps she continued down the narrow peninsula, though soon had to slow to squeeze past a white mini-bus. Its driver she saw to be Angus Caie – Lord Ayrth – in person, a grey-haired common man whom Letheren had had a picture of, along with fuzzier ones of her other marked-down victims.

The wallowing phut-phutting fishing smack off the coast occasioned no special attention in her, for Letheren's sketch of the forthcoming scenario had involved no boats or people arriving by boat.

Lord Ayrth's ancestry did not include, as you might imagine, a long line of romantic and fiercely independent clan chieftains, but a rabble of minor shirkers and skivers from Greenock, the offspring of liars robbers and wedlock-breakers. Lord Ayrth had been elevated to the peerage after a long and illustrious political career spent in promoting the rights of shirkers and skivers.

There was a telephone wire on a row of poles, but no electricity cable. The castle had its own generator.

The road led to a pair of heavy black-painted steel gates in a five foot high stone wall, which crossed a four hundred yard wide isthmus. Behind it were taller steel posts with netting interwoven with razor-wire.

Artemis pulled up and stepped out onto the icy tar macadam. She wore a thick white cable-knit sweater, a white and black shepherd's tartan kilt with its two buckled leather straps over her left hip and its huge safety-pin just above the hem, white knee-length socks with black tabs gripped by her hidden garters peeping out under the turned down sock tops and plain black shoes.

She looked ahead through the vertically-barred electrically-operated gates and a surly middle-aged man looked back. 'End whet does youce whent?' This was no local highlander or islander, but an uncouth Irish import brought via a Glaswegian distillery.

Artemis exaggerated her own Scottish burr to make herself seem more like a native. 'Och laddie, ah kenned this road led to Gaillie Bridge?'

'Na.'

'Ah was goin' to ma wee scon nephew's wi' a bonnie wooden train. Ah'm nee hair to gar trooble withinnen.'

He stared blankly at her.

'Can yer no kythe me tha way?' Having ascertained that she had no business there, he gave her two fingers. 'Skeet, youce flahoolick skirt.'

She had seen all she needed to see, so it suited her to terminate the exchange. She shrugged, climbed back into her vehicle, turned it round and drove away.

The place felt creepy. The goblin on the gate bore the stamp of his employer's disenlightenment and whereas usually you could stroll round Scottish castles and enjoy the scenery, this place resembled a gulag. Behind the wire-topped wall and the second fence of tangled wire two yards further in, the cables of various ultra-high-frequency detector alarms had been visible. These obstacles extended right down to and into the water on either side. Through the gates she had glimpsed the maroon and white castle, but that was not an immediate concern. What she had seen was that the River Ayrth was frozen. A long concrete weir between two shoulders of rock kept it largely salt-free. Today it was a snow-covered lake. She would have to trust that it held until Monday or else consider crossing the weir, though that too might be rigged with traps and wire. The transfluvine approach circumvented the formidable main wall and also the problem of where to leave the vehicle on this exposed finger. The disadvantage was the lack of a road on the other side of the river. None the less, she felt instinctively sure that there lay the right line of advance. The first leg of her assault had been fixed.

She repassed the mini-bus parked on the rough verge and saw Lord Ayrth down by the water's edge with a second man and a pile of luggage. *He* must be the unknown envoy from Berlin.

Artemis would have to extend her four days of holiday. She would ring up the duty nursing officer at North Shields tonight and claim to have caught influenza. Each time there were a few cases about, the nurses created an apparent epidemic by using it en masse as an excuse for some extra leave. Artemis disliked the ploy's transparent lack of originality, but could not improve on it for well-proven infallibility.

This raid would be dangerous and difficult – to a sober mind, chilling. But Artemis knew that once she were zipped up from toe to collar in her burnished and glistening black leather suit, that she would feel transformed and malleable and unscared. Mortality would disappear and everything would be possible.

In the garden, lured by the snake inside her to eat the forbidden apples, Artemis felt good, but unlike Eve she would not repent when the time came, but persist in defying God. Her pistol too made her feel safer and tougher and more intrepid. And the sum of money promised at the end of this particular rainbow would set her up for years, perhaps even for life.

Mr Letheren knew her deepest secrets better than she herself. He was practically inside her and yet for the moment, she did not mind. Helios the sun – he intrigued her – the necessary sub-priest in her soothing dreams, his middle name and the bright and life-giving judge of whom she was a mere extension – his reflecting moon.

The Land Rover rattled round the thirty miles of poorly-metalled and holed roads, cracked and damaged by frosts and seldom patched, to stop just short of coming out on the coast two headlands down from the Mull of Móry.

She drew into a plantation of young firs and consumed her habitual cup of tea and a roll with boiled ham on it.

Beside her lapped the waters of Loch Righ, a sea loch indenting the land by about six miles, yet barely half a mile wide at its neck. On its northern side stood a barren rocky spine about forty feet high, unnamed on the maps and which separated Loch Righ from the frozen marsh of the River Ayrth. She put on the pair of white boots and the hooded white rubberised canvas wind-cheater bought that morning and strolled across the road, through the snow-hidden prickly furze, across brown seaweed-draped rocks to a beach of wet white sand, washed by the everlasting sea. An island in the mouth of the loch calmed its brackish waters in contrast to the white-speckled choppy greyness beyond. Further in, some phosphorescent orange marker buoys in the loch, indicated the nets of a fish farm, the sole sign of life on this desolate rugged coastline.

If it were still, she could row a small dinghy from here to the opposite ridge, scale that, slide down onto the frozen River Ayrth and then cross that to the castle.

Moving back across the gelatinous seaweed-embellished jumble of rocks, she slipped over and bruised her elbow and thigh and wet her skirt. This rubber clothing was cold floppy and though more waterproof than her leather, not emboldening or snug or resilient. Had she slipped on these rocks in her leather, her injuries and discomfort would have been much less.

With the telescope and tripod, she moved through the plantation until she could just see the Mull of Móry round the shoulder of the unnamed intervening peninsula. In a cleft between two elongated tongues of rock, she moved further out and set up the telescope so that it just peered over one of these minor ridges. She trained it out over the mouth of Loch Righ and onto Drumairth Castle.

The castle dated from 1609. It was half castle and half stately home, a combination common in Scotland. Its solid stone walls, surfaced with pebbles except for the quoining, gave it its Gaelic name of 'Artandunan' – 'little fort of pebbles'. These walls were pierced with three rows of sash-windows rather than arrow slits and the little round turrets on each corner had more to do with romantic pretension than the despatch of boiling oil. It was roughly a forty foot cube, painted white with maroon window frames and topped by an array of chimneys and an extraordinary proliferation of aerials. To one side was a quadruple garage, a small whitewashed workshop-cum-store, a stone barn, an oil tank and a selection of vehicles.

Artemis spent forty-five minutes observing it, before the sun dipped down behind the darkening mauve outline of Jura, on this the day before the shortest day of the year, Saturday the twentieth of December. A breeze had sprung up and a damp salt-laden vapour floated inland.

So at a quarter past four, cold and damp, Artemis set off for Loch Eilan and arrived there in a pretty weary state at about seven thirty. The Land Rover was not an easy vehicle for long journeys. The driver's high position rolled from side to side and induced a different type of weariness to car driving.

She treated both her riding boots and her leather suit with lanolin oil, used usually for saddlery. It was absorbed by the leather which in turn became heavier, more waterproof and more easily wiped clean of mud and dirt, but it made it look very dull. That would not do for she wanted these clothes to glint and look belligerent and so an hour later on the spread-out newspaper on the kitchen floor, she smeared them with a clear wax dubbin, which she would rub hard and polish up to a good shine in the morning, to give them a fine soft waxy gloss. Like her coat her suit was made of top-side leather and therefore had its natural grain markings. It had been cut out accurately, sewn with a neat strong stitch and hopefully could take whatever Drumairth Castle might do to it.

After she and Papa had eaten the meal left by Sheelagh, her father went to bed not feeling well. The atmosphere that evening had not so much been bad as non-existent.

Artemis sat in the fire-light with the curtains drawn and watched television. The news repertoire detailed the progress of a series of strikes, the usual tedious menu at that time as mobs of workers held the country to repeated ransom. Michael Rose figured briefly on it, one of the men she expected to meet on Monday evening. The Admiralty wished to place some sonar apparatus on the sea bed between the North of Scotland and Iceland to assist it in tracking Russia's fleet of four hundred submarines, but Rose was against it, describing it as 'provocative' and 'escalatory'.

She pulled her legs up underneath her on the heavy and long dusky blue sofa, which with its four back and four seat cushions of stiff and infinitely durable hide, gave you a comfortable posture only if you did not like softness and sinking.

The weather forecast for Scotland was for cold weather with no gales or storms. Could it be relied upon?

Then came a Richard Burton film. She admired him greatly. His depth made the other actors look like cardboard cut-outs. He may have had some training, but his gravity stemmed from his profound, almost Wagnerian passions. In one scene she wondered if he were not drunk, but still his command were undiminished. The film dealt with an embittered old soldier and a French banker who was a twenty-four carat ball of grease with twisted fat lips like a halibut and it took her mind back to her years spent at the Ecole Ste. Baume in Nîmes.

The burghers of le Midi – and perhaps the whole of France and the low countries for that matter – had seemed to her, beneath a courteous oily righteous exterior to harbour concealed corruptions. Behind their unctuous civilities were mazes of intrigue, echoes arising still from the age-old tensions between *les gros* and *les petits*. The nuns, as if aware of this inevitable imperfection in the human composition, had tried to flee from it into a vault of prayer and meditation. They were partly successful in that the dissembled selfishness of individual taxonomy was subjugated, but it left them austere and withered. Outside the little back-street linen and tin-ware shops near the convent, old women in plain black skirts had sat in summer, knitting with coarse wool and with an unkind indifference in their eyes which had shocked Artemis at first, as if they had finally perceived the lying and unhealthy condition around them and understood that it would never change. What Artemis had liked about the French was their capacity for bold and colourful and grandiose imagination, though unfortunately, something delusory and seedy made their dreams in practice seem tawdry. The French seem effeminate to northern Europeans, because they possess an adeptness at living in a world of fancy – very beautiful to the dreamer, but regrettably inconsistent with churlish reality.

One pleasant aspect of the school in Nîmes had been that on her holidays her parents would usually appear and off they would sally to Switzerland or the Black Forest or Italy.

Artemis parted the curtains and peered out into the darkness. There, there hung a waning and white December three-quarter moon. In two nights' time it mattered that no cloud blotted it out if she were to row across the black waters of Loch Righ and not lose her way. 'Oh fair moon, do not fail your pure daughter,' she said with a preternatural air of melodrama.

As soon as her head touched the pillow, she fell asleep.

Next morning Sheelagh had the day off and Donald went off to Ludlow.

Artemis found the inflatable grey rubber dinghy in the spare room and set about blowing it up laboriously with a foot-pump, to see if it was usable or if she would have to buy another. With a rope threaded through the eyes on its collapsible gunwale and tied with a knot, she dragged it through a freezing mist down to the loch in front of the house. In dungarees, Wellingtons, woolly and red anorak, she fitted the wooden box-seat amidships and athwart, pushed the boat out, climbed into it, put the shafts of the short wooden oars into the rowlocks and after a bit of practice, timed herself across the loch and back.

The afternoon was spent in a little field up near the Eilan Burn, one of their two small one acre fields and the one where her horse used to graze. The weeds and thistles were waist-high now and flecked and stippled thin sunlight shone down obliquely through the tops of the surrounding pines. On the fallen branch of a rotten chestnut tree, she suspended an old plywood archery target and nearby on an old rubber sheet, laid out squares of sticky paper to cover the holes in the target with, her pistol and its accessories. She was attired in her full leather battledress and she practised this time with her thin leather gloves on.

As she knelt down and held the Browning, it occurred to her that it was a trifle large and clumsy for a woman, but none the less she was still very pleased with it. As she loaded two magazines from a cardboard box sub-divided into one hundred spaces for one hundred bullets – ten by ten – a fierce hail storm broke loose with icy ping-pong balls bouncing and hammering off her and the ground for two fearsome minutes. She carried on pressing in the bullets which were staggered alternately – one to left and one to right – and eight per magazine this time instead of five. They should hold thirteen, Mr Letheren had said, but that if filled the springs tended to fail and that in turn caused stoppages. Ten he had suggested was the most she should insert and she settled on eight.

She rehearsed all the procedures. She fired ten groupings of four rounds each at five yards, then the same again with the silencer screwed on. The results were a lot more even than when she had been with the Colonel. She went through some of the drills with her eyes shut. Also she had proven that the thin leather gloves did not impede her when using it.

She packed up.

Sticking up just above the thistles nearby were the two blue wings of her horse-jump. On the ground she found its three blue and yellow striped poles. One day soon, all these things would be tidied up and repaired and made good.

Walking back beside the loch shore, a thirteen hand grey pony came cantering towards her. It must have run away, but no one close by had horses. She put down her things and called to it. It stopped short of her and looked at her with mistrust and fear. Half-expecting a puffing owner to appear, she tried to coax it towards her and catch it, though without tack or a head-collar on, it would not be easy. She clicked her tongue, spoke to it softly and moved slowly closer. Suddenly it turned and kicked her, catching her thigh hard enough to be jolly painful and later bring up a big blue bruise. 'Ouch!' She advanced slowly again, seized its mane and vaulted up onto its back. It bucked about twenty times, but her arms were locked tightly round its neck and she managed to hold on. Then it galloped away and gradually she started to slip off to one side, until she had to let herself go and squirm outwards to land in a bank of heather, as the beast vanished towards the southern end of the loch.

In the early evening Artemis reread yesterday's letter from Denise. Denise had thrown in the towel at Worcester, gone to Italy and met an English civil engineer working on a bridge to whom she had become engaged. She read in yesterday's newspaper too, about a would-be actress who in two years had only featured in one soap-suds advertisement and who now worked on a clothes factory production line, sewing on the left sleeves of girls' blouses. Artemis turned her nose up. No one with a truly noble or artistic calling would descend to that.

As she put on her night-dress for an early night, she reflected that even amongst the supposedly educated, boredom and hypocrisy were almost the standard mode. Very rare was a mind which was true to itself.

* * *

Archibald Letheren and Guy Woollhead, dressed in civilian casuals and overcoats, returned to the black Porsche in Eichenfelsstrasse and sat in it.

'I was in Libya,' said Woollhead, 'in sixty-nine, when Qaddafi made his revolutionary coup d'état. Though it was understood that the army and R.A.F. in Cyrenaica should support King Idris in such circumstances – and indeed only a token move would have been needed to call the bluff – the

Labour government of the day forbade it. A cabinet minister flew out to El Adem to explain to the army and air force chiefs this cowardly and perverse decision, but all the senior officers boycotted him and took a trip out into the desert. So with no one to talk to, he had to fly off home again.'

'A pity they didn't dress up as natives and shoot him. That would have bounced London into intervention. They could have sent a signal – "Minister shot by rebels. Stop. As an interim measure am shelling Tripoli and await your further instructions ... ".'

Snow fell thickly and occasionally Letheren had to operate the wipers to clear their arcs of vision.

'Well, it is number 11A and it is above the rear half of the bank as my source described.'

'What shall we do Colonel? Knock on the door?'

'I suppose so.'

They climbed out again and were locking the car doors, when a woman came down the flight of steps between the plate-glass front of the bank and the colour-emblazoned window of the sports shop.

She wore a white machine-knitted hat with a pom-pom, a fashionable blue and white jacket with an elasticated waist-band, a scarf, baggy blue trousers and white leather boots. Her hair had been woven into two plaits and her face looked doughy and unhappy. She crossed the road to the 'Reisebüro'.

Letheren consulted a tiny photograph, nipped between his fat thumb and index finger and nodded cheerfully.

It was Monday morning.

In the travel agents, the two men pretended to examine a brochure containing pictures of falsely smiling couples in foreign resorts, whilst the girl booked a flight.

'Mittwoch?'

'Ja. Um zehn Uhr von Düsseldorf ... LH 450?'

'Ja.'

'Ihr Name bitte?' The bald young clerk began filling in a booking form.

'Ute Steyer.'

For ten minutes she sat on the bright green plastic chair, whilst the agent scribbled and telephoned and explained some details to her. A small vase of snowdrops stood on the desk. Finally, she put her ticket in her handbag and left.

On the pavement, a man touched her shoulder. 'Guten Tag, Fräulein.' She turned round. 'Heissen Sie Ute Steyer?'

'Ja.'

He gave her a woeful kindly smile. 'Forgive me my dear, my name's Guy Woollhead.'

Ute nearly jumped out of her skin. Her mouth opened.

'Please don't be frightened. There are no policemen with me.' He felt glad that he spent most of his time in an above-board regiment and not in this shifty world of preying on others' vices and foibles. 'My companion over there, is another British Army officer ... Is it possible that we may have a cup of coffee with you?' He took her hand in his and gave it a warm clasp. 'I promise that we won't bring you any misfortune.'

She watched his confusedly friendly face. Her own puffiness had receded under this shock, to be replaced by a wary trenchancy. However, she shrugged. 'Es muss sein.'

So she led them into her flat. A clutter of boxes inside the door, packed up and tied, suggested that a move was imminent.

The two officers settled themselves into the cheap armchairs in the semi-furnished shambles of the poky sitting-room. Ute brought in three mugs of coffee, a carton of cream, a bowl of brown sugar, spoons and knives and plates, some dense grey bread, butter, two sorts of cheese and a liver sausage.

'I am sorry ze place is so horful condition, but I am soon to leave here.'

Colonel Letheren stood up, gave her a brief but touching embrace, smiled and said, 'Miss Steyer, we are indebted to you for the stories you passed to us. Be assured, we will keep your secrets, even if you are doing things which are unlawful.' He sat down again.

'Vot has happened to my boyfriend?'

'Ulrich Schniewind?'

'Yes.'

'I don't know.'

'No. I sink he has been murdered at some place in Amsterdam.' She hung her head.

'Why Amsterdam?'

She sighed and sat down on an upturned box beside Letheren. 'Vee have been making ze hallucogen drugs and selling zem zere ... but zat is feenished now. Zay made people to have vunderful pictures ... Vee put it in zere vine or cola in ze beginning, so zat zay could have ze expearience of it and zen later sold it.'

Her interrogator thought that for one who was involved in such tenebrous affairs, her straight-as-a-die German openness and simplicity were remarkably intact. 'The coffee's good ... or at least welcome.'

'I have done wrong sings, I know. Ten years ago, I voz becoming a nurse and I sort zat people vud be kind and vonting to help uzzers ... I had leeved in a small village in Norse Germany you see and I voz still qvite ... you say "innocent"?'

'Yes.'

'In ze hospitals, boce in France and in Germany, ze doctors seem so nice. Zay say nice vurds and "Morning Ricardo" as if zay are zo friendly, but reelly it is all poison behind zem. Yet I did not see ziss at furst.' She sighed. 'My farzer is a Christian minister, yes? But I found zat life voz not as he had made me sink it vud be. You understand?'

'Very much so.'

'Zen I start to feel zat no vun voz serious and zat men only lied ven zay say zay loved me ... '

'Egotism is the great enemy of fulfilment,' said Letheren and he took her hand, almost without her knowing it.

' ... and zen I become bored about uzzers' tiny hopes and tiny ambitions ... ' She came to a halt.

He smiled. 'Indeed ... there's nothing so common as a unique experience.'

'Vud you like schokolate cake?' She broke free and rushed out to the kitchen to fetch this pre-packed article. She was very much on edge.

They all ate and drank for a while.

'I began to seeing sings viz different eyes. I saw zese lazy people who steal from ze state and vish not to vurk. I see ze doctors giving out ze tranqvillizers viz standard smiles vitch are lies and doing tests to get more money, because zay vont ze big estate car and ze golf clubs. And zay are writing zese research papers viz falsch results to become famous. Vun Anästhesie doctor I know, he makes zese tests on some pieces of bress from ze patient – but ze maschina vitch analeesed zem voz entraining ze air, so ze results voz all rubbish, but still he is publishing.' Her lip trembled and her eyes were moist.

'Zen I voz liking history in school, zo in München, I starting to study an evenings course. But it voz not ze gold pieces of Europe ... ze sublime ideas of Goethe or Creutz or ze noble deeds zat can be making us taller, but ze vor in Korea and Vest Afrikanisch "Kultur" ... how zay cultivate ze yams or burn ze ox dirt ... And teachers who var immoral and are making us today a moral vaccoom, pretend to having morals on sings avay from zemselves in time or distance. And suddenly I am hating everysing and everyvun ... I sink it doesn't matter vot I do to anybody, zay are all so arrogant and horrible.' She threw her head into her hands and seemed to be on the brink of sobbing.

Letheren pulled her round to kneel beside him and he looked at her tear-streaked face. 'Don't worry. Duplicity is harder to spot when we're young.' With the backs of his fingers he stroked her hiccoughing hot cheek.

After three or four minutes, her silent weeping abated and she disengaged herself from him and sat back on her crate again.

'Life is composed largely of things which can be seen as trivial or boring or crooked ... '

'Zen Ulrich came to see me. He voz my cousin but vee had perhaps met only ven vee vur leetle. He voz trained in la chimie and he say he could make a drug vitch vud give people ze *p*sychodelisch pictures in zere heads and vee earn money ... ze lot of money. Ach, vee have met ze many unhuman people and done ze many terrible sings.'

'If any of us looks at himself, if he is wise then he won't like too much what he sees.'

'Yet pleese understand me, I voz in so ... in much confusion. Zo many var glib. Ze French and ze Arabs and even ze Germans too, all sort vee nurses voz only for prostituting. Everysing voz vulgar. Ze talking voz empty ... soulless ... all talked cynically of "love" and not vun of zem reelly knew vot it voz and ... '

The Colonel took her moist hands afresh to interrupt the spiral by which she was working herself up towards hysteria. 'Ute Ute Ute! Don't be too negative. As we drove along the Autobahn this morning, Guy was talking about the Chinese in the Far East. He was saying that in Hong Kong they are so hard and rapacious, but then you go to Brunei where about a quarter of the population has Chinese ancestry and in their robes which range from dusty orange to saffron yellow, they are extremely sweet and hospitable. You have recognised some bad traits and false prophets, but there are good traits and good men too. It's a sort of natural cycle. When we've learnt how unpleasant badness is, we start searching for goodness and redemption and by the time we're old, we're almost back to our childhood again. You mustn't take too despairing a view of what's happened to you.'

Ute thought for a moment. 'I vill make more coffee.'

She went out into the kitchen and they heard the hot water jug start to hiss again and the tap of a plastic spoon against the hopper on the coffee filter machine.

She reappeared with a photograph. 'Ziss is Ulrich.'

The men studied the healthy German Apollo who looked so pleased with himself, standing in front of a whitewashed wall with a tiled top, like the garden wall of a Spanish villa.

'Not in Italia here, but ... er ... Syrie? Near ze Orontes.'

'Aha, the blood red Adonis river. No, I'm afraid we don't know what has happened to him.'

She fetched the coffee.

Letheren had deduced by now, that Ute's principal difficulty lay in finding acceptable outlets by which to satisfy her sibylline sexual currents. Having failed to find a man whom she could trust, she had resorted to that fashionable charade of living the hard life, but it is not given to the finely-balanced feminine constitution to do this and escape damage. Tougher women might suppress their rebellious consciences for a time, but not Ute.

'Zo, some vimmen join sects of bigotting men-hatings or Lesbos or anti-rapists or ban-ze-bomb or become martyrs to some cause zo zay can blame somesing else for zere failures ... but I choosed to become rich.

Zen anuzzer relative appear, my sister. But she voz grown up in ze East. Ingrid is knowing much about ze arms running to ze terrorists ... '

'I give you my word that we won't inform against you. We keep no official records.'

'It is all in your heads?'

The men nodded.

'Ingrid say, "Vot if vee betray ze uzzer corriers and zen *vee* deliver ze veppons and ze explosifs srue Europa and earn much much money?" So vee did.'

'Has any of this gone to Britain or to Ireland?'

'Yes. Ze fiffs and last lorry is in journey now from Türkei to Englant.'

Ute, who felt grimy and unchaste both from all the prodding cockchafers she had allowed through her knickers and from her sordid money-making enterprises, hoped that this confession would herald the start of a return to sanity and happiness.

'Ingrid voz first sending me to Dublin, to meet a man called "Roisin" ... '

'That's a girl's name.'

'Yes. Ingrid says zat his reel name voz "Diarmaid Molloy" ... '

* * *

At two in the afternoon, at Cairndow – half-way between Glasgow and Drumairth Castle – Artemis stopped at a small filling station and filled the Land Rover up with petrol. A little further on near Inveraray, stood a shabby roadside café and rather surprisingly for the season, it was open.

Four lorry drivers looked up from their egg chips and baked beans at the hard ravishing beauty of Artemis's form, as she strode past them and sat at a corner table. On a grey sub-zero December day in a dreary café, here was something worth attending to.

Had they merely seen her figure-head form, they might have gone no further than a few semi-jocular winks or a greeting intended to tease, but with her proud and sexily-carved cast dressed in its gleaming and closely-fitting black leather costume, they thought differently, more unkindly and with relished spite. The semi-shiny subtle potency of her attire seemed to be an external manifestation of a sinister and ardent defiance inside her, just as by analogy the drab cottons and stereotyped artificial suits of more mundane mortals were a reflection of their feeble uncertainties. Nor did it stop at that which might have been justified had she been riding a motorbike or to give protection against extreme weather conditions. Her large bronze belt clasp and her glinting brass spurs were for effect, not function. On the chair beside her rested her black leather gloves and handbag. Not only did this phallic stimulator do no hard labour such as cutting wood or digging potatoes, neither was she good-natured or gentle. She quickly became food for their mental amphitheatres of unbridled beastliness.

Artemis was well aware of the emphatic symbolism of her gladiatorial costume, yet as with anything else which you practise habitually – goodness, glibness, prostitution, honesty, lying – the more you do it, the more it becomes second nature.

'Wha' yer deein' ootsayd wi' me quiney?' called the Aberdonian driver coldly, meaning that he wanted to give her a subduing screw in the back of his furniture van.

'Do you like playing conkers?' asked another and laughed.

Artemis ignored them haughtily and studied the menu of mostly fried dishes.

She thought of her pistol beside her in her handbag as she glanced idly out of the dirty window at the empty and plaintive waters of Loch Fyne and kept an eye on her vehicle as the sullen hauliers went outside to their lorries.

When she had consumed her melted cheese on toast and mug of tea and begun the final leg of the drive out to her assignment, a change of mood crept over her. She was forsaking the commonplace world of transport cafés and insignificant men with their redolent illusions and heading for her own arena of disguise and Deutschmarks, death and devilry, delight and darkness and with this harbinger of thought, a deep slow excitement inched its way through her body, a mixture of alertness and relaxation and a sense of impending danger.

Under her leather suit, she had on a new pair of white lacy panties and a pair of black tights and also different from the night of the raid on the hospital safe was that instead of her school knickers, she had on a pair of black knickers made of the thin supple sheep's leather which was beginning to be used for the newer looser and lighter fashion jackets appearing in the shops.

These underclothes tickled her largish and highly sensitive clitoris and she believed that spontaneous orgasm would start as it had before, but it did not. Instead it seemed to arrest itself just short of the peak of the slide, just before muscular convulsions began and hang there in bedewed and prolonged expectation. She stopped the Land Rover and stiffened. She wriggled her bottom sideways on the hard seat, clung to the large metal steering-wheel with her forearms tensed behind it and her breasts pressing the cross-piece and arched her head and neck backwards, continuing the concavity of her back as she pushed her chest forwards. She climbed out beside Loch Fyne, let the sharpness of the wet cold air regale her and every detail of sea and slashed rock and veiny tree impress her mind with intense and surreal wonder as if moving into another world, but still physically she hovered below the pinnacle of unarriving pulsations. This caesura before the brink declined but continued all the way to the plantation, where she drove carefully off the road and reversed into incomplete cover. She had yet to see another vehicle on this road, either on the Saturday or today.

It was dusk and in the scarlet rays shining over the deep purple shape of Jura, she unlashed the dinghy from the roof and dragged it across the road and rocks to the little light grey beach. She returned with the box-seat, the oars, the two skeins of rope and the red leather holdall full of tools which she placed in the blunt bow section.

The sky was clear, the sea still and only a slight breeze blew.

The wood darkened and the phantoms of night closed in. She felt surrounded by purity, pure herself and sufficiently alone. She went through the elaborate semi-stripping act necessary to relieve herself. The stars sparkled in the dark blue sky. The torch beam caught the false number-plate on the Land Rover. Having decided this time to use some black mascara smudged onto her cheeks nose and forehead, she rubbed this on liberally before pulling on her motorcycle neck-tube and her black woollen pommelless forage hat. Then she strapped on a dark red life-jacket, locked up the Land Rover and pulled on the gauntlets over her thinner gloves. Her handbag was heavy with torches and pistol and magazines, but it was of strong black hide and its broad thick strap travelled round underneath it. She closed all her heavy nickel-plated zips on her leather suit and prepared to move off.

The moon rose at a quarter to six, white with blue smudges like a blue cheese, almost full and unobscured by lumbering clouds as it shone from behind some black spires of rock and a single twisted tree. Its light made a couple of frozen cascading rivulets and some patches of snow shine with a phosphorescent whiteness.

Only now did the muscular spasms start inside her, but with infinite slowness, creating not violent paroxysms of rapture but a sense of prowess and well-being. There had been no external stimulation, no newel posts or saddles or truncheons, only the thrill of anticipated risk and the cold overseeing wintry moon. And on it went without cease, like a very lethargic snake on a long journey.

Artemis pushed the boat into Loch Righ and climbed in. Evenly and unhurriedly she rowed across the water, looking over her shoulder regularly to keep herself well inside the lee of the nameless promontory.

She struggled to pull the rubber boat up well above the high tide mark, slipping at times on the algae and seaweed and sitting down accidentally once in a shallow rock pool. She tied it to a large boulder removed her life-jacket and eyed the ridge above her.

It was not so easy either to scale this fifty degree slope of snow with her two bags and two hanks of rope, but if she kicked the toes of her boots through the hardened crystallised surface of the snow to form footholds, she could make progress although sometimes her footing gave way and she slid down a few feet.

Along the top of the ridge were steel fencing posts linked together by three dense coils of razor-wire, but on inspection no electronic devices. Razor-wire had to be handled with respect, even by Artemis. Its ultra-sharp tinny ragged edges could slice easily through even thick leather if rubbed against it.

She lay on her front, just peeping over the crest and watched for half an hour through her binoculars, having tied her bags and ropes to one of the steel posts.

The hefty medium-sized wire-cutters were the heaviest implement in her red bag. Slowly and steadily, she started to clip pieces out of the lowest spiral of wire, placing the short eviscerated strands carefully in the snow, an arm's length to one side.

The moon shone on the face she had ascended and fortunately, not on the steeper seventy degree face she had now to descend. She took one of the thirty yard lengths of flat red nylon rope, trebly knotted at one foot intervals and tied one end of it firmly to the base of the metal post nearest to her. These posts were set securely in holes drilled down into the rock. She eased herself up into the break in the lower coil of wire and with her handbag trailing beside her, the free end of the secured length of rope in her right hand ready to be drawn out, the second skein over her left shoulder and the red leather bag in front of her, she launched herself from this miniature col to slide head first on her front, down the steep shaded incline of compacted icy snow, digging in her toes and elbows as brakes if she were gathering too much speed. As she set off something tore at her leg. The unravelling return rope snatched itself free from her just before she came to a halt, sprawled out behind a massive hemispherical boulder.

She lay still for ten minutes. Several lights were on in the castle, some behind drawn curtains some not. A few outside lights illumined rather weakly the main gate, the yard in front of the outbuildings and the tall main doors, which with their ornate wrought-iron hinges and sinusoidal tops had looked more like something from an Austrian Schloss. No one could be seen.

Nothing moved. She could see too, that the distant telephone wire was too high and inaccessible to be cut.

She felt some wetness in her panties, as again her persistent delightful and slow-motion orgasms expelled small quantities of warm gooey liquid. It felt pleasantly agreeable. It must be secretions expressed from her sex glands. But it did not matter, as firstly nobody was going to see her – at least nobody who would survive – and secondly, it was all hidden inside her leather clothing anyway.

In front of her lay the frozen river and across it a jetty made of elm baulks, whilst some way to her left was the weir. Rolling over to examine her suit, she found a jagged tear down the right knee-patch caused by a spur of razor-wire, but luckily it had not opened up the main layer of the suit.

She allowed her body to slither forward, down the less steep river bank, over the scentless and lifeless and snow-topped grasses and gorses, which befitted frozen winter. She slid easily over the frosted stones and still on her stomach with her feet bent up, she began to glide across the icy river. It was easy to slide over the pure even snow-dusted ice, but hard to propel yourself. Her elbows pressed downwards and backwards like seals' flippers. Nature seemed so exhilaratingly beautiful and perfect.

The money stolen from the hospital seemed just. She had asked three times to be exempted from the superannuation scheme, but they kept 'forgetting' and continued to deduct it from her pay, as if scared that anyone might be trying to abscond from the state-run ant-heap with its mesh of controls.

That she and Simon had failed to unite, indicated faults on both sides. Her moments of unkindness were not anomalous mistakes, but the revelation of a spoilt selfishness stretching back far into her childhood. His pains were his punishment for not being loving enough. But none of it mattered. It was all unalterable.

On the banks of worn rock on either side of the jetty were more coils of wire, so she decided to climb up onto the planking of the pier, though its foot square elm piles, held together with titanic bolts and nuts, were coated in frozen slime and icicles. With her fingers on the edge of the decking and her legs precariously wrapped round a smaller diagonal baulk, she heaved herself slowly up, planted her forearms on the thick boards, then hooked one leg up and so arrived on the planking. Again she slid on her front along the ten yards of snow, compressing it under her and leaving a wide rut or trail imprinted in it.

She glimpsed a thin stake at the landward edge of the decking and stopped.

The intruder was now fifty yards from the house which lay straight ahead of her and thirty from the auxiliary buildings to the right. Without cover, bathed in pale moonlight and black-on-white, she was quite visible, especially when moving.

She plucked a straw from beside the planking and moving it up and down beside the thin pole, discovered that it supported three naked perimeter wires. Indeed, she then saw that each of the series had been looped around insulating knobs on the slender post. They were probably high voltage wires rather than ones which tripped an alarm. Leather is quite a good insulator though not at very high tensions and besides, her leather's outer surface was fairly damp due to rock pools and melted snow.

The lowest of the three wires ran at a height of eight inches above the ground. On her back and holding the handles of two screwdrivers – which said they would withstand 5000 volts – in a 'V', Artemis raised this wire at its mid-point between two stakes and slid slowly sideways beneath it, with the care of a cat stalking a bird.

She pulled her bags and rope through after her and then crawled on all fours along a swathe of snowy uncut grass, in the channel formed by the silent yet deadly electric wires to her right – now joined by a parallel razory coil of wire which had recommenced at the edge of the jetty – and a simple chicken-wire fence to her left, intended apparently just to keep in the two sheep who kept the grass down round the house and prevent them from being electrocuted.

Behind the barn, the fearless interloper could finally stand up. Her leather skin was wet on the outside, because her body's heat had melted some of the frozen snow and ice.

She straddled the chicken-wire, took her loaded pistol out and deposited her red bag and the remaining skein of rope under the oil tank. Seeing the fuel stopcock beside her, she was tempted to turn off the oil supply and so stop the generator, but that would mean facing her adversaries in the dark and they knew the ground and she did not.

So she screwed on the pistol's silencer and with this in her right hand, her gauntlets in her left and her handbag slung from her left shoulder, she peered round the corner of the barn. She crossed the five yard wide gap to reach the rear of the garage, passed along behind it and turned the corner to survey its second blind side. The two sheep stood there beside a half-bale of hay. They looked at her for some seconds, bleated loudly and jogged off.

Artemis advanced.

Suddenly the invisible front-door opened, footsteps came out and low voices spoke incoherently.

Her heart thumped furiously and her thumb pushed off the pistol's safety catch. She knelt down behind the bale of hay.

'Vy in ze barn?' came a woman's high pitched tones.

Retracing her steps round the back of the garage, Artemis peeped along the gap between it and the barn and saw four figures stroll leisurely across it at the other end, exchanging a few scraps of dialogue.

The barn door creaked open and then shut again.

Artemis retreated back to behind the barn and waited.

A faint peal of deep laughter from inside suggested that some sort of caper was beginning.

The green eyes of a black cat glared at Artemis and it arched its back and miaowed. She gave it a kick.

She dared not risk going into the house at this point, because she might be spotted and there was no way of telling how many servants were still about.

An occasional guffaw or yelp of merriment penetrated the cold night air.

At the back of this barn and above the oil tank, a flight of age-old stone steps set into the wall, with worn treads and no hand-rail led up to a small hayloft door. This was still all on the river side of the outbuildings, away from the house. She stole up these icy steps and sat listening beside the half-height door of cracked and rotting boards. A wind was picking up and the voices inside were indistinct.

With ultra-gentleness she eased back the door by its rusty handle. With an infinitely guarded touch, she lifted the sneck. With the greatest caution she edged the door open degree by degree and then crept with extreme and painstaking care, in onto the dirty wooden floor.

A few bales of straw lay around at odd angles. Artemis crouched on all fours for a time and then lay flat, putting her eye to a knot-hole in the floor. Down below, in the yellowish demesne of a weak light bulb, were the foursome, who had about them that unclean and desolate aura of those who abuse themselves sexually.

When the secret prostrate watcher saw them, she tensed with intransigence – like a mountaineer determined to conquer a difficult peak – for disgust welled up in her. Mr Letheren was right about this ghastly scum. She had had some practice now in felony and did not care what she did to these folk. Still her womb contracted periodically with a relaxing warm and immodest delight. More fluid leaked out into her underwear.

It looked dank and dreary. A central nest of hay had been arranged on an old iron bedstead, amid outdoor tools, off-cuts of timber and two empty cable drums.

Rose lay on his back in the hay in an antique gold smoking jacket and black bow-tie. His tight dark trousers were off and his shirt-tails had been rolled up. He held up his hands as Ingrid with vulgar poses, tickled his chin menacingly with a long dressage whip. 'Am I not vairy beautiful? Can I not break you, you crypto-communist male peeg, viz my Nazi tortures?'

Ingrid in her claret suede pinafore dress, had on under it a white blouse with frilly cuffs and a low-cut neckline plus white silk stockings, a black cloak and a black velvet highwaywoman's eye-mask. Her hair was in a tall bun-like coiffure – all very French Revolutionary.

'Ah my sugar plum tovarisch, the world's sweetest and sexiest, come and be pierced by my Stalinist blunderbuss.'

'You are a Russian peasant. I vont nussing less zan an erzduke to rape me.'

'But we loathe aristocrats! Besides, you're just a cheap tarty vulgar red plastic shoe type of girl!'

She whipped him with moderate severity four or five times and he howled. 'Ach, no peasant gurl can show to you "les fleurs du mal" like I.'

'You wait,' said Rose, 'I will come with all my lawless friends who rioted in Cesford and Broome last week and in revenge, we shall rape you one by one.'

'I vill vip you all to dess. I am a French Nazi marchioness ... une écuyère ... and I vill tolerate no insurrection.'

'I always assume the worst about women. Prove me wrong.'

Ingrid climbed onto the bedstead and took off her cloak dress and blouse. 'Your face has a foxy form ziss evening.'

'He used to be a werewolf,' put in Ayrth, 'but he's not one noooooowwwwwww!'

'For hell's sake, so somesing or I freeze to dess.'

From under his long combed-cotton shirt, Rose extricated and rubbed his fifth floppy member in a revolting display, whilst Lord Ayrth and the fourth man, stood jeering on the sidelines. 'Come on Rosie. You can do it.'

'Can anyvun play ze flute?'

'The flute?' queried Ayrth showing his large mouth and large teeth.

'Like zose snake-charmerers – perhaps Rose's serpent vill rize.'

Whilst Rose's rascally features huffed and puffed in vain, Lord Ayrth with a water-soluble felt-tipped pen, drew a swastika on each of Ingrid's brassière pouches.

Ingrid shivered, bent over Rose and wound her whip thong round his minute sex organ, whilst its owner swore and the two onlookers wearied of the non-activity and non-degradation. The fourth man stamped his feet with cold and said, 'Comm on Rosie, get out of ze pig-pen unt I vill show you.'

Rose's prong had shrunk almost to the point of vanishing. Ingrid kissed his cheek and then bit his lip. He gave a cry, inspected the blood on his tending fingers and said, 'You bitch!'

The fourth man adopted the feet-apart stance of a prize bull, looking on with ring-in-his-nose contempt.

'It's that strap she wound round it,' declared Rose, trying to excuse himself, 'It's scarified it.'

'Angus, you unt Rose go and do ze sings you like doing best and I vill pleese Ingrid.'

So it was agreed. Lord Ayrth and Rose left to wilt and cajole alone in the house, where presumably Rose would play the woman.

Ingrid put her dress back on but removed her panties and then lay crosswise on the bed with her waist at the edge, her trunk curved round and her head underneath it. Her hands gripped the lengthwise angle girder along the edge of the bed and her dress-covered bottom was displayed uppermost. Her bull mounted her, his hands on the floor supporting his upper body. The Admiral thus conjoined himself with the U-shaped Ingrid. As a secret admirer of the Nazis, he liked the image of her being a Hitler Mädchen. With the right lid on the pan, it soon bubbled and boiled. 'Oh-eee!' she gasped. The pretendedly droll house-of-cards Rose she referred to scathingly in German, though the name 'Herr Non-Pop' came out in English. He had said that the cold air out here would do the trick.

The East German pair decided to do it a second time. This time she lay longways on the bed and on her back and after coupling, her short-cropped fifty-year-old German stud rotated to the transverse position and curled his head and neck under the bed. As they adjusted their lie in the freezing mouldy barn, ready to recommence battle, the bedstead broke. The snapped longitudinal girder fell onto the Admiral's nose with the full weight of both their bodies on top of it. The force drove the bony nasal septum back into his skull and into his brain stem. By the time Ingrid had freed herself from under him and scrambled to her feet, he was fitting and turning blue. She heaved his head out from under the bed frame and untwisted his body, but with a last choking frothy snort, he died.

'Grosser Gott!'

She did not scream or shout for help. She longed only to escape from this mess and make it to her secret villa in Portugal and her life there as Gudrun Zapf and that meant thinking before acting.

Artemis understood that she had to tackle her first victims onc at a timc. Shc trod softly but swiftly to thc hatchway and then went down the near-vertical wooden ladder so quickly, that one of its rungs snapped and she fell onto a hay bale. The drop was not far and she managed to keep her pistol trained on Ingrid, who looked up from the comminuted bloody face of her former boss with a gasp. At first glance, this satanic serpent appeared to have come out of the deep in a wet-suit. Artemis climbed over a fallen rafter, hit her shin harmlessly on an invisible rusty plough blade buried in the knee-deep loose hay and brought her silenced gun to within two feet of Ingrid.

'Ach Gott! Bist du ein Teufel?'

'Who is he?'

'Him? Admiral Heidemann? You are ze gurl who killed Penman, yes? Look, you can have ze money ... '

'Where is it?'

'In ze lezzer kitbag in ze dinner-room.'

'How many servants are in the house?'

'Oh ... I don't know. Ze two gurls who made ze food ready, zay left ziss afternoon ... Two I sink? Oh no, pleese don't shoot me. I am only a very small fish ... '

After a sound between a puff and a thud, blood seeped out almost invisibly over Ingrid's claret dress from the notch at the bottom of her neck. She lurched backwards and sat down. Her eyes were startled, unbelieving, almost child-like. After she had fallen sideways and lost consciousness, Artemis stood over her and fired a second bullet, at very close range, into the side of her head. It was just to be sure. When the Argyll and Sutherland Highlanders had found the withered heads of three R.A.F. men on stakes outside a village in Aden and had thereupon massacred most of the villagers, as Letheren had said, no one had thought it wrong except the ever-squealing socialists. Well, Artemis was now similarly administering rough but accurate justice.

So, with Axt gone and this Heidemann who was the unidentified courier from the East, that left perhaps four.

She heaped hay over the bodies and smashed the light bulb with the barrel of the gun. The barn door creaked to behind her and her leather-clad cast moved furtively towards the house's main door, her footsteps crunching ominously in the snow between the half-dozen cars.

She thought how god-like she was. Allure is not static, but is dependent on spirit and circumstance and courage as well as physical form. And the still further extent of the warm wetness in her underwear felt lovely too – literally an orgy of murder was under way.

Wisps of floating fog groped their way across the snowy lawn and round the tall castle and through them the black proud shape of Artemis moved, her mind too disfigured to revert to light. She opened one of the pair of tall main doors and entered the long downstairs corridor. It had low stone lintels, cracked white walls and dirty brown little wall lights. It was friendless and echoing.

The first door in an arched stone doorway, opened into a brightly lit kitchen. Artemis stood there in the pool of light and pulling the motorcycle tube down from her nose and mouth, drank a beaker of orange juice which stood on a table and bolted a small smoked crab sandwich. She blew her nose on a paper towel, ate a chocolate biscuit and lifted the tube back over the lower half of her face. She replaced the two spent rounds from the magazine in her pistol with some loose spares from one of her leather suit's zipped pockets and checked her torn knee-patch, her belt, her handbag, her fine long black leather gloves which she had on and the gauntlets which she carried in her left hand.

On she went, bypassing the other ground-floor doors and climbing the bowed sandstone stairs with their damaged stonework balusters and chipped carved stone shields, to arrive at the end of the much grander first-floor corridor.

She opened the first door, a white one with panels outlined in gold leaf. On the white pile carpet stood a large bed with white coverings. In it Rose and Ayrth were partaking of their catamite practices between silken sheets. An ormolu clock with fleur-de-lis motifs, which stood on a white and gold bow-fronted Louis XIIIth chest, chimed the half-hour past nine.

Ayrth looked up and his eyes nearly popped out. He flung himself over to the bell rope, jarred it frantically and bellowed a queer name at the top of his voice such that it echoed at least faintly throughout the whole castle. Artemis took aim and fired. The first bullet whopped into his pillow, the second hit him in the shoulder and the third, as she closed in and Rose hurled a feeble shoe at her, tunnelled its way into the middle of his chest and finished him.

Rose seemed unsure whether to smile or to try to look offended.

'Aren't you cherubic?'

'What have I done?'

'The bramble bush!' She closed on him. 'The fig tree and the date-palm had no time to rule, remember?'

'Fungus only kills an oak which is sick.'

She leapt up onto the bed, fired into his cowering head and shoved his tottering body off onto the floor with a riding-booted foot. Again for certainty a second round entered his back.

A man burst in with a single-barrelled shot-gun, the surly Irishman who had been on the gate two days before. His throwing open the door, seeing this black apparition with a pistol, closing his gun and firing it accidentally in fright, all happened as an unbroken sequence. The range was about fifteen feet, the aim a few inches off to the girl's right. Artemis was swinging the top half of her body round to fire when the blast ripped past her and she fell back onto the bouncy bed. Her bottom and right hip took a smattering of the tiny ball-bearings from the peripheral part of the spreading cone and twenty or thirty pellets caught her. This could have maimed her but for a number of chance points. The weapon was a sixteen-bore and had been loaded luckily, not with buck-shot, but with the fine number nine skeet-shot. This together with her thick leather saved her. The lead balls were only about a sixteenth of an inch in diameter – which is a little larger than a pin-head – and those which caught her thigh tore into her at an oblique angle and the few which hit her backside, whilst more square on, met double thickness hide because of the large round bottom patch. There were plenty of singed excoriations and pock-marks none the less and a whiff of scorched leather drifted up, but nothing had penetrated and no stray piece of shrapnel had torn a carotid artery in her neck or something similar, as so often happens in shooting accidents. He had blown his chance.

The hydra-headed monster reared up uninjured, aimed her pistol at him, fired and missed. He fled bellowing, 'Rufus, reng to te flahny fezz! Ahoy tere, Drummond!'

Artemis lunged through the acrid smoke and fired her last but one shot as he dived down the stairs, still shouting urgently. She missed again. She had remembered to count bullets and eight minus seven left one. She dug into the compartment of her handbag where the spare magazine was and told herself to keep calm as she changed them over.

Then whirling down the broad stone steps after this wretch who had dared to challenge a goddess in her snug and unassailable leather and exuding an energy and a will-power as if forty Spirits of the Mine were inside her, she ran into two German shepherd dogs which had been loosed. They flew snarling and slavering up the stairs to meet her. She shot one before its jaws locked onto her left thigh, tumbled over in a struggle with the second and landed on top of it – so temporarily hindering its efforts to bite claw and savage her – but she made sure that her pistol hand remained free and poking the barrel into its fur, duly shot it, though not before it had ripped her leather suit over her left breast. For this affront, its mangy form received a second shot.

Thrusting her foot at the boot room door, this high kick flung it open and she saw her slob opponent fumbling desperately with a bunch of keys to open up the gun cabinet for more cartridges. His luck had run out. Lead in the stomach and lead in the head for good measure finished him off.

She recalled Letheren again, commanding her to reload. She obeyed, filling the almost empty spare magazine with its single remaining round, swapping the magazines over again and recocking.

Exiting into the downstairs corridor again and then charging through the door directly opposite, she found herself in a dingy office-cum-store. A telephone on a desk caught her eye and she tore the receiver off its flex. Then behind a rack of cardboard boxes and papers and stationery, she glimpsed a frail elderly man sitting motionless, like a mouse hoping not to be spotted. He had white hair, wire-rimmed glasses, a black waistcoat and trousers and black garters holding his white shirt sleeves. He looked as if he belonged in an H.E. Bates' novel. He was the old retainer, the link with the time when Alistair MacAlister, the thirteenth Lord of Ayrth and the second son of the Earl of Arloss had resided here. He staggered to his feet as if that were respectful and correct etiquette.

'Have you telephoned the police?'

'Yes Madam, just this moment.' He seemed to know that she was just a little bit noble too.

'What did you say?'

'Just that we had an intruder ... and could they come and assist us. I did not know about the firearm Miss.'

'Where's this money?'

'Upstairs, I believe.' He spoke with only a trace of a northern Scottish accent.

'Lay on Macduff.'

He shook slowly, like a man with Saint Vitus' dance as he climbed the stairs.

They stepped over the bleeding canine carcasses and Artemis plucked up her dropped gauntlets. She thought that some grenades might have been useful here.

'Who's this Admiral Heidemann?'

'Is he the foreign gentleman, Madam?'

'Gentleman?'

'No, you're quite right. They all deserve to be shot. Oh the doings which have gone on here! The good Lord must have turned his face away in horror.'

He threw open a pair of tall white-painted heavy double doors and they were in an eighteenth-century dining-room. It had been refurbished perhaps twenty years before, but remained clean and respectable enough with its two glass crystal chandeliers, small stone balcony and floor-to-ceiling windows, heavily braided curtains and polished wooden floor. The Queen Anne chairs with their cabriole legs and white satin upholstery ringed an elaborately carved and inlaid oval table, on which stood a highly-wrought three-branched Georgian silver candelabrum and a gold-crested white porcelain bowl full of large irregular crystals of brown sugar. All that was required was a mellowed violin, some sheets of a musical score hand-written in Indian ink and a frock-coated Mozart.

Artemis repeated her question. 'Who is Heidemann?'

'He came on Saturday, Madam. The new Lord Ayrth went to fetch him. He came about a year ago also. I overheard it said then, that he had travelled on a container ship from Kaliningrad to Boston docks in Lincolnshire and then been smuggled ashore. Perhaps he came the same way this time? As to *what* he is Madam, I have no firm knowledge.'

Opening one door of an ungainly rococo sideboard, he withdrew an orangy kitbag. With her free left hand she indicated that he should undo its spring-loaded clasp. Inside were plastic packets, each containing a bundle of a hundred one hundred Deutschmark notes. Letheren believed that a portion of them were earmarked for the East German President's private deposit account in a London bank and that other amounts were for paying various functionaries to enact tasks which were outside the official compass of the state-run foreign operations.

Artemis asked him who would be in the castle this evening and ascertained that there were only the six of them. She found herself unable to decide whether or not to shoot this ageing servant. As if perceiving her acute uncertainty, he said in a dignified tremor, 'God bless you Madam. Please spare me. I will gladly mislead the police over your description, because in killing these men I do not think you have done anything so very wrong.'

She thought for a moment that she should trust him – Mr Letheren probably would. He was corn not chaff. But the police would press him. She could not risk it. Her own hesitation angered her. 'I am so sorry,' she said with unusual gentleness and then fired three rounds into him to try to make it a quick death. He folded slowly up, collapsing onto the Persian rug with its white and blue and pink and black patterns.

'Manet omnes una nox', she recollected from her Latin lessons. 'One night awaits all'.

She glanced at the neo-classical oil paintings on the wall – one of the youthful Prince Antiochus sick with love for his beautiful young stepmother Stratonice, another of Ondine and a third of Herod's wife Mariamne being condemned to death. She wondered what her father would say about the composition and the brush-work? There was a Flemish miniature of a quiet harbour scene bathed in calm morning light. Had that lout Ayrth appreciated anything of all this?

In a glass cabinet stood an Elizabethan silver salt-cellar and a brooch of platinum studded with a crustacine of glittering diamonds. Should she stuff them into the kitbag, like the money being replaced in Benjamin's sack of corn? No, she was not a wild barbarian.

She left the top floor unsearched. If the police were coming, she needed to depart. As she strode down the stairs for the last time, dragging the kitbag, she wondered if her killing of Rufus Drummond would conjure up a curse. Still, nothing would defeat her. She would overcome any miserable curse in her tough sexy leather!

Outside, a sharp salt-scented wind made her feel purer again, distant from this unspeakable human dross which she had met. Near the oil tank again, she refilled her magazines and recovered the red leather bag and the unused skein of rope.

An aura of numbness gripped the earth. She crunched towards the pier and straddled the wire mesh, but forgot the three high tension wires. They threw her backwards and through the netting fence, like a punch in the chest, expelling all her breath and a squirt of urine. She landed hard on her bottom in the snow. After twenty seconds she had recovered herself. Both angry and shaken, she marched to the barn to fetch a steel crow-bar. With one end planted in the ground, she let it fall against the unseen wires. A vivid blue star crackled before her for some seconds.

Treading along the planks of the jetty, a preludial blast of icy wind hinted at a gathering storm out to sea. Sitting on the edge of the pier, she zipped the pistol with its safety catch on into her right thigh pocket, pulled on her gauntlets once more and threw the coil of rope and her three bags down onto the frozen river. She hotched off the edge, jumping down to join them.

As she walked and slid with some difficulty across to the middle peninsula, the moon abruptly vanished. All was darkness, yet she managed to find the hemispherical boulder and not far above it, the half-snow-covered rope left during her ingress. With her handbag, the kitbag, the red leather bag and the spare coil of rope all dangling from her shoulders, she struggled slowly up the steep slope to the sharp mini-arête, sweating as she tugged on the rope and kicking her toes into the rock's white face of compacted snow.

She navigated her way almost blindly through the tunnel in the razor-wire, groping with her hands to find its limits and kicking furiously at some heinous tentacle which wrapped itself around her left boot and seemed to be intent on arresting her progress. When through, she managed to spin round and complete most of the descent on her bottom and back. She slid down to an audible but invisible Loch Righ, where she slithered over twice on the jumble of rocks and could not find the boat until she fell over it. Cursing the traitor moon and threatening the treacherous algae-coated shore, she dumped her baggage in the bow and using her torch, unknotted the rope which bound the boat to a huge rock.

She was not in a blind panic, but agitated. She knew that the moon had gone, that the policemen might have put their boots on by now and soon be at the castle, that her superb leather had been torn and damaged in a number of places and that the Land Rover lay out on a long and isolated loop of road and so could easily be trapped by a road-block. She felt unnervingly mortal and vulnerable for once and her slow weird orgasms had ceased.

The tide had come in and the boat was near to the water. She shoved it off a flat slimy shelf of rock, put one leg briefly into a thigh-deep wave of water – which meant that a little leaked down between her boot and trouser leg – and scrambled into the dinghy almost horizontally so as not to capsize it.

The only visible landmark on either side of Loch Righ, was the ridge on the finger of land she was sailing away from. There a greyish white line of snow divided a sky of the darkest grey from the blackened peninsula. All she could do was to row steadily away from it and try to keep roughly at right angles to it.

As well as the slow swell of the broad low waves coming in from the sea, there seemed to be smaller faster waves criss-crossing these and sometimes showing a glimpse of white bubbles. They also occasionally slapped against the boat and sent a half-bucketful of brine over Artemis's elbows and back.

Then she caught a crab with the left oar and at the same stroke, missed the water altogether with the right. She nearly overbalanced into the bows and the boat rotated sluggishly. Her marker had gone. She searched all three hundred and sixty degrees of blackness in vain for the snow-capped ridge. She was lost. 'Piss!' Water gurgled along the boat's sides and a slow rolling motion affected the boat as it tilted itself in harmony with the surfaces of the large smoother waves. Should she just sit and wait for the moon or a ghostly iceberg outline of shore to appear or should she try to row in a straight line parallel to the direction of the incoming waves? She felt angry more than frightened and kicked malevolently the vague life-jacket in the bottom of the dinghy. She wanted to fight an enemy she could see, to use her pistol or feminine wiles, not to have to contend with these misty and mystic forces. Was Simon behind this again? She wondered what vow or pact she might make with some dark power, in return for its rescuing her.

Suddenly, as the wind blew into her scowling face, one of the small red luminous plastic buoys of the fish farm's nets bobbed alongside the gunwale. She looked over her shoulder and saw the next buoy and the next. She gave a dourly satisfied smile to herself.

After a few pulls on the stubby oars the flat-bottomed boat slewed sideways and rolled up and down a beach of grating pebbles. She scrambled out and tried to drag the rubber boat up the steep ramp, but her feet merely pushed down piles of the clinking stones. She would abandon the boat. She reached in for her bags. Turning round, her battered and war-worn figure – like a knight having escaped from a massacre – stumbled into a quagmirish gully of sticky mud where a stream ran into the loch and she fell forwards onto her knees and elbows and her handbag and the red leather bag. Swearing a slow obscenity at this latest dose of smearing plastering saturating muck, she stood up just as a wave burst and foamed around her legs.

Turning round to grab the boat, she missed it by a split second as the back-wash launched it and carried it out into the clinging minus nine degree darkness of the loch. Her feet were held as by lead weights in the thick ooze and she could not lunge after the dinghy quickly enough. As if by a magic spell, it drifted out and vanished into the black cotton wool night with an astonishing speed. In it still were the second rope, the life-jacket and *the kitbag*! She knew they would not come back. Like Faust, she had sold her soul to the Devil, only to see the Devil renege on his half of the agreement.

This loss was so immeasurable that no degree of rage or cursing seemed adequate. She let her body finish its forward sprawl to lay flat on the mud and shingle for perhaps three minutes and sensed a cold nagging feeling that her fortune was wholly in the hands of Simon, Mr Letheren and her father. Things succeeded if they *allowed* it. And they let her survive of course to fight their next war. But they also arranged failure, to limit her and chain her to their purposes. They cunningly oversaw each minutest element of her life. 'Oh what frigging rubbish,' she growled, telling herself that it was just a distortion and that they could not really master her. Yet she had survived a thousand risks, killed everyone she had been told to, emerged ready to serve Letheren again and yet lost her own portion of the operation. She brought her fists down feebly onto a small rock near her chin. 'Damn everything!'

She stood up, her drenched sticky thighs sucking at the mud as she did so. The expiring waves lapped and sploshed against the dark wet grating stones, but out to sea she could hear the raging of bigger waves and occasionally in the darkness, glimpse the phosphorescent crests of a breaking roller. Distant thunderous roars dinned in the air and wind-borne spray boomed up over the unseen headland. One such wave came closer in and burst over an invisible reef.

Yet she felt like raging more than the sea, like taking on this courageous contender who had cheated her will. 'I'll even the score!' she spat. 'I shall take on whatever opposes me and have no more qualms about what I do.'

She felt like Hitler near the end of the war, when for all his political cunning, armed might and unutterable will-power, he was being mocked and crushed by a seemingly animated fate. He was locked into a death struggle not so much with communists and Jews, as with some intangible and divergent destiny whose authors he could not get his hands on.

Her clitoris stiffened and engorged. Why could she not fuck everything as measly males did? Whatever they could do with their pricks, she could do too. She was sexier than they! For a moment she nearly flung herself into the freezing water and at the rocks, to do berserk battle with them until either they yielded to her will or she died in the fight, like Cuchulain.

Unsure which way to go in search of the Land Rover, she strode to the right. A faintly herbaceous whiff of pine resin tinged the air, in spite of the wind. She ran into a sapling and lashed it with her filthy gauntlets which she had just pulled off. The aluminium window edges of her metallic and glass box glinted vaguely nearby in the torch's beam. She opened a zip in her muddied exterior and found her keys. The engine fired first time. With her two remaining bags and her pistol on the seat beside her and the headlamps glaring into the blackness, she drove down the twenty yards of slope to the narrow coastal road.

After fifteen miles of freezing jolting and shivering bone-shaking travel over the icy snowy and poorly repaired road, she approached Lochgailhead. This was the first bottle-neck. She had to pass through it. The time was about midnight. As she nosed through it, its darkened solid stone houses slept. Nothing stirred.

Even on the better A83 road though, the possibility of ambush was not entirely past. There is no net of roads out on these sparsely populated western fingers of land and on it went for miles without alternatives or junctions, beside Loch Fyne again, through Inveraray, Cairndow and Glen Kinglas and not until she turned off onto the A814 to Helensburgh, could she feel out of the wood.

On a deserted stretch of this road, she turned onto a side-road marked 'Glen Douglas'. It climbed steeply into Inchgarron Forest, leaving the shore of Loch Long behind. Then spotting a forestry track, she drove along it for a quarter of a mile, before stopping beside the railway – a gash of grey with its two endless silver parallel bars – amid the Grimm-like haunted blackness under the white-roofed eerie trees.

She removed her thinner gloves and washed off the mascara from her face with cold water, soap and a towel. Her exertions had made her moist and together with the influxes of sea water, the penetrating wetness of ice and snow and her own bodily secretions, she felt damp and cold for all the protection of her motorcycle suit, the two pullovers, tee-shirt, knickers and underwear. With the boot-jack from the back of the hard-topped vehicle, she eased off her unzipped but still tightly-fitting mud-covered boots and stood on a rough black and white blanket. She unzipped and peeled off her leather jump-suit with its torn knee-patch and torn breast and dumped this ruined soaked and filthy article on an old sheet. She took off everything down to her underwear and let the welcome wind wash round her and dry her for half a minute, before tugging on a pair of ordinary dry jeans, three varied old sweaters and a jacket. Despite all that her assault get-up had suffered, *she* was unharmed. Her loins ached and she needed a long hot bath, but her beauteous body was unscathed.

She boiled water for coffee and drank three cups and ate two chicken-filled buns and an apple pie ravenously, seated on a rough weather-worn boulder with tufts of heather round it.

She spread a second homespun black and white thin kelt rug over the soiled driver's seat, used rags to wipe the steering-wheel and other controls and put all her bundled-up dirty items into the back of the Land Rover. The mud and dirt from her outfit and bags had to some degree spread itself onto almost everything. This sorting herself out took an hour. All the meticulous cleaning and disposing of things would be done tomorrow at home, not least to try and reduce the clues available to detectives, should they ever manage to pin-point her.

A train burst through the night in a whirlwind and swirled past her on the other side of a fence. Its red tail-light glowed for some time and then died. Perhaps like her, it was a demon able to follow only one course and in the end be eclipsed. Leaning against the squarish front wheel coaming, she devoured a four ounce bar of chocolate and drank two plastic cups of hot water, using the bonnet as a bar. Lastly she climbed up into her blanket-draped seat to resume her journey of retreat.

In Glasgow it snowed heavily again, the wheels giving off a soft furry drubbing sound in the powdered fall, whilst a swarm of white midges hurled themselves at the dark windscreen like tiny kamikaze planes. She seemed to be stationary with her foot on the accelerator pedal, whilst a tunnel of black and white rattled past her.

She had resigned herself to the loss of the Deutschmarks – Letheren might replace them for her she hoped – and with a false glow of well-being and contentment, caused by her great drowsiness and exhaustion, she left Glasgow behind her and headed for home.

## CHAPTER ELEVEN.

Simon stood at the square window with its tied-back lace curtains on either side and gazed out through the two layers of glass at the pewter-grey expanse of Lyndalsfjord, where leaden clouds excluded much of a diffident sun's thin northerly light. A few snow-flakes fell, as if promulgating an early musical echo of the main thematic flood still in reserve.

Closer to him a steep track marked out by bluish imprints, descended with banks of snow on either side which in summer-time would be green and dotted with pink flowers. It ran down to a rather undermaintained boat-house.

The fjords here did not have the soaring Parnassian grandeur of those around Bergen, where enclosing massifs and precipitate cliffs overwhelm the spectator. Here the same jagged Pre-Cambrian sedimentary rocks predominated with their uniform deep grey colour, but the horizon was more open – flatter islands and mountain shoulders less vast and vertical – though the handicaps of sea and weather were equally severe.

In reviewing the Artemis imbroglio – something he could not disallow – he knew that her suffering in the evening would be greater than his in the morning. Yet, he had led an easy and pampered life. He was no Julius Caesar and so understood his failure to belay Cleopatra. The renowned Cleopatra – Cleopatra the Seventh – may have historians divided as to how attractive she actually was, but it was sure that her fascination owed much to her looks being inseparably intertwined with her political ambition and feminine craft.

The single hotel in Namsos could lodge Kim and Adrian and the other 'stars' of Falcus's thirty strong band, but lowlier members had been farmed out to folk who needed to earn a few extra kroner. Simon had been placed with Tryggve and Idunn

Giske, an elderly couple who lived in this old and slightly skewed wooden house.

The woman was small and extremely shy. She walked with her head down as if deformed and was obliging to the point that Simon felt embarrassed. She wore a headscarf on the rare occasions that she ventured out of doors, which was a virtually extinct symbol of marriage – maidens had gone bare-headed. She also used the old-fashioned habit of calling her husband by his surname.

Old Tryggve was a man worn out by a life of hard work. As well as his own job in the sawmill at Grytvatn, he had kept up his father's poor farm for years on an island in the fjord, constructed a byre there for the animals to winter in and so avoid ferrying them to the mainland each winter, built two houses, erected four jetties with the aid of the floating pile-driver from the sawmill, collected a certain type of seaweed for cattle fodder, scythed hay and hung it up to dry, planted potatoes and endless other tasks, almost wholly without power tools and requiring gruelling labour. With his gums receding and little said, he would eat his meals with his horny hands clutching his knife and fork or go out fishing in his boat or fetch some shopping from Skogvik across the fjord or shovel snow – the lesser toils of retirement. But Idunn was long-suffering and kind. She had never been out to work and uncomplainingly accepted life's round of cooking food and clearing away, of having relatives or neighbours visit them and sit round the long coffee-table with coffee and cake to exchange the eternal coinage of who had married whom – the stuff which is so dull when you are young, but more intriguing as you grow longer in the tooth.

Simon had breakfasted early in the main room with its pine walls, its wood-burning black iron stove, its view out over the dismal fjord, its strongly-coloured woven rugs hung up on the walls, its iron and glass oil-lamp suspended over the table and its candles. At the solid table and seated in a carved chair, he had eaten hard dark rye bread with whatever he wished from a selection of hams, pickled fish and cheeses moistened with terribly strong ground coffee which gave you a tendency to diarrhoea if you were unused to it. Whenever he tried to vary the pleases and thank yous by putting a sentence together in Norwegian, whilst meaning to be friendly, both Tryggve and Idunn lacked the imagination to grasp what he was trying to say and so effectively discouraged him.

Filming had again been postponed and no rehearsals were scheduled for that day. Downstairs he put on his padded trousers of blue cambric, his anorak, woolly bobble-hat and mittens. He laced up his hiking boots and pulled over them some stout rubbed bands which Fru Giske had lent him and which had steel spikes on them to grip the snow. He exited via the cellar door.

On this lip of land, beneath rising tiers of crag-clutching frozen silent and snowy blue pines, were two houses. Apart from the Giske's white-painted steep-roofed abode, up and to one side stood a new creamy-coloured little dwelling on a cleared ledge with a railed balcony and large single-paned windows with white surrounds. Tryggve had built it for their daughter Unni, who had thanked them by promptly bolting to Stockholm and living a life of abjuration, the scope of which her parents luckily could not even guess at. So Tryggve had sold his new house to a girl from Skogvik called Helle Eiden.

Helle went to work each day at this hour and had told Simon that he was welcome to drive with her to Høgfoss if he so wished.

She appeared and as in their earlier encounters, turned her head away from him and smiled to the fjord when he greeted her, a response which he found hard to interpret. Either she was shyly and touchingly excited by his presence or she was devilishly trying to lure him.

She wore fur-lined mittens and a red anorak, a wide blue skirt, knitted stockings and thick boots.

The boat-house's frame of fat pine piles and beams, was solid enough still, but its cladding of maroon oil-impregnated vertical planking had faded and sagged. Inside it had a wooden walkway and four boats. She held her small rowing-boat by its mooring rope and nodded brightly for Simon to climb into the stern. Again, he felt that she wanted to speak but was tongue-tied. Water lapped and sloshed gently against the hulls and piles. He pointed to a mould-bedaubed boat resting upside-down on two cross-timbers in this dark and dank cavern. 'Does anyone use that?'

'Unni used to.'

The oars splashed and the thole-pins creaked as Helle rowed with an unerring sense of direction over the green glassy water.

'I've seen pictures of her in the house.'

'We often played together when we were small. On rainy days we sometimes played farms up in the boat-house loft. We used white pebbles for sheep, black ones for horses and so on. Some years a pair of grey plovers used to nest there.'

The boat bumped into an occasional macerated sliver of ice. A mist descended. Only the noises of the oars disturbed the eerie stillness.

'You row very evenly. How old were you when you started?'

'Four.' She smiled. 'My father put me into a boat and shoved it out into the fjord.'

'A hard life.'

'My younger brother was the favourite and my younger sister Gunn was spoilt. It seemed to me remarkable that they had it so good whilst I had it so bad. I had to do most of the chores. I was glad to leave home.' She smiled coyly sideways again.

The mist absorbed Simon's laugh and kept it secret and intimate. He watched her and again she averted her recusant head. Was she the culprit of loving?

A large ugly dark green bird perched on a rock drying its oily wings. Simon did not know if it were a cormorant or a shag. Helle followed his gaze and tried to explain that baby shags would take bits of half-digested fish out of their mothers' crops, but this was too hard for Simon to grasp yet.

Perhaps because he wished to test the water and see if an affair were possible, he leant forwards and placed a soft kiss on her small upturned nose. She stifled a gasp of tremulous delight, but a wistful gleam flitted across her fragile eyes and he knew that he had struck some indelible bond from which it would be difficult to retreat. Helle looked unsuspectingly happy, like a flower poised on the top of a fair mountain.

* * *

The diesel railcar snored and hiccoughed its way through dense blankets of rain over the flat landscape of Norfolk with its ditches and fields of corn stubble.

Detective Chief Inspector Grier alone alighted at Rainey Halt and inclining himself into the wind and lowering his hatted head, trudged the rain-swept three hundred yards to a restored half-timbered Dano-Saxon-pattern farmhouse.

A blue-stockinged sophisticated woman of a superior disposition admitted him through the Tudor-arched oak door with its black square bolt-heads and indicated some pegs where he could hang up his mack. Her name was Sophie Arkell.

A glum convenor at a leaded window peered out at a cat, which sprawled as flat as a mat, edged through the grass ready to pounce on a worm-pulling bird. He rapped the window. The bird flew off and the cat danced in an ecstasy of cheated fury, its malevolent fur standing up on its arched back. The sixty-year-old plump man with his shaggy brows, waistcoated paunch, pendulous chins and finely-striped suit, smiled dispassionately. Like French politicians, he had that look of being fussy and oily and womanish and altogether too astute for his own good. He gave Grier an overdonc smile, perhaps testing his embarrassment.

'How do you do, Mr Vincent?' Grier said, resolutely ignoring the smile.

'No chariot?'

'A long way from Scotland.'

Superintendent Chant, who sat on a carved chest in a beamed recess, smiled. 'Mr Vincent is looking for an expert on Citroëns. He's having trouble with that long grey one of his out there.'

'Yes, I saw it. What does he want to know? How to shorten it?'

Chant laughed. 'That's right. Which end to saw off.'

Grier felt comforted to find that he was not the only one present who was not an over-sensitive Whitehall word-guru.

'Very droll gentlemen,' commented George Vincent with his fulsome and unsmiling smile. 'Now that we are all here, perhaps we should commence business?'

The room with its waxed oak furniture, beams, copper lamps and green dimity curtains, felt cosy and civilised. The four sat down round an oval table with a tray of china teacups and slices of cake on it. Chant, from the Metropolitan Police, vaguely wondered if a concealed fifth person might not be listening too.

'The subject for our colloquy is l'affaire 210121.'

'What?' said Chant.

'210121 is an army number,' explained Vincent. 'Six figures, so an officer's number ... '

'It refers to Lieutenant-Colonel Archibald Helios Letheren,' Miss Arkell said admonishingly to the two puzzled policemen.

'The master of ceremonies in the Penman despatch – Superintendent Chant – and in the slaying of the fourteenth Lord of Ayrth – Chief Inspector Grier – is I believe this aforementioned Colonel. My own interest gentlemen and Miss Arkell's, is to *connect* him.'

Chant explained that Penman's corpse had had pink teeth, a rare but pathognomonic sign of death by violent asphyxia. They also had the murder weapon and an excellent and mouth-watering description of his presumed killer, but no fingerprints nor any clue as to where to search for her. Her first name might be 'Denise'. 'One witness was positive that her skirt came from last autumn's collection of the London fashion house of *Rebus* and we thought this would be a good lead. Fibres from such a skirt were found in the flat. People judged her to be size twelve, but even taking all sizes made – eight ten twelve fourteen and sixteen – only thirteen hundred were sold through sixty retail outlets in this country. The price tag was around £63. But we drew a blank. Either she bought it at one of the two shops which have closed since and scrapped their records or she paid for it with cash – either by chance or by intention.'

Chant paused to take a sip of tea and a bite of cherry cake, making a staggering movement with his hand to indicate the heaviness of this confection, but the M.I.5 people seemed to find this rather infantile and ignored it.

'Although you mention this fellow Letheren, I have to say that forensically there is no evidence for an accomplice, even though strangulation is an unusual choice for a woman. I do concede though that she sounds like bait – mid-twenties, upper-crust, classy, intelligent, sexy plus plus – not the sort of girl you'ld kick out of bed ... ' Miss Arkell shuffled crossly. 'The consensus is that she is English or just possibly French, but not Eastern European.' He glanced at Vincent sharply, as if inquisitive about his real game. 'Penman's surviving impression is that of an antique dealer – the smooth round face of the well-bred crook, good clothes and manners coupled with a rather supple notion of honesty – yes?' Vincent looked as if he could not understand what Chant was saying. 'The possible motives for bumping off this privy councillor I had assumed to be either robbery or vengeance for some out-spilling of his gory sexual addictions, but I take it that we must now add the proviso that some extreme form of political activity is possible?'

The Royal Albert teacups clinked as they were refilled. The police officers were used to chipped mugs and their little fingers did not stick out.

Grier told his tale. Footprints and body imprints in the snow pointed again to a lone woman. The primitive closed-circuit television camera on the main door had caught her vaguely on one of its twenty-second-interval recorded shots, a chilly black jump-suited figure seen from the rear, but clearly feminine with her narrow waist and rounded pelvis. The other three peered for a time at the shaky blown-up dark photograph which Grier handed to them.

Chant observed matter-of-factly, 'She's not just some petty thief or a jealous lover hell-bent on revenge, is she? She's thoroughly trained.'

'About a third of terrorists today are women, Superintendent, often of quite good family too. It's becoming something of an archetype. Often a boyfriend involved has been the initial incitement or a failure with boyfriends has led them to join a cause to retarget their retributive urges.

On the night of the raid on Drumairth Castle, Letheren himself was attending a mess dinner in West Germany, his elder daughter Innogen was playing in a concert in Edinburgh and his younger daughter Catharine Iphigenia, well, we know of *her* whereabouts.' Vincent did not explain this last nuance to his floundering audience.

'She went to school just down the road here, in Slegham,' Miss Arkell said. No one seemed to hear.

Vincent's interlocutions droned on until their barefaced bias overstepped Grier's threshold of irritation. 'If I can just butt in in mid-cliché here, Mr Vincent, the variables you are proposing don't fit the equation. Angus Caie was a corrupt savage. His castle was ringed by an infernal set of traps, razor-wire and anti-intruder contraptions. It took our officers twenty hours to gain access. The dead include an unidentified man with a German tattoo and an Ingrid Axt whom Interpol tell us is an East German spy. The attic was bursting with sophisticated long-range radio equipment ... Any man surveying the scene would have to ask himself, "Who were the baddies and what was really going on there?"' He spoke of the abandoned rope, the clipped wire, the tyre marks and the girl's clothing. 'Superintendent Chant is right, she has been expertly trained, which would mean that you fellows are much more likely to know who she is than we.' His tone hinted darkly at convoluted disloyalties.

Chant remarked to no one in particular, that you only had to pick up a newspaper to discover where Caie's and Rose's sympathies lay.

Arkell titivated her notes with a petulant frown.

'And to accuse my uniformed colleagues,' said Grier, 'of swanning around with blue lights flashing instead of holing up at bridges and cross-roads and trapping her, when we could not even enter the place until the following lunch-time!'

Vincent fell back to a standard smile, as if he were dealing with difficult children.

Rain poured onto the flat lawns round the house and cascaded off the edges of the thatched roof, missing the walls of oak uprights and transoms and their brick fish-bone-patterned infill.

'You may be right,' Vincent confessed magnanimously, 'This girl's victims may not have been men we would have liked. Some may view her as a fungicide. Indeed the Russian Embassy staff may well be as equally worried about her as I am and are equally unsure about what is really going on ... '

'For once,' came Grier's *sotto voce* aside.

'Suffice it to say though, that a number of cabinet ministers are very concerned about these killings and explicitly wish us to work together to compile a list of all possible candidates for this *Letheren* girl or *Leather* girl.'

'Are you watching Letheren himself?' asked Chant.

Vincent shuffled in his chair. 'Sporadically.'

'Is that when he doesn't give you the slip?'

After a time they dispersed.

As Chant drove away he thought about the military, fifth-columnist communists in the government and the Prime Minister's alleged paranoia.

The previous year he had been engaged in an absurd enquiry. It had centred on a type of luminous wand which the army used as night markers. They were shortish rods called Cylume sticks. When twisted a chemical reaction inside made them glow a reddy-orange for eight or twelve hours. It appeared that when Wilson had flown in from the Continent someone had broken one open and poured its contents onto the roof of his official car. In the daylight it was not obvious, but as his cavalcade had driven towards London and dusk had fallen, this vehicle had started to phosphoresce. The party reckoning they were visible from outer space, had climbed out in something of a panic, believing it to be part of an assassination attempt. According to hearsay Wilson expected a bomb to fall from the sky or an ambush to erupt from the next hedgerow. The police had quizzed various flight-lieutenants and army commanders, all of whom had just pissed themselves laughing. It seemed that it was no more than a lark. Everyone knew of the Premier's persecution complex and some prankster had seemingly just played on it.

But Penman, why were the Cabinet so anxious about him? Was he some sort of agent too?

* * *

Simon when small had been fascinated by mines and tunnels and secret underground dwellings. Psycho-analysts would without doubt glibly link it to his shyness and fear of people, describing it as a wish to hide in the depths of the earth or return to the womb. With his toy bricks he would build imaginary self-sufficient subterranean bunkers and think of himself living there in glorious isolation.

The sea mist lifted to reveal the dark white and green lower slopes of the fjord and in these harsh and awesomely arrogating geological confines, he thought he glimpsed something of a rediscovered lost religion.

Skogvik was a cluster of maroon-coloured wooden houses, a post-office and a white wooden church on a few flat acres below a ring of crags. Helle tied the boat up to a stone mole and exchanged greetings with a woman who went past on a kick-sledge. Everyone knew everyone here.

Simon felt very cold. Even if the temperature was only a little below zero, the water vapour from the sea made it bone-chilling, in contradistinction to the higher and dryer more easterly parts of the country.

Beside two rows of named green letter-boxes, stood Helle's rusty old Saab

They left the clutch of houses, the church and the shop behind, thrown down like dice from a giant's hand and not in any discernible semblance of order or rows and drove along the packed snow on the tortuous road which followed the fjord's indented shore.

Although Helle was showing the unmistakable signs of a woman in love, although Simon would move in with her that night and they would from then on spend most of their time together apart from being at work and although she hopped and jumped about so full of life and hope, it would be a couple of weeks before Simon was fully convinced. He had never seen a woman in love at close quarters before and after his Artemis encounter, he had wondered if all women who were not sluts were not as selfishly hard and as hauntingly inaccessible and so for a while he suspected Helle of playing some archly-amusing game with him, of teasing and using him and secretly scorning him. But the evidence of her efforts to please him and her obvious happiness when with him, her saying such things as, 'If I lost you, I should feel I had lost everything,' or 'I love you so much Simon – forgive me that I keep saying it, but I cannot help it,' gradually persuaded him that this was the genuine article.

The ice-tyres of the rumbling Saab, with their cupped metal prongs, pulled them off the fjord-side road and up a snaking shelf of snow-hidden chippings to a low flat building. This was the furniture factory where Helle worked. Outside it had a flag-pole with a Norwegian flag drooping from it, as was quite common here.

Helle unlocked the main door and once inside turned on the lights, a coffee percolator and a gas ring under a kettle of fish glue. She raked out the stove and rekindled it deftly and quickly with some shavings and smaller off-cuts. Simon sat on a three-legged stool and inhaled the sweet sticky resinous smell of newly-cut pine.

Under her removed anorak she wore a voluminous dress of cobalt blue cotton with its sleevelessness and its low square-cut neck revealing a rust-coloured or reddish-brown blouse underneath. It was a modern version of the historic everyday costumes of the last century and before. Her ears bore small round ear-rings of Kongsberg silver with some minuscule Viking design on them.

She offered him her car key and said he could borrow it if he wished to go into Namsos and pick her up again at three o'clock. Concerned that he might be hungry, she opened her lunch-box and gave him a piece of bread with a slice of very salty smoked lamb on it, the sort of traditionally preserved meat which if you are unused to it is almost emetic. They each drank two cups of potent coffee and then she gave him some orange cloudberries, another new food for him, but far more palatable than the salt-encrusted meat.

'These are found in boggy spots in the side valleys,' she said. 'When little, my father often gave me a small pail and told me to go and pick some. Once I felt fed up and filled the bucket with moss and just covered the top with berries. He was so cross, you cannot imagine.'

'Was he a hard man?'

'He was a very short-tempered ox when we were small, but he's mellowed lately.' She pointed to the crumbs down his coat. 'Tut tut. Just like your grandmother.' She shook her head.

'What?'

'My father used to say that to me, when I made a mess.'

She put the string of an old brown leather apron over her youthful neck and tied its tapes behind her back with her slender pale hands.

Her opening up made Simon feel vaguely amative, despite the early hour. He held her unresisting form against a pile of thin boards and a planing machine and kissed her briefly again. She stood breathlessly still, gave her habitual sideways smile to a lathe initially, but then raised her fair lashes, looked at him and gave him kiss.

'Do you want to stay with me tonight?' Things timid and imploring and painful mingled together in her voice and her expression. She blushed. 'I've never said anything like that to anyone else before. You must believe me. Please? It's true.'

'What about the Giskes?'

'Don't come then, if you feel bad about it.' She trembled.

'No really, I would like to ... '

'I shall talk to my mother and she'll speak to Idunn Giske,' Helle explained, almost in an ecstasy of despair.

The sounds of other cars betokened the arrival of the other workers here and Simon left, driving away from Høgfoss, along the shore of a deserted lake and down a twisty scary slope into Namsos, a rather dreary town, especially in December.

In Aursund's Bookshop he bought a rather plainly written biography of Adolf Hitler and two large dictionaries. The sparse amenities here included a public library, housed inside a new concrete town hall, but decorated with pine walls, a large new iron wood-burning stove and historic pewter plates inside show-cases.

Simon sat in the semi-circular wooden chair nearest the shiny black stove with its blue and white patterned woven cushion and read his new book. At the next table, an old woman with a black shawl and her head in a large Bible, muttered incessantly. The librarian watched him suspiciously and followed him if he took a walk between the shelves, as if he were a thief.

The fourth and fifth chapters of his book, dealt with Hitler's life in Graz, Linz and Vienna, then the capital of the Austro-Hungarian Empire. This fitted in with the first volume of *Mein Kampf*, which he also had back at the Giskes' because he had been reading it as a set book for his course at Newcastle. The pre-First World War period of Hitler's life consisted mostly of being a dilettante student, doing odd bits of work and trying unsuccessfully to enter the Art Academy in Vienna and lastly a year in the much more German city of Munich. *Mein Kampf* describes Vienna as a cosmopolitan Babylon and here, Hitler seeing art exhibitions, denounces cubism and Dadaism as symptoms of arrogant depraved and lost human minds. He contrasts too the syrupy end-of-the-century Viennese operettas of Strauss and his like with their trivial plots with *The Magic Flute*, *Aïda*, *Fidelio* and of course Wagner's operas, whose rich subtle atmospheres made the young Adolf feel so pliant and exalted. But what the biography added to this was such matters as the attempt with his flat-mate Gustl, to write an opera on the story of Weyland the Smith and in particular his infatuation for Stephanie, a colonel's daughter, whose distantly seen blonde-haired and erect form had to the young Hitler epitomised everything pure and noble in Germanic femininity. He had worshipped her, yearned for her from afar, written her love-letters and then been badly wounded when he saw her dancing at a ball with various glittering epauletted sneering tin-soldier-like little Austrian army lieutenants, all as alike as peas in a pod.

The engrossed Simon received a bolt out of the blue. He could see this subject making a short film or a television play called *Adolf and Stephanie.* With the scenes tumbling round in his head, he darted out to buy three pads of paper, a cake and a bottle of milk. He scribbled rapidly. Hitler visits the parliament building with Gustl, remarks on the confusion of architectural styles betraying the lack of clear principles and direction and the grandiose emptiness reflecting perfectly the stupefying banality and insincere declamations of its members. Stephanie chooses a dress and talks with her friend about a party. On a building site Adolf is punched and chased off for refusing to join a trades union. He mulls over the discrepancy between socialism's golden words of fraternity and altruism on the one hand and its deeds of menace and terror on the other. He bumps into seedy Jews in grubby caftans running brothels and sees in the Jewish-owned newspapers the sick ideas of liberal-mindedness which seem to support all the contentionist and arrogant sub-factions of society to the detriment of the industrious and lawful backbone of good citizens. They were full too of fatuous articles, for instance, proclaiming that some slimy philosopher – unheard of the week before – had the miracle answer to all the country's problems.

Simon chewed black oval liquorice sweets which resembled goat droppings and wrote madly, trying to put down each line before he lost it.

A wall clock in its salmon-coloured case with a curvy flower-pattern design painted in pinks and blues donged a quarter to three. Gosh! Time to go and collect Helle.

* * *

The lorry swung into its first destination in England, a modern warehouse in Worcester.

On the long overlooking brick-arched railway viaduct beside it, a customs officer dressed in the overalls, donkey jacket and luminous orange vest of a permanent way worker, appeared to be tinkering with the electrical connection box of a colour light signal.

A fork-lift truck off-loaded thirty-five boxes of tinned guavas and four hundred of tinned tomatoes, invoices were signed and the articulated diesel lorry, registration number OF NA 105, nosed its way back out into the traffic.

Telephone calls were made, watches consulted and the army and customs officers watching Unit 2 on the Billing's Moss Industrial Estate outside Rochdale, were alerted.

Unit 2 was one of a row of buildings, built of concrete blocks with prefabricated steel roofing sections on which the rain drummed and outside it stood a sign, 'Bowditch's Rare Hardwoods' and a light van parked on the concrete hard. Inside were a few boards of bog oak and cherry and lignum vitae, some power tools, a telephone answering machine which no one ever answered and three mugs of tea poured from a flask, which were being drunk by two Irishmen and a woman.

Outside again the four customs and army men holed up in a napkin factory were checking their communications. A mile away eighteen armed policemen in three vans fastened on their flak jackets. Crouching double and moving over a stile and along a hedgerow and ditch, thirty-five soldiers from the nearby Royal Engineers' barracks were forming a cordon one ploughed cabbage field back from the rain-enshrouded factory units.

At the large Gossley roundabout, Constable Eastwell in an unmarked Golf saw the Frankfurt company's lorry turn hesitantly off onto a minor road and its brake-lights glow as it negotiated the hump-backed bridge over the canal. Using the additional radio, set to a higher frequency than the force radios, Eastwell pressed the 'send' button.

'Echo Delta four to all Echo Delta units. Over.' A cloudburst of rain made some of the acknowledgements hiss and crackle. 'Echo Delta four. Orange German motive unit with a red and grey Austrian trailer, registration number Oscar Foxtrot, November Alpha, one zero five, has just left the Gossley roundabout on the Riderwood Road. Out.'

The rain poured down the soldiers' necks. No one was going to escape a cold today. Thunder rumbled like artillery support. A spasm of lightning hovered over the horizon.

Siobhán Quigley read aloud a small newspaper article about a bunch of Spanish fishermen who had flouted British authority by fishing off Cornwall.

A diesel engine shuddered and growled outside. Jim Gawley went to operate the aluminium roller door. The other two, like amoeboid blobs of jelly, took up their stations by the hoist.

The lorry accompanied by a cold wet draught, reversed itself inch by inch into the hollow womb. Its only remaining cargo was four roughly squared boles of timber.

Running feet were all around them. The order 'Freeze' had replaced the age-honoured 'Hands up'. Surprise, desperation, fury and hate all quickly succeeded one another on the Irish gang's faces. They were handcuffed, searched and separated from one another within ninety seconds. A customs officer with a flash camera blitzed away furiously in every direction.

With the side tarpaulin loosened and rolled back, a police sergeant with a power-saw cut into one of the trunks, producing a shower of sparks as it hit something metallic.

'You bloody lunatic,' yelled someone else, 'You'll blow us all up.'

A convoy of vehicles took away the captives and the German lorry driver. A painstaking study of the industrial unit, the Irishmen's van and the lorry and its load would proceed more slowly.

* * *

The film-makers were lunching on boiled fish – which had been stored in an alkaline solution making it soapy – and mashed turnip. It was yet another Norwegian dish which was an acquired taste and not exactly delicious if you were not used to it. Simon had put a lot of salt on his to try and disguise the sliminess, but the grains had largely bounced off onto the table.

'I suppose it is *table* salt,' thrust out the slinky-eyed Kim, trying to touch his knees with hers under the table, but Simon was having none of it.

'Are you flirting with your knees or just exercising your leg muscles?'

'Adrian's had a letter from his wife,' Kim replied. 'She's pregnant. 'I should think it's highly improbable that *he's* the father, wouldn't you?'

'Maybe she sees him differently to you.'

Nearby, Sir Robert was talking about *Egmont*.

'1570. The Low Countries are restless under Spanish overlordship because of religious intolerance and infringements against their local customs. Their cause is championed by two noblemen, William the Silent – the Prince of Orange who later became the first Stadhouder of an independent Netherlands –

and Count Egmont.' An insect crawled disrespectfully across a page of Goethe's script in front of him. 'In an age when most minor nobles sought posts as secretaries at princely or ducal courts and acquired the niceties of etiquette and polished manners, Egmont is an anachronism. He is still the rough-shod lord-of-the-manor of a century earlier.'

'Get her to orgasm?' whispered Kim, 'Unless giving her the shudders counts? He must rely on foreplay if he ever gives her any satisfying stimulation.'

'Also, Egmont holds the naïve belief that if you say what you feel in your heart, then everything will turn out all right. His faith is proved to be misplaced and as the friction escalates between the overweening Iberian masters and the ever more resentful populace, his lack of subtlety makes him a handy scapegoat. He only sees this at the end, when he is already condemned.'

'Do you think a red three-cornered jester's coxcomb with a bell at each corner would suit Noddy Sir Robert?' muttered Kim, but unable to elicit a response from Simon, she switched over to sudden anger. 'What is the matter with you?' she hissed.

'So whilst he fails by the worldly yardstick of success – in contrast to the shrewder William the Silent, who eventually gains the upper hand over the Spanish – he is none the less the hero for Goethe, who considers his irreproachable honesty more of a universal virtue than the prejudice of pressure-group politics. For Egmont, defeat and failure were the truest path.'

The company were now eating biscuits and Gudbrandsdal cheese with some cheap German Tafelwein dragged expensively from the clutches of the state alcohol monopoly.

Kim was turning her nose up at Simon with feeble disdain. 'You needn't have any delusions of grandeur. I don't know what makes you think I want to bonk with *you*!'

'Oh nothing, nothing at all.'

Men who were attentive to Kim were 'wonderful', those who ignored her 'odious'. Simon was being relabelled from the one category to the other. He had seen as she had spun her webs, how bitterer than death was her mind.

'So one and all,' Sir Robert concluded his speech, 'after reshooting scenes 14a and 14c this afternoon, we are finished. Those of you not involved are free to disperse as you wish. I wish you all a very happy Christmas and I look forward to our meeting again in Elstree on the seventh of January, to see the results of our labours.'

Neither the food nor the hotel were conducive to sparkling congeniality and both the applause and the replies smacked of inertia. Also the usual bickerings and under-the-surface rivalries had soured the esprit de corps. Kim for instance had wanted the part of Klärchen, the affectionate but undemonstrative lover of Egmont who with her humble clear-sightedness, unimpaired by pretentiously genteel aspirations, was to Goethe what Solveig was to Ibsen. Sir Robert had given her though the minor part of the Duke of Alba's grasping mistress, where she only needed to be herself, but that had not stopped her from back-biting the whole time against Miss David who was playing Klärchen.

Simon, now ensconced with Helle, returned to her house. He rowed back in the failing twilight from Skogvik towards the luminous bluey-white snow on the opposite shore and the two lighted houses, compressed between an inky sky and black water.

The large main room with its kitchen off was upstairs in Helle's house and the bedrooms and store-rooms downstairs.

The pine walls here were whitey-yellow and edged in straight lines, not the dark varnished pine of the Giskes' house with its convoluted beadings. Also here were no ornate silver-edged photograph frames containing faded portraits, nor lace curtains suggestive of turn-of-the-century German houses, but dried orange and blue flowers, good modern beech furniture and a tone of bright and clean simplicity. On the light oak floor were blue and orange rugs. The beechwood-framed sofa had orangy-red dimpled leather cushions on it. The blue-shaded wooden side-lamps were romantic, as were the two fat blue candles in their stocky heavy brass candlesticks – Norwegian sitting-rooms rarely have centre lights – and all was reflected in the shiny polished glass of the large balcony windows. It was homely, an island of seclusion hemmed in by the invisible rocks and waters of the fjord.

Because of her lowly origins, Helle valued highly what she had gathered and her busy nimble nature kept everything in beautiful order.

If Helle could speak any English she were too diffident to try it. Besides, she and Simon had no trouble at all in understanding one another. Sometimes he would point to something and ask her what it was and when she said it, repeat it. That she found even such repetition a pleasure, proved her to be in love. Also whilst in the evenings they sat on the sofa and she crocheted or carried on knitting a patterned pullover she had begun for him on a large circular needle, he would read history books aloud to them both.

*Adolf and Stephanie* had been written in one day, rewritten and polished the second and typed out the third. Today Sir Robert had flatteringly told Simon he thought it concise colourful and workman-like and offered him £1,000 for the copyright with an undertaking to film it during the coming year. It would of course be only a short low-budget piece, but

Simon felt very gratified not to say relieved to have earned some money.

Sitting on the sofa with Helle, her fingers touched the nape of his neck and stroked it and wandered through the short stubble of his hair, a novelty still easily able to please him. It delighted him intensely to be so spoilt and tended so wonderfully by a pretty girl who adored him and wanted solely to make him happy – so much so that her possessiveness was not yet evident.

'Where does love come from,' she asked, 'God or the Devil?'

Simon laughed.

She looked cross and yet happy. 'You have me over a barrel,' she told her own vexed mind. 'I should have been cleverer and kept my silly mouth shut and pretended I was only a little bit interested in you! But it is no use. I cannot hide it.'

He laughed again in triumph.

'You know when you're onto a good thing, you crafty Englishman.' She fell limply into his arms and he drew designs and circles on her smooth back inside her blouse. A measure of temporary comfort spread over her. Before she had never let anyone touch her, but with Simon she never hesitated nor ever withheld herself. 'I will always be only for you.'

She skipped off to boil cross-sections of unsmoked salmon and small potatoes and to cut up two tomatoes for their evening meal, eaten off blue earthenware plates on the sofa with light blue serviettes and solid silver forks with tightly-knit curved depictions of the Norns on their handles. After this came coffee and a chocolate cake she had baked that morning.

Helle was tallish, twenty-four and with short-cropped blonde hair on her squarish head. Had her pale and unmade-up face not been pretty and rather elfish, she might have appeared unfeminine and dull. Her body was slender but boyish, undeveloped and unvoluptuous. She contrived both to look girlish and to behave girlishly with her child-like and passionate and uncamouflaged emotions. Norwegians are generally unadventurous, unassertive and uncomplicated and Helle was consistent with this. Eight hundred years ago the stuffing fell out of them and they retired from the centre stage of history to sleep in the wings.

Simon saw his lover's pale forearms revealed by her pushed-back cardigan and blouse sleeves as she sat beside him with her cake plate on her lap. He touched them gently and felt their soft fine hairs. Helle held her breath in frozen ecstasy. He saw her long lithe legs and touched her rounded knees above her knee-length socks. He slid his hands up her long firm thighs and under her baggy skirt. She put her plate down on the long glass-topped coffee-table and then sat still, tense and smiling and hopeful, as if paralysed by a curare dart.

She went to bed with him nightly without any moral qualms, yet she was one of those women who are almost asexual. Her happiness is connected wholly to being loved and not at all to receiving orgasm. Had she been a ballet dancer she would have appealed perhaps more to women than men, for a purity so unseductive and guileless.

'Your skin is as fine and smooth as a very soft and tight-fitting leather suit.'

The candles flickered and they kissed in a long and gentle manner, falling inseparably sideways onto the sofa cushions and ending in slow and easy and amateurish sex.

Later, whilst she knitted and he falteringly read out loud from a book about the Italian Middle Ages, an idea for another short film about a court intrigue surrounding Joanna the First of Naples, one of her lute-playing courtly lovers and the fleeing Pope Clement the Seventh hit him and again he scribbled away on numerous sheets of paper whilst his inamorata nuzzled her nose round his ear and neck.

'You need children Simon. They would be good for you my wounded sparrow.' Helle thought of the little white-painted church in Skogvik and hoped that Simon would soon propose to her and that they could marry there. 'What is it? What has happened to you, to make you so hard?'

* * *

The black lacquered wrought-iron sign read 'Iserkirchgasse'.

Catharine passed under the bullet-pocked stone arch into the courtyard of slippery icy cobbles. In the middle stood a bare apple tree and two empty stone flower troughs. She pressed the plastic bell-push of number two, a two-roomed stone doll's house.

Christopher Roden opened the low-lintelled medieval door and peered at his caller through thick-lensed small circular glasses. He looked like a bachelor with his skewed tie, rumpled shirt and cardigan which had doubled in size at the first wash.

Catharine smiled. 'Is this your book?'

His forty-year-old face wrinkled and squinted at the blue tome. He held it, examined its title and opened it. 'Yes. Where did you find it?'

Roden was English, small and wizened, like a pickled pixie.

'May I talk with you for a few minutes?'

She scraped the snow off her boots on the iron scraper and ducked inside the snug cramped downstairs, where a dark table and chairs and a bookcase, though tidy and clean, needed some flashes of colour and feminine decorative imagination to make them more homely. French windows looked out onto a tiny garden, where there was just enough room to hang a hammock between two cherry trees in summer. An English newspaper lay in an armchair.

'Sit down. I don't very often have visitors. I left England years ago because of a disappointment and vowed never to go back. Tea? Rhubarb tart?'

'Yes and no, please.' She took the 'disappointment' to mean being deceived by a woman. Either loneliness had made him rather peculiar and nervous or vice versa. Catharine raised her voice so as to be heard through in the tiny kitchen. 'You asked where I found the book. Does the name Ute Steyer mean anything to you?'

'No.'

'Ulrich Schniewind?'

'Yes. I work at Heugel Pharmazeutik here in the city. Schniewind worked there too until a year ago, when he was sacked. It would be about then that my book went missing from my office.'

'I'm sorry, I haven't introduced myself properly. W.D.C. Sleigh from the West Mercia Constabulary.'

'Christopher Roden. How do you do?'

'I have flipped through your book and in chapter fifteen – on the synthesis, esterification and methylation of butyrophenones – a lot of lines have been high-lighted in blue. Is that your doing?'

'I don't use high-lighting pens.' He set down a brass tray of tea things on the gate-legged table and a rather burnt slice of rhubarb tart for himself. 'Cordon noir cookery.'

'We suspect Schniewind of manufacturing a drug ... possibly an hallucinogenic one.'

Roden looked at her womanly face, her loose blue skirt with small black and white geometrical designs on it, her open dark and light blue anorak and under it, her white angora woolly over her pretty but breastless body.

He refocused on the book and found some hand-written jottings in a margin. 'What's this here? A benzene ring with a bromine atom in the para-position being substituted by a side-chain of propylated ... ? Temperatures of ... ?' He suddenly raised his right palm to his forehead. 'Of course! It's all perfectly clear. Three months ago the police department in Hamburg sent us a circular asking us if we knew of anyone who might be making quantities of an illegal hallucinogenic compound. Their forensic people said it burnt with a mint green flame and they thought it was a butyrophenone structure, but it had been mixed with other complex but inert organic compounds, to make it virtually unanalysable. It had some trendy street name ... "Blue Gold" or something ridiculous. The taker should sit down in quiet and undisturbed surroundings and make himself feel relaxed and comfortable, perhaps with some music they said, before taking it by mouth, otherwise it would turn out more nightmarish than agreeable. It gave vivid visual images of animals and plants – or if a "bad trip", monsters and goblins in science-fiction caverns.

Now I now recall, that such a substance was discovered accidentally at Heugel's about three years ago. I cannot recollect the exact formula off hand, but it would have been of this type. You would need a good quality pressure vessel, but they can be bought easily enough ... some glassware and then if you were not too fussed about impurities, you could do it on the kitchen table.

So Miss Sleigh, we've solved your puzzle.'

*　　*　　*

On Christmas Eve morning Helle and Simon borrowed Tryggve's motor-boat and went up the fjord a long way to see some pre-historic rock carvings on a sheer cliff face which dropped vertically into the water. The light green crusts of mould half-hid the not very impressive crude deer and fishes and circles, but the water underneath them seemed to be still as by magic and on the slopes above, small firs watched in deathly silence, heavy with undisturbed snow.

In the afternoon they went to Skogvik church – for Helle was moderately religious – and like many of these churches, it was believed to be on the site of an earlier temple to Odin. In 1860, someone had found a partly rotted wooden effigy of a head behind the altar.

Several hundred candles flickered, the Puritanical sermon was inevitably long and dull, but some of the carols were melismatic and their words unstereotyped.

'Fair is the earth, splendid God's heaven,
Bright is the soul's pilgrim way.
'Mid the earth's riches, touched by its leaven,
We sing of paradise today.

Seasons shall come, seasons shall pale,
Young follow old paths along.
Echoes from heaven, never shall fail,
To sweeten every pilgrim's song.'

Helle thought of a wedding here, with Simon, herself in her regional county costume of assorted blues and silver jewellery, the priest, the two legally necessary witnesses and a ring. She would marry him now, if possible – her gift from the Mind of God.

In the pew in front of them sat a whole row of her aunts, women with leathery faces, some kindly and some dissatisfied, but all joined by unspoken undercurrents to the mould and stone upon which they stood and to the folk-lore embedded in the rainbows in the spray from the waterfall and in every shadow and nuance of life. Their names were Ingegerd, Jorunn, Borghild, Frøydis and Torveig.

Through a deathless twilight Helle and Simon rowed home to presents, roast pigs' ribs and a Christmas tree with white lights and miniature Norwegian flags on it.

Simon burnt his tongue on the food and she inquired why he insisted that Englishmen liked hot food and then every time she served it hot, burnt himself?

Simon kissed her delicately on her small nose and watched the strange joy form in her, a calm glow which spread right down to her toes. But then a darker thought broke out in her mind and she reciprocated his observation of her, attempting to decipher his thoughts.

'I went out with a boy once, for about a year. I thought too that I was beginning to love him ... but I see now that I didn't know then what love was.' She hesitated. 'Tell me about your earlier girlfriends, Simon.'

'There's nothing to tell.'

She gave a half-smile and peered assiduously into his eyes. 'My wise Augustus, what are you thinking?'

'I was just changing thoughts.'

'What to?'

'The new one still hadn't arrived.'

'What from?'

'I forget.'

'You sly-boy ... the sweetest on earth.'

'Only when you are with me. You must be the ingredient which sweetens,' he complimented her.

She laughed briefly, not foolish enough to listen to flattery, nor did she ever make the mistake of trying to be learned. She was far too shy to be called a goddess, but it was equally clear that she was not unchaste.

She went to a chest downstairs. It had iron bands and handles and was painted a leaden blue-grey colour – or 'farmers' blue' as it was known there. She brought up a photograph album and showed him pictures of her childhood and the boys and girls she had gone to school with.

'Helle, I did once love a girl ... but nothing happened.'

'Why not?'

'She refused to see me.'

Helle found this puzzling. He who had knitted Simon together had dropped no stitch. 'So it is her you really love and I am just a replacement?' Her sadness was ruly but her pain unblunted. She burst out sobbing.

'That was some time ago. I don't think about her now.'

'You would enjoy talking about her I think,' Helle said, but allowed him to cuddle and comfort her.

The house was wonderfully cosy. The insulation was such that an electric radiator downstairs on half a kilowatt kept everywhere warm in spite of the sixteen degrees of frost outside.

He cleared away the meal and she brought out the dainty white Porsgrund bone china cups and saucers, small silver teaspoons, her grandmother's old German coffee pot, a plate of varied biscuity-like cakes she had baked, a dish of decorated and coloured marzipan shapes, a conical cake made up of almond rings and a bowl of dark and bitter chocolate Madonnas and whales and trolls.

'What was this girl's name?'

'Artemis.'

'Artemis.' Helle repeated it as if savouring a new food. 'It sounds very high-class.'

'She was classy, but bad.'

'But you loved her.'

'Yes.' Seeing that her fragile arms and chest were quivering inside her soft blue dress, he held her and tried to change the subject.

'You use me ... soften me up with kisses ... ' But again she let herself be soothed, helpless to resist.

Simon watched her pour the coffee. Everything she did was done well and with flair and she had that artless talent of concentrating entirely on the task in hand. Should he settle here in tranquil obscurity with this loving but possessive woman? If so, he would have to love her well too, or later she would grow vicious and resentful. He told her that he *thought* he would like to marry her, but that he needed to return home first for a week and ponder it.

She viewed this as wine laced with poison, delight tainted by danger.

'When you are not by my side, I think all the worst things – that you are grown weary of me and won't come back ... '

'How about a honeymoon in Ecuador? It's warm there, even at this time of year. My sister, who's a lot older than I, is employed in the British Embassy at Quito. I've never been across the Atlantic. She says that the towns are squalid and violent, but that the pink and grey Andes and the blue Pacific are very beautiful.'

'It sounds enthralling, to ... have you all to myself for two whole weeks!'

On Christmas Day, nothing happens in Scandinavia. After their usual breakfast of orange juice, coffee, new rolls, boiled eggs, cheeses and a runny strawberry conserve made of uncooked pulped strawberries stirred with sugar, Helle and Simon went out on long narrow cross-country skis, dressed in bobble-hats, mittens, ski-suits which stopped just below the knees and long thick patterned socks.

They left the boat and herring-boned up a steep narrow shelf, stopping at the top for breath. A pure white plateau lay before them, edged with distant sleeping firs and gripped in a deep solace, gloriously remote from the chaos of aggressive minds, from strident and perturbing oratory and enchantingly isolated still from the hellish tomorrow which all noisy and assertive demagogues promise us. Here were no transparently pushy Kims, invoking dirty thoughts and spurring on toads to jump on top of them and deposit their sperm-laden fluids between their legs. This stillness seemed to defy the egocentricity of atheism and say that tenderness and regard and intimacy are the everlasting values and that innocence and deep understanding may go hand in hand.

As they propelled themselves over the dry and rather resistant snow, a single line of half-submerged footprints appeared. They led to the trees and a frozen stream which had trickled down a narrow ravine until winter's paw took it in its grip. On a rickety suspension bridge, wide enough for just one person, stood a scantily-clad wild-looking man of over two metres in height. This was Mad Martin. He lived in an abandoned cattle shelter up here – a few rude beams and a roof with turf on it – and he used to go down in the daytime to knock on folk's doors and eat huge meals which they gave him. Helle talked to him for a time and he was as docile and meek as a little child.

Simon stood apart, feeling contented and pleasantly boy-like, though less boy*ish* than before. He remembered Goethe's adage, 'New love, new life'.

Yet first, he had to see Artemis once more.

He pointed to the masses of icicles hanging over a distant mountain and asked Helle if it was a waterfall.

'No,' she said, 'That's the hair of a troll.'

Dusk would soon fall, although it was only two o'clock. They set off home. He had promised to do some snow-clearing for the Giskes with one of those broad aluminium shovels.

'Is that a waterfall then?' He indicated the thinnest of streams dripping over a ridge.

'No,' she said, 'That's a goat weeing.'

As he looked at the trees, he said to them inwardly, 'Oh Artemis ... I must ask you one last time, because it is you whom I really want.'

## CHAPTER TWELVE.

On Christmas Eve on Ward 4, Artemis was on early duty. The day unfolded for her with that poignant clarity which men say they experience before battle or when near to death. Reality seemed slow and vivid with nothing insignificant or common about it. Ordinary dull mortality receded as if ushering in a calm before the storm – the overture to some dramatic climax.

Pink and blue streamers criss-crossed between the trusses under the high ceiling, a blue Christmas tree bearing silver baubles stood sentinel-likc beside Sister's desk at one end of the long Nightingale ward, the Salvation Army brass band appeared and played *Hark the Herald Angels Sing* with the bass notes reverberating from a double-bass trombone and a prominent B flat trumpet playing a descant line and an effulgent afternoon sun streamed in through the tall windows between each bed to cast white rhomboids on the polished parquet flooring.

Ward 4 was considered the best in the hospital. Its sister, Carole Brumwell, kept superb order without hassle or bossiness. Her dulcet tones encouraged a cheerful seemliness even amongst the less responsible staff. Her one eccentricity was a hatred of cockroaches. She would pour ether on them and they would turn over onto their backs to protect themselves, but then unable to right themselves after it had evaporated would die. The cleaners complained in vain that the ether marked the floor's oak blocks.

Student Nurse Boden and Staff Nurse Way were making beds together, folding back the starched white sheets and tucking in the scarlet blankets.

'Why don't you ever come out with the rest of us, Nurse Boden?'

'Well ... I'm busy ... I'm writing a book.'

'Oh. About what?'

'Um ... It's about a pink elephant, who wanted to be the first pink elephant to swim across the English Channel,' Artemis explained with gravity.

'I see,' said Philippa in an undertone.

'He drives down to Dover in his Skoda and is one third of the way across, when he meets a French pink elephant swimming the other way.'

'How does it end?'

'That is a secret, Nurse Way,' she confided. 'You'll have to buy the book to find out.'

On the wall above them, a stone lyre-shaped tablet thanked Moura Lympany for giving a benefit concert here in 1938 and raising £601.

'Someone tried to force their way into your room on Sunday night.'

Artemis blanched.

'Doctor Khan it was, with a long ladder reaching up to your window. Christine Lockwood called the police and in his bag they found a wedding dress, a bottle of champagne and a revolver. In his cell at the police station, he produced a syringe full of thiopentone which he squirted into a cannula already in the back of his hand and killed himself.'

'Did they arrest him *before* he entered my room?'

'Yes.'

Artemis breathed out with silent relief.

The surgeon whose male ward this was, Mr Sword, appeared with a medical student to do a ward round. A mellowed and unpompous man with a sharp eye for distinguishing genuine suffering from self-abuse and idleness, he ensured propriety and good morale in his wards by not allowing them to degenerate into doss-houses.

Sister Brumwell in her medium blue dress, white pinafore and intricately folded white hat, held her clip-board and went round with the chief.

Initially all was affability – a remark of encouragement, a query as to whether Mr English still lived in Collingwood Street, a proverb – and then came Mr Brush, a proudly boorish Yorkshireman.

'Good afternoon Mr Brush. And how are you?'

The correct answer to this question was, 'Fine, thank you Mr Sword.' After all, Brush had had his hernia repaired and the wound was healing well.

'Cor, still bloody sore!'

Sword's cheerfulness vanished. His mid-fifty jowls fell and his shaggy eyebrows jutted forward like awnings. 'Look here Brush,' he growled, 'you've had your treatment. You can get out and make room for somebody else.' He swung round to Sister. 'It's no pleasure treating these sort of people you know. No grit at all.' Sister smiled inscrutably.

Artemis was in the ward kitchen, standing beside the stainless-steel table-top and counting the bottles of milk, loaves, eggs and cubes of butter which the porter had just delivered. Nurses then were not allowed to sit down. The only exception was if feeding a poorly patient, so that they did not feel they were being hurried.

She went to intercept a cockroach crossing the floor, but then suddenly and decorously stopped to let it pass. 'Good afternoon Simon!' she said.

The ward was still and the patients, who occupied about a half of the two rows of neatly lined-up beds, were all tucked in and awaiting the chief's progress.

Mr Sword's Pakistani houseman had belatedly joined the round. An unproven suspicion existed that Mr Sword was racist and certainly he tried to avoid this fellow.

'So Doctor Mohammed, how do you think we diagnosed Mr Fairless's tumour?'

'By scan, Sir?'

'No, I didn't use a C.A.T. scan nor a dog-scan. I used my hands Doctor, my hands. Where are you going to practise, in the United States? There they start with fifty tests on the patient and if it doesn't give them an answer they do another fifty and if still they don't know, they actually look at him. But good for business no doubt – expensive these tests.

So, here we are with silent obstructive jaundice. Now if we *can* palpate the gall bladder, what is the rule which says that it may then be a tumour in the head of the pancreas, Doctor?'

'Sorry Sir. Don't know Sir.' It was Mohammed's destiny never to know.

'I don't know how you expect to pass these examinations if you can never answer these questions.'

'Would it be Courvoisier's Law, Mr Sword?' asked the student.

Sword chortled and turned so that Mohammed could not hear him. 'That's it! I'd forgotten myself.' He turned to Mr Fairless. 'So Mr Fairless, your wound's healing well. Eat up your food, especially the meat and the fish and the nurses'll start getting you up for small walks tomorrow.'

Mohammed asked, 'Excuse me, Sir. Have I seen these patients also getting hypersplenism, isn't it?'

Sword thought for a moment. 'Your experience in this field Doctor, has again been unique.'

After the last patient – a fellow with an obturator hernia – Sword left the ward and in the draughty main corridor met the old orthopaedic surgeon Mr McNeill. The two gossiped and emitted smothered guffaws. 'Mac the Knife' spent most of his time at a small private clinic doing unnecessary operations for large fees. He was bald, slightly nondescript and had a cheesy smile, yet was held in some respect for he could be nasty if he put his mind to it. Behind them a brass plaque read, 'The telephone was donated by Lady Ailith Still in 1922'.

At three o'clock the split-shift nurses returned, Sister gave the report and Artemis left.

In the blue and cream half-tiled corridor with its strong smells of the antiseptic carbolic acid and camphor and with odd bits of apparatus parked in its recesses, she saw Mr Sword talking and thought of her grandfather trying to press him into marrying her mother. He was well-liked especially by the theatre staff. On Friday lunch-times, before he went up to his boat at Blyth, they would make him something to eat and not just a sandwich but ham and eggs or whatever.

Up the broad stairs, the menu outside the self-service dining-room offered a choice of grey-green greasy Limpopo pie, a chicken leg fed on fish meal and garnished with a sprig of festive holly or a boiled kipper with grated cheese all accompanied by peas and potatoes. Artemis chose the latter and in the almost deserted canteen ate with Sister Burch, who though not dating from the Boer War as rumoured, had put patients under their beds during air raids in the last war and worked for a time with two army surgeons in Catania after the Sicily landings. But she had become lost and confused in the modern unordered and undisciplined world, where you went to parties seemingly to get drunk and vomit in your host's freezer box. She climbed out of her office window now on the paediatric ward when she heard the new young smooth consultant coming to do his rounds, because she could not stand him and left the staff nurse to go with him. It had been she too who had interviewed Artemis back in August, the two of them sitting alone at one end of the long massive table in the oak-panelled boardroom, with its gilt-framed and oil-painted long-dead surgeons and an old tattered banderole hanging aloft. Plywood partitions were now converting this into yet more offices. Artemis felt she were seeing the twilight of a passing and very different world.

Neither she nor Sister Burch could find much to say.

The Sister peered down at the fob-watch pinned to the top of her apron. 'If you'll excuse me Nurse, the train to Bedlington leaves in half an hour?'

Had she lived thirty years earlier, Artemis thought, she might have liked nursing – but not now with today's ungrateful rabble and the lack of pride and belief born of insecurity. Nowadays no one told you, 'Do this. This is your duty,' and so you drifted along aimlessly as an easy prey to some or other vice.

Artemis left the hospital too and with her hands thrust into the pockets of her black tightly-belted leather coat and flakes of snow drifting down in the darkness to land on her hair and on the red black and gold shawl draped round her neck and shoulders, she kicked her way through the new white rugs of snow both in the hospital yard and in the cold dark alley. A hint of manic nonchalance hid a deepening and all-engulfing despondency in her.

As she fished for her key to the nurses' home in her little red purse, which was worn almost black in places from repeated fingering, she realised that two men in raincoats were stood by its high blue door.

'Good afternoon, Miss. Tynemouth Police.' The speaker produced an oblong blue warrant card and Artemis glanced at it in the thin light from the lamp above the door.

'Good afternoon.'

Her heart paused for a few seconds before recommencing its beating and the contents of her bowels turned to liquid. In her travelling-box were her pistol and a new leather suit and boots.

'Would you know if a Miss Victoria Inall lives here?' asked the second looming grey face.

'Yes she does,' averred Artemis.

She let the three of them in and switched on some lights in the broad gloomy and slightly dilapidated hallway.

'Top floor, turn left and it's the end room.'

They thanked her formally and clattered off up the stairs.

Artemis took some mail from her own pigeon-hole and as both letters in Victoria's slot were from Barclay's, she took those too. In the first-floor kitchen she removed her coat and placed it on top of the post. She stamped her foot to try to prevent an involuntary tremor from spreading up her leg.

The descending detectives tapped on the open door and entered this brightly lit and spacious room with its tubular lights, kitchen table, ironing-board and cooking facilities.

'She's not in. You've no idea where we might find her?'

This mundane statement sounded inadequate before this apotheosis of lithe sexual beauty. She stood there in her finely-striped uniform dress pinched deeply in at the waist and supped a glass of milk. Something of encumbered confrontation hung in the air. She imagined that both men felt icily virile and that either by himself might have tried to hog her or to persuade her to sit on his eager cactus. For her part she understood their restriction of circumstance and smiled sympathetically.

'Almost everyone's gone home for Christmas, though the senior sister on duty in the hospital should give you her home address, Officer.'

The temptations of her firm sexy outline were bad enough for their souls, she thought. She transposed her faint smile into a paraphrase of something more cryptic and belittling. Artemis had no white image left – only the black form – though as with Hitler, of whom the word 'evil' is so often used, she was in her own dramatic estimation, simply an ardent idealist. Yet she was nearing the point of ignoring how others regarded her and of not acknowledging the deepening ill-grace and unhappiness in her own mind. If you do not see these warning signs as measures of something bad, but only as bright and vital aspects of your true self, you are heading for catastrophe.

'Thank you,' said the policemen with uneasy politeness, for their weather-vanes of instinct were warning them against her Siren-like allure.

As they clattered off again down the second flight of stairs, Artemis muttered to herself, 'Enjoy your dead-end trail.'

One of Victoria's official letters was a bank statement which correctly catalogued the opening deposit, the huge health authority cheque, the massive cash withdrawal and the small positive residual balance. The second communiqué stated with impersonal brevity, that 'the possibility of irregularities pertained to the above enumerated cheque' and would she contact them at once to 'discuss it'. Artemis set fire to these documents using one of the cooker's gas rings and watched them burn in an empty soup tin beneath the extractor hood.

She took a melon from the refrigerator – no one had molested this as they had sunk teeth into her cheese – and with a bread-saw she bisected it, scooped out the stones and cut a saw-tooth pattern round the top of each half, mixing the left-over triangles with halved maraschino cherries to refill the scraped-out middles.

She opened up a Christmas card from Veronica Whale, a girl she had been at school with and perhaps exchanged a 'good morning' with about once a term. In the card was a photo-copied personal letter in which Veronica 'deplored her shyness in her school-days', wished she had been 'more gregarious' and hoped they would 'all meet up again soon'. She had also bought a *Rupert Bear* quilt for her bed! Artemis recalled a little school play they had both acted in in the fourth form called *What Margaret took off*.' Yet this circular letter was a testimony to Veronica's cracking up, especially when you bore in mind that another eighty had been sent out. The card too was amorphous and neurotic, with a white hand reaching out for a black one and some nonsense in it about 'symbolising our need for human communion'. Artemis threw it in the bin. Grown women really should not play such childish games. They were just as much sly plotters this Christmas as last and not likely to alter drastically by the next. The two would have nothing in common if they met. Veronica was a puerile defeatist, frightened of men, unable to manage the sexual field and full of soppy ideas, whilst Artemis was nail-spittingly stand-offish. With the exception of Denise, the only people whom Artemis could talk to sensibly seemed to be older men.

She thought of the two policemen searching for Staff Nurse Inall, who unbeknowingly were really hunting for her. If one had come alone, would she have tried to entice him into the spiritual dangers of sex? They were her foes after all and she wanted to ensnare them into injuring themselves, as Xystia had hoped to tempt Christina of Bolsena into self-destruction. Besides logically, if she intended to love no one and live by auto-sex, what other uses were there for her Terpsichorean poses and her vagina?

Her second envelope was postmarked 'Ludlow' and came from her father. In semi-legible writing on thick expensive paper, badly folded and blotted with a dried tear mark, he told how he had visited a man who sold second-hand Meccano and amongst other pieces, had bought a rare part 119, an eleven and a half inch circular girder only made pre-war in the dark red of the 1926 – 1934 period and in near mint condition. She mused over how marvellous it was that he could be so pleased over something so simple – yet perhaps he had not much else to be happy about? In fact was he really worried about her and therefore talking about anything else which came into his head? Was he really restraining an impassioned torrent which said, 'Oh Artemis, whichever way I turn at night I cannot sleep. My breast is raxed with fear for you my beloved daughter'?

Pure-hearted girls it seemed should float on a cumulus of romantic mysteries and ambiguities. But why? Why must *she* be good when men could be faithless and bestial and that was quite in order?

She wiped her nose on her small lace handkerchief and reflected more comfortably that men were weak and indecisive and foolishly fearful of the shadows of sin. No Pied Piper's illusory dance would mislead her. No staid and mediocre ideal would detract her from her soaring aims.

Artemis's last envelope had a 'Norge' stamp on it which she suspected meant 'Norway'. The card's outside had a reprinted painting on it of a wooden cabin in deep snow with children and a Christmas tree outside it. Inside, under a printed 'God Jul', it said 'Love Simon' and there were four kisses. What was *he* doing in Norway? Had she turned him into a troll? Had her sorcery been successful? Or had he turned her into a stone perhaps? Or had she always been a stone? Had his defeat been a Pyrrhic victory for her, the price of rebuffing him ruinous? And had it set him upon some exciting path of adventure? Restlessness crept over her. She wished to be back at Loch Eilan again, scheming how to wrest wealth and fame from a spiteful world and planning Simon's downfall.

An auxiliary nurse called Gail Fell sauntered in, wearing a cream dress with shoes, a belt and a handbag all in matching red plastic. She thought this to be stylish. The dress was a thin nylony affair which ensured that the outlines of her brassière and panties were easily and tastelessly visible as they cut into her fat. She was busty, vain and fond of admiration. Artemis's secret name for her was 'La Limace,' which meant both a slowcoach and a slug. Gail for her part thought Artemis to be a cut-glass prig ... or was it a pig?

She was like most Tyneside girls, extremely laissez-faire. No lewd or obscene suggestion would shock them. They might say 'no' but would not be outraged. Of course Goldstraw and his type would say that that was what was good about them. That was the start of a relationship, not the end of one.

Gail threw her leather coat onto a chair, a cheap rough one which though nominally black had a hint of greyishness in it and was matt and with a long split up the back. It did not fit well nor gleam like Artemis's and the most you could say about it was that it looked common and raunchy.

'Hi Artemis, I've just been out with Angela for a few lagers. They've made me go all woozy.'

'Eureka,' commented Artemis drily.

'Oh, a man rang earlier. He didn't give a name ... said you'ld know who he was. He's coming to visit you this evening.'

'Thanks, though I was expecting him actually.'

'He sounded posh. It must be *nice* to have boyfriends loaded up to the hilt.'

'In Scotland we say "up to the kilt".' Artemis gave her an ironical smile.

Gail munched a piece of left-over toast from the draining-board. She belonged to that class of females who if accused of inciting harassers or pesterers would protest that she had no idea what you were talking about, yet was able swiftly to denounce other girls for similar antics.

'I think Russ in the boiler-house's fallen for me.'

Fallen? A big drop. Had he broken a leg in the process? If he fancied stoking Gail, thought Artemis, she doubted whether he would have much competition.

'He might be at the Eustacia Arms later. I've put a frilly bra on.'

'I can see.'

Gail looked crossly at this stuck-up prude. 'Why are you always so cutting ... ? '

Artemis was tempted to say that the bra was more cutting, but reined herself in, even though she was indifferent to Gail's estimate of her. 'You're misconstruing me, really. I hope you have a nice time.'

Like many Tynesiders, Gail though hard-bitten, wore her heart very much on her sleeve and a touch of kindness would have gone a long way. She was teetering on the brink of feeling undesirable and it would have been generous on Artemis's part had she shown some goodwill or given her a bit of friendly advice.

'Have you seen my chunky red sweater about?'

'No.' Artemis hated the in-vogue word 'chunky' which was lately applied to everything from sweaters to marmalade.

'I hear you're on Brumwell's ward now?'

'On *Sister* Brumwell's ward, yes.'

Gail clanked a milk bottle against a glass. '*Sister* or not, I think she's ignorant. She never says "hello" to me in the corridor.'

'She often walks past me too without saying "hullo", but I'm not offended and she's certainly not ignorant. That's just your misconception.'

Gail shrugged awkwardly. 'I think she's élitist.'

'A pity there aren't more élitist people about.'

Gail wrinkled her nose up sourly because she had failed to draw Artemis into her grimy web of back-biting. 'You're a bloody snob too,' she spat.

'Just shut up and buzz off!'

Gail's face looked murderous, stung by this wasp.

Artemis returned the glare. This gall-bag ought to go and work in one of those dishonourable nursing homes, where she could whine and loll and smoke in cupboards, steal money out of senile old women's handbags or when they died swap over their gold jewellery for those gilded plastic imitation pieces found in party crackers.

Scowling, Gail seeped off.

They had come within a whisker of having a scrap.

Artemis too after a drink of water snatched up her coat and marched upstairs to her room, something detestable and savage swelling up inside her caused by an infuriation with the success she suspected Simon to be enjoying.

With the angle-poise lamp tilted against the wall, only a ring of white light diffracted into bands could challenge the shadows. Artemis meditated on the paths of radical evil – how to become Nemesis the Goddess of Vengeance – and strike at Simon. She did not furtively relish others' misfortune in general – and in this she were less perverse than many around her – but in this coming and inevitable struggle, she could not be hampered by the fear of harming others incidentally. Simon must suffer both mental torment and bloody bodily wounds if he was as she now believed, the originator of her failure. Her strict and independent aspirations were not to be forbidden by that half-wit.

Yet the more she considered it, the more she saw that Papa and Mr Letheren too were forcing her to kneel and obey like a slave girl! *Why*??? They possessed some sort of magic between them which skilfully hemmed her in and steered her.

And these three supreme arbiters were like fish bones sticking in her throat.

A stylus-like shadow on the wall moved a little. 'Mene mene, tekel upharsin' – the writing on the wall, the allusions to disaster and the knell of death which the doomed queen could not decipher. The head might err if not the heart, but the heart had been stifled. It told her to marry Simon for it knew the hope which the head did not see! 'Oh my fairest saddest child, write to him and ask forgiveness,' it called in anguish in sibyl-like dislocated incoherent prose, loaded with undampened pain.

She knelt and unlocked her trunk and extracted a large flat polythene-wrapped parcel from it. Yesterday she had driven down to Northampton, to the factory which had made her first leather suit and which she had since sunk onto the bottom of a deep part of Loch Eilan tied round a large stone. She had coaxed the manager, using that half-smile of hers which drove men mad with desire, into selling her its identical twin as a retail sale and had been to Hawkins Boots too and bought a new pair of replacement top quality black leather riding boots. She unpacked these items, sniffed them, fingered them, held them to her warm cheeks and to her body as a girl in love must touch and possess her loved one or as a cat ritually urinates on things to label them. She had always liked the feel and lustre of leather – the blue leather sofa at home she could remember stroking when only three years old, saddlery, her orangy-tan school satchel, shiny well-worn dog-eared and with her initials 'A.O.B.' embossed on it in gold. She liked stone and gold and oak too, but leather she adored. The power of this obsession was enough to quell any dissent from her soul.

As a schoolgirl at Fort Augustus, she had gone by bus once a week to a private drama lesson still in her school uniform of a tartan pleated skirt, a white blouse and a pullover all in the school colours of black blue and white. But the visible items were a black hair-band, white knee-length socks and the standard black gabardine school mack with its belt and hood which with its dark tartan lining hung buttoned on below the back of the collar. She would sit on the ribbed seats of the archaic bus with her satchel either on her lap or beside her. A gangly local schoolboy named Stephen had occasionally dared to sit beside her. Once he had even tremulously offered her a mint, but he was far too nervous to ask her out. In any case she had been disinclined to be helpful and besides the school never granted exeats on such grounds. Yet she had known even then, that she were waiting chrysalis-like for something else. Now all that had been revealed to her – the effects her body could exercise on men and the dread excitement of doing wicked deeds when dressed up in leather – but in those formative years the notion of leather emitting overtones of toughness and sexiness, of its suiting her pale and untender and Mephistophelean beauty had been only a latent horizon, a vague adumbration.

She caressed her new leather rig for a time and the surging toxins of envy subsided. The restoked fires of a full-blown pride made her feel delightfully soothed and eased. An unabating tide of omnipotence fizzed in her blood and made her sure that she would never surrender to any sniggering smirking dross. She must rise again and in dark enterprise conquer. Especially she needed to tackle those unbearable threats and taunts in the shadowy darkness beyond, to leave the claustrophobia of everyday tedium, to leather and beat into submission those sub-human forces which were blocking her path. Her breast thrilled rapturously. ‘Come on Mr Letheren. Come and see me again. Tell me what havoc I shall wreak next.’

She put on her new attire and looked over her shoulder in the mirror, to view her creaking glistening image from all angles in an orgy of self-love. It was stiff, whereas its predecessor had begun to grow suppler with use. It could keep out ineptly wielded sticks, chains and kicks. Penises would stub themselves helplessly against this tantalising defence and fail to penetrate the thick double layer under her pubis where the front zip's lower end was embedded beneath an extra strengthening fillet. She put on the bronze-clasped belt. She slid her hands over her taut leather curves in gratified delight and oscillated her hips in defiance of that triumvirate of tyrannical males, no of *all* males and the *whole* world.

Leather had become an outward extrapolation of her willful pride and the fury incurred by her reversals. It was made for her and she for it. It was her right and unique spiritual gallows. It was symbolic of her essence and an expression of her dark alliances thereunder. On her behalf it seemed to say, 'Look at my brave and dazzling mistress in her sexy tough black leather. She challenges you all to dare to oppose her.'

Undressing, she saw that the brown pensile outpouchings in front of her armpit had shrunk to small reddish spots.

She took a soapy perfumed bath and washed and combed her shortish hair. She put on an alarmingly short and previously unworn dress of glazed black moiré patterned with awned barley heads in silver glitter and pulled in at the waist by an aluminium chain. With black tights and shoes, argentan bracelets and a long silvery neck-chain and ear-rings, dark red lipstick and blue and black eye make-up, it was an outfit which left little doubt as to the wearer's intents. Lessened were her stiff gait, her arched neck, her coy floating eye and her stern reserve, yet she still retained her striking beauty despite the signs that she had become debased. She appeared like a high quality guy, a sylph-fury, a girl ready to be disreputable or like one of those vivid fiery whores who had danced for the chieftains of the Black Sea tribes and who – before the Bolsheviks had eradicated them or forced them all into boiler suits – had given such wild colour and unequivocal life to the music of Russia's minor composers.

Tonight she would repel civilisation and embrace barbarity. She *wanted* to be a tart. She wanted to seduce Letheren, to lure him into shoving his muscular male missile into her virtuoso form, into bedewing his potent sweet and life-giving oily balsams inside her and in so doing, into triggering those addictive florescent ecstasies within himself which would drag him down into her dark chasms of insatiable night where she would drown his virtue.

She borrowed a red Hessian cloth to drape over her travelling-box and on it set out the halved melons, a bottle of wine, glasses, Ardennes pâté, biscuits, cheeses and two small bowls of bloated water-laden imported strawberries sprinkled with nuts and cream.

She would flirt with him and set light to his testosterone propelled rocket and prove to herself that she were sexier and more irresistible than other pitiful fallen travesties.

Colonel Letheren knocked on cue. If he seemed mildly startled by her gaudy rig-out, he too wore pretty eccentric garments. Tonight over a tabard of dark red knitted cotton, blue breeches and black boots, he had on an old large oiled mack like a green carapace.

Artemis bade him enter her den. He discarded his mack and sat as before on the edge of her bed, his warm and strong presence born of hardship and suffering, glowing like a shy fire-ball. She loathed this invasion of light and smiled crookedly in unison with his wary benevolence.

'I replaced the shredded spare tyre for you,' he said as they swapped over the key of the Porsche and the key of the Land Rover.

'Thank you ... my overseer.' She used her deeper register, which she knew on stage to have a more expressive timbre. 'Or ought I to say, my sorcerer?'

'A very amateur sorcerer as yet,' he remarked.

She sat down in her easy chair and told of the night at Drumairth Castle and of the wave which had carried away all her loot. 'How is it,' she demanded, 'that I succeed masterfully in fulfilling *your* portion of the operation, but fail to extract my own tribute?'

'Ah, don't be begrudging. Everything is unfolding as it should and all can end well for you *provided* that you soften your heart a little.'

'I cannot help being severe.' Her dress's hem had receded up so far that her white panties were easily visible through her tights. She smiled at him suggestively and writhed, concealing her anger.

'Selfishness turns us into drudges. It is love and sacrifice which lift us up. If you put a bit of warmth and generosity into what you soever do, it might repay you more abundantly.' He took her slender hands and she knelt before him. 'The police seem to have only a very sketchy description of you and no leads. I have interceded that the blame – if there be any – is on my head. Even Rufus Drummond, I accept wholly that guilt too.'

'He might have described me under pressure.'

'Surely. In the last war, on a mission into the southern Sahara, we ran into a score of Germans by accident and they surrendered. We could not take P.O.W.'s with us so we shot them ... Humanity and the rules of engagement say you shouldn't, but what else could we do?'

Artemis had no interest in moral dilemmas. As a fair Egeria-like nymph she would captivate the affections of the feudal Numa, carousing at sunset in mystery and beauty. A lily-white doe with a snake nourished in her bosom – that of avenging those responsible for her failure – made her feel sweetly poisonous and brilliantly ghastly.

'I have about one and a half million Deutschmarks in a Swiss bank, which ought to make good the contents of the lost kitbag. But to earn this sum, you have to take a trip to Liverpool. It should be a piece of cake for you my conscience-denuded and leather-encapsulated Caliban, but none the less, beware of over-confidence.'

'I plan thoroughly.'

'I can see that.'

She stood up unexpectedly and sat down beside him like the spider beside Little Miss Muffet. This dark calculatrice wrapped her arms round his shoulders and neck. She kissed the clean-shaven leathery skin on the side of his face, well-tanned and supple like an old soft leather bag and hoped for a satyriatic response.

He turned his head and smiled forlornly. What had happened to the aphorism that women with skirts up run faster than men with trousers down? Clearly it belonged to an evanescent era. Today men with running-spikes on, might just if they were quick, escape girls with next to nothing on.

She seized his head and kissed him again, more intensely.

They watched one another's eyes – but it was she who was obsessed. 'The occasional stroke or touch is acceptable but no physical intimacies beyond that are.'

Women often made first-rate agents because they did not have the moral inhibitions which plagued men. Letheren was ever dithering because he was hounded by ethical qualms.

He feared that if he committed the least untruthfulness, he would be punished with a restive and unbecoming spirit. For his great responsibility he was held on the tightest of reins. Any instant misused or word wrongly uttered cast a black spot on his life.

He gave her his salty walrus smile, which she ignored and without impediment sent her hand diving swallow-like under his tabard. Though surprised by these changes in her, he was swift enough to deflect this molestation.

'Sleep with me,' she pleaded with extemporary sweetness. 'Do you hear?'

'Artemis ... !'

'Do you have ear trouble?'

'Oenone ... !'

'No. The trouble's further in than your ear,' she lambasted him.

'Miss Boden ... !'

Hormones were hissing and foaming inside her. She stood up, switched off the lamp, pulled off her tights and panties and trembling with desperation, toppled him onto his back and clambered on top of him in a frenzy.

He bestirred himself to parry and fend off her hail of assaults, fighting her as one gently restrains an epileptic.

'For goodness sake, cuddle your Teddy girl.'

'I am too big for soft toys. I need *hard* toys.'

'Give all this to the boy who ought to have it.'

'There is no such boy. You are my beacon. I feel a zeal for your rays.' She tried again to grip his sexual bibelots.

Her dexterity and strength were considerable, but he rallied himself for a counter-attack, entangled her in a blanket and then turned on the light.

In between her attempted accolades and unceasing struggles, he thought that as his love for his children was a borrowed analogy of God's love for us, so her disavowals attested within her the negative and destructive existence of wickedness ... and how weak it was.

Finally tearing herself free from the twisted blanket and giving up, she seethed, 'Confound you, you scrott-bag. Do you hear? You pathetic wizard!' Then unable to endure any further rhapsodic orations, she flew out of the door and down the stairs.

She dived unseen into the darkened box of the unused games room and came to rest with her forearms on the invisible baize of the snooker table with her head hanging limply down. Her fiery and unsatisfied neophyte enthusiasms waned temporarily.

Why had she been incapable of devising a delicious enough snare to overwhelm him?

She hooked herself tentatively up, so that the corner of the billiard table might chafe her genitalia through the hem of her mini-dress. Her hands gripped the cushions, but it was not satisfactory, not the same as having a man inside her or as being dressed in her evil black leather. She abandoned such a dirty and pathetic idea. Girls who did such things were those who nourished tawdry romantic fancies about castle-owning hunkish princelings being besotted with them, not seeing that with their fat blank faces and nasty thoughts, no such encounters were likely this side of eternity.

Up in her room, the Colonel drank some of the wine and devoured biscuits with smoky blue cheese and some grapes.

He mused that Artemis, woman-like, knew what she wanted and would be deterred only by practical limitations. She saw life simply as a roulette wheel with no principles involved. She would try hard to win, but the outcome of her sorties she would regard as being pure chance. He guessed that by rejecting Simon she had prompted her most sacred ambitions to misfire, yet if she would not be tamed nor forgo the mantle of war, then he could use her all the more readily to engender bloody ends to his son's killers. After all, she felt no compunction about being cruel or unkind. The dark bathos of her reprobate mind was untouched by contrition. 'Och bairn, yer're nee goo' ... but I trow ye'll turn afore yer dee,' he imitated a Scottish accent badly.

Artemis heard two male voices enter the adjacent room. She stood and listened in the darkness. Both were radiographers. One was an amiable and polite Negroid fellow called Fred Cadman, renowned on the golf links for miscounting his strokes. The second was a chap from Sunderland or a 'Wearwatter' as the local girls would have it. He was Howard Pike, a decidedly bumptious and ungentlemanly boor with a kit-car and whose jokes were both smutty and unfunny. His girlfriend was called 'Dizzy Lizzie' or more unkindly 'Sweaty Betty', a moll who hated other female toads nearing her scummy pond. They were apparently discussing a new colleague called Gotthard whilst waiting to meet their girls.

'His jokes aren't bad.'

'For a German.'

'Is he a tosspot?'

'I don't think he drinks at all. When I'm a chief, I shall re-jig the adverts so that only sweet and pliable young damsels can apply to work in the department.'

'With emoluments to match?'

'*I* shall be the emoluments.'

Fred's lass, an enrolled nurse called Annora appeared and the one pair left.

Artemis struggled. Her near uncontrollable cravings made her want to seduce Howard and yet he was so awful ... God! What should she do?

It is a great paradox that proud-hearted girls spurn men who love them and go wild about those who refuse them. Yet in the end they are humbled either by love or ruin. The vain young maiden boldly rides her chariot along the sea-shore, shunning men's approaches, until a secret and terrible fire breaks out in her heart which she cannot quell – she is overtaken by turbulence – the righteous vengeance of Aphrodite.

Howard and his girlfriend Lizzie went round usually like Siamese twins – inseparable, nauseating and even smiling in concert as if controlled by a single brain.

Artemis hated them both for their pretended turtle-dove courtship and for their insipid smugness. How could anyone so revolting think so highly of himself? And yet even though in three days' time she would be in Liverpool in her malevolent black leather, still she needed some vicious caprice now. Should she wreck their pseudo-heaven?

She sauntered through a door and met her skulking prey. She smiled lop-sidedly as Howard looked up from peeling a tangerine in the empty common-room.

Howard noted her cool patrician loveliness clad in such unusually captivating and wanton clothes. He smelt the astringent Cinnabar perfume dabbed behind her ears.

A seemly air hid at first her dark tangy urge to make trouble. She lingered and eyed him. 'Hallo.'

'Hello.'

'No Christmas revelry?'

'Er ... later, I hope.'

'Sin lies mixed with its own fruit.' She nodded at the tangerine. 'Where's Elizabeth?'

'Er ... she's grinding up some egg-shells and potato peelings for her mother's hens. She'll be here in twenty minutes or so.'

She danced in front of him, keeping her feet still whilst rocking her middle like a boat at sea. He looked slightly pale and ill.

'Am I making you sea-sick? Come through here.' She took his hand and led him dumbly through into the unlit snooker room, where as she attempted to pin him against a wall, he flinched, fell back into some heavy and long-unwashed curtains and nearly lost his balance.

'Oh, I am sorry,' she whispered in fulsomely bitter tones.

'What did you want to show me?' His voice trembled with moronic flatness.

'How to play billiards ... ' she said with mock passion.

It was totally dark.

Howard swallowed as the remarkable truth dawned. He knew that she would be scornful of base attentiveness, but perhaps she did want him to be attentive to her base. 'Ah ... Artemis, I can g-give you both quality and quantity,' he tried to tease her bawdily.

'Of what? Kisses?'

'I wasn't thinking of kisses.' He seized her. 'Under the snooker table?'

She could pull whatever faces she wished to in that lightless and dimensionless void.

'So you are really a bad girl, yes? A vampire?' he exuded through unseen clenched dull yellow teeth and between lilac folds of lip as his breathing deepened.

'I'm not sure.' Out of the blue she felt less like yielding, but rubbed his penis-bulging front with her hand before recoiling. She suddenly regretted her scandalous intents.

'I don't mind being a cuckold ... especially for you. It won't take long.'

He kissed her unexpectedly on the mouth and she felt her lips burn. 'No. Get off.'

'What's the matter?'

Quite abruptly his vileness became so overwhelmingly apparent that she changed her mind. She just could not do it and so spoke secretly to her inner self, to the Spirit of the Mine, 'Rescue me from this need. Arrest it until Liverpool, please. Calm it till then or anyway unleash it in some other way.'

'So I'm the lucky one, eh?' He tried first to pull her down onto the floor, then to press a lewd thigh in between hers and lastly to push a hand into her vulva but met with strong and strenuous obstruction at every move. 'Well, I suppose you had to fall for somebody one day ... just yield girl ... what is it?'

'Because you go round with dopey simpering Lizzie, there must be something wrong with you.' Shame seized her. What had possessed her? 'No it's not that. I'm sorry Howard. I didn't mean to lead you on.'

'What were you doing then?' Now awakened, he tried to forge ahead.

'No, you gnat!' She forced him back like a demon.

Sod it all. Virtuous men shrank from her and roused her to a terrible if secret fury. Scum-sacks could not wait.

'Howard – you who are one of the world's great undiscovered personalities – go back to Lizzie. Forget this ever happened.' She prodded his chest with a forefinger.

Her attempted miserable trick had been an anticlimactic flop. Worse had been the exposure of her need and susceptibility. Her face was white and ghastly, bled of humanity and revealing a body of only vulgar flesh. It did not matter that she was a lone frigate detached from the fleet – some people are meant to lead such lives – but without proper exchanges of affection, she would end up as a gutted wreck.

She marched up the stairs with a stateliness she did not feel to face again that swine Letheren.

Before she even reached the top of the stairs, the puff of her bluff and show had deflated itself. She wanted to burst into her room, throw herself at Letheren's feet and ask him to forgive her or pray for her. Yet why? Why should she show remorse? Why?!! She could behave as she wanted to could she not?

Letheren put down a nursing magazine which he had been thumbing through. The main headline read, 'Shock Irony in Crisis Drama'. The entire contents seemed to be based on false perceptions about what confers health and longevity written by practitioners with over-inflated notions about their own importance. The answer seemingly was not to live a right life, but to avoid eating red meat.

He had with him a photograph of Nicholas in combat gear on top of his Chieftain tank in West Germany. Its name was 'Enyalios' – an epithet for Ares, the god of war. He peered at it and it reminded him of what he was doing here and indeed of the risks which Catharine and Innogen were also running. And where was Artemis, that succulent incubus or insolent succubus?

She held herself in check as she entered the room, but avoided his gaze and in the wash-alcove behind the fitted wardrobe pulled her panties and tights back on and straightened up her dress and ornaments. She called out with nervous aplomb, 'So then, brief me about Liverpool.'

When she returned to his arc of vision, his face focused on hers with sobriety and sadness as if the events of the last half-hour had not so much repulsed him as brought him nearer to her plight. She wished she could command him to stop gazing with that unwanted sympathy, but she could not. She hated herself for her vassal-like weakness but some unruly vagary made it so.

She found herself apologising for her behaviour. 'I am so confused about how to live both a right and an exciting life.' She mentioned Denise's experiences at teacher training college.

He sighed. 'I sometimes hear these dyed-in-the-wool lefties vying with one another to sound the most moral or ultra-liberal and wonder if one day they'll look back and cringe that they ever uttered such spurious hog-wash.'

'I suspect not. The great division in the modern world seems to be between straightforward realists and sightless counterfeit purists.' The squad of self-styled Leninists whom Denise had encountered, had not seemed even to be sincere about their ill-conceived anti-nepotistic stances, but had viewed it more as a vindictive tactic in their class war. She filled her glass and drank some wine.

Her visitor remarked that it was desirable to live lives which were tinged with a bit of solemnity and quiet splendour.

'Is there any truth in these rumours about a planned military coup in recent years?'

Letheren smiled inscrutably. 'It was discussed, sometimes seriously, sometimes playfully. And the government did become agitated, paranoid, even fearful. Knowing this some bluffers – in the best Agatha Christie tradition – start laying false clues.' Suddenly he smiled broadly.

'So it was just a leg-pull?'

'I think so. Well, where would it go? Firstly we're royalists and this shower are Her Majesty's elected ministers. Secondly, coups gain popular support by liberating, not be setting up dictatorships. And thirdly, who would be appointed to govern? No, we old-school simple buffoons know we have to suffer the taunts of the smarmy bombasts gracefully. Hopefully their machinations will rebound on them one fine day.'

She sat beside him and they clinked glasses.

He continued abstractedly. 'The disquiet with Wilson's troupe is genuine enough and perhaps some have held out the hope that they might influence him or make him seem unbalanced ... though some of the tricks were a bit thin really. Once the Defence Secretary – a signed-up member of the Communist Party by the way – visited Aldershot and there was a line of armoured cars waiting with number plates such as KGB 1, 1 VAN, RUSS 1 A, TSR 2 ... '

'And he pretended not to notice?'

'Yes.'

'What was the TSR 2?'

He smiled at her. 'A hedge-hopping tactical bomber. It was one of many futuristic military projects which were axed in the mid-sixties when the socialists got in. Not only did they cancel it though but also ordered all the jigs and templets to be destroyed ... It is really that sort of detail which proves their communist sympathies and belies their protestations that such decisions were solely economic.'

'They do need money though to support thousands of idlers and single mothers.'

'True. Engineering the social balance. Multiplying the indifferent types who are dependent on all their new benefits and who will thus always vote for them in future.'

'Struggle, achievement, etiquette ... of no importance?'

'It seems not. Money will soon be the only thing that counts. Still, let us turn to business.' He produced new photographs for her and together they combed through the strategic and tactical minutiae which lay ahead of her.

As he departed he held up a finger and said in an aesthetically austere voice, 'Artemis, all sin is forgivable except that of blotting out right emotion.'

He was gone.

The rite, the reinvestiture, the incantations – all were complete. Whilst her Prospero drove away in his reclaimed Land Rover, Artemis thought of her promised money. But it was not the money which counted, it was the recharging of her strength, the mysterious reaffirmation of that ability which allowed her to ride out again to battle, self-confident and caparisoned in her deadly leather. She would surmount every obstacle, tussle with each puny bedevilment and act sinfully as was her wish.

She thought of Howard's Lizzie, renowned for trotting out threadbare and trendy utterances based on obsessions about the rights of the individual and leftish politics to try and shape a personality for herself, unaware that such nonsense in fact obliterates the true self.

This thought made her decision easier. She had reached a watershed. From here onwards Artemis would be her own true self. There would be no more hesitations or compromises – never.

She wrote a letter of resignation to Matron.

* * *

Ulrich had not resurfaced.

Ute with both grief and relief in her heart, the senses of loss and freedom, knew he was dead.

In her red Renault with its snow-tyres on, she drove to Lake Constance's Austrian shore. It looked unfamiliar in winter for she had not been there before except in the autumn. The cows were indoors. The grassy erratic knolls and wooden houses had been mostly hidden under the even blanket of blue-tinged snow and the waters of the lake were seemingly bluer because of the snow.

In the small Alpestral village of Weidorf, where a score of wooden chalets had white yule-tide lights glowing on trees in their front gardens, she swung off onto a steep tributary road which climbed the side of the Heifels Ridge.

Her car was lucky to make it round the double hair-pin, where you had to sacrifice practically all of your momentum and again to claw and slip at least half of the way up the even steeper spur to Ulrich's dwelling. This track, poorly surfaced with only some compressed stones, lay under deep undisturbed snow.

In her blue leather suit and black leather boots – mementoes of times spent with Ulrich – she waded the last fifty metres through the white and grey shaded undulating drifts and gave a brief shudder at the coldness of the air.

The small wooden building with its steeply-pitched roof stood on a rocky shelf, well-sunned in summer, overlooking a snowy landscape but backed by a rising forest. The drooping fir boughs were motionless and untainted snow had obliterated the ankle-deep and untended weeds on the plateau round the cabin. No one had been there recently.

Leaving an ungainly messy scar behind her in the otherwise flawless expanse of snow, she made her way round to the back of the house where silent and eerie saplings encroached. A small foot-bridge over a frozen stream, led into the forest and to its deer. Under the trees, the snow was thinner and patches of dark green moss and clumps of minuscule white flowers were to be seen.

She let herself in without picking off her well-fitting driving gloves, stamped the snow off her fur-lined boots and looked cautiously round the cold quiet interior. There was even frost on the inside of the windows.

This house had been the office and store of the Wilsattel Manganese Mine until its closure at the turn of the century. Outside the slag and the debris of the other structures had been cleared and levelled and sprinkled with grass seed and gravel and geranium tubs.

Inside it was really one room except at one end, where a sleeping platform under the roof's apex rested on top of a narrow kitchen and bathroom, with a ladder up to it. But it had been attractively renovated with varnished new beams and trusses and double-glazed windows with blue duchesse curtains. This cosy nest included a sofa and coffee-table, a television and hi-fi set-up, books, shelves and a collection of beautifully painted lead figures – troubadour, princess, knight, milk-maid, strolling player, woodcutter and cobbler.

Seeing no cause for alarm, she turned on the electric heating, made some coffee and found an almond cake in a tin.

In the small stone hearth, she put her arm up the chimney and pushed back the steel occluding plate. Some dirty snow fell down. Beginning with the desk, she lit a fire by burning every item of paper, every bill and every letter she could find, adding some sticks and logs from the neat pile in the corner, to keep it going.

In the kitchen she slid to the two heavy bolts of the main door. In the bathroom, she rolled up the green mat and revealed a manhole cover in the floor, its aluminium edging interrupting the mosaic of small glazed ceramic floor tiles of pale greens and whites. This could be lifted up by its two stainless-steel rings. Ute climbed down the vertical steel ladder into the cellar, smaller than the little house above, because the old stone foundations had been lined with half a metre of reinforced concrete. She turned on the glaring light. This low and cramped room was neatly ordered, for Ulrich could be strangely meticulous about things which he was proud of. There were shelves with tinned food on them, clothes, candles, light bulbs and stationery. In one corner on a piece of spare carpet stood skis, pails, a palliasse and two gas cylinders. Ute lugged all this to one side and uncovered a heavy black steel trap-door. To release its plain smooth solidity you had to operate a cylinder lock hidden beneath the wine rack to which she had a key. Then by standing on the black square, by a system of well-oiled counterweights it swung downwards and backwards under the floor to expose a second ladder and a sub-cellar or rather a man-made cave. One end-wall was of massive grey ferro-concrete and on it was a light, but running away from it was a dry drift of argentiferous chisel-hewn rock – one of the old mine galleries. Here stood a small hefty work-bench of black oak, rows of punches and files and chisels and an old boar tusk, saws and planes and clamps and further in, lengths of timber and mild steel and phosphor bronze and boxes of blocks and bolts and nuts. It was a nuclear fall-out shelter and a hidden sulphurous chasm of Nibelheim, where goblin artisans and deformed smiths might make magic brooches and rune-engraved weapons for the gods of Valhalla, bent over anvils and forges and labouring in the depths of the primeval earth.

The hill was of impervious rock, so no water dribbled into this sombre, blocked-off tunnel. In a dusty crate, lay a cache of chemical retorts, condensers, glass tubes, iron pressure vessels, electric heaters and thermometers.

Firstly she carried up twenty-six variously-sized jars and bottles of reagents and emptied them carefully down the toilet with frequent flushes before replacing the empty receptacles and the other equipment near to the door, ready to take it in her car to some distant tip in Germany or France. She found the note-books with their records in and the detailed recipes for producing EF31A and placed them meticulously on the fire. Ute gathered up a few pieces of clothing which belonged to her and also took a few favourite items to remember him by.

Her aim was that when either the police or Ulrich's parents appeared here, they would find no evidence of his drug-synthesizing activities, nor his arms-running, nor his secret money hoards and as little as possible to connect him to Ute.

Her hair was swept back into a bun, but her body seemed lifeless and egrimonious. She looked as if she were more unhappy than she realised.

She flipped through his two photograph albums, reviewing all the pretty spots throughout Europe which they had visited together, before reluctantly burning those too page by page. She made some macaroni cheese in a saucepan and ate it off one of his heterogeneous assortment of plates. Then she trudged back and forth to her car with all the incriminating material which she had assembled. Finally, she raked through the ashes of the fire, closed the chimney shutter, switched everything off and tidied up.

As she drove northwards through Germany, to the home of her adoptive parents in Fassberg, her prime emotions were of relief and gratitude. She knew from the papers that Ingrid had been shot in Scotland and that she alone had survived. She felt a debt to some guardian angel, which had to be repaid by resolving to live more honestly and decently and she was willing to humbly oblige. She would have to sell the villa above the Roman-tiled roofs of Hautfort-St.-Gildas in southern France, for living there by herself would only mean night-clubs in Monaco and the awful life of being a wealthy whore. Expensive presents from Monte Carlo for her parents lay on the passenger seat beside her.

As she sped through a misty dark forest she remembered a side road which led to a lovely lake, but she was frightened of becoming stuck in the deep snow and besides, some of this chemistry rubbish might float and spoil the countryside. She found the answer whilst filling up at a petrol station. Just beyond it in a quiet darkened lay-by, stood a rubbish skip and in it she dumped all the unsightly and incongruous abominations of the EF31A process.

It was still perhaps just possible to settle down with one man, have children and behave herself. Certainly she wished to renounce her former life-style and try.

Christmas in Fassberg was a time of partial reunion, meat and potatoes without wine, prayers about bad thoughts entering the human mind more readily than they departed and how Christ's coming uniquely could save us from being overwhelmed by them.

On Boxing Day in Der Alte Fassberger, a single-storey bar-cum-café which she revisited partly out of teenage nostalgia, she found it almost empty. The only folk she recognised were three young men she had been at school with, though she did not know them well for they had been the shy triptych, nervous where girls were concerned. None the less they greeted her pleasantly and invited her to join them. The conversation verged on the dull, but at least there were not those nasty leering sneers on their faces, which told you exactly what they would say about you after you had left. These fellows had a degree of respect for women and sexual affairs and a thoughtfulness about the everyday matters which they discussed.

She drank coffee and ate a pineapple and grape and banana fruit salad with cream. For the first time in her life she felt more ready to appreciate the qualities in her strict-minded father and in these unprecocious contemporaries. One of them drove a diesel engine for the East Hanover Railway Company, stuttered slightly and had had a disastrous two month marriage at some point in his past.

The deep homely impulses of Germanic femininity were coming to light in her after a decade of repression. Stability, a home, children, unspectacular friends to pass the time of day with – such were her thoughts turning towards. And if her husband were humble, unvirile and earned little, at least she had her gold coins which she would retrieve from under the patio stones and her other investments with which to discreetly brighten life up a bit. And she would not have to vie continually with fifty other trollops to keep him.

* * *

The black Porsche swung off Brownlow Hill opposite the rotunda-like Roman Catholic cathedral, into the Liverpool University campus and pulled up in the dark shadows beneath the old red-brick anatomy building.

Artemis locked it and walked away into the foul and deserted night. In the light of a street light the slanting flakes of sleet and rain could be seen.

She wore her new black leather suit and boots and over them, a size fourteen black nylon coat-length cagoule instead of her usual size twelve, to make herself less conspicuous in this grim and hostile city. The cagoule had red strings both to pull the hood tight round her face and inside the garment to pull the waist in and a red zip at the front. The melting sleet coursed down off this black outer covering's lower hem onto the knee-patches of her leather suit and her shiny well-polished riding boots. By pulling down a little on her handbag's shoulder strap, it moved to hang a little more behind her than at her side.

The clock on the Gothic Revival university clock tower said six o'clock, which was still a little early for the brothel off Fryer Street. She splashed through slushy puddles, rejoined the main road and after a few hundred yards went into an old-fashioned public house called the Admiral Hood, which had ghastly scroll-work tiles round its door and clumsy stained-glass tobacco-darkened windows. On a conviviality rating of nought to ten it was off the minus end of the scale. The modest patronage clammed up instantly when she entered, as if she had interrupted the proceedings of a criminal information exchange, which she probably had. Artemis could see only men – crafty thieving dogs filled with a hard concentrated sneakiness. This animal pit contained no festive scents or merry vistas. The stares of this dross, those of ravaged smirking criminally-addicted wolves – men who if they did successfully steal a few thousands would instantly blow it on bingeing and women in cesspits in Copenhagen – were of loveless humourless and unremitting brutality. The disguisedly lecherous barman, who usually ignored strangers and would not serve them, supplied this disdainful beauty with an orange juice and a cheese roll on a paper plate. He gave her her change reluctantly. She walked sedately between the grey twisted seditious faces, the centre of rapt enmity, as an exotic bird amongst jackals which by its extraordinary exterior amazes and paralyses those predators.

Her intuitive warning mechanism was not defunct, but the impulse to flee was overridden by her supreme arrogance. She remembered her last school play about the October Revolution and wished that she had been a tsarina, able to send in her Cossack horsemen to hack down and squash this iniquitous poxy scum. Forty eyes watched her neat and alluring feminine movements from all points of the compass, as she opened the brass clasp on her black hide handbag and felt inside it, but they did not know that she was checking her pistol. Her leather creaked as she sat down on a side-bench, even though she had treated it with lanolin oil and polished it thoroughly with wax – for Artemis was equally energetic and practical where dull though necessary tasks were concerned, as with doing things she enjoyed.

Ashtrays had been screwed to the tables and everything in this bar had been as far as possible made unstealable and indestructible. Her unconcealed pride had conjured up their fury as meekness might have dampened and dispersed it and an unspoken sequence of half-winks and intercalated cave-man nods had established that when she rose with her nose in the air and left so elegantly, she would be followed, beaten up, robbed and her pretty face scarred. But something happened to put this plan into disarray.

A freckled red-headed barmaid in a short pink and green dacron dress and with a slovenly toe-dragging step, a haggish face, veiny legs and an appearance of sexual uncleanliness, tripped over someone's outstretched foot with a tray full of empty glasses and bottles. The commotion was spectacular and the shrieked accusations delightful. Whilst the termagant and the beer-spattered scouses bawled fluent obscenities at each other, an unseen Artemis stood up and despite her slinky obdurate uppishness, departed unnoticed. A man in a crumpled purple suit and a tie – a token gesture of civilised existence, a sort of cynical parody of the accepted forms – flicked a blob of nasal mucus into the barmaid's eye and she in return stubbed her fag into his leery smarmy face, before dropping it into his ale.

Outside in the rain Artemis studied her street map of Liverpool, memorised the first section of the route out to Fryer Street and set off through Utopia Precinct, a 1960's council development of concrete and colour-panelled utilitarian flats, constructed in the Russo-Assyrian architectural style and already gone to seed. Those windows which had not been boarded up had no flower pots in them, nor neat curtains. The door handles were unpolished and skewed. Indeed there were no signs that the inhabitants had any flair or pride. It was a grim and unkeepered menagerie.

She turned right into an alley. On its concrete walls, vivid graffiti overlaid blotted out faded graffiti. She felt the murky tendrils of malignancy, a sullen soporific servility congesting the air and a lurking threatening lawlessness waiting to pounce. But she felt secure. Her own zestful graceful evil, defended by black firearm and black leather, could counter any squalid undisciplined louts who dared to challenge her.

Two youths had sprung up behind her, like maggots out of putrid matter, whistling with deliberat e insouciance.

The snicket narrowed and led under a building. Artemis turned a corner and there stood a gum-chewing Negro in a torn plastic jacket, the sleeve sewn back on again with string, lolling in training shoes and blocking the aperture into the next street. Two behind her and one in front – it was no doubt a well-rehearsed manoeuvre. A number of windows loomed above this stage, unblessed boxes with tightly-drawn curtains of Hong Kong printed calicoes, but no one behind them would of course ever see anything or know anything.

Artemis felt unafraid. A warm surge of confidence came to her. She was a goddess and would not lose. The threesome grinned, especially the Negro. They had caught an enemy in the class war, a Fascist sow, an object to be hated, someone to mug and to rape. The Negro relished the flavour of her rare beauty, her alabaster skin, her undeturpated vagina. She backed into a blind subway which led to a rubbish collection area.

Her assailants moved casually in after her, into *her* trap, for she did not wish to leave dead bodies where people might fall over them too soon. The swaggering testy defilers advanced abreast. An obtusely-flavoured smile flickered on Artemis's face in the deep brick-walled gloom. The Negro thought her bottom looked like a big fleshy black pumpkin and he intended to truss her and piston it with his big shiny aubergine and then slash her under-side with his hooked knife.

At five yards they did not see her leather gloved hand dip into her handbag and produce her silencer-fitted ready-loaded ready-cocked pistol. She flicked off the safety catch, parted her legs slightly, took aim and fired, hoping that none of their dirty blood would splash back onto her pure face or new cagoule and boots. After three thuds – one per chest – she moved forwards and shot for the second time the motionless but alive bodies in the head at point blank-range. Without her realising it a short contemptuous snort escaped her. She changed magazine, recocked her weapon and pocketed it, before tugging on her new gleaming pristine black leather gauntlets and dragging each corpse in turn by the ankles deeper into the shapeless recess of the refuse enclosure. Here she overturned soggy cardboard boxes and plastic sacks of household rubbish to cover them and found it strangely pleasurable – unlike the boredom of watching it on television. It was proper justice too, not faffing around in some court-room whilst an addled magistrate allowed villains to exploit all the law's weaknesses with an enfeebled benignity which just refused to see evil.

'Such audacity,' she sighed, as she set off again through the maze's dreary intangible darkness. She was the tall pine tree in Aesop's fable and these envious prickles would never cut her down or see her humbled.

Her gauntlets appeared clean, so she refolded them and tucked them back into her handbag's large back pocket. The rain trickled down her beaming moon-like face and her black cagoule and leather boots. In the electrine mist of the tall sodium street lamps on Smithdown Lane, cars swished past through the black slush, throwing up a fine spray of vaporised dirt.

She imagined herself sitting on the blue sofa at Uanrig House with Simon beside her. She stroked him tenderly, whilst he kissed her and worshipped her and from a cuddling position, pushed her over. Should she have accepted him and tried to be more kindly and forbearing? The fire burnt cosily and she were in early pregnancy and not in this inhuman hell. Had she made a mistake and if so, why could she only see it now? But why also, were there only two divergent extremes – the one of love and meekness and forgiveness and the other of red-eyed and white-faced pain and leather-inspired wrath? Why could there be no compromise, a blend of affection and pride? Why not? She hated milksop Simon and always would hate him! She would go the other way and fight until she won, despite the dangers!

Her heel skidded on a slush-coated lop-sided paving-slab and she fell flat on her back. This unleashed an internal tirade of venomous threats against those cunning forsworn fairies who dared to try and admonish her, yet who were beyond retaliation.

She stood up angrily, but had immediately to jump back over a small garden wall as a growling green and cream filth-washed bus approached, throwing up the whole gutter full of water in a fountain over the pavement. She crossed over the road, turned left and then left again into Fryer Street.

Fryer Street was not Prince's Park – magnificent Victorian shipowners' mansions turned into bed-sits, along tree-lined boulevards – but one strand in a poor 1870's web of cramped terraced workers' houses near Edge Hill. Artemis passed two burnt-out car shells, dripping tyreless rusting wrecks and a stretch of torn-up pavement, all this the grisly remains of a recent minor riot. Again she saw Cossacks, firing once into the air as a warning and then charging an unrepentant mob who jeered from a concatenated barricade of hijacked lorries. She heard the rattle of sabres and saw the glint of stirrups and spurs and saddlery, the bloodily massacred limbs beneath the horses' hooves, the flattened carved-up upstarts –

how exhilarating it would be! A part of her wished she were a male. She had what psychiatrists call 'penis envy', the female desire to be aggressive.

On she went, along the dingy scary street. She waded through the shallows of a flood, where in a dip a drain had blocked. It was dark and frightening here, very few lights shone dimly in houses and all the street lights had been broken. Clouds hung low overhead and poured down icy darts of sleet.

Saint Helena's Grove, a short cul-de-sac off Fryer Street, consisted of two short blocks of narrow-fronted houses facing one another with most of their windows boarded up. Discarded chip papers, canine excrement and items of refuse littered the steeply cambered road surface, which had many of its cobbles missing.

Inside the pitch-black smashed-in doorway to an empty number two, she put on her motorcycle neck-tube and woolly hat and peered out at the just visible snow-flakes touching down to merge with the black slush. She took off her cagoule and with its inside outside, folded it up tightly and pushed it too into her overfilled handbag. Her pistol was in her right thigh pocket which remained unzipped. With a hitch she adjusted the height of the deep tight bronze-clasped black leather belt round her waist and in her scrupulously calculated underwear and woollies, moulded on the outside by her intensely black relucent chromed leather, as in wet clay by the hand of a master potter, she gave a self-satisfied little smile to herself and moved off. Like a warm and even mawkishly stimulating electuary, her pride bolstered by her pistol and the vulgar lustre of her black leather vesture, cosy and corsleting but not too tight, sent her forward with a beating heart, exited and unhesitating, to effect Mr Letheren's hazardous demands. She set out to kill with this misalliance of fragile strength and overestimated self-worth.

The diminutive front gardens were bounded by low brick walls, whose iron railings had been taken for scrap during the war. Number eight's garden had bushes and weeds spilling out of it. Her boots splattered the slush to one side, compressing it and squirting it out from under their steel-tipped leather soles and steel-arced leather heels.

She noted the drooping red blanket hung up at the front downstairs window as a substitute curtain, with a light shining through it. She rapped the stiff iron knocker on the peeling door.

After fifteen or so seconds it creaked open and a woman of about thirty with dyed auburn curls peered out, her face at once lewd and insipid. She waggled her droopy naked breasts until she saw that it was not a customer on the step. Artemis wedged herself into the shutting door, feeling ruthlessly tough and utterly undefeatable in her leather cavalry uniform.

The copper-head turned to shout for assistance, but Artemis said hastily, 'It's all right. I've come to see Eoin Prior.'

Eileen O'Shaughnessy stepped back and admitted the shoving caller. 'Arghhh,' she smiled as she buttoned her blouse up, 'Opp te stairs, enn fierst on yer lift.'

Her inspissated face watched the lithe shiny black gazelle move onto the stairs with some residual apprehension, for like all whores her ability to sense perversity and danger was finely tuned. Eileen gave a flabby frown to the door as she shut it. She and the other two Irish prostitutes here were used to the signs and effluents of sexual pollution, but not those of these menacing macabre I.R.A. characters who visited their temporary lodger.

Artemis strode up the bare boards of the groaning stairs, her hard riding boots echoing noisily. She knocked firmly on the first door on the left, a varnished brown oblong in a patchily damp cream wall.

'Ah, come in Patrick ... Who in the name of Beelzebub ... ?'

Downstairs, Eileen sauntered into the back kitchen, where a portable television transmitted a pop-music programme from its corner of the table, flanked by dozens of half-empty sauce milk and alcohol bottles. She tipped half a scuttle of coke into the rusty stove, for it was chilly if you were only half-dressed, even for a hardy Kildare lass like her. A cloud of coke dust blew back into her face, its small particulate carbon specks sticking to her loud pink facial cream. 'Argggh, fock!' she scowled and slammed the top iron plate back into its hole with the two-pronged lifting tool.

She felt ill. She had had a lot of green discharge from her feminine passages lately, smelling like a leaky abscess. She lit the gas stove under the chip pan and began peeling some potatoes. Like a rat with plague, she wanted to retreat to her hole and nurse herself.

Prior sat on the edge of a low grubby bed in the small front bedroom, which he was paying very well for. It boasted unvarnished floor boards with a solitary synthetic hairy orange rug in its middle – a wretched attempt to create an air of high living and exotic taste. The plaster was wet and crumbling under the window sill and a number of tawdry pictures of nude women in obscene poses graced the walls. A one-bar electric fire glowed in the corner. The drab and squalid atmosphere could scarcely be exaggerated.

Prior looked as sour as a crab-apple and beside him sat a rather plain slouching girl with a page-boy haircut. Another man with a grey drawn bloodhound face, sat on a chair. The threesome played a desultory game of Turn Eight, in which they had lost interest. Prior sloshed some more whiskey into his white enamelled mug and sipped it.

'Be Jaizu's bullud, weer's focking Beeg Pat?' muttered O'Shea, like a fallen wizard who lacked the panache or verve to curse effectively any longer. 'Te man must be a-knowing' 'at tiss is hextremely hurgent!'

'Hmmm. I hope it's not the only thing that's urgent,' simpered unsexy Maureen meaningfully, as she stroked Prior's back.

'I trust he's not gone off to Gweebarra Bay again for the pissing weekend!'

'Ah, oi'm sure he'll 'a' not Eoin ... or if he hezz, only fur a short weekend.'

They heard the front-door knocker give two metallic dunks. O'Shea moved to the window and parted the thin rayon oblongs, but could not see the caller in the darkness.

'Focking snowin' still.'

'But it isn't that cold,' cooed Maureen to Prior, 'At least I hope it soon won't be.'

'You heard what he said? Blue ball weather.'

'Oh no. I'll keep them pink for you.'

'I was referring to the golf course!'

'Take your coat off Eoin ... '

'Give it a rest, woman,' growled Prior irritably.

A knuckle tapped on the door and in burst a pistol-holding black phantom.

O'Shea and Prior knew that if they both dived for her at once, probably one of them would be shot but the other overcome her. The lunging O'Shea being the nearest, took the first bullet in his massive inner-tube gut. Prior stumbled and fell over the card table, as Artemis stepped back a pace into the doorway.

Maureen sat petrified and gave a brief weak squeal, before her spindly legs shot out stiffly in front of her and her hands went up to her waxy face.

A second bullet thudded into Prior's shoulder and a more accurately aimed successor bored its way into his skull. Artemis had recognised this malefactor-in-chief from his photograph. A longer shriek from Maureen ended when she was hit twice in the chest and O'Shea too then took two further round-nosed cylinders of metal. Prior received the last round from this magazine via his left eye-socket.

Across the landing Fionnguala Kennedy was busy under a customer. Her lair was adorned with grubby little items of supposedly erotic paraphernalia for her clients to choose from. A brilliantly coloured poster curling at the edges and a spot-light pointing at the floor filled the room with a feeling of bizarre and shadowy expectation. Just as the lonely little Inland Revenue man began to puff and grunt, Fionnguala heard Maureen's squeal. An illogical intuitive streak in her warned her that a British assassin was in the house. She tossed off her man and stood up into her plastic high-heeled shoes of a reddy-orange colour so bright as to be almost phosphorescent. She jerked her nine inch brown leather mini-skirt down to crotch level and with some of the tax inspector's ejaculate trickling down her leg, strode out with livid burning eyes.

On the landing she saw Artemis ejecting the spent magazine from her pistol and through the open door, O'Shea's blood-drenched head. The pink eye-shadow and purple lipstick, misplaced and misjudged effort at any time, looked like a Red Indian's get-up as she flew at the intruder with her claws extended and her face twisted.

Elsie McAdoo – or Fionnguala Kennedy as she styled herself in Liverpool – could still see the day when her brother had been found guilty of murder at Belfast Crown Court and sentenced to eighteen years and outside that Protestant mob shouting, 'String him up!' If she had had a machine-gun she would have mown all the bastards down on the spot. As it was she had gone berserk and come round later with a prize black eye and a hideous gash on her leg. The oppressive British were the cause of all her troubles, the reason for her horrible low existence. It was they who had made her wretched and denied her elegance and wealth.

Full of such swirling furious hatred, all targeted at this black viper before her, this living mindless lump of flesh – easily capable of murder or bestial brut ality – launched itself at Artemis. The chance had come to strike a blow back at those who had reduced her to a sewage pool, unable to love or be tender or be moved by beauty.

The pistol fell onto the floor boards and the two women wrestled and struggled frenziedly soon ending up on the floor. The Irish wild cat for all her strength, could not easily hurt Artemis. Kicks and scratches did not touch her body and she defended her eyes and face well. After two minutes of flailing gasping threshing and tumbling, Artemis prevailed in the battle to get on top and banged Fionnguala's head savagely many times against the wooden floor, until her victim seemed no longer to respond sensibly. Then as Artemis crawled across the boards to recover and reload her pistol, Fionnguala leapt up again and landed on top of her with a jolt which sprawled her out flat with her head over the top of the descending stairs. Some of her handbag's contents too had spilled out, including length of nylon rope. Grappling and slithering, they went down the whole flight head first and then at the bottom stood up and staggered back and forth like drunks, until Artemis eventually, with eyes like black ice-cubes and full of crazy boiling fury, succeeded in snatching up the cord which had accompanied them down the stair-treads and in looping it round Fionnguala's long scraggy neck. With the ends wrapped round her gloved fists, she heaved it tight.

A groggy Fionnguala, staggering round and momentarily with her back to Artemis as she lost her bearings, saw a piece of flex flash before her eyes and then bite into her neck with terrible force. She tried to grab it but could not. She tried to put her hands over her shoulders and grip at least one of Artemis's hands, but could not. She squirmed about like a landed shark. She feigned unconsciousness and slumped backwards into Artemis's chest and stomach, but Artemis knew she must sustain the strangle hold for three or four minutes. Fionnguala tried desperately to kick backwards but with no effect.

Copper-headed Eileen appeared from the grimy kitchen and watched with open-mouthed rigidity for some seconds as Fionnguala's bloated face turned the same colour as her lipstick. Then Eileen screamed, repeatedly and hysterically.

At last Kennedy twisted round and caught one of Artemis's black leather pincers, but it was too late. She felt faintness pass over her and she sank to the ground.

Artemis tore upstairs and seized the pistol and her second magazine which still contained two rounds, though tripping on the top stair and falling flat on her way. She raced down again and shot Eileen. She tried too to shoot the apparently dead Fionnguala but the Browning jammed. She released the magazine and pulled the slide back to eject the stuck cartridge case. Back upstairs she spent some minutes using a pocketful of loose rounds to recharge both magazines and thus reload the pistol. Downstairs, she checked that it was working properly again by firing it twice at Kennedy. Whilst picking up the items spewed out of her handbag, she suddenly saw the aghast tax inspector peering timidly out onto the landing. The nine-millimetre semi-automatic was coaxed into discharging itself twice at him too and with a long gasp he sank spirally onto his knees, bleeding invisibly yet restfully from his chest.

She moved quickly but not hurriedly through every room, starting with Fionnguala's whory den of sad trinkets and underwear and chests of Victorian drawers and a mirror in which she saw her own sleek deity-like and evil beauty. She smiled briefly. As she went round, she would sometimes shape that smile of pseudo-sadness at the lifeless masks of her victims and say, 'How unfortunate.' Alternatively she would pronounce these shagging scum scavengers and curs, doomed to be too undeferential to accept their true lot as bottle-washers, to have been rightly killed for their presumption and by her, this scion of true nobility as she believed herself to be. She donated ready criticism to their faces. 'Even when given money and education, you just throw it away.'

In the kitchen she threw a basin through the television screen which imploded into a dust of fine glass particles. She overturned the flimsy tubular-legged table with its myriad greasy bottles, saw the chip pan with its fat now near to the boil and poured it over the lighted burner so that a woof of flames and belching black smoke engulfed the room. She slammed the kitchen door behind her. At last her gritted teeth relaxed slightly and she let out a sigh of relief, her task once again fulfilled.

This was though a night of terror. All present in number eight had felt their heaving agonising Mother Earth speak to them to forewarn them and now Artemis, Letheren's Caliban and the Spirit of the Mine's pupil, sensed too, like the German soldiers on the Eastern Front facing the Slavic hordes, that the battle was far from over.

She left. Outside again, the night was black though a small crimson eddy of flame glared already in the lounge window.

At the entrance to the cul-de-sac stood seven youths, shuffling about and loitering beside a wall. The silencer had been on her pistol throughout, so they had heard no shots, but the screams had aroused a curiosity in them and anchored them there for a while in vague anticipation of entertainment.

These youths were nobody in particular – just unemployed malodorous petty thieves and intimidating chanters – a part of Liverpool's unsavoury majority.

They saw this prccocious Aphrodite stride forth with their leering pining quality-starved eyes and saw her lewd leather sheen rippling and glinting in the minimal light. They tensed themselves and formed obtrusively an irregular phalanx to block her path. Their hopes were not disappointed. Her arrogant neat lovely face and form, her conical teasing breasts, narrow waist and smooth rounded hips, approached them in the biting night air. These slavering dogs growled and gargled. They moved to encircle her. They could scarcely wait to accost this archly proud goddess. Their coarse paws itched to maul her slippery leather-covered body. Their rough lips longed to fumble and slobber over her delicate and unabused features – so extraordinarily unmarred and ruthlessly attractive.

She smiled coolly but ruefully, as if to say to a moved but inexperienced lover, 'Don't be silly. It's so easy. Let me show you.' She stopped. They stopped and pawed the ground. She had only four rounds immediately available and here were seven street-wise skunks. She must not let them sense when her gun were empty. A slushy snowball slapped into her shoulder. One urchin jeered weakly. She responded with a grin of secret exuberance at this ungrateful council of vermin-ridden rodents who now stood at six paces. The chief thug strolled nonchalantly forward. The Browning reappeared. Chief Thug halted. Artemis lifted her black handgun swiftly, aimed and fired. The leader folded up and rolled backwards in the wet snow, clutching his throat, his dark blood flowing copiously out of his slack mouth to join the thin grey trampled pulp. An impressive opening. The skirmish had commenced. His mates stared in disbelief at their skin-headed bone-headed leader, shot by this horror-story character. One dropped his glasses. He picked them up nervously and wiped them. Artemis grinned indulgently. Their bravado had gone. 'Cross the road you dung.'

They were uncertain how they ought to handle this intrepid opponent. Plots starring cool tough men should not develop like this. A second of their number sagged unexpectedly. They were about four yards from her and on three sides. If they moved simultaneously they would get her, but each trembled and flinched at the thought that he might be the next one to draw her fire. She waved her pistol-holding hand to suggest the desired direction of motion. They sauntered off.

'Don't turn around,' she commanded.

Like resentful sheep, they obeyed. She picked the straggler off, then the next one bit the slush.

By the time they had guessed what was happening and twisted round to look, she had changed magazines. They ran. A bullet caught one on the elbow, but these remaining three escaped. Artemis smiled, started out for her car and promptly slid over again on the packed mushy snow, because the smooth leather soles of her boots did not grip well. Her satisfaction changed to a vehement outburst of swearing at this ice for continually daring to humiliate her. She sprang up, brushed some of the wet crystals off her bottom and strutted off out of Saint Helena's Grove and across Fryer Street.

Nobody in this sort of area rings the police for anything and as the crackling fire in the concierge Kennedy's brothel was adjacent to no one, probably not the fire brigade either.

Artemis considered that she would soon be on the end of some stupid police hunt, when rightly she should be receiving a medal for ridding society of a dozen murderers and parasites.

A strange survival instinct and animal awareness lurks in these nefarious warrens of anarchy and depravity and at the behest of certain whistles and calls from the fleeing three, creepy-crawlies started to appear out of snikkets and ginnels and from behind rows of lock-up garages. These fiends might steal from and knife each other readily enough as a rule, but in the face of an alien invader they banded themselves firmly together.

A hundred yards up Fryer Street she saw the pack assembling – only eight so far, but there was evidence that others were preparing to come out and join the mêlée. One carried a machete, a second a crow-bar, a third a huge stick, whilst a fourth had a mere knife. They seemed to be leering slimily, in readiness for the ritual killing of a higher being to a rhythm of merciless and fatal beatings. Sadistically, they would want to cut to pieces this brave heroine, who had dared to show them their own lowness without apology.

She felt her heart throb with defiance, but she had no more than thirty rounds of ammunition left. Artemis felt like having a tantrum and taking them all on, but she saw that she had to retreat ... at least for the moment. It needed tanks and infantry to deal with this. When she was an empress, she would send one of her armies here to destroy this despicable place and all its creepy bilge rats.

She marched across a small patch of slippery muddy wasteland behind a boarded-up ransacked Baptist chapel and levered herself up onto a six-foot-high wall built of blocks of browny-red sandstone. This was not easy. Only the dire necessity and the fear of the closing mob urged her on to superhuman efforts. She clawed savagely at its top and heaved herself up, scraping her breasts up and down quite a few times before finally getting one leg up with an immane struggle.

Forty feet below her in a cutting, ran the electrified main railway line out of Lime Street. She glanced round. No one was about. No one had yet spotted her. Straddling the wall she applied the safety catch to her pistol and zipped it into her suit's thigh pocket, then with her gauntlets pulled on and her handbag's strap hoisted over her head, she hotched off onto a strip of wet snowy tufty weeds.

The cutting had been dug by sawing out huge blocks of red sandstone, so the walls were not just steep but vertical, except for small ledges and irregularities.

She jumped down another three feet onto a narrow shelf and stood there with her feet apart and her back pressed against the wet abrasive sandstone face behind her.

An overhead wire sang. The pantograph of a locomotive running light, coming in down the incline, threw off a huge lingering blue meteor from the overhead electric wire and this illumined eerily but prettily the further thirty frightening feet which she had to negotiate to reach the track bed.

The thought that she might die or be put in a cage having done Letheren's dirty work again, spurred her on to greater courage. She turned around slowly, knelt gingerly down and with her fingers clutching the edge of this sill, lowered herself towards a second ledge eight feet below. When her arms were fully extended, she let go and scraped down the gritty face, fearful of toppling backwards and outwards. She edged her way along this next lip to a small recess beneath a bridge. Here she could lean out and embrace a thick vertical 'I' girder, one of a pair which were underpinning the inner end of a cantilever bracket which in turn held a colour-light signal. Having gripped it with her arms, she wrapped her legs around it too and then slid down it like a fireman's pole, only more slowly for she used its greater friction to retard her rate of descent. At the bottom she continued motionlessly to clutch it, as a passenger train glided past. The titanic engine had a blacked-out cab and its rheostats hummed and whirred and clicked.

Three minutes later came a short goods or possibly a permanent way maintenance train drawn with minimal speed by a diesel engine obeying the two orange circles of another signal ahead in the gloom and behind it trailed faithfully the blackened steel underframes and axle-boxes of the wagons which it hauled – six open wagons and a bogie bolster.

As this last long wagon clunked past, she scrambled up out of the trough with its discarded beer cans and old prams tossed from above, up the rampart of the large rust-stained granite chippings of the track bed, up onto the concrete sleepers and deep heavy rails, to grab the rear buffer beam's greasy coupling hook with both hands and with serpentine acrobatics to manage to first swing her legs up onto a buffer and then to heave herself legs first, across onto the wagon's flat surface. With a gasp of relief she sat and looked back. No one appeared to be peering over the bridge's parapet or down from the adjoining sooty walls.

For a few minutes she lay flat on her back between the two chained bundles of bright steel strip – like spaghetti still in the packet – and recovered her breath. The train's rattling echoed less as the cutting opened out into the sprawling emptiness of Edge Hill Station and they swayed and screeched over the innumerable pairs of points of the large junction and marshalling yard there.

When they had passed Sandown Park she turned her stiffening cast over and crawled forwards along the wet sandy and splintery forty feet of wooden decking, interrupted three times by the thick transom bolsters on which the two sheaves of steel bars were laid, but without it excoriating the knee-patches of her superb quality leather suit in the least.

At the leading edge of this mammoth wagon, she stood up and leant across to the rear side of the open wagon next in line. The freezing wind swirled and eddied around her, but her leather suit and undergarments kept her still reasonably warm and only round her neck where her suit's collar gave way to the porous wool of her neck-tube, did she feel its draught. She stood on the two nuzzling left-hand buffers to bridge the gap, before spanning the three feet high end-boards of the wagon with one leg on either side and ending up in the company of a load of planks of imported Swedish pine. Because these thick yellowy resinous planks were shorter than the wagon, there was a space for her to stand or sit in. With her forearms folded on the steel edging on the top of the wagon's side, she peered into the darkness and saw a green light shining ahead of them. She rested her chin and nose on the moist rain-bedewed smooth leather of her sleeves and again smelt the pungently sour tanning fluids. As the engine passed the signal, it switched to red. They were picking up speed now. She had evaded her trivial pursuers, as Artemis Boden was bound to do. Only the recovery of her car posed a minor difficulty.

Her murders were as nothing. No bad conscience troubled her about them. The deadly sin she strove to escape from was her refusal to give herself to Simon. Selfish pride had masked her biological and spiritual yearnings from herself. She had blotted out the tall white spirit which she should have been and because that height was very high, she had slipped not just into the dull dreary round of no man's land, but into the dark negative etching of herself, a pit of terrible depth. Yet the tragedy was inside her mind and not in her deeds. The folk she had slain had long since been abandoned by God. The manager at the leather factor's in Northampton had had a black eye from being recently beaten up by animal rights activists. There was no shortage of people about with too much money and leisure, who sought outlets for venting their own pent-up spites. Artemis had not been a fatalist before, but she were becoming more and more convinced that her course had been predestined. Every stitch of this tapestry seemed to have been woven together to allow her to follow this most exceptional of paths. Stomach pains, depressions, headaches and such minor ailments as are usually sent to admonish us for entertaining wrong attitudes were strangely absent in her. No physical curbs had been imposed.

A bat flew past. She cleaned her greasy gauntlets as best she could on a wad of paper handkerchieves. In the bottom of her handbag she had a tin of orange juice and a bar of marzipan chocolate. She dug these out and consumed them. It was still spitting a light mix of sleet and raindrops.

The M62 motorway under construction travelled along beside them for a while, then small ill-lit commuter stations – Roby, Huyton and Rainhill rolled past. The heavy rails alongside trembled on their bed of large rock chippings and like a tornado, a passenger train hurtled past, a fifteen second buffeting whirlwind which left strong vortices in its wake.

At St. Helen's Junction they slowed abruptly and just beyond it rumbled and slewed and lurched into Bold Moss sidings, where they lost more speed and clunked to a halt. A smattering of yellow dots, less than half a mile behind them in the gloom, indicated a town. This was Sutton and St. Helen's Junction Station lay on the edge of it.

The coast was clear. She clambered over the wagon's end onto a buffer, lowered herself to a sitting position and jumped. She ducked under a parallel row of stationary bogie well-wagons, her leather boots causing the granite ballast to grate and rattle slightly. She crouched here, thinking how in films it was always men and never girls who did such deeds as this, yet really if you were adequately dressed there was no logical reason for it. Women usually had on hats with silk ribbons which might become soiled or tights or thin cotton frocks which might tear, but if clothed like Artemis, there was no difficulty at all. Even it was quite thrilling to be able to move in this cold and alien world.

Footsteps approached. She lay flat, the sharp-edged lumps of stone pressing into her soft body. The footsteps went past.

She emerged on all fours on the other side of these wagons, then crossed over the two empty tracks of the main line in the darkness before sliding on her bottom down the melting snow of the embankment. She moved through some bare stalks and reeds which nodded with incomprehension at this intrusion into their line-side domain and then followed the post and wire fence back towards St. Helen's Junction.

A tall clump of weeds stood guard where a drain ran into a culvert and here she paused to put on her black cagoule and remove her gauntlets – to look more like an everyday human being.

She approached the bridge where the railway passed over Helena Road and just before it, slithered down through some untamed bushes whilst keeping an eye on the terraced houses opposite to be sure that no one saw her. She ended up beside a bridge pier, crossed Helena Road with the bridge to her left and then walked up a steep footpath on the opposite side of the road, between two high walls of blue engineering bricks, up onto the station platform. The platform and the brick waiting-room were deserted.

By the pervading greyey-orange vapours of the sodium street lights, she surveyed herself. There were several streaks of rust or grease on her boots and her clothing looked a trifle clumsy and heavy, but it was a filthy night.

At the platform's farther end and to its right she found a gloomy and equally deserted cobble-stoned station forecourt where a single Ford Granada taxi waited beside a bent taxi rank sign and a hooded telephone. It was exactly nine o'clock and beginning to rain more heavily.

Artemis tapped on the window. The driver awoke from a doze, evidently surprised to be disturbed here except by the telephone.

'Are you for hire?'

'It says "For hire", don't it?'

Artemis suppressed a desire to beat his head in and climbed into the back. 'Liverpool please.'

It crossed her mind that she could ask him to stop at some quiet spot on the way, shoot him and then commandeer his vehicle.

'The University please. How far is it?'

'Eleven ... twelve miles.'

The black metal box rattled and swished westwards, whilst earthly stars – the pricks of artificial light – gave the drab cold world only the bleakest and gauntest of images.

When Artemis was on her expeditions, she felt neither happiness nor unhappiness. Her thoughts were alert but not original nor lively nor amusing. She was wholly alone but not lonely. She were used to being alone and the barren and unloving wastelands of such dark nights did not frighten her remote soul. In fact such isolation, terrifying to many, excited her inside her warm and seemingly invincible leather.

'I hear there's been some shooting in Liverpool tonight?' she prompted him, to discover if he might have identified her.

'Don't know. I only listen to the sport on the radio. Everton's pissing lost.'

'I beg your pardon?'

He did not bother to explain. 'You're well dressed for the weather.'

'My moped's broken down.'

In Liverpool she asked him to drop her off in one of the deserted little service roads between the different faculty buildings of the University, just round the corner from her Porsche and paid him generously with an old note.

No one saw her slip into her unvandalised Porsche.

Artemis left Liverpool by travelling northwards through Bootle, to give Edge Hill and Fryer Street the widest possible berth, before once more driving up to South-West Scotland.

She did not stop for fuel or food, for she knew that her description and particularly that of her clothing would be in tomorrow's news.

Artemis reached her home on Loch Eilan at about one thirty that morning.

* * *

The enormous crimson ball of the sun sank behind the deep blue melancholy sky-line of minarets and office buildings.

Colonel Letheren and his daughter Catharine walked arm in arm with the chilly Bosporus to their right and a great rampart gouged and cracked by cannon balls to their left. They passed by a gate whose gargantuan lintel bore a renovated blue frieze with an inscription from the Quoran on it in gold Cufic script. Apparently it read, 'The heart of wisdom is the fear of

Allah'. Archibald compared it to the Christian 'The fear of the Lord is the *beginning* of wisdom', which to his mind seemed far more sublime.

They turned a corner and some way ahead through a screen of cypresses and palms glimpsed the Golden Horn.

'I think Ute Steyer will keep silent. She wants no more trouble, but simply to survive and enjoy what she has won.'

They emerged from beside some hanging gardens to wend their way via quiet back-streets to the main railway station with its swarming life and hubbub.

Catharine stopped to buy a bag of hot chestnuts from a gipsyish girl with a barrow and brazier. This girl flirted furiously with two excitable native admirers, batting her long lashes challengingly. She still found time though, both to overcharge and short-change this mute tourist. As she oscillated her hips from side to side, her grilling stand suddenly collapsed in a shower of sparks and hot dust and she screamed hot-blooded Turkish abuse at everyone around her.

The smells and glitter of poverty and warmth seemed to be one with the Turkish soul. They blended with the shoddy night bars under the trees, the demonic whores, the tatty fretwork around the cafés, the cheap scents and the vague lawlessness of the evening air. Unlike in Germany, where they were unhappy non-natives amid the mirage-like wealth of the twentieth century, here unsevered and undisplaced from their own milieu, their uncorked innate wildness flowed freely.

The Letherens were staying in the Hotel Bactria, a modern establishment designed for Americans, with bidets and air-conditioning. In the restaurant the English guests ate juicy burnt lamb with onion quarters and slices of tomato on kebab skewers with South African wine of dubious authenticity. Catharine washed a few clothes out in their bathroom and they went to bed early on the Sunday evening, the twenty-eighth of December.

The next morning they went to a northerly suburb of the city, to Haluk's Car Rental, run from an old wooden house with a ramshackle concrete garage beside it with riot-proof barred windows. Haluk, a smiling but wily businessman, appeared and Letheren negotiated with him in Arabic for one week's rental of a smallish Fiat camper-van. Afterwards they bought sleeping-bags, a primus stove and a crate load of provisions which they put into the back of this vehicle.

By mid-morning they had crossed over into Asia. Here apricot peach and cheery trees grew round many of the houses softening the residential panorama. A carpet of purple-leaved wild flowers stretched beside a railway line as they headed eastwards towards Ankara, using roads once travelled by Christian pilgrims and crusaders, by Alexander's army, Urartian merchants and warriors of the Chalybes tribes.

Up from a mildly cool Damascus, a pale blue Rolls-Royce drove through the wasted interior of Syria, a wilted landscape which had once been a part of the busy and thriving Hellenistic and Classical worlds, but where the civilising inroads had slowly died until the olive-presses lay broken and only the cicadas grated forlornly in these sadness-beset doldrums.

At a green spring, near the faintest traces of a long-lost Roman imperial road and a cluster of osculatory pink desert flowers, al-Uzza ordered a halt. His chauffeur and his body-guard took a hamper out of the boot for him and he sucked noisily at chicken sandwiches, at delicious chocolate-coated orange-cream biscuits and at illicit and unholy champagne.

Al-Uzza made a call from his back seat telephone.

On the limousine rolled to the soberer commercial city of Aleppo for an overnight stop.

The Letherens headed south from Ankara, up onto the vast Anatolian Plain. They shared the driving and given the rough state of the roads, made good time.

They overnighted in an infertile valley of sagy greens and contorted tufa, between the northern end of a great lake marked as Tuz Gölü and a ridge of foothills, pitching camp by a shrunken river with a bed of yellow and grey pebbles. The last vestiges of daylight glowed on the thick snow of the outlying peaks, stars shone timelessly and on a hillside a faint square of light oozed out of a solitary cottage.

Lamb neck chops with chopped onions bubbled in a saucepan on the primus stove. Catharine inquired about Hassan al-Uzza.

Her father cut some wedges of coarse bread to eat with their primitive stew. They were huddled beside their rented vehicle.

'Some of these nomadic tribesmen, who have no aptitude for civil administration or business – indeed who even despise such things – find Islam to be an attractive religion because it supports a state of continuous warfare. There have been chivalrous Muslims such as Saladin ... but al-Uzza and his type, whilst they may like to pretend that fighting and conquest are still in their blood, are just as much under the sway of greed and their own power dreams as is most of the world today. Military prowess and artistic prowess count for nothing in this age of prurient desires and international control games.'

With their stew and bread they also drank red wine, like a eucharist for pilgrims heading for Jerusalem.

'The strength of these Arabs lies in their sturdy peasant hardihood and their stern materialistic faith, not in their harsh view of God, which is far less transcendent than ours.'

Next morning, Letheren bathed briefly in the winding icy stream, whilst Catharine made tea and cheese buns.

They drove back down to the main road against a back-drop of white highlands with straggly sheep dotting the arid lower slopes and continued their journey southwards with the Colonel map-reading. An occasional plot of stunted fruit trees or a wretched village of mud and wood hovels went by, until after three hours they neared the edge of the great flat empty plain. Mountains loomed ahead. They crossed a single-track railway line and passed through a small dusty town, then after a few kilometres swung off onto a side track. The camper-van wound up a snaking track and after ten minutes pulled up behind an axleless shell of a lorry with much of its bodywork rusted through. They hid the van amid bushes and sandy hillocks with tall weeds.

It was noon. They had two hours to prepare. With the necessary minimum of equipment they slithered down a small scree-slope, jumped over a stream and climbed up a steep rocky hillside topped with irregular crags like a row of broken teeth. They reached a side-gorge where spray was blown back up at them from a stream, frothing and tumbling over a precipice, Advancing into this chasm through a sward of mulberry trees, they came to a bubbling spring set in a green grove. To one side were the remains of a small enclosure of weathered rectangular grey blocks, the temenos wall of an ancient shrine with lilac flowers sprouting oddly between the dislodged masonry. Moss and bracken covered the ground.

There Catharine waited, cold in her navy blue coat and white knitted scarf and mittens, seated on a cyclopean cube of stone and looking out over the southerly edge where the usual path of approach led up from a winding road. This minor road lay on the opposite side of the hill to that from which they had come and carried on past the sanctuary, upwards into the snowy peaks beyond. After a time the girl stood up and walked back and forth, stamping her feet occasionally but still watching the road periodically.

The bullet-proof Rolls had stopped in the nearby village. The body-guard had to keep on his toes as a posse of sullen but volatile and penniless youths gathered and glowered with envy.

'The Qaimakam of Aleppo is an important man,' said the chauffeur as he reluctantly handed over a note or two and then a gold coin in mistrustful and grudging barter for directions to the forgotten temple. As they moved off, a large rock dented the car's boot.

The chauffeur found the mountain track but missed the faint footpath on the left and continued upwards and through the snow-line.

Al-Uzza intended to ask Ute about the disastrous end to the fifth arms shipment, but still to offer them a contract for two further shipments, if she could allay his suspicions adequately. Reverting though to the immediate difficulties, he cursed his chauffeur and demanded he turn round. As they attempted a five-point turn at a passing place on this snow-packed and unbarriered section of road, clinging to the face of a curved mountainside, they simply slid off the edge.

Catharine had watched the car advancing uncertainly. Higher and higher it went, its exhaust echoing softly like an airship's bass drone off the rock wall beside it. Then it stopped and the next thing she saw was it leaving its icy perch. A door flew open in panic, but too late. No one managed to leap clear. The heavy beast nose-dived onto the uneven white rocks below. It ricocheted off one jagged surface, somersaulted off a second and crumpled into a third, creating a thin trail of dust or moisture before ending up out of sight.

'Pappa,' called Catharine's undulating sing-songy voice, 'You can come out. Look.'

They watched a small pillar of vapour settle. No need to use the rifle, which an officer in Cyprus had secretly brought by boat to Istanbul. He had intended to pick off al-Uzza and his assistants whilst the former spoke to Catharine.

She took the rifle and set off down to and across the narrow road and along the steep obstacle-strewn slopes, to identify the men in the unignited vehicle and ensure that they were dead.

Letheren turned round and read the worn engraving on the broken altar stone. 'To her bright image nightly, Sidonian virgins make songs and vows.' Between the symbols of Hesperus and Phosphorus – the evening and morning stars – also in Greek capitals, was inscribed the name 'Artemis'. A boar lay pierced with lances, wolves were gored by a gigantic mould-spotted bull and a maiden in an Ionian robe looked on, chiselled in relief. A breeze wafted through the alder trees and the waterfall hissed softly, where in this enchanted place long-forgotten priests had once watched over their hallowed books and ancient treasures and sacrificed to Artemis, the Goddess of the Moon.

Once we lived in forests and ate acorns and wore skins and always in the Germanic or Anglo-Saxon soul is a piece of this lurking, yet the crystal clarity of the Greek mind is universal.

Letheren saw things from his early childhood, things he had forgotten he knew – blackboards with childish scribble on them, all perfectly part of an inevitable evolution – and he felt strangely light-headed. He saw Artemis Boden in her lethal leather. She would not drift through life aimlessly, but either love much or hate much and it seemed she had rejected love. He had seen this when Innogen had bodefully first named her and known that she would end on the borders of sadism in an arcane auto-destruction, whether he used her or not. He saw his wife

Anne on the day he had first met her, not self-elevating or quick or strong enough to be a goddess but equally appealing in her passive and right-hearted unassertiveness. Her blitheness had been reticent, her goodness unspoken and unburdened by renown and her cordial behaviour the summoner of good fortune. Her spare time she used to read and not to be drawn into idle talk. This was the sort of woman to marry. Good women are not 'moral', they are good through right instincts. Women who pretend to be 'moral' are just trying to gain credit for limit ations which they cannot escape from anyway.

Catharine reappeared with al-Uzza's passport. 'The Rolls' shell is in a nosc-down position in a hollow of sand and fine gravel under the snow-line. Al-Uzza and his two servants were already dead. Their spines had perhaps been broken, but al-Uzza too had had the large vessels in the left side of his neck cut on the torn metal of a door and his dark blood had gushed out into the damp terrain.'

Letheren threw his rifle and the spare rounds into some undergrowth in the gorge.

By three o'clock they were heading for the peaks of the Taurus range which guard the Cilician Gates and via this narrow defile, they left the hinterland for the rugged littoral of Asia Minor. Rivers tumbled down between rocky pinnacles and through immense canyons clogged with pine and myrtle.

They dropped four thousand feet onto a plain with ribbons of water and flocks of sheep and villages in which they glimpsed smoke pots of baked clay, evidence of bee keeping and the cultivation of olives, lemons and lentils.

Outside Tarsus they stopped beneath some silvery-grey walnut trees to brew tea and eat oranges and figs from their crate.

They drove on to Mersin and in the harbour between the fishing boats and oil tankers and caiques the evening ferry to

Famagusta waited. They left the van in a side-street and sailed to Cyprus. From there, with its R.A.F. base at Akrotiri, they should soon be home.

## CHAPTER THIRTEEN.

Many recently sawn tree trunks lay in piles beside the track and stretches of shuttering and loads of road-stone were further evidence of the first steps in the restoration of Uanrig House, which Donald Boden had initiated. A shrinking melting topping of snow capped a few bare patches of earth.

A Land Rover moved slowly along this track, its driver on unfamiliar ground. It stopped at the front of the stone house. Innogen stepped out in a smart black woollen coat and black fashion boots. Between the two plain Doric columns she pressed the non-functioning bell-push and after an interval banged with the bronze knocker.

Artemis opened the door. Behind her Innogen could see the three-stage oak staircase, the oval gilt-rimmed mirror and the three ascending paintings.

'An envelope for you Artemis.'

Artemis took it and opened it. It contained a cheque for one and a half million Deutschmarks, which had been signed by A.H. Letheren.

'The payee's name has been left blank, so you can use a pseudonym. My father recommends that you keep the money in Switzerland.'

'Thank you. Would you like a cup of tea or some rice pudding?'

'That's very kind of you, but I have to be in Glasgow this evening for a concert.'

Despite this superficially credible excuse, Artemis sensed under the quiet grave diplomacy, that she were being avoided like something black and sticky. Innogen of course, was far too well brought up to make such a refusal obvious, but that only added to Artemis's displeasure at being slighted.

Innogen with her pale blue eyes and fair placid face, looked at her. She held out her hand and gave Artemis's limp hand a modest shake. 'Thank you. Bye-bye.' She enunciated it with an overtone of finality.

Artemis watched her drive away, annoyed that she had not uttered the first deft insult. But it was too late and that made her even angrier.

Dark cloud formations had swept in from the West and were starting to shed a lot of rain. In the gilt-rimmed mirror, her own imposing splendour seemed suddenly to have shrunk.

The rain rattled violently against the kitchen windows as Artemis heated up some of yesterday's rice pudding in a saucepan with a splash of milk to moisten it. She had felt fairly relaxed that morning, but Innogen's visit had perturbed her. Was Innogen too a part of the conspiracy against her? She had Robert Falcus in her pocket, that was clear. Was she the slave of the three males or their commander-in-chief? It was so hard to fathom which of them was the head of the snake. By setting out the pieces on Papa's chess-board and playing a made-up game with them, she deduced that Simon was the real genius behind the plot.

Simon was staying with his widowed mother at Green Leys Cottage in the village of Estcott in North Staffordshire. He had committed the cardinal error of mentioning this 'girl in Norway' in passing, an allusion to which mother had instantly locked on, ever fearful for the esteemed letters after his name. Being good-natured original and a sort of silly yet thoughtful self-effacing dilettante counted for nothing. You must have status and the trappings of success. All must seem outwardly grand, regardless of how inwardly dull it actually was. For a whole day her dissatisfied mind did not float back to its favourite vain dreams of those ghastly chic fashions and church hall dances of the 1930's, but instead accused him of 'turning away from the plough' of 'disobedience' and 'ingratitude' as she sensed that he might abandon his course at Newcastle.

'No pretty picture of me in a gown and a hood of many colours on degree ceremony day, to show to your "friends"?' said an emboldened Simon.

She changed her tactics to tears.

His elder sister Lesley, he knew, had long since wearied of trying to win approval by complying with mother's manipulative whims. Only little brother Laurence's misdemeanours were easily forgiven and forgotten, anything which Simon or Lesley did out of line being scored indelibly into the maternal memory – two black sheep and one fleecy little white lambkin!

He had studied German *not* because he wanted to visit Germany and show off that he could say 'I want a bottle of whisky' in their tongue, *nor* trot out those hideous commercial or political clichés about marketing or public relations, but because Lessing and that period of German drama had fascinated him. Yet hardly any of his course work made him all excited and shivery or pulled him a bit further up the hill of wisdom. The modern texts were all tricks and no substance, the lexical history, Middle High German orthography and proto-Germanic substantives could only be tolerated in the smallest of doses and his heart wanted to drop it and explore other fields.

No sooner had he left his mother's in his rented car, than he felt calmer and more rational again. He lurched along Hay Edge and turned onto the main road beyond White Cross Grange. The forced veils and duplicity faded readily enough before his own straightforward emotions and plain thoughts. He felt that he would not mind if he ended up sweeping floors, just as long as he was not involved in hollow powder-puff promotions or sham geniality – anything free of lies.

The automatic choke finally sorted itself out and he headed for Scotland with an improved smoothness of motion.

Innogen had been gone less than an hour, when the knocker thumped again. Artemis answered it wearing her MacRae tartan skirt, an off-white pullover, long white socks and dainty black slippers like leather ballet shoes. She looked quite schoolgirlish and serene.

Simon oppositely seemed to have grown taller, his clothes hung more easily on him and his manner was more natural. Kim and Helle in differing ways had cured his stage fright, his false starts and his falling over himself.

'Hullo.' She gave him a serrated smile. 'You've come home from Norway?'

'Briefly. To see you.'

'What an honour. Come in. Leave your shoes on the mat if you don't mind.'

She sat him on the dusky blue leather sofa in the rather dowdy and old-fashioned pink and blue drawing-room and went out to the kitchen. Simon felt instantly at home, instantly in love with this house and everything in it, not only because it was his beloved's but because it was so beautifully peaceful and mellow.

In the kitchen Artemis gripped the back of a chair, trembling as she boiled water and set some slices of fruit cake on a plate. She would listen to what he had to say. Perhaps she would have to give in, say she loved him and yield to him.

Simon saw that if she did surrender, he was in for plenty of volcanoes and eruptions as she tried merely to use him and resist actually loving him, but he was willing to try and bear with that because he knew that the heights of joy he might reach with this woman would quite surpass that possible with any other girl. She would cleave his soul, render it blackly dynamic before the devil and disarm it to whiteness before

God, whereas with another he would merely follow life's tedious round. He thought of her sexy body which might rightly be his and imagined Adrian describing her as 'one of the world's most delectable iced-buns'.

She entered, put down the tray on the coffee-table and sat down on a pouffe well away from him.

'I've been living with a Norwegian girl.'

She shrugged.

'She's a lively girl ... practical ... loving ... '

'Marry her then.' It sounded both sarcastic and offended.

'I'm considering it ... but I still feel for you ... '

Just as he was about to stand up and go over to her, to take her hands or even embrace her, she unconsciously pre-empted him by rising to switch on a couple of lamps on side-tables and to tear off the calendar to read Tuesday the thirtieth of December, with a show of indifference as if she were waiting for him to say something of interest. Outside, an abrupt twilight had fallen over both forest and loch.

He sat dumbly for a few seconds, before seeing that words were inappropriate here. He sprang up and tried to corner her and give her forceful and incessant kisses. Fleeing capture, she darted round the sofa, but he vaulted over it and arrested her. She wriggled violently against his grip of her wrists, avoided his looming lips and nimbly evaded the arm which sought to seize her round the waist. She was no brown leaf to be blown along by the autumn wind, no sapling to bow and loosen and break her roots in her clayey maiden soil. Simon tried to bring his chest to touch her firm breasts, to hold her tightly and to kiss her, for he thought that then she might go floppy and cease to resist.

Artemis saw with alarm her nearing solemn concessions. She could not even harm this attacker by seduction as with

Colonel Letheren or Howard in North Shields, because he was her legitimate lover. In a last fling of resistance she threw him back with vigour, overbalancing him so that he sat down firmly on the end of the sofa. But she had no more defensive forces in her. She waited for his next advance, ready to soften and kiss him.

Yet Simon saw no outward mark of this threshold and he did not feel justified in struggling further with her physically, if she showed no sign of weakening. He was not a Red Army soldier, who regarded rape as the rightful winnings of the conqueror. He said, 'Oh well, if you don't wish to give anything ... '

'Only if I *must*,' she said coolly, hovering on the verge of cracking. But no, *he* must persevere and *she* must be won.

Simon lay slumped listlessly on the sofa. He had given up. 'I would have given everything for you,' he stated retrospectively, like a king who has lost an empire. 'Everything.'

This pathetic worm, failing just at the vital moment. Come on, ravish me you wretched louse! 'Puh!' she said haughtily and then enigmatically, 'The mountains which divide you from bliss!'

'What are they?'

'Your feebleness.'

He failed to understand her clue.

She yawned.

'Are you tired?'

'Yes. Are you awake?'

'Yes.'

'Awake but dead.' She sneered slightly.

He looked puzzled and stood up to leave, whilst she leant with provocative impassivity against the far window.

But he seemed to have made up his mind, to have wearied of her games and as he let himself out, utter rage swept over her. Why had he not persisted and slept with her, this midge who had sabotaged her acting career? Did he expect her to run after him, as all other spiritless girls did these days? Should she beg his mercy or his love? Should she crawl to all those pruritic film directors he had set up against her? Why had his will snapped at the crucial point in the battle? Or was it timed just to torment her? Anyway, he deserved to lose!

Her face turned dark and ugly. Why had she not shot him? Why had she missed this golden opportunity like a fool, mesmerised by his magical powers? She hurled herself face downwards onto the sofa and beat it angrily with her fists. She had let Innogen slip through her fingers too. Two out of four she could have netted today, both the master genie and one of his spies. Why had she not seen it? Why?! Why had that huge patch of mud on the track not bogged them down? Why was everything on their side and nothing on hers?

Simon drove away with the feeling of a man who has failed at a major interview. As the smoke of pique and pride clears, he sees that it was the inevitable result and he feels released and eased. He felt glad for Helle too, she who could not comprehend her love and flitted between joy and vexation, hanging on his every word and unstintingly sharing her all with him. When he had left she had plucked at her cardigan in despair and been very downcast. 'I am frightened that you will not return to me,' she had murmured, 'But I shall sit and wait and hope that one day you will come back.'

Some time after the rising whine of Simon's car engine had faded in the distance, Artemis stood up from the sofa and kneeled before the fire. She rattled the ashes through the fire-bars and placed three half-logs on the glowing remnants. 'Love! What deluding rubbish,' she whispered. Even if it did exist, the climb to it would be too arduous and humiliating for her proud spirit to acquiesce to. 'I shall live without love or die in the attempt!'

As the flames took hold of the log on the left, a strange shape danced above it indistinctly.

'So Artemis,' she mouthed to herself, as if the puppet of an unseen ventriloquist, 'you belong to the Spirit of the Mine. Now that that silly interlude with Archibald Letheren is over, you can turn to your true purpose. You must rid yourself of these three *good* men who are curbing you and making you ungraceful because they envy your loveliness. Then the smell of arc lamps, the thrill of grease-paint and the stir of the audience ... The path of being a great actress will substitute other passions for those of your outings as a black leather knight. But firstly, kill Simon, the head of the three *wise* males.'

'But where shall I find him?'

Her subconscious produced no answer to this query, so she stood up and drifted out to the kitchen, but as she crossed the hallway, there on the large rug lay a bent copy of a journal called *The Dramaturge*. It had fallen out of Simon's jacket pocket as he had tied his shoe-laces. A hand-written note protruded from its centre pages and read, 'The Annoch Lodge Guest House. Telephone Newton Stewart 440. One night. Single room.'

Artemis picked up the telephone and dialled. A man's voice at the other end answered through a yawn.

'Good afternoon. Do you have a Mr Simon Collett staying with you, please?'

'Er ... yes, but ... oh, I think he's just coming through the door now ... '

Artemis put the receiver down.

She drew the sitting-room curtains, made some coffee for herself and sat down on the sofa. So, the Spirit of the Mine could assist her. She felt suddenly more confident, more buoyantly wicked again. It was possible for her to wrong-foot them too, instead of them constantly wrong-footing her. Outside the dull daylight faded as the sacred darkness advanced. Perhaps magic could win over love in this forthcoming guerre à outrance? The Annoch Lodge Guest House was just a few miles along the road from here. She ran her tongue round the inside of her cheeks and tilted her head back. 'Oh my sweetest, you are not going to get back to your little farmyard wench in Norway. Oh no!'

The logs spluttered and spat, as f rejoicing with her and conferring calm upon her.

Her calm disappeared though, as thumbing cursorily through *The Dramaturge*, a small head and shoulders photograph of Simon appeared on one of the news pages near the back. With his chin propped up on his fist he smiled restrainedly out at her. Under him, was a half-column article mentioning briefly that his first television play, *Adolf and Stephanie*, was scheduled for filming in March, directed by Sir Robert Falcus and that he was working on a second screen drama, *Joanna the First of Naples* and currently living in Norway.

Artemis ripped the magazine into ribbons in an ecstasy of fury, flung the pieces on the fire with trembling hands and swore copiously. Should she kill him or should she go to the guest house, say she would marry him and give him hell?

She put on her black leather coat, her thigh-boots and gloves and a scarf, put up the fire-guard, locked the house and drove off in her Porsche in the drizzling misty blackness.

The headlamps lighted up transiently a wooden bench on the lawn running down to the loch. When a toddler she had sat there with her mother on sunny summer days and been read to. It had a little plaque on it, 'Made from wood from the *S.S. Llandovery Castle*. Scrapped at Inverkeithing 1953.' She remembered one pop-up book about an Arabian djinn named al-Manat. It had been her favourite book and though unable to read, she had known exactly when to turn the pages. She had played together with her father there too, with her toy animals and wooden bricks.

Before going to see Simon, she drove into the village of Dulloch and stopped beside the churchyard. All was silent except for the patter of rain. Only the odd blot of snow like spilt milk glowed in the gloom, but along the sodden paths she walked until she found by blind instinct her mother's unkempt grave at the end of a row. Artemis knelt on the untidy grass and dead weeds in front of the drunken stone, her knees dimpling the soft ground slightly and her bottom on her heels. In an urge to cuddle her mother, she changed to the erect kneeling position and folded her arms around the flat wet headstone and touched its slimy surface and an ivy creeper growing across it with her lips. She wished she could cry.

'Mama, please help me. Please tell me what to do and how to love.' She pressed her breast against the gravestone, but she heard no answer. 'I know you loved me. You spent so much time with me. You did not just say "Oh how clever" and turn back to chat with your arty friends. You taught me to bake, you corrected me, explained things ... Please guide me now.'

In the dense darkness with the rain dripping off the intangible shapes of the trees, she waited for some minutes for a sign or a word. All was silent.

Intending to walk around the churchyard and then return, she stood up but after a few paces collided with an invisible tar machine which some bastard builders had parked under the trees. She grazed her forehead against it and removing a bitumen-smeared glove, felt the sticky black goo both on her brow and down the front of her coat. What would happen next? Would she slip over into a pile of manure which the gardener had conveniently left hereabouts or have an accident and wet herself? And was this the response to her pleas?

Shaking with anger, she strode back to her mother's plot and grabbing the top edge of the stone, tried vainly to push it over. Things were not as they seemed. She pushed and pulled at the stone but despite its tilted angle, it would not budge. Tremblingly, she turned round and shoved her bottom against it.

That arch-magician Simon, whose seeming frailty she had so badly misjudged was behind all this. She would engage him mercilessly with the boundless force of the Spirit of the Mine. Power did not reside where you first thought. Like wizards who could change shape, Simon had assumed the form of a mouse, whilst truly he was the potentate of a thousand natural entities. And he was attempting to destroy her for refusing to become his slave. Here lay the ultimate battle. The notion that belittlement should sometimes be borne to atone for some misdeed was not a thought readily acceptable to Miss Boden.

Then as she pushed backwards more fiercely, chafing her bottom against the skewed slab as if to destroy it by friction or abrasion, her right heel suddenly slipped forwards and she sat down in the weeds.

A distant dog barked with a wolf-like howl.

* * *

In the City Hall the rondo movement of the evening's first symphony was under way. Innogen sat patiently in the back pair of violas during a sixty bar pause, whilst the serried cellists beside her scurried away like madmen.

The programme was based on the in-vogue 'rediscovery of Mozart'. Whilst he had written a few great works, been a capable orchestrator and had a good grip of the abilities of the different instruments, the Victorian view that much of his canon was tuneless and stereotyped seemed to Innogen to be correct. Beethoven had by his emotional articulation, quite superseded him. In this piece they were playing, nothing made her go all tingly and light-headed, which it ought to with a composer of his supposed stature. She lifted her bow for the next flurry of unmelodious arpeggios.

Behind her were the double-basses, old sweats with droll faces, hoping to be out before the pubs shut. To her right were the oboists, serious men with goatee beards, slightly supercilious attitudes and a tendency to despise the audience. The Japanese conductor swirled about like a man being overwhelmed by missiles. Every fourth bar he tossed a hank of black hair back out of his eyes and sweat droplets flew through the air. His death-throe facies of passion and ecstasy seemed to Innogen ingenuine and to someone of her breadth and fidelity, such pretence was deeply appalling. Perhaps the poor man acted because he did not understand real feeling, because he was yet another of these technical prodigies, a house built on sand. Even worse was that no one else seemed to share her disquiet.

But for this indifferently executed performance, which also failed to inspire belief that the true spirit of the work had been brought out – if indeed there was one – the audience clapped excessively and the awful round of hand-pumping and false smiles took place.

* * *

Artemis left the utility room, having dumped her tar-bedaubed gloves and coat there following her mishap. A quiet but deep-rooted rage had slowly but surely taken possession of her.

In the mirror – apart from the bruise and a black bituminous smear – her face as by an optical trick looked brutal and haggard as never before. She dabbed turpentine onto her face to remove the tacky dense petroleum residues.

'So you think your star is in the ascent, do you Collett?' she slavered as she reheated some of yesterday's stew in a saucepan in the large and attractively sombre kitchen. 'Well, I'm going to slay you tonight ... pluck you from the constellation of victors.'

When she sat at the table to eat her quick meal, the first three lumps of meat were gristly, the stock fatty and floury and the potato displayed a huge rotten blue bruise. She made a firm mental note to have a blazing row with that insolent Sheelagh when she returned from her New Year's holiday. Papa was ridiculously lenient with her. Anyway, she would soon be rid of him too. Perhaps his train would crash on the way home next week and save her the trouble. Yes, she would be glad when he was dead and out of her way, so why should she not say it? He had failed her too – a traitor who had joined Simon's camp.

As she left the kitchen table with jerky movements, she semi-accidentally knocked the bowl of stew off in a trajectory which ended on the thick floor tiles where it broke.

'Clean it up,' she commanded a non-present Sheelagh,

'Clean it up yourself.'

'Do as I say. I don't clean floors.'

'That's the worse for you.'

God, she would sort this Celtic dryad out when she saw her next. Perhaps she too was one of Collett's spies? She had always assumed in her conflicts with Simon, that her one ace was his not *knowing* her weaknesses, but if every tree and stone were on his side, besieging her with his black arts and trickery, only her own self-faith and self-courage and one great hammer blow against the god himself could wreck this creeping and invidious alliance. She in her tough sexy leather would bring to a fiery and cataclysmic end once and for all, all his hateful legions. She thought of all those trees out there, leering at her and watching her.

She restoked the fire, made some cocoa and sat on the sofa to work out in detail tonight's attack.

If you left Uanrig House by the main track and at the main road turned left in the direction of Newton Stewart – which she rarely did – after about four miles through the forest, this Annoch Lodge lay back from the road on the left-hand side. The manager's office and the single story moulding shop of a derelict brickyard had been renovated in the 1960's to create a motel. The robust stone shells had been filled with shoddy teak veneers, tea-making alarm clocks and remote-controlled television sets. She must break in in the middle of the night, stab or shoot him and remove any papers he possessed which referred to her. She had mastered the art of burglary now. She would break in between two and three o'clock in the morning via some flimsy back toilet window, find his room number from the desk register and with a spare or master key, enter the lair of the fiendish serpent and kill it. If she were caught, she had merely to say that she were his girlfriend.

She recalled Innogen in her new-looking black woollen coat – it had nice simple lines and suited her tall figure ... and yet why had she not chosen leather? Was it cowardice? Was she frightened of wearing leather? Did she regard it as dangerous – especially to her soul – or did it simply mean nothing to her? Or had she decided to rely instead on these mysterious notions of 'love' and 'goodness'? Was she able to yoke such misty forces and if so how? But Artemis could not understand such things, whereas leather she understood well. In that she would tremble and feel delight. In it a wondrous ecstasy would subsume her, a limitless and unbridled rapture overwhelm her with its intoxicating potency. In it you could defile yourself and defy the whole world ... nothing else could ever be compared to it.

On the northern side of the main road lay areas of forest and heathery moorland, scarred by gullies, boggy and very humpy and uneven, noted for deer and edged with pig-netting set back from the road. On the southern side it was virtually endless firs and there was only one turn-off she could think of in the propinquity of Annoch Lodge and that was a Forestry Commission access with a locked gate. There seemed to be no hidey-hole for the Porsche. Yet as the snow had all but melted, she could go on one of Papa's semi-veteran motorcycles. The large scale Ordnance Survey map of the area reminded her of a feature she had forgotten.

Beyond Annoch Lodge was a stippled red bridleway, rather overgrown in the days when she had ridden her horse there, but passable for a motorbike. It ran round behind the water-filled marl pit, the three or four round bee-hive kilns and the ruined excavator shed of the brickworks and eventually joined a track which headed eastwards – skirting various craigs and cairns – to the southernmost tip of Loch Eilan. She could seclude her motorcycle in some trees and bushes, just off this track.

Her violent shaking had reduced itself to a minor tremor and her deep pantings of savage fury abated to a breathing pattern just slightly deeper than usual. Artemis put on a pair of floppy Wellingtons and her black cagoule and turned on the lights for the yard and stables.

Like many men born in the 1920's, Donald Boden had been fascinated with mechanical feats and achievements. He had always had a large collection of Meccano and also motorcycles had been one of his hobbies since his teens.

In the stable used as a workshop, the grill-protected yellowy lights enabled Artemis to survey his three chargers – a Sunbeam which had been in pieces for a while, the Ariel used by her on the night she had tried to leave for Robert Falcus's party and a 1964 Aermacchi 344 racer. Her father frequently spent a day dismantling cleaning and reassembling some component, so they were quite well maintained. On the bench and on the shelves all the tools and spares were laid out neatly, many springs and nuts and washers stored in pre-war 'Wills's Cut Golden Bar Tobacco' tins. These were orange with a red line round the edge, for what 1930's tin or packet would not have a line round the edge? She picked up a bright red and gold Nimbus badge to pin on her suit like a brooch. Artemis had not ridden the Aermacchi before, but its sleek powerful and weapon-like lines made her darkly excited. Tonight she would feel very feminine but also quite masculine.

She unscrewed its two number-plates and pushed it into the yard. The rain had practically ceased, though there was a thin mist and the temperature was falling sharply.

Her weight was scarcely enough to depress the kick-start, but it started with the second stiff kick. She filled the petrol tank up from an ex-army jerry-can and then sat on the saddle and played with the controls before having a brief practice on the loch shore. With these older vehicles, the layout of the controls was far less standardised than it has become since and on the Aermacchi, the foot-brake and gear-change pedals were on opposite sides to the Ariel. The Ariel had its gear-pedal on the right and the brake-pedal on the left – a common arrangement on older British bikes – and consequently a number of times, she pulled in the clutch only to mistakenly brake.

She parked it on its stand in the yard, closed the two halves of the stable door, went inside and turned off the outside lights.

On the sofa she tried to read some of Luise Gottsched's *The Siege of Corinth* in translation, a rather stilted static neo-Greek drama, supposedly modelled on Racine, but ended up dozing for about an hour.

When she awoke, here eyes focused on the fire. She knelt before it. She was going out to execute her should-have-been lover. She felt no hesitation or compunction. He had haunted her and dared to exclude her from the stage. He had by his sorcery reduced her to desperate hopes and ignominy. The Spirit of the Mine rightly demanded of her from the flames – flickering on her white and terrible face like an oracle – that in sinful revenge she should destroy those bewitching and paralysing sages, Collett, Letheren and Papa. She intuitively knew, that this night would be long and fearful, yet she felt good, she felt strong-willed and she felt sure of herself.

For an hour she made general preparations, polishing and checking and setting out all her uniform on the bedspread on her four-poster and the chairs in her bedroom and filling her handbag with a glass-cutter, torches, a dagger, two screwdrivers, keys, sticky tape and the pistol's spare magazines. She put some food and drink into a small dark plastic bag and strapped both it and her faithful solid handbag onto the frame behind the Aermacchi's saddle. In the kitchen she ate a plate of mushy peas and half a grilled turbot with a hard roll.

She washed her hair with a herbal shampoo and ran a bath into which she tipped a whole bottle of perfumed emollient bath oil. She soaked in it for half an hour and watched how with her breathing, the water ebbed and flowed round her breasts and on and off her stomach, as around small tidal off-shore islands. She felt in the middle of her back, a partial recurrence of those fungus-like pendulous growths. The soapy water seemed to accentuate their sliminess. They so hideously blemished her exquisite form. And Simon was behind this too. She recalled the wretched Christmas Eve in North Shields, when she had let Howard escape harming himself through not sexually raking him. As a fornicating roe-deer she should have been brave enough to have made it happen. Her life was slipping by, empty and miserable. She did not care if she had to fight an army to reach Simon tonight, she would take on any number of his malformed goblins.

After she had put on a pair of plain white cotton panties and a white brassièred top, she applied an ocean of Chloé perfume, a vast excess because she wanted to feel very feminine and Cleopatra-like. For the same reason she fastened on her white gold neck-chain over her plain black tee-shirt and slipped her three rings of red gold, electrum and platinum onto different fingers. She considered using her mother's wedding ring too, but after the events near the grave, rejected it. She put on her hockey socks, her black leather knickers, a red woolly and round her neck the knitted 'tube'. She enjoyed dressing up for great occasions. A premonition eked into her mind that she would win every battle except the one she was now embarking on, every fight except the one which really mattered. On went her elbow-length black kid evening gloves and then her gleamingly lubricious black leather suit, down the legs of which she shook clouds of sorbefacient talcum powder to stop it sticking to her should she sweat. She did up its five zips. It induced a savage rage in her, delightfully wanton. She would contend with whatever awaited her out there! She snapped to the neck-stud of this pliant black leather armour, pulled her black woollen hat on and draped a black and red patterned headscarf round her neck, pinning it together at the front with the cast metal gold and red Nimbus badge. She had bought a new belt too, less deep than the other so as not to rub the under-side of her ribs, but again it was of thick black hide which gripped her tightly round her girth and had a heavy brass clasp, zoomorphically etched with a hart. She tugged on her stiff size seven riding boots, which came right up to the knees and zipped them tightly up the inside calf and buckled the thin trouser straps inside their tops. Lastly, with a new pair of long-cuffed black leather gauntlets, she was ready.

As she preened herself in the mirror, she was very conscious of the intertwining of her sexual allure with her beauty and her vanity and she liked it.

Artemis was not going to allow Simon to orchestrate her downfall any longer.

* * *

Innogen had walked back from the fracas at the City Hall, through the streets of Glasgow on this frosty starry night with one of the bassoonists, Christiane Unger, who was a fellow music student.

At the university hall of residence where Christiane lived, Innogen bent over the guests' book in the bare and inhospitable porters' lodge and signed it with a scratchy pen, unaware of the janitor's leer. This man, fiftyish, rosy-cheeked and with black hair slashed with a silver streak was an unhelpful go-by-the-book fellow. Behind the desk two cleaning girls with pails and mops were sat smoking. They glared at the two students with those sullen stares used by low people who are trying to be disdainful in difficult circumstances. Innogen regarded them with slightly puzzled sadness. They looked a bit silly and unsure of themselves, the sort of girls who could not really care less about anything and who would start having affairs not out of right impulses, but simply out of curiosity and a wish to feel more 'mature'.

In Christiane's box-like second-floor room, they sat down with a dim lamp on in a corner, biscuits cheese and tea and listened to a record as a prelude to chatting, as students do the world over.

Although Christiane was of a wholly German family, they had lived in England for some years and she understood the English way of speaking. You were not taken too literally, as is so often an obstacle when Germans converse with the English-speaking peoples. Also in common with most of that small band of German Anglophiles, the aspect of the slovenly and chaotic Britons which had appealed to her was their failure to take rules and bureaucracy too seriously. Order and officialdom ought not to intrude too far into human affairs.

When thirty minutes of Purcell's *Dido and Aeneas* and some food and drink had induced a degree of relaxation into the two girls, they began slowly to practise that art of exchanging thoughts. That is to say that they started with small remarks about whether Prof. had granted Innogen her year's sabbatical for taking part in her play in London, the scarcity in the shops of browny-pink cardigans and whether Dr Huntbach was merely nice or too nice, but with the aim of probing their way forward into articulating those small niggles round the borders of their hearts – life's emerging new imperfections – as yet not wholly identified or voiced. They did not bandy pseudo-erudite assertions gleaned from others and which did not emanate from their own feelings, nor did they rap their fists on the arms of the chairs and pretend to be terribly excited about things which really grown women should not be excited about, but they wove together a dialogue which was unbigoted, eclectic and not disturbing to the spirit.

Their first main subject revolved around the staff members of their music department, who for all their civility and well-intentioned aplomb gave you the feeling that if you did not maintain a certain distance, you would lose something of your independence and integrity of mind. It had something to do with their homage to the tin god of public relations and their institutionalised self-interest. They might be proficient in their musicianship, but they were not great men and their emotional depths were impaired. This seemed to be the key to why Beethoven and Wagner were so often accused of being unreasonably curt and rude by their biographers.

After a period of fumbling and hesitation, their dual meditation moved thoughtfully on to evil people and their need to continually seek new victories to hide from themselves a looming and painful void. Yet in their bones, these men know that the end of this line of hollow conquests will be a terrible and infinite darkness. Also the good bit in them wants them to *lose* the battles, in order that they may be forced to abandon their shallow and blighted careers.

'At school, we performed Euripides' play *Electra*,' said Innogen haltingly. 'Now Euripides was not satisfied – as was Æschylus – with the notion that the mother-murder could be simply ascribed to duty in obeying a god-given command. He wants to know what *sort* of woman could premeditatedly commit this act. This matricide, this killing of one whom nature says we should love, is a dire sin and a mind-deranging horror. No god of light could demand this, he seems to say, only a supernatural demon – which is a personification of other influences ... such as feelings of bitterness or envy or seeing your youth wasted. It is a womanly revenge sprung from desperate hopes or false oracles which tell her she has been wronged. “Electra” means “the unbedded one” or “unmated” ... I suppose “unsatisfied” and hence haunted, poisoned, intolerant of poverty, constantly brooding about love and hate.’

Innogen herself was the antithesis of all this. Her life was characterised largely by abstinence from thrills. Her time was spent heating up a tin of soup or writing out a page of music. And asceticism opens up springs of quiet succour. God took centre-stage in many of her thoughts and consequently her external circumstances seemed less important to her than they would have to most of her contemporaries.

* * *

In the tenuous gloom of the unlit stable-yard, Artemis straddled the Aermacchi’s hard pappi-filled leather saddle as it stood there in its wraith-like greyey-silver hues. Her gauntlets filled with dangerous fingers, clutched fiercely the handle-bar grips, whilst she raised her right leg and then her entire cast heedlessly onto the kick-start, ready to set out and destroy the ostensible cause of all her misery. As the engine erupted into angry life and Artemis urged the bike forward off its stand, she felt an almost masculine prowess surge through her leather-encased body.

The temperature had just dipped below zero and a thin mist pervaded the night, intensifying the darkness and making it penetratingly cold and damp. But Artemis felt snug and formidable as she rode out past a pile of dirty refreezing slush, where her father had cleared some snow and the dark loch and the dripping trees. Something of a breeze had sprung up too.

The time was a quarter past eleven, too early strictly speaking, but she would use the surplus up in making a meticulous and scrupulous approach, dealing with any impertinent hindrances or even just lying in wait. Her suit’s pockets carried her spare keys, her watch, some money and her pistol.

Along the eerie half-reconstructed track, skirting planks and pyramids of road-stone and pools of mud, went the Aermacchi, welded together as one with its aggressive mistress, whose entire moral disinhibition shaped them into a fearful and pitiless unity.

Out on the two-lane main road she increased her speed. The tall black pines on either side swayed and swished in the windy night, whilst Artemis in the swathe cut between them felt supreme. It would be another flawlessly executed foray – it *had* to be! The coarse vibrations of the high performance engine were transmitted up through the handle-bars to her shaking arms and via the saddle and her wide leather-covered rear to the rest of her frame, giving her a thrill similar to the canter before an impending cavalry charge. No other vehicles shared the road with her. In the distance she saw a hint of moonlight in a navy blue opening at the end of the forest.

Artemis throttled back minimally. The illuminated sign of the Annoch Lodge Guest House was easily visible and set back from the road were the rebuilt two-storey office and the long low building with a couple of faint lights glowing inside. On the gravelly forecourt four cars were parked, grey in the paltry artificial light but with one resembling that which Simon had driven. A third of a mile further on, where the bridleway should have joined the road by piercing a broken stone wall, a new vehicular entrance was under construction. The two sweeps of kerbstone were in place and the unmade-up surface between them, marked off from the main road with a few grey cones, dipped down and out of sight.

On she drove without slowing, downhill with the trees opening out and an odd crag overlooking the numerous bends, until a couple of miles further on she saw a small meadow with an open gate. She braked almost to a stop, did a U-turn and swung into this fallow field, pulling up behind a dense hedgerow and switching off the engine and lights.

Last summer, she recollected, there had been a planning permission controversy about establishing an outward-bound school on the old Slegarrie Brick Company's land behind Annoch Lodge. The plan had included a camping site, hostel, facilities for rock climbing and abseiling on Ben Greet, canoe training in the flooded marl pit, orienteering in the forest and so on. Clearly it had gone ahead, but would there be anyone there, a night-watchman or a warden in a temporary residence? 'Damn it,' she seethed. These locations needed to be reconnoitred first in daylight.

On both sides of the road near Annoch Lodge – though set back ten or twenty yards – continuous fencing stretched for miles. As she had no intention of walking all the way from here, she would just have to pull off onto that half-made road, roll down it as quietly as possible and hope that either it was deserted or that no one heard her.

The mist had become patchy. A waning moon, between a half and a quarter and veiny and looking poorly, shone dully and intermittently down on Artemis in her field. It seemed larger and nearer than usual though, as if curious.

Artemis, more familiar now with her snazzy bike's controls, leapt up to restart it. She did this a second time and a third. A telegraph pole seemed to be watching her. If you were on a push-bike and it punctured, it did not matter beyond the inconvenience as you had not set yourself up as some supreme invincible deity, hence there was no humiliation ... but here? It started on the fourth kick. 'You were just in time,' she muttered dourly to it. 'But next time that won't be good enough. I expect you to start first time ... in fact perhaps simply at my command, without my even doing anything.'

She returned towards Annoch Lodge. Some way before, she switched off the lights and rode warily by the faint metallic green light of the moon. Then she cut the engine and coasted, before pulling off between the dimly seen cones onto the new road. The gradient served her. She rolled gingerly down the hill as it swerved gradually round to the left. The gallium-green pall of moonlight made the rank weeds and matted grass appear to have been anodised with silver and even the shapes of the churned-up mud looked like something precious and coated in chrome. Roots, leaves ... all seemed to be frozen or sleeping, but were they really only in a bewitched trance under Simon's spell, waiting to come to life and trip her or ensnare her at his bidding? Everything here might be on his side, but she did not care – she would take on everything and win!

On her left the dome-shaped kilns slid by, almost submerged in undergrowth of jungle-like density. Her tyres sometimes crunched softly over stones, sometimes ploughed their path through a thin coating of mud. On her right came the foundations and the beginnings of walls of two buildings, a darkened fibre-glass portable office, a cement mixer, a hose, a stack of timber and some pallets laden with breeze-blocks – the usual spread of a building site.

At the end of this sketched-out snake of road was a patch of raw earth where a tracked shovel stood with one of its cab windows glinting in the moonlight and beyond it and its drum of diesel oil, a couple of bushes. Artemis thought to conceal her Aermacchi in the tufty grass and heather between these two spreading thickets and here began the inevitable sequels to her heaven-abhorred arrogance.

The moon faded behind a cloud. Artemis unexpectedly felt the front wheel dip down into a ditch, not previously visible from a distance because it was screened by thistles. She stamped on the brake, which turned out to be the gear-pedal and so too late, rammed on the real brakes. The bike was tilted too steeply downwards for her to hope to push it back out, so she allowed it to complete its descent into the trough.

The traitorous moon reappeared.

Artemis did not swear, but her heart thumped with an ominous force. She sat astride the saddle as if mesmerised by her monstrously antagonistic fate, though secretively and subconsciously she had expected opposition. It resembled the night she had become stuck whilst trying to leave for Robert Falcus's trivial audition, except that then her sin was fresh and not fully ripened. Then as now, she had sallied out *not* under Mr Letheren's auspices, but she would win without him! She must prove to herself that that were possible. And this time she would not weep. She was a real woman now, ready to clap her hands together and throw her head back with derisive mirth.

But before she could move against Simon, she had to extricate her motorcycle and she wanted to avoid starting it up. She tried to push it up the side at an oblique angle, but she lacked the physical strength and no matter how she heaved and cursed and grunted, it made only minor progress and then it skidded down sideways again.

Next she thought to build a ramp for it, so she walked up and down to the piles of building materials four times, for two long planks and some bricks to support them at their mid-point. But either the plank twisted over at the crucial moment or she missed her footing and slipped or her boot became entangled in weeds or her strength failed her at some awkward angle. When it slithered down on its side for the eighth time, her anger knew no bounds. 'I'm not being pissed on like some play-thing,' she simmered, falling onto her knees in some icy dock leaves. Her arms and thighs quivered with violent rage. 'I'm not going to be made low ... sweating, shoving, humping bricks like a slave ... ' she breathed furiously.

Deciding to pause and think, she rolled onto her back, lying flat in the shallow ditch and staring up past the tops of weeds and trees to the clouds and the moon. How many other girls in Britain would be doing anything like this this night? You could probably count them on the fingers of one hand. The place seemed silent yet aware.

She wondered if the foreman's hut might be a listening post, placed purposely to intercept and monitor her defeat? No, that was ridiculous. There was no real reason to suspect human presence. There were no lights anywhere, no parked cars with managers screwing their secretaries inside and Annoch Lodge was perhaps half a mile away across acres of saplings and rubble and weeds. Yet Artemis sensed that Nature was looking on with a silently supercilious grace, even perhaps the faintest whisper of disparaging laughter, as she struggled and stumbled and sprawled herself headlong on the base earth.

She stood up and eyed the dim abject outline of her bike. 'You are *going* to move,' she murmured her dire threat slowly, 'because I am Artemis Boden and *nothing* is going to thwart me!'

The tracked shovel up above her caught her eye. It seemed to have eyes and to be exuding a quiet sneer. She waded up towards it, climbed onto one of its tracks and searched in its engine with a gauntleted hand, until she seized hold of some ignition wires and ripped them out. She sat in the cold dark comfortless cab and with a spanner, found accidentally by sitting on it, smashed its gauges and dials. With that slow motion of unquenchable rage she strode up to the foreman's cabin, took up a brick and hurled it against the glass window of its door. Being made of perspex though, it made the brick rebound harmlessly. She savagely tried the handle of this site office door and found it had been unlocked all the time. By feel and the vaguest of shadows, she found a bag of sugar with the tea-making commodities. She walked elegantly back to the loading shovel and standing on one of its tracks again, she emptied this kilogram of white crystalline granules into the fuel tank, so that when run the engine would gum itself up with sticky burnt carbonised sugar.

'So you sodding bulldozer, you don't laugh at me again or I'll completely beat you up.'

On reviewing her motorbike's predicament, she decided that if she started it she might coax it to propel itself up the less steep wrong side of the ditch. It would then end up on a shelf, but if she made an opening in a crumbling rough stone wall she could then drive it round over safe ground and using part of the old unbulldozed bridleway, return to the spot where she wished to park it. She would just have to chance that no one would climb out of bed or bother to investigate a minute or two of her bike's engine revving.

She walked over the route to ensure that no more traps had been rigged up to trick her and then lifted out twenty sharp-edged irregular mossy stones from the wall to make a gap in it. As she undertook this labour, she saw above her the blotchy green one third moon and the light blue pin-pricks of stars in the blue-black sky and further down the hill, a pathway of glittering light clove the water of the flooded marl pit and made some small islands in it look like giants' stepping-stones across a platinum lake.

Artemis righted her racer.

Out of the blue she felt good again and mounting her scintillating grey and silver bike in her shiny black protective attire, an air of discreet hubris and toughness and challenge surged into her features. She took off her hat which marred her feminine beauty, her hand flipped out the kick-start, she put the gears into neutral and paused.

Throwing out an ominous smile – like a gauntlet of defiance to the world – she kicked the kick-starter down savagely. It started.

The thin spears of moonlight gleamed both on the bike's grey gloss and polished steel and on her subtly lustrous pitch-black leather.

'Right, you are going to do what Artemis tells you. If you *dare* heed Collett's wishes, that mis erable male, I'll leather you to liquid metal, I'll frazzle you to a scrap-heap. If you *dare* to disobey me in my tough black leather, I'll leather you into milk tins ... into atoms ... !'

Artemis undid her suit's collar-piece, tucked in the loose ends of her headscarf and fastened it again. She adjusted her pose so as to be bent taut and low over the steed, her breasts almost touching the petrol tank, her round rear well back on the saddle and her thighs splayed. After she had engaged first gear, she placed her widely spaced feet again beside the rear wheel and twisted the throttle with great determination.

Her irate fingers slowly released the clutch lever. Without lights the Aermacchi growled along the ditch. She veered it deliberately to the right and then swerved to the left across the bottom of the trough, before attempting with a frenziedly shrill engine note to free her trapped charger from this hole. With jockey-like expletives and urgings it just made it. Its rider helped it over the one residual layer of stones in the breached wall and then accelerated it over the rough ling-swathed slopes to where she had originally meant to be and switched off its ignition.

As she eased it back onto its stand between the two bushes, she congratulated herself on the good effect of her blunt menaces and immense will-power. She felt decidedly satisfied. She had shown that she *could* win, if only she demonstrated sufficient resolve.

Standing beside her dark warm machine, she took off her gauntlets and rested them on the saddle. A pleasantly cooling breeze flowed round her. Unzipping her left groin pocket, she took out her watch and peered closely at it. It said a quarter past one. Perfect! She would have a snack and then advance on foot to the guest house. She ought to arrive there at about two or just after, which was exactly as she had planned.

Unlashing her two bags, she extracted a well-earned tin of grapefruit juice and a thin bar of bitter dark chocolate.

* * *

As Innogen walked through Glasgow's tomb-like streets, deserted except for the occasional drunkard, she remembered how when small she had stood on a troopship's upper deck with Catharine – for the officers' cabins were the best ones – watching a crane swing a selvagee of kitbags across from the dock-side to the hold. One kitbag had fallen into the water and the sergeant-major supervising it all had roared with laughter. When they had arrived in Libya though, it was the men who had done the laughing, for the missing kitbag turned out to be the sergeant-major's. Her sister and she had had the top deck practically to themselves to play on – a far cry from modern sardine-like cruise liners. She could still see too the great Rock of Gibraltar passing by in a morning haze.

She had left Christiane's at about one o'clock, but on entering her own flat at a quarter past she felt strangely sleepless. She changed into a pair of Prussian blue cotton pyjamas, made a cup of tea and toasted a muffin.

On her sitting-room wall, as she sat by the light of a lone candle, a gaily coloured reproduction Italian Renaissance painting set on wood of some musicians and singers in a palace garden glinted and looked down upon her.

Britain had broken her treaty obligations in not using both her infantry and tanks from the Tobruk area and her fighter squadrons based there, to oust al-Qaddafi's followers and restore King Idris. The government of the day in London had been so corrupt and infiltrated as to be incapable of any bold or forthright action. Downing Street – with its seedy self-seeking and suspicious associates, all seemingly with links to KGB officers in London – had decided simply to pull out. Was that failure partly responsible for Nicholas's death? Had that sullen and rather anti-European people been abandoned to a wrong régime and that in turn spawned its curse's reward?

She tried to say her little rosary of Paternosters and Ave Marias, but found it unduly hard to concentrate.

The neighbouring flat's occupants had some music on and as often happens, the faintly heard tones seemed sweeter and more mellifluous than the piece properly heard would have done.

As Innogen's mind imagined exquisite cadences and sweet-sounding arcs of soaring beauty, she seemed to move up a path on the side of a mountain, higher and higher until she reached the peak in an ever more tranquil and benign light. From this high aiguille she could see many lands and cities and palaces. She saw lush forests and arenaceous wastes, tossing oceans and coloured birds, all tamed and all comprehensible. She saw a Ptolemaic court and a Seleucid king on a terrace, heard foreign tongues and the noises of cave-men and as the varied fire and meaning of every age coalesced into a single and flawless entity with all prejudices and wrongs perfectly cancelling one another out, something hovered behind her left shoulder.

Innogen felt afraid and dared not turn round.

She saw Artemis, in whom differing elements both did and did not want to kill her loved ones – for no one is wholly evil – and in a leather outfit she was indulging in a tantrum which would be impossible in more ordinary clothing.

Something was behind her still – no cowardly minister nor moribund official sent by an unsupernal legal system, but a strange and soliform light. A weak roseate glow in the window was perhaps a reflection of it.

'Innogen?'

'Yes?'

'The suppliant who asked for vengeance upon her brother's slayers?'

'Yes.'

'It has been done as you wished.'

The sun of just spirits, immured in its holy hill, had shone out.

Innogen permitted herself a small breath.

And as she sat in the wake of being touched by something very good and very great, her solemn and sovereign countenance darkened. She asked too, for her who had been the instrument of revenge, that tonight her wickedness would come to a head and the trail of exoneration and forgiveness begin.

'Tonight, would her bubble be pricked.'

* * *

Artemis had zipped her watch back into her suit's left pocket, deposited the chocolate wrapper, the empty drink tin and her hat in the plastic bag and was shouldering her handbag and preparing to pull on her gauntlets, when a voice from nowhere said, 'Good evening.'

She nearly fell over with shock.

A feeble torch beam flickered on and moved hesitantly up and down her sensually sinister shape. Her right hand slid down to her thigh pocket for her pistol, whilst her left hand fumbled in her handbag for *her* torch. She shone it at them. Two pink oval faces were dimly discernible four yards away. Whilst their torch played on the Aermacchi, she slipped out her pistol and held it behind her back.

Unknown to Artemis the stony slope behind the new buildings was being used by a public school army cadet force for a winter training camp. The thirty-strong contingent in their eight tents had heard nothing until the shrill screams of the 344 c.c. engine had rent the night. Then one of the two masters and the S.U.O. had pulled on a few clothes with a weary but necessary inquisitiveness, for there had been some I.R.A. activity on the British mainland recently.

Artemis imagined that these spectators had witnessed her embarrassingly mortal efforts in the ditch and heard her obscene utterances. They had watched her damage the mechanical shovel, spotted her motorcycle without a number-plate and most inexcusable of all, seen her being humbled by fate.

Maddened and heartless, she strode two paces towards them and shot them almost without a qualm, for no one could be allowed to live who had seen her perversely mishandled by nature. Four silenced shots from a wobbly right hand despatched these curs, but the first flash of orange flame which momentarily lit up the twosome, gave the second target a chance to bellow a warning to the field below and his sleeping-bag-engulfed comrades. His yell ended with a tailing off, yet deeply pervasive groan.

Yet her shooting was unsteady. Both were clipped by each of two bullets but not fatally wounded. She kicked the bodies with a snarl, as from a mere three hundred yards away came urgent shouts from the secretly bivouacked sleepers. Patches of light moved behind canvas walls and kindled shafts of torch-light jerked visibly about in the open.

'Damnation,' mouthed Artemis in an extended syllable, as she hastily relashed her bags back on to the bike's rack, resheathed her pistol, tugged on her gauntlets and sprang astride her bike. It failed to start until the fifth kick and Artemis leaping furiously up and down on it, scowled like Richard III over her shoulder at her closing multitude of foes on Bosworth Field.

Despite a near paroxysm of temper, on the pretext of self-preservation, she elected to abandon her real quarry that night. She had downed two more of Simon's acolytes – the stage-manager himself, the régisseur, could wait till another day. She must retreat temporarily from this unnumbered army of puerile males.

The police coming from Newton Stewart would take at very least fifteen minutes, so logically she ought to have gone home as swiftly as possible via the main road, but as one of the cadet force's Land Rovers started up somewhere down beside Airiekells Bundle Plantation, a dread of being rammed came upon her. She feared too – wrongly – that the boy soldiers' leaders might be armed and she believed from their shouts, that they were closer to locating her and cutting her off than they were.

She therefore chose the cross-country route, the once familiar bridleway which led to the southern tip of Loch Eilan after a distance of three or four miles and which was too narrow for a four-wheeled vehicle.

Off she set, skidding slightly in a deep splodgy rut made by an excavator's wheels, causing droplets of liquid mud to fly up and speckle her pure black leather boots and thighs. She entered the old and seldom used path between an amputated hedge and a wall. It was waist-high in kelk and rosebay and with a floor alternately turfy and sticky. With moderate agility she steered her motorised beast downhill, through a pebble-filled clear burn and then uphill along this track as it climbed over the tapering lower slopes of the Rig of Deesmoor. Beside it were odd rocks between one and four feet tall, lying amid ferns and broom. The path had irregular and sometimes slippery hidden bumps and ten miles per hour was a realistic maximum speed. Tufts of gorse scratched at her legs and as she strained to see the way ahead, she thought for an instant that she saw pink stars in a deep blue heaven. Tired fencing posts and the bared boughs of winter bushes appeared to have the deep black-brown colour of polished ebony in the fitful moonlight, but otherwise – apart from the occasional cobwebby grey edges of boulders – a featureless black sea hid the clues to the earthly maze before her.

Yet as the motorcycle mowed a thin swathe through the wilted weeds of late December, at a lurching but steady second-gear pace and she successfully distanced herself from the swarm of disturbed ants, she grew angry with herself for having shown fear. Her subconscious had wanted her to flee, because it saw that in failure and humiliation lay the release from this unending night. Her conscious hubris might be bent on victory or annihilation, but near to the brink her almost suffocated soul made her irrationally incur defeat, because then only could she be saved and a gradual restoration of light found.

'I'm braver than you, Collett, you master sorcerer, because to counter my plots you have to use legions and in the field even then you don't win. I'll take you on and all my other relentless foes.'

Yet however much Simon might control things outside her, it could not be his fault that she had felt afraid. Also, she inexplicably 'forgot' to look out for a side track to the left, missed it and immediately found herself slithering down a steep squelchy gully with her wheels locked and her heels gouging the mud to help her brake. She came to rest a few yards before a tiny bridge of three rotting railway sleepers over the smallest of streamlets and the motorbike stalled.

The track she had passed had led round to the woods on the western side of Loch Eilan. She should have taken that path round to Uanrig House, driven the racing bike into the loch and then gone inside and put on a night-dress. Then if a police search-party had come she could have opened a window and looked bewildered, for at this stage there was no reason to connect the occupant of Uanrig with the shootings. The Aermacchi would never make it back up the slope which she had just skidded down, nor was it possible to ride or even walk round close to the loch's western shore, for there were many acres of dense head-high briars there, impenetrable even to this wild goddess in her daring and resilient leather.

Again she saw that Simon could not be blamed for this error. It had been *her* decision, *her* oversight. With this thought came the disclosure that her mind was at war with itself. Some rebellious fragment had undermined her all along. It was not just that regardless of what she selected to do, Collett's knaves and sprites had every angle covered, there was treachery inside the fortress as well. The besieging army outside had the clandestine support of the strategists within. Suddenly she knew that nothing mattered anymore, that she had inevitably lost ... yet ... her reckless pride refused to allow the surreptitious saboteurs to conquer. She would burn the citadel herself and take these good fairies with her.

The damp night air was subglacial. Freezing vapour condensed onto her black rippling leather suit's colder outer surface as dew, to make it sparkle magnificently in the moonlight. Only her boots had lost their gleam, their lower halves being caked with mud.

She raised a smooth bulbous-thighed frog-like leg up onto the starter to jerk her mount back into life. At the first kick it spluttered unpromisingly. She fiddled in its innards, opening the choke a little and trying sweet thoughts whilst stroking its petrol tank fondly a couple of times. 'Perhaps instead of a man, I could live with you?' she said. Her bike would not be an equal of course, but a well-treated vassal – just like a man in fact. A couple more effortful kicks still produced no real signs of life.

She knew that its failure to start was not really a mechanical hitch. True a motor engineer might look at it afterwards and say, 'Oh, the sproggle pin's worked loose', but the deeper question was, 'Who had made the sproggle pin work loose?' No, this was spiritual. It was a war between her and the insolent and uncurtailed fairies who lived in the rocks, between her and fate. She knew too that both this motorcycle and her defiant leather were very closely linked to her pride and arrogance.

Why were girls so weak? Why was she not a male as well as a female? Why did she not have a big penis like men, to fuck everything which obstructed her? Why did women feel so incomplete alone and only able to fulfil their ambitions through the agencies of men? She would have to use her clitoris to fuck with. This was her penile missile, her male assault gun. She felt it stiffen and elongate and she imagined it to be larger and more throbbing than it was, ready to attack and destroy things, like males did with their penises. Her whipped-up tensions were demanding release.

Was the mud gloating? Were the rocks sniggering? So what? She would return soon and beat them up. Nothing was going to put her down! Even if the gods were involved she would not surrender. She would take them all on.

A remote klaxon squawked in the clear night.

She sat forward on the saddle and leant forwards over the handle-bars, so that the pommel at the front end of the broad hard leather seat chafed her vulva slightly. As the bike rolled slightly forwards, propelled by her feet, a minimum of friction and rocking initiated an orgasm and instantly she felt less impotent. A surge of crude relaxation flooded through her and she felt gloriously and perilously poised beside some dark abyss of limitless pleasure.

'Be good to me,' she whispered gently to the Aermacchi. 'You can have sex as often as you like with me, Artemis, the ultimate in feminine sexiness.'

She raised herself up for another superhuman endeavour to depress the start-lever with vigour and this time the engine fired up and burst into action. So, finally she was ready to move off over the narrow bridge and down the last hundred yards to the loch's shore's southernmost point.

She advanced to a strip of muddy gravel beside the lapping surface of the loch. The slopping of the wavelets, rushing inside her ears, produced a ravishing magical effect. Artemis felt that ensconced in such a pure domain, free from the man-made foulness of cities and towns, that she too must be pure. At this spot eleven and a half years ago, she, her mother and her aunt had come by rowing-boat for a picnic. It had been a lovely sunny day – rare for Scotland – with wild roses everywhere and the scents of honeysuckle pervading the breeze and even the usually clayey ground had been dry and cracked.

The banks round Loch Eilan fell more steeply into the water at this southern end than at the flatter and more open northern end.

The terrain's contours in this region were formed by the gashed and eroded underlying rock. It determined the layout of ridges and lochs. In the hollows and on the less exposed slopes, a smearing of bluish-grey clay had been left by the last passing glacier and because of the currently wet winter, this was very water-logged and this present night had not yet frozen it.

Even now Artemis's most sensible course would have been to run her charger into the water here and be rid of it, walk back up the gully and turn back onto the missed track, which ran along above the dense brambles until it lost itself on the more open forest floor. Then she could follow the shore round for two and a half miles and reach her home. It was the shortest route.

The fragrance of her own perfume washed around her. She wantonly mulled over unbounded obscenities to tease and subdue that part of her which had so treasonably risen up on the meritless Collett's side. She smiled as she guessed at what would be happening in the area about her. They would never put her in a cage. She would die first. A light tinkling laugh flowed artificially from her lips. Simon had visited her yesterday morning in a pair of *rubber* boots! How did anyone who wore anything as pathetic as rubber, expect to win against her in her tough black leather? 'He will never uncork me. I'll let anyone else in, but not him. And why aren't all his vile little elves grateful to me for postponing his execution?' She glared wildly about. 'Or do you see that as marking a fatal weakness in me?'

She dismounted, propped the bike against a lone tree and climbed astride a vast rock. 'You might please me, if you stuffed a slippery spike into my craving and lovely form,' she said to it, shuffling up and down and daring fate with her outrageous wrongness. 'I don't give a toss any more! I'll do whatever I like.'

What did it matter what befell her anyway? And besides, those nurses in North Shields were always at it – horizontal sport with any priapic male to hand – two layers of hot meat separated by a cheesy sauce, like lasagne. Why should only she be chaste?

Despite the morass of sturdy thorns to her left, to her right on the eastern shore, the trees came all the way down to the water's edge. She intended to ride along the sloping floor of this pine hanger with its masses of exposed but scarcely visible gnarled roots, up to the northern end of the loch and then walk back down the western side to her house.

She knew that her bike's high-revving engine would greatly help any search parties in locating her, yet furtively she craved the thrill of confrontation. She could not bear to sit still a moment longer. She did not merely anticipate difficulties, she self-deceivingly sought them.

She jumped down onto the saddle once more and raised herself up onto the kick-start, but her soiled boot slipped off. She swore. She kicked it over four times without result. She closed the choke, in case she had flooded it. After further fruitless kicks she paused. A conflagration of anger seized her, accompanied by deep tempestuous breathing and a furious tremor. She gripped her rebellious charger as if ready to murder it, kicked its engine violently with the heel of her riding boot and swirled round looking for a rock with which to strike it and pay it back for this rash effrontery. Unable to see one, she pounded the petrol tank with her fist, leapt on it again and after another dozen vicious stamps on the starting lever, it reluctantly but finally complied. Her unbridled sexual ire again set off an uncultivated and prolonged orgasm inside her. 'You abject disloyal slave,' she seethed, 'You do as I say!'

Without lights still, for the moon was at last cowed and faithful to its mistress's commands, she steered the obstreperous Aermacchi round to the right and moved off under the canopy of tittering pines, but immediately became stuck in a boggy depression where another tiny burn crept noiselessly and unseen into the loch amid a few clumps of reeds.

Once again though, it seemed that with grit and an inflexible strength of mind, she could sway the matter in her favour. Crouched tenaciously over her ripping ranting beast, it slowly clawed its way out of this shallow ravine and up between the erect stately tree trunks. The thrill of raging unceasingly, of rubbing and tweaking her distended clitoris up and down on the smooth leather saddle, of adding new crescendos on top of still unabated ones, welled inside her pelvis in a gross burning cataclysm. She meant to sustain this until she, Artemis Oenone Boden, had thrashed and thwarted all of Simon's upstart fays.

With judicious idlings and cautious accelerations she pressed on for about two miles parallel to the eastern shore, though with frequent downward slips of one wheel or the other under the black panoply of interlocking branches. The moonlight on the face of the water could be seen down and to her left, like a wispy silver dust.

Then there came a stretch of shore line where there was an enclave of ancient blackthorn bushes, a salient in the pines. If she kept far enough up the incline, she could skirt round above the upper limit of this recess and to achieve this, she angled the Aermacchi just slightly more up the slope. After some progress the rear wheel suddenly spun and skidded off an ultra-slippery root and Artemis was thrown down on the uphill side of the 344.

She sat there unharmed with a tolerant if slightly slit-eyed smile, as she glanced about for some tangible kelpie. The moon feebly illumined her darkly pale and flinty face and under it, her sheer black leather also mirrored it resplendently. With her doubly gloved hands she tried to grip the offending root and tear it out of the ground ready to leather it to pulp, but her mailed slender extremities could not hold it firmly enough. Then her foot inadvertently dislodged her bike, which started to slide slowly and erratically down towards the clusters of heavily intertwined blackthorns. 'Stop,' she commanded it amiably, but it ignored her.

Softened by distance, another pair of unabrasive intermingling and discordant klaxons reached her ears.

'I don't care a cuss,' she smiled genially again. 'No army's going to overrun the court of the Empress Artemis.'

A knotty root pressed innoxiously into her left hip. She stood up on the matted pine needles and mounds of clay, tried unsuccessfully to brush some wet soil of her suit's rear and then half-slid and half-walked sideways down the slope to where her bike had come to rest against the wickedly barbed thickets. With splenetic exertions and profane rhetoric, she pulled it upright and then when she had bounced up and down on it again twenty times, it eventually deigned to start. But there was no room to manoeuvre, the gradient here was particularly steep – not the fifteen degrees so far encountered but nearer thirty – and the need to move up the line of greatest slope in order to leave this little pocket and clear the next clump of thorns, made the task nigh impossible.

'Mooovvveee!!!!' She nearly burst in a climax of choking fury and for one miraculous instant, it seemed that she had done it.

They began to growl and crawl out of their notch, the front wheel on the verge of being lifted up in the air. But even her will-power was not quite enough. The engine stalled and they slipped backwards, the rear tyre hit a thick spike-laden stem and with a short 'Pssss,' punctured. They toppled over and she found herself prone on the hard slimy-silken clay which had caused this disaster. 'You offending filth,' she purred, her lips only an inch from it.

Rolling onto her side, she wrenched at the pannier-frame's straps, ripping one of its buckles off as she did so. She tore free her handbag and slung it over her head like a bandolier. A thin whippy branch with long thin prongs snatched at her neck-scarf and rent it. Incensed, she turned over and for a brief minute fought this contemptible bush as if it were Collett himself. It was after all, an extension of him. It was yet another of his minions. She clutched at it and kneed it and elbowed it repeatedly like a crazed and bucking Bacchante.

'Sod you, you vicious and unremitting thorns!!! How dare you bugger up my plans and not Simon's or Innogen's? Answer me! Who controls you?'

When Simon wanted her to be somewhere, such as at home yesterday morning, she of course was. When she wanted him somewhere, she could not arrange it.

The sprouting creepers seemed to be suddenly looping themselves round her legs and tangling with her arms. She fumed in a renewed and even more livid fit. 'Why is everything pissing on me? I'm going to piss back!'

With gasping yet almost enjoyable hatred she felt and heard these pricks scratching and poking at her. 'I shall win by black magic and my infallible black leather.' It really did not matter what tried to thwart her. She was just going to prevail.

She reflected that when she had set off to Sir Robert Falcus's party and become stuck, she had sat down and wept. There was no danger of weeping this time. Artemis had come a long way. Now it was an exciting and bold paradisiac to be struggling ceaselessly with fate, where every battle was akin to a new shot of nepenthe for an addict. Nothing mattered any more, just absolutely nothing. Consideration of the Robert Falcus fiasco though, did prompt her to brood on the perfidy of the Spirit of the Mine. It had promised to shield her, to make her the Queen of Night and where was she now?

She forced her way through a thinner screen of thorns – going backwards to shield her face – then as she turned, in front of her lay a steep drop with a patch of black nothingness at its foot and the glistening lake beyond. A large black crow flapped noisily up, its wings creaking as if it had hinges which needed oiling. She sat down on the rocky edge and pushed off like a skier on a ski-jump, intending to slither down on her feet and bottom, but a prominent branch jutting out from this face, caught one of her boots and like a stung horse bucking, or as if catapulted by a judo throw, she turned a somersault and landed eight feet below on her back, cracking a slender branch as she fell on it.

Quite unhurt, she lay on her back in a soft spongy bed of motley wet icy thistles, growing on a damp swampy expanse of soil. She sat up and squirmed round and some smaller twigs snapped.

Three flashing blue lights threw sweeping wands across the loch, like luminous helicopter blades beneath the water. She watched them move along the last stretch of track on the opposite shore, up to Uanrig House.

She stood up. The mire squelched a little underfoot. She waded briefly in the shallows of the loch to dissolve some of the thickest ooze off her boots and with her shredded scarf wiped some of the dirt off her gauntlets before flinging it away.

The hiatus in the trees here occurred because the ruins of a castle intruded. The foundations of a circular tower and a short length of wall had been almost certainly abandoned before construction had proceeded very far. It appeared on no map.

Artemis walked across the thistle-carpeted mud, aware as well of her Chloé perfume, of the acidy eggy smell of the gas bubbles being freed as her boots squeezed the saturated ground. She reached up to the edge of loosened rubble of the wide-topped circular tower base and after several attempts, heaved herself up onto its disintegrating and bramble-enveloped flattish surface. She hotched round on this thorny uneven masonry, her feet dangling over the loch into which it protruded and her back against the revetment of spilling briars, until on its opposite side she jumped down, tripped and fell onto her knees in yet more briars.

The now stationary artificial blue lights flashed distantly and coldly from outside her home, outshining the weak moon.

Artemis felt contented and more sure of herself again and even sexy in a placid sort of way. She recited to herself a piece from the translation of Luise Gottsched's *The Siege of Corinth*, where Psammetichus realises that destiny intends Corinth to be destroyed by her revolting colonies.

'Splendour here would have
No virtue on this wicked hill.
The gods' admonishment is more
Far-seeing than the hopes of men.
In Ionice will I trust
And take Ogygian puissance from
This scene. Let mad inglory reek
And ruin come. Let Eurytis
With hate and animosity,
Lasciviously and power-crazed,
Then steer to its intended doom
Our town and all her wayward flock –
For in one omnipotent hand
Is all and so I fear no more.'

She pressed on along the water's edge, her boots sucking at the bog and leaving black holes behind them. She met a barrier, three rusty strands of barbed-wire on rotting posts. She sat heavily on the top wire to bend it down, straddled it and so stood in Uanrig Estate. On she went through the more thinly spaced trees. It bored her, all this tedious walking. She craved some new contest.

Could she ring up Simon in the morning and invite him to breakfast at Uanrig and then murder him? No, it was too late for that.

Her easy indifference started to ebb away again. She felt supreme and perfect and formidable. A small amount of pleasantly warm sticky exudate had been secreted by her sex glands and moistened her panties. 'My penis is bigger than Simon's,' she said and by perpetual repetition of such phrases, she induced yet again into her body those heightened pre-sex urges and compensated for having no man inside her.

There was one way still to rescue herself from all this. She would compel the Spirit of the Mine to give her her dues. She was no less a god than it. Her egotheistic fury would surpass all bounds. She would enter its sacred cave, which last time she had not dared to do. She would grapple with it and defile its abode in uninhibited war, from which there could be no turning back. She should not die in shame and utter disgrace, but conquer the whole world. She would soon finish off too, all those stupid blue-bottles who were prowling round her house. Artemis was not going to allow it. When the Spirit of the Mine was sorted out, chaos would break loose on all her enemies. She ran into a small tree stump, knelt down and hooked herself up on it. A mild discrete feeling inside her lower body told her that spontaneous sex was again imminent.

She saw a torch beam. She heard an oath as a burly Scottish police sergeant's foot sank into some unseen peaty water. The thin constable with him took care not to laugh.

Artemis lay flat on some mossy grass behind a tree trunk and an ugly straggly bush. A puff of cold wind blew off the loch. The ground was freezing. The tinglings of fulfilment still racked her body. She removed a gauntlet and took out her pistol, an act which this time seemed to be psychically coupled to her orgiastic writhings. As fatso's bulky body loomed closer and an outline took shape, Artemis took aim and squeezed the trigger. It refused to budge. The ill-equipped officers moved obliviously by. Shc flared up, still unable to fire it, repocketed it and put her gauntlet back on.

She crept on, deeper into the police net, approaching the northern end of the loch where the Eilan Burn trickled into it. She moved further away from the water, deeper into the cover of the trees. She knelt down behind a weed-sprouting rock to fix her bearings. The moon had vanished behind wind-driven clouds. The eerie pulses of blue light revolved above her. She moved behind a small ridge and proceeded north-westerly, until treading on non-existent ground, she fell into the scooped-out gorge where the Eilan Burn ran.

A dense matt blanket of blackness obliterated her sight. The Spirit of the Mine was at hand and trying to repel her. But nothing frightened or curbed her now. She stood up and strode cautiously forwards, like one on a rope being lowered into a void of deep and drowning darkness. She felt her way with her hands between a jumble of gritty boulders. She slithered on a slimy flat rock in the stream and bruised her elbow and well-padded hip. This was it. Here Artemis in her black leather must be avenged on *all* her enemies. She stood up only to slip immediately again and sit in a marsh of greasy liquidy sludge. She clambered over a fallen tree. It sparked off her umpteenth wave of escalating fire, a cyclical hay-wire convulsion which made all her giblets burn within her. These contractions became so shocking and excruciating this time as to seemingly numb other parts of her body. She crawled shakily across the plateau. A twig poked her in the face. Her rasping breath drowned out the tinkling waters of the burn. As if a fifty pound block of lead were on her back, she struggled on through the oozy weeds using her leather elbows and knees to propel her form inefficiently forwards. She hauled herself over the flat altar stone. Creepers tried to obstruct her ingress into the thick black choking denseness which surrounded the unbounded darkness where she knew the mine adit to be. Hissing with implacable rage, she groped her way in inch by inch.

'Out of my way, you miscreants! I've a bone to pick with your lying master.'

Her head could have been inside a box for all she could see. Her slime covered leather suit and gloves scraped over the once hewn galena. She smelt the minerally dampness and lay still awhile, resting her wool-covered chin on an undirtied part of her crooked leather forearms. Her heart beat so rapidly.

'You have been weak,' said a soft voice with a slight echo. 'You have failed.'

'Come here you swindling imp!'

Something laughed a little. 'A long time ago, some Romans came here and sacrificed to me on the stone. They called me Mithras and they chanted animistic liturgies amongst the encircling silent trees. Once they slew a white bull in my honour, another time they slid up and down on a greased bull-hide with a young maiden and often they poured out libations of oil or milk for me.'

'They could not have served you better than I. You enticed me with your pagan tricks!'

Again came that depreciative laugh, calculated to infuriate. 'You enticed yourself. Now get out.'

'Don't warn me. I fear nothing now.'

'Can you fight the green-gunge goblin and the gritty grackles? They are not asleep like the sun and the leaf.'

She clawed her way over a pile of fallen stone which half-filled the narrow tunnel.

'My rocks will impede you and finally as "Mithry-Addy" I will keep you out.'

Water dripped from the roof onto her back. 'I'm going to leather you to destruction!'

Another immoderate orgasm seared up through her, as she squirmed forwards in an ultimate volley of furious rapture.

Something thick and rubbery pressed her left thigh. At first she wondered if it were just a sodden crease in her macerated leather or even a tear letting in wet filth to her pure body, but it was external and moving.

'Sod it! I'll find you! Artemis Boden wants to fight you.'

The strong muscular thing was now between her thighs. It must be the Spirit of the Mine's penis.

'You won't enter my luxurious vagina. My supreme leather will defend me.'

She tried to twist over onto her back, but the passageway was too confining. In front of her she felt that there was no ground. Here a vertical shaft descended. Artemis groped about and found a small rough cube of stone which when dropped, plopped just a few feet down.

A sudden movement again between her legs, primitive and powerful, ended in the faintest of stinging sensations behind her left knee. Unsure what was happening but unable to turn round, she could only open her legs a little and try to put an arm down her back to reach that area.

A black viper had sunk his fangs into her. They had easily pierced her tough leather and the vein-dilating venom had entered her body.

Unexpectedly, it shot across her back and past her head. She tried to grab its unseen looping form as it slithered by, its hidden yellow zig-zag the emblem of its fiery curse.

A giddy warm feeling spread across her chest and then diffused itself into her limbs. She twitched her eyelids, as if to ward off some agonising herald. Her heart faltered and seemed to stop. Oh God, was this it? Was this the end of the endless night ... or the beginning? She felt urine trickling into her underclothes. Could Simon really do all this to her? Would he really become a well-known playwright and live in Norway shagging a troll? She laughed and cried. She had lost. She could not catch this unearthly spirit and extract from it her rightful tithes. No matter what, she had to surrender. Perhaps goodness really was the only way to win? In the marrow of her bones something willed her back from that last leap out into the nebulous void. Her heart seemed to be beating again, quickly if weakly and she sensed a strange calm sweep through her head.

A long way behind her a faint light flickered. A dog barked. A cup full of sour wine seemed to fill her mouth. As we live so we die and as we die so we stay. And this was not the way to die.

## EPILOGUE.

Artemis put down her book – Marcel Pagnol's *L'Eau des collines* in French – stood up and gazed out of her big first-floor barred window at a bed of budding roses and a creosoted fence in the grounds of the psychiatric prison. From her cell she could see a dove-grey stone church and a red-flowered cornfield beyond the fence.

After six months her hair was now long again, hanging in a schoolgirlish plait. She wore her charcoal dungarees with the red stitching and the two square pockets on the front also sewn on with red thread. These were on top of a thin white polo-neck woolly and thick black socks used as slippers.

Those jangling keys, like something from a hackneyed film, rattled outside her door and a warder let in Dr Caspar Box, who greeted her with his well-oiled clinical smile. Artemis returned a smile of exaggerated sugariness. Dr Box switched off his smile and looked grave, for he knew that this was a difficult cas e.

'Don't you like my nice smile?' she asked sadly.

The protracted court proceedings had finally ended in March. Artemis had been here for three months, but so far it had failed to impair her extravagant loveliness.

Dr Box, who smelt slightly of coffee and musk, seemed confused. He sat down on the white metal chair at the white-painted table in this cell, which despite its plain white walls and ceiling, white bed-linen and white cupboard, was quite large and airy and pleasant. He pushed an algebra book and a note-pad to one side. On it in her hand was jotted the integration of $\cos x(\sin x - 4)$. Here he had no imposing swivel armchair, no carved desk, no overcrowded bookshelves behind him, no etched copper plate to attest his manifold qualifications.

Artemis sat on the edge of her bed, crossed the ankles of her outstretched legs, hung her arms down to cross over loosely on her thighs and watched her toes wiggle inside the thick socks.

Dr Box was in his forties, bald with long greasy sideboards and a small tapering beard. He wore tight white trousers, a flowery-patterned pink shirt and a white tie. His face was long and gnarled and did not of itself exude kindness or wisdom. Large veins coursed across his temples and he had a pair of metal-rimmed spectacles which he kept taking off and on, as if he himself suffered from a nervous tic. This would be his fifth session with her, a most interesting case – not because he felt compassion or wished to help her or anything naïve like that – but because the hints of nights spent in black leather committing unearthly and sensual crimes sounded morbidly tantalising to his unhappy mind.

Artemis though, was far too sharp to confide any of her intimate feelings to this unwholesome weirdo. Being about four times as intelligent as Box, her psycho-analysis of him was making much faster progress than his of her.

'Well Artemis,' he began, for it was all informal first name stuff here as everyone was so full of profound understanding, 'our earlier meetings haven't been very fruitful, have they?'

A right spirit had restored itself in Artemis. The traces of her few weeks of frenzied debauchery, though present were slight. 'What is there which needs to be said? The sun is shining ... and it would be enjoyable to go out for a walk.'

'Indeed or take a drive in my new Vulva.'

'I take it you mean "Volvo".'

'What did I say?'

'Never mind.'

'I'm so sorry. I think I used the wrong word.'

'But it *was* the one which automatically popped up into your psyche as you unreeled the sentence.'

'A meaningless slip. My work intruding into everyday conversation again.' The stock smile was on display once more. 'Anyhow, how are you feeling today?'

'Restless.'

'You might feel less restless if we exorcised your demon.'

'Does "exorcising my demon" mean me taking you out on a leash?'

He sighed heavily. 'Artemis, we are here to help you come to terms with whatever it was which caused you to exhibit such an extreme behavioural disorder and from that base, to develop ... '

'What does it mean, "come to terms with"? Something has happened. That's that.'

The only point he had so far established about discussions with this girl was that they must be wholly irrational. 'In the deeds which you have committed, must lie the clues to your difficulties. We can either try to extrapolate backwards or begin in your infancy or youth, or all of them – a three-pronged attack – but we can't make pies without meat.'

'Custard pies?'

Most exasperating of all was that he could not decide if she were a ruthless animal lurking mockingly behind an appearance of good breeding or if she were really putting a composed front on over fears and fantasies which she dared not face.

'I think that the obstacle to openness between us may be that you regard some matters as too shameful to discuss. Your background, if you'll allow me to say so, is very bourgeois and I don't doubt, full of value judgements. You're probably too morally opinionated and blinkered.'

'*Me*? *Moral*?'

He flashed his smile again briefly. What a tough nut this was to crack. 'Bodily needs – the sex urge if you like – are natural enough in a young woman. It may be simply a question of growing up a little, of admitting such things to yourself in order to avoid the deviations you've had of confrontational masochism.'

'Women are not masochistic. That's a popular view I know, but wrong. In fact the contrary is true. We're more concerned to protect ourselves from harm than men, I would say.'

'Is that why you wore black leather so much?' He moistened his lips and leant forward.

She smiled disparagingly. 'You ought not to believe all you read in the newspapers.' She would not ordinarily have shown any interest in this pimple of a man, but her material was rather limited today and would be so for the next three years, until she could dance in the fields and the woods again and escape these awful creeps.

'When I was a house surgeon, a girl who was a motorcycle stunt rider came into the orthopaedic ward for the tenth time and someone said, "If she's not in action, she's in traction." Now ... '

'But presumably she wasn't *seeking* injury.'

'Perhaps when you were out at night – doing whatever you were doing – you never *sought* physical injury, yet I believe you subconsciously craved humiliation and revelled in the chaos of violation.'

'But if *you* have no moral position, what do you mean by "violation", Dr Box? Surely violation implies morality – that some deeds are right and some wrong? If you don't believe in any set of rules, then there is no framework to violate. At your last visit you were taking a highly moral stance on the rights of ... was it black immigrants? Yet where sexual behaviour is concerned, you repudiate morality. It doesn't add up.'

He suppressed a sigh. 'Tell me about anything. Tell me about your earlier aspirations in life if you wish. Start anywhere.'

'I wanted to become an actress.'

'Aha – you liked dressing up? Knights, milk-maids, fantasy worlds?'

'Perhaps.'

'And did you want to extend these characters into real life situations?'

'I don't think so. Surely though the point is not the clothes or the actual act committed – dressing up in a ballerina's tutu and fishing-waders and raping a dead pig or whatever – because that is merely an eruption of a simpler problem ... The key is the lovelessness or the receiving of unkindness or the anger over some thwarted ambition say, which generated it. The form of the external manifestation is fairly unimportant.'

'A debatable point, I concede. However in most women such crises show themselves in less aberrant ways than yours. They kick their underlings around, have a row with their husband ... '

'But does that matter? One man likes motor-racing, another ancient Tuscan ... it just is so and you cannot really say why. Yet both are equally liable to be troubled.'

He looked deflated. He had almost squeezed some deep confession out of her there. 'Can I suggest that you felt upset on leaving finishing school to discover that male virility is aggressive and that sexual lust is aroused usually by spite and rarely by tenderness? These unpleasant realities would be conflict-evoking with your staid and indoctrinated upbringing. I *do* understand that. When we're young, we're idealistic and stumbling too quickly into too many iconoclastic discoveries, can throw us off the rails. With your love of the stage you then transmuted this clash into a physical contest, where you are dressed up as the dark secret heroine fighting men who represent these threats.'

'I made *one* error. I know where I went wrong. I'm quite happy to tell you, but you won't believe me.'

He gave her a watery smile, implying that he was prepared to hear her inexpert opinion.

'I refused to marry the boy whom God wanted me to marry and as a punishment for that disobedience, I was flooded with turbulence and sightlessness.'

A particularly taut smile struggled to conceal his view of her religiously prejudiced conceptions. Certainly that school in Nîmes had a lot to answer for in all of this. 'This Sainte Thingummy school ... '

'Sainte Baume.'

' ... was it a convent school?'

'No.' Artemis saw his thoughts and shrugged wearily.

If he liked to sun-bathe in his own importance, there were few enough rays coming from her. 'Look, we are both tellurians, so ... '

'I could be an angel? They do sometimes appear in human form.'

'Do you regard the world as a threat?'

A dismissive shuffle of her body implied that this was a stupid question.

'You are awash girl, with a genetic uneasiness and experiences which you interpret as suspicious.'

'It's not genes or imaginings. There *are* bad people about, so of course the world's a threat.' Anyway it was with creepy-crawlies like him around.

She felt herself although outwardly female, to be secretly half-boy and half-girl. She smiled tartly. His advice was utterly useless. What she needed was to live a right life.

How could he crack the falsely ethical ground under her feet? 'Let me put a different view-point to you. Stand back, take a relaxed view of this "good" and "bad", think more of "pleasure" and "pain", of effects and not of edicts carved by God on some tablet. Suppose you just enjoyed yourself, said what you really wished to, did as you wanted to with your own body, experimented ... '

'Be wafted about, be drift-wood, swim with the tide, be free, take licence ... be nothing. Freud was wrong. *We* shape our environment, not the other way round. We *are* responsible for our choices and our actions. Without that, civilisation is meaningless. "Good" and "bad" *do* exist. You are not helping anyone by saying they don't. Without them all would be just a shadowy grey land. I know that because I came back from the boundary in the lead mine of my own free will. I came back towards the light.'

Box did his best to look impressively sceptical. He was after all, the 'professional'. He saw not that her greater gravity and depth might mean that her views were nearer to the truth. 'Your concept of life has very little freedom in it.'

'Perhaps freedom is just more ways in which you can go astray. You say you are promoting liberty, but are you just helping people to destroy themselves? Perhaps you hate virtuous minds, because they silently show you your own corruptness?'

'I shall pretend I didn't hear that.'

'Try being silly instead. Silliness is an essential element in discovering civilised living. Licence isn't.'

'I've been looking at a new book on schizophrenia. One section in it describes girls like you – those ... '

'Has the second copy arrived yet?'

' ... with a strong masculine element in them ... which by the bye is known as "penis envy". Your motorbike got stuck in the mud, yes? You put the psychological penis on to conquer with but it fell off. So instead of a conqueress you became a failure.'

Artemis considered giving a scornful laugh of incredulity, but saw that it might be taken as a sign that he were nearing the truth. Instead therefore, she said, 'Dr Box, have you ever seen Loch Ness?'

'You liked to feel masculine and aggressive, didn't you? You liked the motorbike's image of power. You liked to imagine yourself with a penis attacking things, yes?'

'Loch Ness? With its ruined castle?'

'Let us talk about leather clothes, shall we ... not shoes or gloves, but larger items such as coats, skirts, motorcycle suits et cetera? Would you agree that they are connected with a desire for aggressive sex?'

'They might suggest such to some, but not necessarily.' Under the table she could see that in his tight trousers, his penis had just stiffened. Clearly the subject of leather meant more to him than her lovely and picturesque form. She would extort some suffering for that slight.

'When you pulled on your ... '

'Listen, Dr Box. Let me draw an analogy. Say our conscious thoughts are the surface of Loch Ness. You psychiatrists want us to put on our diving gear and plunge down into its depths to get to know our monster. But are you really false prophets seeking excuses to navigate into and mull over others' depravities just for the morbid satisfaction of debasing everyone? Is it not really wiser to stay on the surface enjoying the half-sheer fern-covered Scottish crags, the colourful sail-boats, the idyllic bluish banks of wild flowers .... and then the monster below – which after all is subtly connected to the whole milieu – will gradually metamorphose and become mellower and less threatening? Perhaps the more you look into horrible things, the more horrid and vicious they become? And perhaps the more one looks at the fair and the tranquil ... '

She had turned the tables. Box recognised that all this was uncomfortably near to the truth. He was in fact covertly planning to write a book about her and give it the attention-grabbing and erotic title of *Leather* and make hopefully lots of money out of both her and out of his own particular fetish.

'Why are you curious about others' grime? Why do you need to expose ignoble traits in everyone? Is it to try to excuse something in yourself? You say, "Delve into the slime and really get to know your devils so that they become less frightening," but is that a good idea? Why not discipline your mind to stay away from the hideous and the sordid?'

'But you did not choose that path, did you?'

'That was perhaps a mistake.'

'An inevitable mistake?'

'Cicero I think, said that goodness needs practice. We do commit blunders.'

He needed a quantity of her analects for his intended compilation, but she was being distinctly unforthcoming. 'Artemis, tell me what you felt when you were wearing your leather get-up and I will tell you an intriguing story.'

She looked at him distrustfully. 'Have you come to cast your swine-like thoughts before my pearls? It is I who am enlightening you, not you me.' If the poison of craving power was still in her blood, it was dormant. Outwardly she appeared quite graceful again. 'No. Things are clearer and simpler than you believe.'

'Humph! What do you think you know about these twisting tunnels? I could talk for hours about your psychological kenogenesis and ontogenesis, but I don't. I keep it simple.'

'Your ideas are too complex, too tortuous ... you move in an obscure world of dissembling half-shadows and false goals. Your Austrian founder, "Zigzag Fraud", lacked ideals. It is unwise to conjure vacuous theories and it leads nowhere to try merely to penetrate someone's ultimate ambitions.'

Box was having a rough morning. He had walked into a door-post first thing and put a star-shaped crack into one lens of his usual glasses. His first patient had up-ended his desk and started smashing up his office before the orderlies had arrived to pin him to the floor. And now this slippery girl was running rings round him. Then out of the blue she handed him a spontaneous insult which really stung.

'Besides, you're not fit.'

He was so angry he wanted to march over to her and hit her, but as the 'carer', the 'sympathy giver' he of course had to control himself. 'You do know that you're suffering from an acute psychosis?'

'What does that mean?'

'It means you need help.'

'Is this "help" as meaningless as your term "support"?'

'No one can stand alone. You need leading through your own mine-fields.'

'I have books ... my instincts ... '

'You need *human* help.'

'My father ... ' She stared at him thoughtfully. 'I think you're the sort of man who makes approaches to women, not because you want to bed them but because you want them to move forward and show an interest in you?'

'You said on Wednesday, that during your childhood, that when you had had a nose bleed, you used to spread the blood all over your bedclothes to extract as much sympathy as possible from your mother. Now that is a sign of insecurity and ... '

'Why? Do you have to prove to yourself that you are male? Is it vanity or are you impotent?' A sudden thought flashed into her mind. 'Or arc you frightened of homosexual tendencies inside yourself?'

Beyond this over-perceptive probing was a worry about his research. Two years ago he had allegedly achieved a 'great breakthrough' by culturing *in vitro* glial cells from patients with endogenous depression and showing that they contained raised levels of 3-methyl-hydroxytryptamine. Then last month some Australian dingoes had queried the validity of his work. As other scientists were embroiled through having used his fraudulent cell lines as their starting point, the profession would be seriously displeased. Curse these uncouth wallabies from the antipodes! Fortunately the press were still well-disposed towards medical men – lawyers could be bent and policemen crooked, but doctors were good and compassionate and high priests not to be blackened. But still, his colleagues would *know*, however good the cover-up. They would have forgotten the extra research funds which his 'success' had brought them.

Box suggested that she consider 'her options' very carefully. 'Where do you want to be in ten years time? What sort of person do you wish to be?'

'Hopefully not one chased by Russian spies.' This was devious, but a part of a fiction which she felt obliged to sustain from time to time, because at her trial her insistence that she had been acting in self-defence against sinister left-wing pursuers had undermined much of the prosecution's vehemence.

'Are they not just figments of your illness?'

'Axt, Heidemann, Rose ... figments? Of course they're all your ideological bed-mates. We know which side of the fence you types are on.'

'Typical! You have bloody everyone pigeon-holed.'

This institution was set in a corrie a few miles from Reedsmouth. Artemis drifted over to the window and watched a gardener hoeing in the distance in the balmy July sunshine, utterly impervious to this false counsellor's advice. 'I am a Spartan goddess and Spartans think of duty not choice in a crisis ... not like those smooth Athenians. From all our conflicts too with the Helots, we are the only Greeks good at night fighting. You're an Athenian. No wonder no one trusts you.'

Suddenly he was sick of words and sick of losing. How he wished he could screw this Venus de Milo, this truly exceptional stiff and aloof sex-object, for when all was said and done this was what all the fancy terminology was really about, was it not? That was what everyone wanted. That was how to cure your female patients, yes? He felt agitated and deeply lonely. He was considering suicide.

'Why don't you take the tablets we've prescribed?' he said irascibly. If he could hook her onto this dope, he might manage to break down her hang-ups. Then who knew what might happen? Hatred would inspire him. It would be a delightful change too, from the unvaried lack-lustre ritual with his bored wife.

'You haven't told me what they're supposed to do ... and incidentally no, you can't have sex with me.'

This was the last straw. His face looked very ugly as he stood up. 'There is no point in me wasting my time, trying to help somebody who just fundamentally does not want to be helped!'

She turned coolly to face him. 'My father visits me regularly and brings piles of books, paper and pens ... and his love. They're good for my mind ... not your zombie pills.' She turned back to the window.

'Just stew in your own gory juice girl!' He marched to the door and shook it angrily. 'Warder! Hurry up! I'm a busy man. I've a committee meeting in ten minutes time.'

He reached his office, which oddly had an outwardly opening door, to see that some wit with an indelible pen had changed the 'PULL' on it to 'BULL'. He sank into his chair and muttered, 'You fucking vicious little Nazi bitch!'

Artemis poured herself some tonic water. She knew that her wrong act had been refusing Simon, yet oddly that was not why she had been tried. Modern law was all about the arbitrary application of abstract rules, not about right and wrong. She considered her punishment just – an unusual attitude these days – though not for the reasons cited by the court.

She recalled her first day at Sainte Baume when eight years old – the sixteenth-century cloth merchant's house with its central courtyard and stone steps and balusters. Should she tell Box next time what she really thought of him? Should she be 'judgemental'? 'No, let's not jump the gun,' she said to herself, 'at least not verbally.'

Artemis had repented of her wrongs and felt forgiven. She had lived out her rebellious and egotistical fancies and been humbled. She were now more ready to serve. The pot-holing amphetamine-like madness of the Spirit of the Mine was history. She looked forward to becoming exalted in another way, to being a non-bewitching yet human girl.

She studied for a further two hours, for she hoped to retake Latin and mathematics 'A' levels and Greek 'O' level next summer and to apply to university when released.

Her father visited her faithfully twice a week and he arrived in the early evening in her Porsche 911. He understood something of the truth now and was not angry. On the contrary he just loved her and encouraged her to hold out. With good behaviour she ought to be out on parole within two years, unless Box meanly blocked it.

Papa had long since banked in a Swiss bank the cheque which Innogen had brought, so financially all was in good shape.

Before her surrender, Artemis had dropped the pistol and its magazines down the flooded shaft in front of her and although she had confessed to certain crimes, she had kept mum about her connections with Colonel Letheren. Her accusers too did not mention him, for had it become an espionage case it would have collapsed through witnesses who could not be called or who were forbidden to speak. Her defence had been aided too by a number of chance revelations in the press at that time. The most notable of these was that Hugh Gaitskell had probably been poisoned by a conspiracy of Russians diplomats and left-wing parliamentarians at home, though other rumours and suspicious links brought a sleazy network of leftist activists at least partly to light. With the trial's ramifications into Caie's and Rose's activities, the case had proved quite uncomfortable for the Government and all this had worked in the defendant's favour.

Donald Boden had become a very reclusive man. He no longer worried about having the right-coloured socks on. His daughter kissed him fondly when he arrived. It seemed odd that they were now closer than for many years.

She poured tea and he unwrapped a walnut and cherry cake. He had to find things to say as her life was naturally pretty empty. He talked this evening about his war service. From being a pay clerk in a factory in Andover, he had been called up, trained as a signalman and then put on a draft for Iraq with 50 Operating Section. Artemis listened with genuine attention as he relived those exciting and novel years. They had embarked at Prince's Dock in Liverpool on the fifth of December 1941 and sailed in passage with the large convoy WS 14. All those liners and fast cargo ships had created such a stirring sight and moved him deeply. They had sailed out round the North of Ireland and down the centre of the Atlantic, even having the battleship *Ramillies* in company. 'I had always loved ships. I had read about them avidly – and suddenly to see all these merchantmen of the Blue Funnel, Elder Dempster and Union Castle Lines ... and to be part of it ... We refuelled and revictualled at Freetown and at Durban had a pay parade on the beach. There was concern at that point in the war that the Germans might break through the Caucasus and capture the oilfields in Iraq, so we disembarked at Basrah and drove up to Kirkuk. Whenever the lorries stopped – even in what seemed like a sand-blown wilderness – within minutes there would be natives there selling us oranges and cooking chickens ... ' He could still remember their faces and would occasionally paint a scene from those not-so-far-off memories.

Listening patiently to his modest adventures, Artemis understood with greater clarity the lost world which Innogen's father had been struggling vainly to uphold.

Three loads of granite blocks had arrived for building a little jetty out into Loch Eilan not directly in front of the house, but fifty yards to the North, blocks cut from the granite quarry at Creetown. Two local men were renovating the lime-whitened Easter Tickell Cottage. The money in the bank in

Zürich was doing something. Not all her effort had been wasted.

They did some maths together. She showed him how to integrate various trigonometric functions and he tested her on declensions of Greek substantives.

When Box was mentioned, he said, 'Ken Dodd is supposed to have remarked that the trouble with Freud was that he'd never played to the second house at the Glasgow "Empire" on a Saturday night.'

'That's good. That's very good.'

They talked about the Aermacchi. He had taken it to bits with his 1931 set of Abingdon King Dick spanners. Soon she would be fine again.

She watched from the window as he drove away. A crimson sun was setting over the wood of olive green trees. Another day had almost passed.

She lay on her bed and thought of the great quandary of when to be forceful and when to be submissive. Violence did not befit the lowly – for instance Rufus Drummond – but for nobler spirits there were times ...

Even though she had known it to be wrong, nihilism had six months ago seemed preferable to being debased by failure. A reckless orgy of envy and fury had spilled over and pulled her onwards.

A book from her childhood flashed before her. Saint Hild and her sister were baptised as young girls because they were grand-nieces of King Edwin of Northumbria who was converted in 627 at Goodmanham. Despite this, they had still thrown corn onto a sacred stone or sneaked out to pray to Eostre when there had been a full moon. A few lines of an Anglo-Saxon chant had been below a picture of them kneeling by the stone.

'Straight and strong Eostre, awake!
To stir these earth-fair bundles,
In winter-time.'

Power corrupts all but the most devoutly religious. If Box queered the pitch by saying that she were still unstable and in need of further therapy, what could she do? Damn the modern world's bogus use of democracy, utilising it as a widespread cover for selfishness, the settling of scores and greed. Could she ever be happy in a society which hated aristocracy, artistry, war, horses, saddlery, ladies, love and picty?

She remembered standing in her hard gleaming leather beside the dark warm Aermacchi behind the Annoch Lodge Guest House and thought of a line from the Iliad, 'They pulled up their chariots by the ditch's edge and crossed on foot, dressed in their armour.' How would she fight her future battles?

* * *

Ten summers later Archibald Letheren was paddling in the shallows at the edge of Ullswater with his trousers rolled up. With him was a very happy-natured six-year-old in Wellingtons, called Tom Slade. He was Innogen's eldest child.

Above them, a white sun ruled a powder-blue hemisphere, above a brown hem of hills. Night had diffidently withdrawn herself from such a brilliant sun. The water of the lake glittered in gold and blue rings round their legs.

On the light green turfy shore, on a slab of whinstone, they had made a little fort of sticks and pebbles. Inside it were six lead camels, four pack-mules and eighteen contraband-running Arabs in white jellabiyas from some villainous tribe in

Muscat and Oman. They had placed them round the walls with their minute rifles.

Letheren picked up one of the inch high figures. 'This fellow, with his curved sabre and his red keffiyeh w'aggel, shall we say he's their chief ... their Mansab?'

'What shall we call him?' asked Tom. '"Ambrose"?'

'How about "Hassan Qasim al-Uzza"?'

Tom gave a brief peal of laughter, as if he had heard a joke.

'That's an Arabic name. You say it.'

'Hassam Quass Alluzzy.'

'Very good.' Letheren stroked his jowls which had some blue fluff on them from shaving with a new towel.

Tom looked round at their ship floating on the lake. 'How would Hassam say "water"?'

'"Myah" ... at least it was in Egypt.'

They had a wooden aircraft carrier, which was about three feet long and half as wide and this they had launched and towed out. It was light grey and black with a dark blue flight-deck marked out with white and yellow lines and it had on board five silver Sea Vixen fighters, five grey commando helicopters, a couple of dark green landing craft, an orange crane, some grey life-rafts and a White Ensign at the stern. Mustered on deck were a few sailors and naval aircrew and about thirty marines who were due to take part in the assault on the mud fort. It was a solid ship but its details were not exact nor strictly to scale. Rather like Victorian toys, the emphasis was on providing fun and not on great precision. Letheren had made it thirty years before for Nicholas, but recently taken it out and touched it up. Its name was *Eagle*.

'Look,' said Tom indignantly.

A large black oil beetle was crawling through the casbah, knocking over some of the Arabs.

'Grrrr,' said Archibald to it threateningly, as he tried to persuade it to climb onto his finger.

'Don't kill it Grandpa, you'll hurt it!'

Letheren smiled and threw it away into some gorse.

Yet its black lustrous form had reminded him of Artemis Boden and she in turn of the story of the Cretan Princess Pasiphae, a girl of legendary beauty. Her father, King Minos, had summoned many princes to sue for her, but it had amused Pasiphae to lead them on a little and then haughtily dismiss them. Aphrodite the Goddess of Love, angered by this abuse of love's sacred tokens, punished her for this calumny by setting in her an infatuation for a certain white bull, which lived in a meadow near her father's palace. Each day Pasiphae would spend her time caressing it and weaving garlands of blossom for it and eventually she gave birth to the Minotaur, the beast which was half-man and half-bull. How well the Greek tales depicted the courses of action and reaction which govern human existence, thought Letheren.

He looked down at the boy, assiduously lining up the toy figures. Like Nicholas, it seemed that he would not be clever. Yet there was already more than enough cleverness in the world – what was missing was a sense of fun, a sense of adventure and integrity.

Letheren brushed away a tear, bent down and hugged his grandson fondly.

THE END.